THE MARSHAL'S LOVER

BY JO GRHAM

"**I** will have to sleep with him," I said. "I confess my skin crawls at the prospect."

He waited and said nothing.

"It is possible," I said slowly, "That the Philadelphes are not all hot air. It is possible that they have some actual knowledge that is important." I did not know how much he knew of our lodge, or how much he believed, but I found it impossible to believe he knew nothing, as close friends as he and Lannes had been for years. "I will need to find that out. There are two pieces, sire. There is the political conspiracy which may cause much trouble, and there is the possibility that they are indeed using some actual efficacious method."

"And you can do both," he said. "That is why I need you, Madame St. Elme."

"I am yours, sire," I said. I took a deep breath. "Marshal Ney...."

"Is about to receive his orders for Spain," he replied. "It's a mess, and Alexander must have his Hephaistion!"

I opened my mouth and shut it again. There was no reply possible to that.

"Ney will take a corps command in Spain this summer, and while I know you would like to follow the army, you may have your own work."

I nodded. If we were two men we would not always be posted to the same command, and one could not whine about it. "So he has broken my heart. I will need to tell him that."

"You will need to enlist his assistance, I should think," the Emperor said. "If it is to be plausible. And I will send you to my sister, Elisa. She's in Florence and is well known to have a soft heart. You have impressed her with your sad story and she will give you a post as a reader in her household out of pity for the cruelty of men!"

I thought he was getting a bit carried away in the melodrama of it all. "She knows?"

"She'll know you're my agent and that she is to render any assistance possible, personal as well as financial. But she won't know the details of your assignment. No one will."

I would leave for Florence at the beginning of May on the Emperor's service with a license to kill, spy and magician.

For Melissa Scott

L'audace, l'audace, toujours l'audace!

"I have lived many lives. I have been a slave and a prince.
Many a beloved has sat upon my knee
and I have sat upon the knees of many a beloved.
Everything that has been shall be again."

William Butler Yeats

Northern Lights

"Colonel Corbineau and Madame St. Elme!" the major domo announced, and we proceeded through the door, my hand on his arm, to greet our host.

The ballroom was lit with a thousand candles, one of the finest houses of Warsaw thrown open for two nations to welcome the Emperor to Poland and to begin the season of Carnival. Chandeliers shone while beneath them on the elaborate parquet floor a hundred people swirled to the strains of music provided by a chamber orchestra. Gorgeous uniforms glittering with gold braid and brilliant color contrasted with white dresses worn by young women, with the rich velvets of the Polish nobility, with brocade frock coats and frothing lace. It was a magnificent sight.

No less magnificent was my escort, Jean-Baptiste Corbineau, now a full Colonel, whose splendor put mine to shame. He was with Klein's Dragoons now, rather than chasseurs, and had traded blue coat for forest green with scarlet facings. He also had rather a lot of gold braid on everything, though the crowning glory was his tall brass neo-Grecian helmet with a scarlet plume and a band of faux leopardskin.

I, on the other hand, wore my only presentable dress, the silver gray satin, but it was a color that suited me well and was the latest style from Paris, having been made as a knockoff of Leroy only the previous summer. The ladies of Warsaw were either madly making over court clothes of years gone by or driving their seamstresses to copy Parisian styles as quickly as possible. Many of them were quite lovely, but I preferred the ones who either adopted simplicity, as one cannot go wrong with white silk, or who unapologetically wore the splendors of the bygone era in all its charm, wide lace collars and velvets like something out of the Thirty Years' War.

There was something distinctly appealing about pale skin rising out of a square black velvet neckline…

At the base of the staircase our host waited. Charles Maurice de Talleyrand, the Foreign Minister, did not look the least put out by my presence, uninvited though I was. Rather, he seemed amused. Dressed in an impeccable coat of dark red velvet that suited him well, he bent over my hand politely as I curtsied. "Madame," he said, his mouth twitching with what might have been a suppressed smile, "I am most pleased by your hair this evening."

"Thank you, Your Excellency," I said, with an answering smile. "But I fear it is nothing to what my hairdresser in Paris may accomplish!"

At that he did laugh. "Colonel Corbineau, you are a fortunate man."

"I am aware of that," Jean-Baptiste said gallantly, though he must have been utterly confused by the exchange. And so we passed within, as there was a press of guests behind us.

The ball was already in full swing, the Emperor present and chatting with Prince Borghese, his brother-in-law who was wed to his sister Pauline, and another man I did not recognize but that I guessed to be a Polish nobleman.

"What was all that about?" Jean-Baptiste asked me under his breath.

"A very long story," I said. Jean-Baptiste's brother Claude was over by the windows. "Dance with me and let us lay your brother's mind at ease."

"Claude won't be happy thinking I've an expensive mistress who takes all my pay," Jean-Baptiste said philosophically. "But I suppose it's better than the alternative. Hold on. I need to take my spurs off so that I don't catch your dress on the turns."

I waited while he sidled up to the wall and unfastened them. "Why are you wearing them anyway? It's not as though you need a horse at a ball."

"They lend a certain something," he said, standing on one foot and hopping about a bit.

I refrained from observing that what they lent was a certain aura of the ridiculous. That award should go to Marshal Murat, who appeared to have a leopardskin flung over his shoulders. It went well with his long pomaded curls.

"There." Jean-Baptiste dropped his spurs into the bucket of his hat, which he carefully arranged on a chair by the wall so that the plume would not be crushed. "Now we can dance."

"I do appreciate your care for my skirts," I said.

"At your service, dear sister!" he said, presenting his arm with a flourish and leading me onto the floor. "After all, you are here tonight to do me a service."

"Two services," I said. "Providing an escort your brother will find acceptable, and having a look at this woman you are so worried about."

"But I'm also doing you a service," he pointed out as we made our way onto the dance floor. "After all, it's something to attend a royal ball in Warsaw, isn't it? Especially when you weren't invited and I was?"

"It is something indeed," I said. How many times would I have the opportunity to attend a gathering like this? Even after so many years of scaling and descending fortune's wheel, a royal ball was not a common occurrence in my life.

"Ah, there she is," Jean-Baptiste said more or less at my ear, turning me about in the dance. "The Countess."

She was not beautiful. From what I had heard I expected a breathtaking beauty, the kind of once-in-a-century loveliness that launches a thousand ships. Her hair was dark honey, that shade between blond and brown that comes when blond children's hair darkens with age, the color of my own when it wasn't bleached with sun or something stronger. She had broad cheekbones and a roundish face, clear fair skin with high color, a blush rising pink in the heat of the ballroom. She was a lovely young girl, but it was not true beauty, only health and youth that would pass far too quickly. At forty-something Josephine was beautiful still, blessed with good bones and features that aged well. At forty the young Countess would be nothing in particular to look at.

And yet. Watching her from across the ballroom, glimpses caught and obscured by passing dancers, there was a firmness to her pretty bow-shaped mouth. There was a tilt to her chin, an expression…. She was nothing like Josephine, born to captivate as surely as any favorite of an ancient court. She was twenty, and yet her eyes were old. She watched. She measured. Behind wide blue eyes like cornflowers there was a mind wide awake. She was modest, her white gown simple, dressed like dozens of women there, and yet she shone like a star come to rest in a flowerbed. Not a rose. She was not a rose, opulent and sweet. She was some more prosaic and sturdy plant, a morning glory that climbed the house and wreathed all in green leaves long after the blossoms of morning had closed.

"That one," Jean-Baptiste said. "That's Countess Walewska."

"So I see," I said.

"What do you think?"

I shrugged. She sat with the matrons, an embroidery hoop on her lap. Surrounded by old women, she almost glittered. As of course she would know she would. Surrounded by maidens, she would be one blossom among many, one more fair-haired, pink-faced girl of twenty in a white dress. Surrounded by old women clothed in mourning, she illuminated. "She's pretty," I said.

Jean-Baptiste looked at me keenly. "And that's all you've got to say, Elza?"

"What do you want me to say? I think she should do something with her hair. Those ringlets are a bit too young for a married woman."

He snorted. "I got an oracle all the way to Warsaw to tell me that?"

"What do you want me to tell you?" I asked, reaching for a glass of champagne proffered by a passing footman. "I've seen her for five minutes across a crowded ballroom without speaking. You've got to give me a bit more to go on."

I turned so that I could at least see her across the room again, my gray satin skirts flowing with the breeze of passing dancers.

"The Emperor is in love with her."

I took a sip. "This week." Her head bent over her needlework, so serious, so matronly. "He has mistresses. Josephine knows that. They have an understanding—actresses and singers, pretty and entertaining, and none of them very long. A few weeks, a month or two. He's generous and none of them are the worse for it. And neither is he." I refrained from saying that I should know. That week in Milan was more than six years in the past, and my relations with the Emperor now had little to do with it.

Jean-Baptiste shook his head. "You don't understand. This is serious."

"Because she's married? Because she's Polish?" I shrugged. "I don't see how."

"She says no."

"Then what will come of it?" I had certainly never known him to force himself upon someone unwilling, and indeed I would find it most unlike him. Besides, why should he? There were a dozen women in this room who would delight in his attention on any terms, and as I said she was no great beauty.

"Would you say yes?" Jean-Baptiste looked at me sharply. "Given you have the Marshal?"

"That's immaterial," I said, lifting the champagne glass again. "No one is asking me." In truth, the situation would be very awkward. But I did not think it likely to arise. I was much more valuable to the Emperor in other capacities, and he did not mix war and love.

Jean-Baptiste turned, blocking my view again with his gold-laced shoulder. "He's never carried on like this about someone before. Never. He's acting utterly ridiculous, making a fool of himself over her."

"Well, what does she say about it?" I tried to angle around again so that I could at least observe her. Another young woman had come in with a baby, a pretty child a bit less than a year old dressed in white lawn and blue ribbons and was leaning over her, the baby reaching out arms for her. "Is that her child?"

"Apparently," Jean-Baptiste said dryly. "Though her husband's seventy-five if he's a day. Very rich."

"Of course," I said. That went without saying. How else should a man of seventy-five have a wife of twenty? Now she was taking the child from her friend, holding it on her lap facing outward so that it could watch the dancers, raising pudgy hands entranced, her hair falling forward on her shoulders. A chill touched me, the familiar hint of the uncanny. *A white gown, a little boy on her lap facing forward, knees squared, hair escaping from high pins and falling across her shoulders....*

"She looks quite the Madonna," Jean-Baptiste said cynically.

"All that is good and pure compared to all that is lush and corrupt."

It was gone. He had interrupted me before I could follow. "Jean-Baptiste," I said sharply. "Will you be silent for one minute? How do you expect me to see anything if you will chatter?"

"I thought you couldn't see anything."

"I can't when you're talking!" I handed him my empty glass, my voice low. "Bad enough that you expect me to see something in a ballroom full of people! Now give me a moment's peace if you want me to see anything."

"I just want to know if she's bad," he said. "How hard can that be?"

"Bad as in an agent of evil?" I rolled my eyes. "No, Jean-Baptiste. She's not an agent of evil. But what she is and what will happen, good or ill, is far more complicated. There are patterns within patterns." It was irritatingly large and irritatingly out of reach, like looking at a stone and being expected to see the shape of the mountain. What happened here changed the future just as surely as what happened on the battlefield, the shades of what might be drifting through the ballroom like a whiff of powder smoke. Vast chains of consequences centuries long, thousands who might live or die, nations that might be born or conquered....

"He wants you to talk to her."

I closed my eyes. What could he not understand about being quiet for a moment? "About what?"

"About anything. You know none of the ladies of the court speak Polish."

I didn't open my eyes. Jean-Baptiste stood beside me, close enough that his sword brushed against my skirts, as though he were my lover, a real and constant presence. The dancers moved like ghosts, like shadows reflected on the tall windows closed tight against the winter's night. And still I could see her, burning like a brand. "Doesn't the Countess speak French?"

"Of course she does."

"Then he doesn't need a translator."

"I think he's looking for a reference."

My eyes sprung open. "And he thinks I'll provide him one? And that this is any way to impress her?"

Jean-Baptiste shifted from one foot to another. "You and the

Marshal are very happy."

"Michel is not paying court to Countess Walewska," I said. "Michel isn't even in Warsaw. He's in Silesia facing off the Russians, which is where I would be if I weren't needed in Warsaw! I don't see what Michel has to do with anything."

"You left your husband to be the mistress of a general and you're very happy."

"Ah." I looked across the room to where she sat, the child on her knee, laughing with her friend, young and unafraid and unblemished. My voice was very even. "And so I am the ideal person to persuade her that throwing away her position and her future to be the lover of a man who will doubtless tire of her in a few months is a truly excellent decision." I turned my eyes to his face. "No."

"Just no?"

"No," I said. "I won't do it."

"He wants you to," Jean-Baptiste said. "And are you not his in all things?"

"Not in this," I said. "I won't be his procurer."

"Elza, you know he'd do her no harm," Jean-Baptiste began.

"I'm sure they'd have a lovely few months," I said. "And then what would become of her?" There was anger in my voice and I was not sure how it got there. "You have absolutely no idea the things I have done to survive. You have seen me happy and beloved, but you did not know me when I was twenty-one or twenty-two. You have no conception of what life is like for a woman who has turned her back on respectability and is left to her own resources."

His eyes ran over me from the gilt pins in my hair to the ruby at my throat, gray satin dress with its absolutely simple neckline, nothing of the harlot about it, sumptuous in its simplicity, champagne glass touched with gold in my hand. "You don't seem to have done too badly."

"I haven't," I said. "But most of my friends are dead. One was beaten to death by a lover. Another overdosed on laudanum. Another killed herself. Another disappeared when she had nowhere to live except under a bridge. Where do you think these women come from, these scraps who live on scraps, who trundle about half mad with disease? They're the ones who lose." I shifted, my skirts rustling like the tail of a cat lashing. "I'm both lucky and strong. But most never last this long."

Across the ballroom I could see the Emperor talking to Marshal Davout, the taller Marshal's head bent to his, profile classically fair. His expression was animated. Whatever Davout had said, it made him smile. He turned his head and his eyes caught mine, smile broadening with recognition.

I sunk into a deep courtesy, acknowledgement of Imperial favor. It might simply have been the desire of an aging courtesan to catch his eye. Of course Jean-Baptiste knew better. My oaths to the Emperor had little to do with our current flesh and much to do with promises I had made more than two thousand years before. Or so I believed.

He nodded, that magical regard encompassing me, and then turned back to Davout.

"Most die," Jean-Baptiste said thoughtfully. "But you dance with kings and princes. Would you say the odds are worse for a harlot or a light cavalry trooper?" He shook his head. "The boys I started with are dead too, Elza. And here I am, thirty years old and a colonel. It's a fine thing to be lucky and strong. You'd have it no easier if you were a man."

"Believe me, I am learning that," I said. I shook my head. The young Countess was talking with her friend, not even glancing in the Emperor's direction. "But is she lucky and strong? Better not to chance it, and I do not say that lightly. It is easy to say, at twenty, that one will be among the winners, but the odds do not favor the gamester. The house almost always wins." She was not beautiful, and yet....

"Do you wish that you'd stayed with your husband?" Jean-Baptiste asked quietly.

"I don't know," I said. Another footman approached with a full tray, and I traded glasses. "My husband was in his thirties. I had no reason to think that he would die young and free me in a few years. If I had known that..." There was no point in speculating on what might have been. "But if, as you say, her husband is seventy-five, is it not likely that in a very short time she will be a widow of independent means? Then she can do as she likes."

"What about love?" Jean-Baptiste asked.

"What about it?"

"Does it not figure in?"

One of Berthier's aides hurried up to the Countess, bending over her hand to introduce himself, and I watched her face suddenly go white, all color draining from it.

The dance ended rather abruptly, but I hardly noticed and doubtless would have tripped had not Jean-Baptiste dragged me off the floor. "Careful," he said, steering me around a lady in scarlet velvet.

The young aide took the Countess' hand and led her onto the floor where a contredanse was forming up. "What..." I began, but then I saw. The Emperor had gotten up and came out, the aide stepping gracefully aside as Berthier, Prince Borghese, and Murat made up the quadrille with an amazingly quickly assembled collection of Polish ladies. The Emperor bent over her hand, and I saw the color rush back to her face, as though this were the thing she had both anticipated and dreaded. He turned her into her place, his other hand behind his back, all of that fatal concentration bent on her, and she looked up, her eyes not leaving his.

"Oh dear," I said quietly to Jean-Baptiste. The Emperor was a horrible dancer and it was all the others could do to prevent collisions in the figures. And yet....

The Countess turned, her arm extended, her fingertips just touching his. She did not smile or speak, and yet it was as though thunder rolled beneath the earth. We watched them move through the figures. Except in the turns when they must, they did not look away from one another though only the tips of their fingers touched. I saw him speak, only a few words, no doubt some commonplace pleasantry.

She replied. I could see her lips form, "Thank you, Sire."

Turn and turn and turn again, light on her feet as a dancer caught in some ancient temple frieze. The music ended. The Emperor stepped back and bowed. She curtsied. An old man stepped out from the sidelines beaming, his white hair caught in an old fashioned queue, white lace falling over his hands, her husband, pleased at how well his young wife had performed.

"Oh Jean-Baptiste," I said.

"You see?"

"I don't know what I see," I began. My eyes slid past them to the ballroom doors, deferentially opened by a pair of bewigged footmen for a group of officers coming in. The first... My heart skipped a beat.

He wore his dress uniform as he should, cream colored knee breeches and an evening coat of dark brown velvet, a waistcoat embroidered with gold. Gold oak leaves adorned his collar, red hair closer cut than usual, showing off the lovely lines of his face attenuated by a winter campaign. He was looking around the room, looking for someone.

For me. Michel's eyes met mine and his entire face lit up, a smile in his eyes that was only for me, a caress that did not leave my face as he made his way around the perimeter of the ballroom.

Jean-Baptiste might have said something. I didn't hear it.

He stopped in front of me, towering over me by five inches for all that we both wore slippers. "Elza."

"Michel."

"Good evening, sir," Jean-Baptiste said. Apparently he couldn't hear Jean-Baptiste either.

Such warm eyes. He looked thinner, though summer's sunburn had faded. His skin was redhead fair, crinkled at the corners of his eyes. The music had changed, Polonaise to waltz, and he reached for my hands.

"In front of everyone?" I whispered. "Michel, this is not discreet. Aglae..."

"Is in Paris." He took my hands in his, drew me in with his arm about my waist. "And I don't care."

"I've missed you too," I said, and surrendered to his lead, spinning clockwise inside a counterclockwise circle, the ballroom moving in reverse order to individual couples, a dizzying dance perfected in Vienna and given to causing swoons from one end of the continent to the other. Princes and generals rotated by like shooting stars, gold and blue and scarlet blurring together. The Emperor and his marshals, nobles and magnates and churchmen of Poland, lancers and hussars and all the rest, girls in their white dresses, all swirling together on wings of music, while Michel held me against him as though the world might end. We moved together sweetly, precursor of that other dance. He smelled like orange flower water and horses, and I bent like a reed to the wind. No one could play me as he could, an instrument in his hand like a flute or a sword.

"God, I've missed you," he said.

"A thousand times each day," I said.

The Countess was a blur as well, golden among the women, looking up as we passed with a strange expression on her face, as though a bell had sounded somewhere far away. But what could I matter to her, a foreign Aphrodite she had never met in the arms of a man she had never seen before, gilded butterflies in my hair?

Davout and Murat, Jean-Baptiste and Max Duplessis, and the Emperor watching with a fond and expansive smile, as though he were the patron at the feast....

"Why are you here?" I asked.

"The Emperor called me in for a staff meeting," Michel said. "Lucky me." The corners of his mouth twitched. "It's cold in Silesia."

"And you think you'll have a warm welcome here?"

"I know I will."

"You think very well of yourself," I said archly. This was our game, our dance, the consummation never in doubt.

"I thought you liked the best of the best," he said.

"And that would be you?" My smile deepened. It was dizzying, swirl within counterswirl.

"You know it is."

"I do," I said, and drew closer, my face almost against his shoulder. "My Michel."

It was bitterly cold, Orion riding high over the rooftops of Warsaw. I was quartered in the palace itself, a small room right up among the chimney pots, but I was lucky to have it, something owed to my unspecified services. I'm not certain who the servants thought I was. If it were only that I were Michel's I would not warrant a room in the palace.

My maid, Claudine, had lit the fire and it glowed in the small grate in a friendly fashion, the big carved bed piled high with blankets, warm though the frost sat heavily on the window. It was the seventeenth of January. I locked the door behind us, Michel swinging his heavy velvet cloak over the back of the sole armchair before the fire, his dress sword at his side. Once he had traveled without such state. I'd hunted all over Munich to find proper shoes for him, counting dress uniform and sword a lost cause, but that had been six Christmases ago. Then he had been a young general of the Republic. Now he was a Marshal of France. We had been through a great deal since then, and had even parted for two years when I refused to marry him. Now, perhaps, we were past that, even though he had married Aglae and we had made a mess of everything.

And yet some things had not changed at all. When I reached up to kiss him it was as heady as it had been then, and as tender. He bent his forehead to mine, his hands cupping my chin as I stretched my arms about his neck.

"Your hair's grown out again," he said.

"It does that." I smiled and dropped my lips to his palm, kissing the sensitive center, nipping at the skin between thumb and forefinger with my teeth.

His breath hissed, and I felt his hand tighten at my throat. "I hoped you would be here," he said.

"He's run me ragged since Jena," I said. "What with one thing and another. But that business is done and I hope to have a rest." Michel did not ask me where I had been or what I had accomplished. Perhaps I would have told him and perhaps not. I had been on the Emperor's business, and the less said of that the better. Michel knew the shape of my work, as I did his, but not the specifics. That had been the case since I had become the Emperor's agent, a spy who worked for him alone, rather than through the Minister of Police. Michel knew that I was not at liberty to discuss the details of my assignments, and he did not ask.

"So you are simply here to be an ornament to society?" His callused thumb traced the shape of my lower lip.

"I hope so," I said. "But one does get lonely on leave." My eyes flicked to his, conscious of the quickness of my pulse against his palm.

"And what do you do about that?" he said, stepping a little closer so that I could feel his body along mine. "Lift your skirts whenever the whim takes you?"

"More or less," I said. In truth it had been three long, celibate months, but I would never say that. It would sound as though I were pining for him. "Any handsome fellow home from the field…" My hand slid down the front of his waistcoat, fumbling at the buttons between us.

"A girl could get in trouble that way," he said somewhat breathlessly.

"Could she now?"

"She might bite off more than she could chew." He tilted my head up and bent his face to my throat, kissing where the pulse leaped, following the chain of my pendant down between my breasts.

"I imagine she could," I managed. I could not get to those buttons, ivory satin covered buttons on ivory satin, too slippery to undo with one hand.

"Someone who is not so nice…."

I gasped as he lifted my breast roughly, thumbing the nipple to attention as he pulled at my neckline. The dress couldn't really stand it, and it was my only evening gown. "Between the bedposts," I said. "Naked."

"If you like."

It was a four-poster with very sturdy columns and a turned crossbar between them, all elaborate knobs and whorls, just across my belly as I stood at the foot of the bed, divesting myself of the last of shift and bustier. I looked up at the posts speculatively. "I don't think I've got anything…."

He unwound his elaborate cravat. "Just hold onto the posts and imagine." He had shed coat and waistcoat and sword, and there were more pieces to his evening ensemble than to mine.

"What is that for then?" I asked as he folded the cravat.

"This," he said, and laid it across my eyes.

"Oh." I closed my hands around the carved posts as he tied it behind my head, careful not to pull my hair in the knot, the knob of the crossbar against my lower belly. Blindfolded, the kiss of cool air on my skin seemed sharper. Deprived of sight, other senses intensified.

He tugged on the blindfold once, then stepped back. I heard soft sounds, unidentifiable, my breath in the silence. Intense, this nothing. Intense, this absence of touch to go with absence of sight, legs apart, arms stretched up the posts. Waiting. Waiting. My breasts tightened, nipples responding to the cold, and I felt the telltale warmth begin between my legs, ripe with anticipation.

"You look like a sacrifice to some pagan god," he said, and I knew he was watching me. He was seeing every change, every flush, every desire written on my flesh.

"Yes," I whispered.

"Some terrible sacrifice," he said, his voice moving as he walked around to my left. "A woman left bound between two trees in the forest, given to the creatures of the wood." His fingers traced my spine from shoulder blades to waist, and I jumped. "To the monster. To the beast."

"Given to the beast," I whispered. "Just punishment." I could imagine the starlit wood, the silence of the forest. And the sound of approaching footsteps.

"Sacrifice and payment," he said. "Her flesh to appease the beast." I couldn't tell exactly where he was. My entire body strained to know, still holding onto the posts as though bound there. I wanted the warmth of him. I wanted to know where he was. And yet there was nothing. No touch. The beast simply watched me, deciding what to do.

"Yes," I said. "To appease the beast."

And there was his hand at my cleft, reaching between my legs to grasp me by my pubic hair, sharp and startling and painful, his other hand pushing me forward against the knob of the crosspiece.

"Soaking wet," he said, his voice a low rumble behind me. "You want this. You'll even take a beast."

He was naked against me, the sudden shocking feel of his body against mine, hairy chest against my back, as though it really were the lord of the forest who stood there, or some minotaur out of legend, half man and half creature.

"Beast," he said, and drove into me from behind, pulling me back onto him, his calloused thumb against my pearl.

I shrieked, holding onto the posts for dear life. Bound between trees in the wood, the monster's enormous prick inside me....

"Knowing," he said breathlessly, "That it will have you over and over. It will take you until you beg and plead and still...."

"...and still," I gasped. In this mood it would not take him long.

"And still you'll come for it, come with that creature...."

"...come for the beast," I said. And he would. He would make me. He would make me as often as I wanted. Not yet, not enough, but for more than long enough. He thrust again savagely, the knob of the crosspiece against my bladder, sweet pain and tension.

He gasped and stiffened, undone, his hand suddenly stilling and I let go and took it, lost in the fantasy of the creature in the wood, the one who I might never see. The rush of his warmth, of his release, staining me, marking me his....

"Don't stop," I said.

"Never." His breath was rough and he leaned against me heavily, his face against my neck. "Never."

"The creature is without mercy," I said.

"And before the dawn comes you will weep," he said, reaching about me and grasping my breast roughly, as though it were some monstrous hand that clutched at me, nails scratching my flesh.

"Yes." The pressure, the helplessness... His other hand moved again, the back of his knuckles parting my nether lips, and I ground down against it. So close. And not quite.

"Given to it to satiate its lust..."

"Yes." So close. So wet. So dark and bright. The world dissolved and I clutched the posts, wrung out again and again, great rolling spasms that shook me.

"And again," he said, his thumb pressing inside me as I ground against his hand. "Without ending."

I threw my head back, another storm taking me, held up by nothing except the posts and his hand inside me, my knees giving way, shaking in a high wind.

"There," he said smugly as I leaned against him. "There." He stretched his arm up along mine, as though he undid invisible bindings. His big hand caressed my wrist, caressed each finger and unclenched them from the post.

I reached up and slid the blindfold off shakily, finding my feet beneath me again. "Oh my God." I turned against him, chest-to-chest and belly-to-belly.

"Good?"

"Good," I said. I put my arm about his waist. "How is my favorite beast?"

"Cold," Michel said. "I should have thought of that before."

"It's Warsaw in January," I said, making my way gingerly around one side of the bed. "Perhaps next time something under the covers, so my poor beast doesn't freeze!"

Michel dove in on the other side. "Your poor beast needs considerably more fur if he's going to haunt the forests of Poland stark naked."

I settled down beneath the blankets, the firelight burnishing his hair with bronze. He held out his arm to me and I curled against his shoulder, nose against his flesh, warm and seamed with one long, pale scar. I twined my legs with his, cuddling together tight and safe. He yawned.

"Well, then," I said, and closed my eyes.

Patterns in the Snow

I dreamed, and in my dream I was a child again in Amsterdam. In my dream I walked through the house my father died in, the one my mother called cursed. I went down the hall, everything monstrous and huge, just as it had seemed to me when I was eight years old, antique black teak paneling absorbing the light of the candle I carried. In my dream I walked through it in silence, knowing that my father was dead.

As happens in dreams, one place becomes another with a thought, and I stood in the nave of the church. I stood among the mourners, and my father was dead. This was his funeral, I thought, looking up at the painted ceiling far above. My father was dead, and I dreamed of being a child at his funeral, a black clad, golden-haired little girl standing among my brothers and sisters.

Only that could not be right. I had only my brother Charles, and he died before my father. I had been the only child at my father's funeral.

Yet there they were, two sisters and three brothers, walking with me down the aisle toward the front of the church to kneel in prayer together, all of us fair, my sister's long pale hair hanging loose. My sister stood beside me, my age exactly, her hair the same color as mine, her eyes the same shade of sapphire. "Our father is dead," she said. "He has died for his country, and we are all that is left."

"I know," I said, and felt tears start in my eyes.

"We are all that is left," she said, and her gaze did not waver, my sister, born in the same year, born under the stars of winter. "Our country is dismembered by our enemies and our people ruined. There is no one left but us."

"And what can we do?" I asked, my voice that of a child, clear and dreaming. "We are little girls, not soldiers."

"We must ask Her," she said, and her eyes sought the front of the church.

Behind the altar there was a vast icon, the Virgin enthroned with Her Son on Her lap, robed in a blue so dark it was almost black, spangled with gold like a thousand starry heavens. Her skin was mahogany, dark as an African's, two long scars marring one cheek. At Her feet sat the orb of the world, and behind Her long curtains susurrated, moving in a silent wind.

"We must ask Her," my sister said, and took my hand to lead me forward. "We asked Her before."

"We did," I said, and I followed, making the genuflection at my sister's back as she sunk to her knees.

"Mother of the World," she said, her child's voice firm and clear, "Maria, Queen of Heaven, listen to your daughter!" She lifted her face and her eyes were bright with tears but none spilled down her cheeks. "Not for me, but for my people! Not for me, but for those who weep! There is a wind through the world, and it is blowing!"

I caught my breath, words returning to me as though long forgotten. I knew what she would say before she said it.

"Not for me, but for freedom! Not for me, but for our survival as a people! I call him by his bones, by his bones that rest in our soil, by old blood spilled on his behalf long ago, by his name and by his oaths! Come to me."

"Come to me," I whispered. A memory, a ghost. *What wind is this that shakes the flames? It is the wind from Egypt….*

"Come to me," she said, and lifted her eyes to the icon, to the living woman who bent Her scarred face over my sister's head in unsmiling benediction….

I woke in the gray silence of dawn, the sky soft and close beneath clouds that had rolled in, lavender tinted. There was frost on the windowpane, tracing shapes along the glass. Beyond, the elaborate chimney pots gave off the smoke of morning, fires kindled in the rooms of the palace. It must be well after seven, and yet all was still quiet.

Normally the Emperor was up at five, and heaven forbid any in the entourage, great or small, lag in bed until after seven! However, whether at the behest of Marshal Berthier, or because of the late nights the court had been keeping, the Emperor had decreed that he would work privately in his office until ten, and therefore there was no need for a full staff before dawn. Small comfort for his valet and the cook who must make his coffee at five as usual, but it was a gift to the rest of us. Certainly my maid, Claudine, wasn't awake yet.

Michel was still asleep, and how not? He'd ridden in from Silesia the previous day and then been up half the night. Presumably the staff meeting was scheduled for afternoon. He was sprawled in the very middle of the bed on his stomach while I had curled up against his warmth, toasty and comfortable despite the chill of the room. The fire had died down to ashes. I slid out of bed without disturbing him and wrapped up in my rose velvet dressing gown, sliding my feet into last night's dancing slippers as proof against the cold.

I stirred the fire gently, putting more kindling on the coals and encouraging it to light. The servants probably did not like it that I had driven a hob into the woodwork of the mantel in order to hang a kettle, but I had to have some way of at least making a cup of tea. I put the water on as the fire blazed up and sat down in the armchair and stretched my feet against the fender. The thin soles of the dancing slippers were worn nearly through. I should have to have another pair before long.

The strangeness of the dream stayed with me. I leaned back in the armchair, my head against the collar of Michel's evening cloak, watching the flames leap, kindling catching quick and bright from the coals. Life from death, the story of the phoenix, born of fire…. Why had I dreamed of a sister? I had never had one and not particularly felt the lack. Also, this girl was very particular, not merely a generic sibling I might have imagined, but a real child, the dream clear and bright as memory. Only it was no memory of mine. Why should I, brought up Dutch Reformed more than anything, imagine that lush icon of the Madonna, dark-skinned and gilded with precious gold? That was no part of my story.

And yet it was someone's. I was certain of that. This was no mere fancy but a weaving together of stories, a true dream born of something I could not put my finger on. Who was the girl and what had we promised Her in times past? And what had that to do with the present? Not for the first time I wished that I had had the opportunity to learn from Dr. Mesmer, that controversial physician that Lannes and Noirtier had worked with in Paris. Noirtier had promised me an introduction, but I had not returned to Paris for more than a few weeks in the year and a half since then, what with one campaign and another and one piece of business and another.

It had been difficult enough to see Michel. In this year and a half he had fought two great battles, at Elchingen and Jena, and we had utterly crushed the Austrian Empire. The Holy Roman Empire, that rotten colossus that had stood for a thousand years, was no more. The Austrian emperor had ceased to claim the crown of Charlemagne, ceased to claim the right to govern the Continent in the name of God. Instead, sovereign principalities that had long wished freedom from the Hapsburg dynasty were on their own, and rulers like Max Joseph of Bavaria were glorying in their newfound independence. Other states were bound together in various alliances, including the Confederation of the Rhine. The most powerful state, of course, was Prussia, which still bitterly opposed us, and for good reason. They, along with Austria and Russia, had benefited from carving up Poland scarcely twenty years ago.

A century gone, Poland had been one of the proudest kingdoms in Europe. While the Thirty Years' War had decimated the entire center of the continent, destroying cities and farms and people alike, nigh to dropping millions back into the Middle Ages, Poland had stood to the side, her strength a buffer against the Tartars to the east. But all things decline and fail, and by the time my father was born, Poland could no longer defend her own borders. His mother was Polish. I knew that, just as I knew that I had been named for her, a pretty woman who had made her way in the world as mistress to a Hungarian noble who had cared for her and her son until his death. My father had been left alone in the world at thirteen, the ward of a maternal uncle who was a hired sword in the service of the Czar. That was what it had come to by then.

He had taught me a little Polish, something I found very useful now, as almost none of the court had any at all. It came back to me swiftly, as things learned in early childhood often do, and here, looking out at the rooftops of Warsaw, I wondered about her, that woman who shared my name who had died a decade before I was born. Had she gone with the Hungarian for money or for love or for sheer survival? I remembered that my father had smiled when I asked about her once, fingered my long blond hair where it fell out of its ribbons. "Fair like you," he said. "Hard but not cruel. My father was fire, but she was earth. Storms could break themselves against her."

Was that why I dreamed this now, some lost memory of early childhood stirred by the sound of voices speaking Polish, something buried in the blood that answered to the church towers of Warsaw against the winter sky? It was true that I liked it here, liked the temper of hussars in their brittle pride, impoverished boys with a nobleman's name and little else, determined to win back their country from Russia and Prussia alike. They appealed to me, gallant and stubborn, hard drinking and hard riding. Antique rooms and antique manners, women in their made-over court dresses from the last century, making do with their chins high and their beauty as their chief ornament…oh yes, it appealed to me. I should be proud to claim kinship, though I doubted they would feel the same. I was hardly a virtuous Catholic girl.

The future of Poland rested in our hands. We had won the section partitioned to Austria, and had made it the sovereign Grand Duchy of Warsaw, but two of the three sections remained, divided between Prussia and Russia. Would the Emperor restore those sections as well? Would he back the patriots who dreamed of Poland reunited and restored as a nation? We had been welcomed in Warsaw as liberators on that hope, the best chance those rash boys and wise minds alike could see—Napoleon stooping like an eagle, a wind through the world in whose wake their land might again flourish, an ally who might drive their foes before them and restore all.

…what wind is this that shakes the flames…

A breath from the dream, a fragment of words that escaped me even as I tried to capture them.

…it is the wind from Egypt…

Some part of a play? Lines I had heard performed somewhere once? And yet I had done Antony and Cleopatra dozens of times, two different scripts by two different masters, and those were not the lines. It was not even in that ponderous translation of Shakespeare, "come dear lady, the day is done and we are for the dark," which had sent shivers up my spine. Why did it make me think of Antony and Cleopatra when it was no part of that play?

Michel stirred, turning over, and I opened my eyes. A thin stream of steam emerged from the kettle. I got up and made tea, poured the pot to steep with strong Russian tea. I had only one cup, so if Michel wanted some without calling for Claudine he should have to share. In any event, he preferred coffee.

He was looking at me as I poured my cup, his hair mussed and a day's stubble blurring the lines of his face. "What time is it?" he asked.

"Not quite eight," I said. "You've had a good sleep."

He groaned and flopped back among the pillows.

I came and sat on the end of the bed with my cup of tea, tucking my feet under me. "It's still early for the court." I could hear small sounds now, the footsteps of servants moving about, the clink of a coalscuttle being hauled up the stairs to one of the upper rooms.

"Late for me," he said. "How is the Emperor?"

"Indulgent," I said, taking a sip. "But then he's entirely enamored with Countess Walewska."

"Who?"

"I doubt if you noticed her last night," I said. "A pretty blonde."

"Oh." Michel shrugged. The Emperor's assorted amours did not interest him very much, except as in they disturbed Josephine, which is to say very little. An infatuation on campaign was nothing to the Empress.

"He's mad about her," I said. "He met her last week at some function or other and was entranced. Corbineau is worried."

That at least warranted a sharp look from Michel. "Corbineau? What the hell is he worried about?"

"I can't make any sense of it," I said, taking another sip. "He asked me to See for him, to take a look at her for him."

Michel propped up on one elbow and reached for my cup, which I gave him with a smile. "What did you see?"

"Nothing," I replied.

Michel frowned. "Isn't that unusual?"

"I suppose," I said. I hadn't thought of it that way. I had blamed the noise and the crowd. Corbineau wouldn't stop talking. But perhaps that wasn't all. "I couldn't really See her properly. It was like looking at a rock and trying to see the shape of the mountain. What you see is too small to give you any true sense of the whole."

Michel's eyebrows rose and he took a sip and handed the cup back to me before he continued. "A Companion?"

"I don't know," I said slowly. "Something. Something deep." I took a sip of tea and gave it back to Michel. "But I don't see what danger she can possibly be. She's a young wife that the Emperor is enamored with. Maybe she'll yield to him and maybe she won't, but I don't see what possible difference it can make in the long term."

"You underestimate other women," Michel said, sitting up and tucking the coverlet about his lap. "What possible difference can a campaign infatuation make? How about Roxane? You're the one who told me I had to read Arrian's Campaigns of Alexander. She was a campaign infatuation that changed the world."

"I do not underestimate other women," I said.

"You do." Michel cupped his hands around the tea, mostly leaves in the bottom now. "Just because she's not waving a saber doesn't mean she's not dangerous. Look at Josephine."

"Josephine isn't dangerous."

"Not to you," he said. "She likes you and you've given her reason to trust you. But she's not harmless. She's the one who sent Madame Tallien to the country and kicked de Stael out of town, not the Emperor. And the Emperor's sisters aren't exactly harmless either. Pauline may be all right, but Elisa is the Emperor all over again and Caroline is a sleek, well-fed ermine ready to go for the throat."

"I thought you liked Caroline," I said.

Michel shrugged. "She's pretty. One can't help but notice."

"It might be the transparent bodices," I said wryly. "But lovely breasts don't make her dangerous."

"How about dabbling in the legacy of the Pleiade?" Michel said. "She has her own pet fortune teller according to rumor. Elza, you're not the only Dove in France. Caroline may be more interested in advancing her own interests and her husband's rather than the shape of the world to come, but I wouldn't dismiss her."

"The shape of the world to come," I said. "That's the question, isn't it?" I looked at him, his legs crossed beneath the covers, tousled red hair and square jaw, my on-and-off lover of six years. "What will the map look like when we're finished with it?"

"I don't know," he said seriously, "But it will be a change as profound as Charlemagne's, as Caesar's or Alexander's. The world will be changed and it will never go back to the way it was."

"No matter how much some wish it," I said. That at least required no Dove to know—the old powers of Europe had deeply vested interests in the way things had been done, in pretending that one could simply render it 1700 again, undo the mighty tide of revolution, ideas and books and all.

"But who wins and who loses?" Michel said. "That's what's up in the air. The Poles...."

"The Poles want a piece of it," I said. "They want to harness the flood." There was something there, some story of an ancient kingdom fallen into disrepair that hoped to ride the crest....

"I'm all for that," Michel said. "We need allies and they're good ones. But getting Russian Silesia back is going to mean kicking the Russians so hard in the ass that they can't find their asses again, and that's not easy work." He looked at me. "And you know who that will fall to."

"You," I said.

"I'm the one with an army corps sitting next door. I'm not afraid of Von Bennigsen, but I'm not thrilled with the idea of taking him on before spring either. The weather's awful and the fodder is scarce too." Michel tipped the cup hopefully, but there was nothing but leaves.

I got up and refilled it from the pot. "I think the Emperor plans to winter in Warsaw," I said.

"And if I can thank Countess Walewska for that, I shall," Michel said. He grinned at me. "A few square meals, a few dances with a beautiful sacrifice...."

"Is that what you call that?" I said. "Rather more than a dance, my beast!"

"So I hope," he said. "And the staff meeting isn't until two."

As it happened, the staff meeting lasted barely an hour, and Michel was back at his own rooms by four, flinging his hat on the sideboard in his rather larger suite in the palace as I looked up from my book. I had curled up in a chair with a light collation and a rather dog-eared copy of *Therese Philosophe*, which no doubt had occasioned a scandal when it was brought into the palace thirty years earlier.

I looked up as Michel came in. "Back already?"

He nodded, a perplexed expression on his face. "The Emperor asked for my verbal report, which is the same as the written one I gave him yesterday. Which is not materially changed from my report last week because we're in winter quarters. The only change is that some few of the wounded men have returned to active duty, and thirty-odd men are on sick leave with winter influenza. Why this required reporting in person in Warsaw is beyond me!'

"Maybe he plans to discuss the spring campaign with you later," I said sensibly.

"That could be." Michel sat down on the other end of the settee, and I slid my feet over between him and the back. "It's two or three months yet, but it's certainly worth talking about. We're going to need some intelligence about the roads east of Działdowo. Our maps are from the 1780s. I can't tell which roads are capable of handling an artillery train. I told Berthier I needed to get back to my troops. They're in winter quarters near Działdowo, between the Prussians and Warsaw. I don't like being gone very long."

"I know," I said, reconciling myself to another long absence. I had no assignment from the Emperor at present, but until I did there seemed no choice but to stay in Warsaw.

"You could come with me," Michel said. I looked at him and he shrugged. "It's winter quarters, Elza. Nothing is happening. We're sitting in a small Polish town. It's not as though the Emperor can't find you if he wants you, though he seems remarkably busy at the moment."

"I've noticed," I said.

"He sent Duroc with a letter and a bouquet today. She turned him off."

I blinked. "She told him no?"

"Apparently," Michel said. "But unless you've something to do with all that, there's no reason for you to stay here, is there?"

Nothing except a nagging feeling that I should, though what I had to do with any of it entirely escaped me. "No," I said. "There isn't. I'd be delighted to come to Działdowo with you."

WINTER

All the way from Warsaw to Działdowo the rain was rolling, a gray screen across the landscape. We expected snow in mid-January, but it warmed unexpectedly into heavy rain on top of the snow already on the ground, turning everything to a morass of mud and half-melted snow. I left my dresses behind in Warsaw with Claudine, and a good thing too. There is no place for Madame St. Elme here, only for Charles van Aylde, that handsome Dutch volunteer who had attached himself to campaign after campaign. Not that Michel's staff did not know I was a woman, but for the most part they were used to me and the ordinary soldiers no doubt assumed I was a civilian valet or the like. Given that some of the marshals were known for traveling with extensive household staff, including cooks and footmen, a civilian valet provoked no comment.

Działdowo was an unprepossessing small town home to a thousand people. No doubt in summer it would have appeared picturesque, but in winter it was miserable. Our tents were lined up in neat rows in field after field, fires smoking sullenly in the steady drizzle. The village itself was little more than a hamlet at the intersection of two roads, a stone inn, a stone church, and a few houses about a square. Many of the other houses had roofs of thatch.

And yet it was strategically important. The roads that had given the town its inn, that had given it a name and a place on the map, were beyond critical. Here the road from Warsaw came down from the hills and woods into the plain, and here it divided in two, the left arm running northwest to Gdansk and the right northeast to Konigsberg. If either the Russians or the Prussians wished to march on Warsaw they should have to use this road. Our troops stood astride the junction. Not that anyone truly thought that the

Russians would begin a winter offensive. The terrible state of the roads would weigh more heavily on them than us, as they should have to move and we should only have to hold firm.

Word had spread from Warsaw what we were about, and for the most part the Poles were glad to see us. The hatred of the Russians runs deep in that part of the world, as after all it had only been twelve years since the last war, since Poland was erased from the map and ceased to be an independent country. Even in the inn in Dzialwolo they had horror stories to tell of Cossacks and the Russians, awful stories of livestock slaughtered and left to rot, daughters raped, and barns going up in flames. More than once I envied Michel that he did not understand enough Polish to follow most of these stories.

He sat beside the fire in the inn's main room, his maps spread over the table before him, nodding seriously at a story told by the innkeeper's wife of atrocities perpetrated on her family and neighbors by the Cossacks. Colonel Dery and Dr. Duplessis, who did not understand any Polish, were eating bread and creamy cheese at the next table. We were paying for provisions, of course. These were allies and Michel was very strict about looting, as the citizens of Bavaria could attest, and our purse was fat enough. But there is no buying what there is not, and one look at the stores was enough to give me concern. I did not see how we could pass the winter here, not two months more at least on the foodstuffs there were, and the situation with the fodder seemed even more dire. This was not a wealthy area and it simply could not support our numbers. Dery and Max were eating, Michel was nodding seriously though I doubt he understood one word in six, and I wished that I did not understand quite so well.

"Lech found her body three days later," the innkeeper's wife said, her lips pursed tightly. "We never knew why they did it. Wasn't it enough just to rape her and kill her?"

Michel said nothing, just nodded again seriously. He understood her tone, the expression on her face, even if he could not follow the story. She needed to tell this to someone important, to a general glittering with gold braid, to the man who stood between them and the Cossacks presently, needed to tell this story of brutality a dozen years old. And so he listened and didn't hurry her. He nodded and showed respect.

This is the backside of war, always and forever. These are the ashes that are left, the survivors still caught in horror even as they go about living.

At the next table Max and Charles Dery burst out laughing over some joke of their own, neither of them understanding a word of Polish. They didn't understand, but at least they might show some respect for the old woman's grief and bewilderment. "Be still," I said to them in French, "the poor woman is telling the Marshal of her niece's murder!"

They hushed then, Max and Dery, like schoolboys caught talking out of turn in class. I saw Michel's eyes move to me and then back to the innkeeper's wife. He wasn't angry at me for calling them to order. Max and Dery both knew me, and Max at least had had reason to work with me in the past, in Boulogne on the Emperor's business. They treated me like an odd kind of creature, half soldier and half mother, for all that Max was the same age as I.

The innkeeper's wife noticed too. She finished her story, and with an expressive shrug for the cruelty of the world, turned away.

"Come and sit by me, Mother," I said, sliding down the wooden bench and making room for her at her own table. "I have brandy in my flask that I will be happy to share. It's a wet day."

She looked at me suspiciously for a moment, taking in my shorn hair, man's trousers, blue jacket with no insignia, and finally my woman's face. "Are you his wife?" she asked.

I met her eyes squarely. "No, Mother."

"Ah." She shrugged, and then lowered herself onto the bench next to me. "You are going to get yourself in trouble, young woman."

I passed her the flask. "I think that cow is already out the barn. I have borne two sons, Mother."

"So have I. And two grown daughters as well. I am thirty-four, you know." She looked at me sharply.

"I did not guess," I said, but secretly I was appalled. She looked ancient, bent and arthritic, with white hair and fingers gnarled with arthritis, and yet she was only four years my senior, I who could still dance all night and ride all day.

"You are not even French," she said.

"Dutch," I agreed.

She stared at me again, looked me up and down. "Your accent

is very bad."

"But not so bad as these French," I said, taking back my flask and drinking from it "To your health."

Her eyes were sea green under all those wrinkles. She tipped her head towards Michel and Max and Dery by the fire, the courier just coming in. "Are they serious, these French?'

"They are serious about being rid of the Russians," I said truthfully. "I have talked to Prince Poniatowski in Warsaw. He is serious."

"And your Emperor?"

I took a breath. "I do not know," I said. "He is no friend of the Czar. If we can defeat the Russians we will. But if we can—that is a thing I do not know."

"Ah." She was silent for a long time, taking my flask back and turning it in her hands. Then she got up heavily. "Maybe it will be better. Maybe it will be worse." She gave my flask back to me and went back to her kitchen.

After that it did not stop raining. Everything was soggy and mildewed. Blades rusted in scabbards and even my stockings mildewed. In short, we experienced discomfort, but not real hardship. Four days later a letter from the Emperor reached us, brought by a young chasseur filled with his own importance.

Michel read it in silence by the fire, the light glinting off the buttons on his coat and making planes of his face, his long greatcoat swaying. Carefully, he refolded it and looked up. "Thank you for your promptness," he said to the chasseur dripping on the floor. His trousers were so muddy that one could hardly tell what color they originally were. Half of the roads between Działdowo and Warsaw were all over him. "You may rest the night here. I will have dispatches and letters for you to return with in the morning. Dery, see to it that this man has a hot supper and a good bed tonight."

"Sir." Dery led the courier out, shutting the door behind to keep the warmth in.

Behind Michel the stag's horns on the wall were thrown by the firelight in a shadow three feet high, as though he were wearing an immense pair of antlers himself. He went to the fireplace and poked at it a little with the fire iron, the sparks shooting up the chimney and making the shadows on the wall move like live things. "Elza," he said, but did not turn, kicking idly at the nearest log.

"Yes?"

"The Emperor hopes that I am well."

"Well, you are, aren't you?"

"Yes." He kicked at the log again, and the sparks illuminated his face in a flash before they died. "This is poor countryside without much for them to do and with far too little to eat. In a week the complaints will start coming in -- stolen chickens, noisy brawls. If I don't hold it down then, in two weeks it will be worse."

"You will hold it down." I crossed my legs on the table bench. "You always do."

He looked around from the fire, throwing his face into shadow. "Such faith in me. Elza, I'm sorry I dragged you down from Warsaw. You could be dancing with generals right now."

"There is only one general I want to dance with, and he's right here," I said, smiling at him. "Believe me, I would rather be with you."

He handed the folded letter to me. "What do you make of this?" he asked.

Quickly, I scanned the pages, squinting in the poor light. "That my eyesight is finally beginning to go." I frowned as I read the conventional phrases, the cheerful scrawled signature. "Maria Walewska gave in," I said.

He looked up. "Where do you get that?"

"He's delighted. Look at that flying N. If she were still saying no, he would have such a crabapple up his ass about it by now that his signature would come out little and squinchy."

Michel roared as I meant him to. "There is no one like him, is there?"

"Not on this earth at present," I replied.

"He has a more complicated personal life than Zeus on Olympus." Michel came and sat across from me, turning my hand in his, covering my fingers with his long ones. "I can hardly blame him. Surrounded by sycophants and fools every moment, cut off from everyone by court intrigue and ceremonial, isolated like a lion in a cage in the zoo. None of us can bridge that gap, even if we want to. He has put himself at the top of a tall pillar and now even

Josephine can hardly reach him. Elza, he wants to be a man again, a man and a lover and a soldier. I am far luckier than he is. I have never aspired to a crown."

"Better not to," I said. "Companions should know better than to grasp for that ring of fire. Better to take the honors that come one's way with grace and leave the rest."

"As you say." Michel closed his hand around mine. "I have a feeling that something is wrong, something with nothing to do with the weather or the fodder and the rest. Read for me, Elza."

"My cards are upstairs." I said. "I'll go and get them if you think it's important."

Michel smiled ruefully, still covering my hand. "It's a little unbalanced, isn't it? A rational man in this day and age packing a soothsayer along like Wallenstein or Julius Caesar?"

I shrugged. "If it worked for Wallenstein and Caesar, that's good enough for me. They were both successful, weren't they?"

"They were also both assassinated."

At that I felt a moment of chill, a hand at my back as though something pushed at me that I could not quite remember. "Come upstairs," I said. "I'll read on the bed. Better that no one see it anyway."

He followed me up and sat down on one side of the inn's best bed while I got the cards from their layers of oilcloth and silk, shuffled them feeling their familiar smoothness beneath my fingers. "Ask your question," I said, closing my eyes and letting their touch absorb me. "And don't ask something enormous. You know I won't get anything that isn't vague that way."

"What is going on in Warsaw?"

I shook my head. "That's precisely what I mean by enormous. Thousands of things are going on in Warsaw, Michel."

There was a sudden knock on the door and I started, opening my eyes. As Michel stood up I swept the cards together underneath my leg. He opened the door. "Yes?"

Dery stood on the tiny landing outside. "Sir, I hate to interrupt, but we have a complaint from two citizens. They claim that some of our troopers used part of the thatched roof of their house for fodder."

Michel put his hand to his forehead. "All right. I'm coming

down. The roof?"

"The roof, sir," Dery said. "I know that fodder is short…."

"But we can't eat the roofs. Yes, I know. A general order on the issue of roof-eating being forbidden…" I heard his bootheels loud on the stairs as he followed Dery down.

I held the deck, feeling it warm in my hands, and then on impulse turned the first card over, the one that should have been the root of the story. The sun shown brightly over a garden in bloom, a boy and girl at play beneath the blue sky. Happiness unfeigned, the return of joy…. The Emperor was happy. It did not take the cards to say that. And yet there was something that touched me with cold--boy and girl twins beneath a cloudless sky, laughing and running with no knowledge of that which might come….

I put the card back into the deck and carefully shuffled before I put them away. After all, Michel had never spoken his question aloud. It might have been anything. It did not necessarily have anything to do with Countess Walewska.

Michel came back an hour later shaking his head. "We're going to have to move," he said, coming in and spreading his map over the bed. I was washing out shirts in a bucket and hanging them to dry as best I might against the back of the chimney of the fireplace below as though I actually were his valet. "We can't stay here, not for two more months. There's not enough to eat."

I spread his shirt against the warm stones, smoothing the wrinkles out. A hot iron was probably beyond me, but he truly didn't need to keep that state in the field. "And then what?"

"Torun," he said. "It's a much larger town and it's not very far. But it will have better stocks and since it's on the river it's easier to supply. We'll move out tomorrow."

"I thought the Emperor said we were to stay here," I said.

"If Von Bennigsen marches on Warsaw he'll get to Torun before Działdowo," he said. "It's safe enough. And if we stay here we won't have a horse fit for battle come spring. Not if we eat every roof in town."

The next morning we broke camp at dawn, the usual chaos of moving out of an encampment we'd been in for some weeks, thousands forming up into columns for the road, followed by the living monster that is the baggage train, sutlers and wives and wagons of all kinds, provisions and personal belongings and children and pets and the rest. Max rode with the medical wagons in the back. We had no wounded with us at present, as they had all been sent to hospitals in Warsaw, but we did have a number of men on sick call with one thing and another, mostly respiratory illnesses that surfaced every winter, and so his duties continued even on the march.

Michel rode to the fore with his staff, and I could hardly join him there, though I certainly did not want to confine myself to the back of the baggage train. Instead I fell in with Dery in the squadron of hussars to which he belonged.

It had cleared finally, and the rain had frozen, making a fine tracery of ice on trees and earth that melted as the morning passes.

"If this keeps up the roads will be a morass," Dery said. As though they weren't already, I thought. Days and days of rain on top of melting snow meant that in some places the mud came up to the horses' knees.

I nodded, dropping behind him. It did not look good for me to put myself forward too much, especially when we had seen no action since I came down from Warsaw. I did not want to engender resentments.

I slowed Pomme just a little, and we slipped into the first rank, riding in loose order wherever the solidity of the road surface permitted. The hussar on my left, hardly more than a boy, smiled a little shyly at me, as if uncertain whether to dare a greeting or not. He looked vaguely ridiculous in his fierce costume and struggling moustache, as though he would be much more at home mucking out stables in Toulouse. I wondered how old he actually was.

The morning drew on with a five-minute halt for water later. I took advantage of the halt to check the condition of Pomme's feet, an action that won a look of approval from Dery. He had not been Michel's aide long. It was always like that when they did not yet know me, and supposed I must be different than I am.

Pomme nickered softly and butted against my shoulder. I leaned gratefully against her, looking into one intelligent brown eye. We got on well. Before Pomme had been mine she had been Corbineau's, a strained relationship at best as each strove for mastery. I had bought her from Corbineau a year ago when it became clear that my beloved Nestor was no longer up to the rigors of a campaign at twenty-three. Nestor, in turn, had been sold to Gervais Subervie and was currently enjoying his retirement at Subervie's parents' inn in Gascony, where he was teaching young Master Jean Subervie, age five-and-a-half, to ride.

I swung back up again, trying to look easier than I felt. During the stop my muscles had frozen up a little, which was what I deserved for the months of not riding enough astride while on the Emperor's business, and I could feel the ache along the insides of my thighs. However, at least my courses had decided to absent themselves once again, as they often did on campaign. It did not bear thinking that there could be some other reason for it.

While we were mounting up Michel rode up with three or four other men, his chief of staff and an Imperial Aide-de-Camp I did not know. I made myself inconspicuous behind a tree lest he tell me to move to a position further in the rear, back in the baggage train where I ought to be under any circumstances.

Michel drew rein to talk to Dery. I only caught a few words across the distance—Dery had sent out a fan of chasseurs ahead of the column an hour previously but they had not yet reported back.

Michel nodded. "Not time enough yet," he said to the Aide-de-Camp, and they moved on, past us toward the head of the column.

We swung back onto the road under a brightening sky. It looked as though the sun were beginning to break through the clouds, a welcome change from the days of rain, now and again peeking through scudding low veils. Somewhere ahead somebody began a bawdy song, but was hushed with the reminder that the Marshal and his staff were just ahead. I whistled under my breath, and Pomme pricked her ears, dark hairs on the tips in contrast to her silvery gray coat.

"She's a pretty one," the boy next to me said. "What is she?"

"Part Lusitano, part who-knows-what," I said, reaching forward and patting her flank. "She's a good horse."

The boy looked doubtful. "Bit small."

"Not for me," I said. I've never liked sheer size in a horse. I preferred intelligence and speed rather than sheer power.

Ahead, a faint flash among the trees caught my eye. Dery was coming forward along the side of the column keeping anyone from straggling and pulled up beside me. "Did you see that?"

"Yes."

The boy looked bewildered as Dery nodded abruptly and touched his heels to his horse's flank, spurring up towards the front of the column, maneuvering around the ranks carefully spread out to take advantage of wherever the road's surface was most solid. Before he reached the first rank and the staff ahead the woods erupted with gunfire, powder smoke rolling forward in a cloud as the reports startled birds from the trees.

Beside me the boy sank slowly in the saddle, blood streaming from his mouth and shattered jaw as he fell towards me, his eyes wide with disbelief.

Pomme shied at the falling body, nearly going up on her hind legs, and I pulled her hard to the right toward the trees that verged the road. The reins were in my right hand and beneath me Pomme danced to avoid the corpse beneath her feet. I touched my heels to her and she pushed toward the trees that lined the road to the right, their interlaced branches bare with winter.

They were beyond the trees. I could see them now, men kneeling in line to reload, the rank behind standing, and I knew I was marked. I hauled on Pomme hard, putting the trunk of a big tree between me and the ones I could see.

And not a moment too soon. The next volley crashed into us, the screams of a wounded horse mingling with the cries of men. Dery was shouting orders and in the woods I heard answering shouts, words I didn't understand. Whether they were orders to reload or fall back I could not tell.

Suddenly Pomme reared, backing frantically. In our cut toward the trees we almost stumbled over one of their men reloading, the wadding gripped in his teeth. With a cry he threw the gun down, reaching for the long knife in his belt.

I wasn't certain how my saber came to be in my left hand, as I didn't remember drawing it at all, though of course I must have. As Pomme came down I struck him across the face, leaving a bloody ruin and a sickening grating on bone that almost tore the hilt out of my hand. I jerked it to free it, propelled forward by Pomme's momentum.

Behind me I heard Michel shouting, "Get off the road!" his voice carrying over every melee. In any case, the firing was sporadic, one or two shots here and there as men had reloaded, punctuated with the different report of one of our officer's pistols.

I wheeled about, raising the saber to guard, the blood running down the channels of the blade and soaking my glove, looking about the wood. The underbrush was sparse, bare and broken branches and drifts of last year's leaves, little enough cover. I could see that they were pulling back, pale sunlight glancing off fixed bayonets as they backed away. There were two on foot ahead fighting with a mounted hussar who had broken through, his scarlet pelisse bright as blood in the wood. I ducked under a branch and rode at them, taking the first from behind, his arm going slack as I severed the tendons in his shoulder with the first downward swipe while the blood from the severed artery fountained in the air.

Then I was past him, stirrup to stirrup with the other hussar, a man whose face I knew but whose name I did not remember.

The firing was sporadic, and there were no others near except the dead and dying, so we turned back toward the road. Michel rode up at a canter, bared saber in hand, and for a moment I did not think he recognized me, so intent was his face, stern and serene at once, incongruous amid the carnage. Without a word he rode past and with a shrug the veteran and I wheeled to follow. My left wrist hurt. I must have twisted it on the recovery to guard.

The firing had stopped. There were eight of us together now, other troopers forming up. Dery and Michel had spurred up the bank further along, where it was steeper, pursuing them into the woods with the rest of the troop. On the road there were six red-jacketed bodies in the mud, one struggling while his horse stood over him, head down and stirrups empty. The veteran dismounted, squelching toward him. Behind me I could hear the frantic whinny of an injured horse. As quickly as it began it was over. The acrid powder smoke was blowing away rapidly to the east, leaving the road bathed in winter sunshine. I let Pomme pick her own way up the bank.

"Russians." Dery was dismounted, speaking to Michel, prodding at one of the bodies with one toe. Michel had not dismounted. "A foraging party, I should say, not a movement en masse."

Eleazar was used to the smell of blood and stood perfectly calmly though mud and gore coated his white socks. "I expect," Michel said. He raised his head, the pale winter light glancing off his hair. "They've the same problems with food and fodder that we do."

"My thought is they mistook us for a supply train and then got a nasty surprise," Dery said.

Michel nodded. "No doubt. Have someone ride after Lieutenant Montreux and his men and tell them to come back here. There's no point in chasing a few stragglers all over the countryside." Then he turned Eleazar and rode toward the back of the column, where the bodies were.

That night we were in Torun, a good-sized town on the banks of the Vistula River. The rest of VI Corps had caught up to us, and the elements that began the day in the rear had passed through and were five kilometers ahead of us, camped in the muddy fields just above the river's floodplain. It was a pretty medieval town laid out about the river trade, with red roofs and two bridges that spanned the swollen waters. Here they were less glad to see us than in Warsaw. The town's burghers were Prussian and Protestant, and while they did not love the Russians they did not love us either.

Rather than headquartering in an inn, Michel chose instead to take possession of the town hall, having ample room within its sturdy confines for all the staff and a considerable guard that would not have to be divided overmuch. Of course others would be quartered in the town, in inns and other public buildings like the old barracks, but he resisted groups of smaller than ten, a measure of caution that he did not usually display among friends. Dery and a number of others were detailed to acquire bedding and other necessities while Michel met with the town fathers. It said something that he required no interpreter. They all spoke German rather than Polish.

For my part I hustled his actual bodyservant, Courrèges, about until he managed to make up some reasonable semblance of a bedchamber for his master. Leaving him to the end of that, I went down again to the largest meeting room to see if the burghers had gone and if our staff were meeting and if anyone had found any dinner.

Michel had laid his maps out on the largest table and there was a huge fire blazing in a mantelpiece adorned with an elaborate clock and matching candelabra. We might have been in Munich.

Dery was leaning over the maps, munching bread and sausage. "Foraging parties tomorrow, sir. Here and here," he said, pointing with one greasy finger.

Michel stopped pacing and looked where he was pointing. It wasn't much after eight, but it seemed much later. Pomme was long since settled in the nice warm stable. "Very well, Dery. Mounted parties only. In case of any heavy resistance."

"Our scouts have encountered no further activity, sir," Dery replied, taking a swig of the beer at his elbow.

Michel began pacing again. I was certain that he had eaten whatever he was going to eat in about three minutes. "Don't let the regular companies press any further ahead. Send a message to Corbineau that I mean him too. We are not going to spread out all over the countryside." He glanced up and saw me standing in the doorway, then looked back at Dery. "It's too uncertain this far north."

"Yes, sir," Dery replied and began rolling up the maps.

"Write it out yourself. Just tell Corbineau to camp and stay where he is. I know he can't resist scouting, but tell him to be extremely circumspect."

"Is there anything else?" Dery asked, looking hopefully towards the kitchens. He must have had hollow legs. He always seemed to be hungry.

"That is all," Michel said. Then quietly he added, "And then get some sleep."

The door closed behind Dery, and for a long moment there was only the sound of the fire. "You have not got the blood off your face," Michel said, brushing at my cheekbone with one hand.

"Oh that," I said. "I must have wiped sweat out of my eyes."

"Upstairs," he said. "There is a fire lit there too. If you will stay, Elza?"

"Where else would I be?"

"I will be up in a moment," he said. "As soon as I've spoken with the sergeant of the guard."

The room was warm, sturdily built with modern windows with many panes of glass. There was a bed with clean linen sheets turned down, and heavy shutters on the window to close against the cold. There were candles in a brass holder and a wash basin and pitcher. Courrèges had finished his work and gracefully departed, something of a first for him. I stripped off my gloves and washed my face and hands. Michel was right. I must have wiped my face with my gloves.

Down the hall in the other rooms I could hear the rumble of men's voices, surely the best sound in the world.

I took off my coat and draped it over a chair. My wrist was still sore, though there were no bruises that I could see, so I hung the sword belt beside it and stood looking in the glass over the mantel.

I heard Michel's familiar step at the door, and then he came in and closed the door behind him, looking about as if surprised by how warm and inviting the room had become. Outside the rain had started again, blowing against the window in great bursts of wind, not quite cold enough to freeze. He came and stood beside me, reflected in the glass. The candlelight cast a strange sheen on the mirror's surface, burnishing it like metal instead of glass, rendering my eyes huge and feral.

"Courrèges has done a good job," I said.

He slid his arms around me over my tailored waistcoat and neckcloth, his chin not quite tilted up to rest on my head, almost exactly a head taller than I. "He did," Michel agreed.

In the mirror we looked so odd, Michel now lean as a whiplash, cheekbones carved out of marble, hair falling forwards to cover where his hairline had begun to recede, me slight in the white shirt and waistcoat, androgynous and pale, hair darkened by the damp. Erastes and eromenos.

"Tired?" he asked.

I nodded, leaning back against him.

"Sleep then." He turned away from the glass and blew out the candles. As I finished undressing I heard him sit down, the heavy thump of each boot hitting the floor.

The boy from the road was once again before my eyes, falling silently as a tree, with no blood at all, no wound on his face.

"I have ruined my gloves," I said.

"I have some leather soap for Eleazar's tack," he said. "You can use it."

He turned down the bed. The rain spattered against the glass, now with the faint ticking sound of ice. I stood considering whether to sleep in my shirt, but it smelled too much of other people's blood and finding my bags in the dark seemed like too much work. Instead I dropped the shirt on the floor and slipped in beside him naked, his arms fitting about my waist again. I hardly felt his arms around me before I was asleep.

Eylau

The Russians went on the offensive and it was Michel's fault. Our sudden move northwards and the aggressive mettle of our scouting parties signaled to Von Bennigsen the beginning of a winter offensive, so he decided to jump first. It was a logical conclusion, given our victory at Austerlitz the previous year—a battle fought in December in horrible weather against all expectations. It was reasonable for him to conclude that the Emperor intended the same again, a lightning strike in the depths of winter when no one would expect it. Some of our advance scouts, especially of Klein's Dragoons, to which Corbineau belonged, had pressed as far north as Lidzbark Warminski, well beyond Russian lines, and indeed almost to the Baltic. Certainly we had concentrations of troops who had gone up the eastward road from Działdowo to quarter in Olsztyn as we had gone to Torun, and how not? There was nowhere in Poland that 25,000 men could go into winter quarters in one place.

A letter came for Michel from the Emperor, a formal, stiff letter in Berthier's hand demanding that he come to Warsaw immediately and explain why he saw fit to disobey a direct order instructing him to halt VI Corps and go into winter camp rather than moving without permission. He left immediately for Warsaw and I did not accompany him for what would certainly be an official reprimand at least. My presence would do him no good and might do him harm if it seemed that he was passing his time in frivolity rather than tending to business.

Instead I remained in Torun with Dery and Max Duplessis, waiting to see what would happen. It was nearly a week before word came. On the 31st of January a courier arrived from Warsaw, his bags bulging with dispatches and mail.

"Not too grim looking," said Dery to Max.

"Yes, but where is the Marshal?" Max wondered out loud.

I didn't think that his absence was a good sign. The courier dismounted and hurried in to report to the Chief of Staff. With a look at one another, Max and Dery followed after. If he had been relieved…. Scuffing my boots in the dirt of the stableyard, I crossed the courtyard and went into the stables. If he had been relieved, I would return to Warsaw.

At the sound of my step Pomme nickered, sticking her head over the door of her stall. Gratefully, I went in to her. I'd already brushed and curried her, but I picked up the comb again and leaned against her side, brushing with the grain of the hair and she turned her head and bumped me, pushing me back a step. The brushing was soothing and it gave me something to do other than worry about things that could not be helped. I brushed her entirely again from nose to tail before I heard the sound of voices in the courtyard and Max opened the stable doors.

"Elza?" he called.

"Yes?"

Max came down the row to the door of Pomme's stall and leaned over the door. "It's not as bad as it could be," he said.

"What happened?" I asked, looking up, Pomme nudging at my hand.

"It was an official reprimand. The Emperor asked him what it was about the order 'stay where you are and do not move' that the Marshal did not understand, and that if he did understand it, why he took it upon himself to ignore his orders without even politely informing the Chief of Staff that he intended to move." Max sighed. "I imagine the Emperor was very upset."

"I imagine so," I said, thinking that livid was probably a more likely word. "What did the Marshal say?"

"He took it on the chin," Max replied. "He apologized and took full responsibility, and offered to accept dismissal if that wasn't good enough. Otherwise, he said, he would make up for it by winning the battles of the coming campaign."

"That is like him," I said. At least it was not a dismissal.

"The Emperor seemed satisfied," Max said with a shrug. "He's coming down himself. The Marshal is to hurry to Mlawa and our cavalry is to go to meet him with everyone else following after.

We're opening a major offensive. That's what the orders were that the courier brought. We're supposed to get on the road tomorrow."

"The Emperor is coming down?" I asked. He'd made it perfectly clear he wanted to winter in Warsaw.

"Not to VI Corps, but he will take command himself. I think he wants to wrap this whole thing up as quickly as possible."

"I wonder where I am to be," I mused. Of course there was no letter for me in the packet, or Max would have given it to me by now.

Max shrugged, his gray eyes alight with mischief. "You're always welcome with the medical wagons. No need to sit in Torun, is there?"

At dawn the next morning our cavalry left Torun, heading south down the road we had arrived by to return to Działdowo and take the eastern fork as far as Mlawa. Needless to say, the medical corps did not move with such speed. It was three days before the back of the baggage train pulled out, on the fourth day of February. Much as I enjoyed Max's company and considered him a friend, I chafed at the delay. When at last we did get on the road they were in a dismal state, as we followed our own artillery train. When a road that was only mud to begin with has been covered in snow, then doused with rain for a month, and then frozen hard, and then torn up by artillery, it is not precisely easy going for heavy wagons. A day of that and I was done, and I said so to Max, riding up beside him as we broke camp the next morning.

He shook his head, the winter sun glinting off his glasses. "I didn't expect you'd stay," he said. "Give the Marshal my best and tell him we'll be there as soon as possible." He glanced up at the pale sky, clear except for a few high, thin clouds of the kind called mare's tails. "Hopefully we'll catch up before the weather changes."

"It looks fair," I said.

"It won't stay fair," Max said. He dropped his voice. "I've a talent for weather, so M. Noirtier says. There's snow off to the west. I'd bet my pay on it."

"Wonderful," I said. "How long do you think?"

Max looked at the sky thoughtfully, eyes like a hunting bird scanning the heavens. "Maybe day after tomorrow. We'll move as fast as we can."

"And so will I," I said.

I took no one but my Saxon groom, Hantz, whom I hired in Magdeburg in the fall. He spoke only passable French, but he did know the roads in this area, having traveled them in years past. It was, after all, only a short distance down to catch up with our cavalry, and from the way things seemed to be shaping up, the decisive engagement might not wait on the arrival of VI Corps' infantry, much less our poor baggage train plodding along in the mud, last as usual.

It took all day to retrace our steps to the road junction and set out on the eastward fork, though night caught us before we had gone far and it seemed best to simply sleep rough. Perhaps it would have been better to stay in Działdowo, but a sense of urgency caught at me that was only partially fueled by Max's predictions about the weather.

Early on the morning of the 7th I woke in the chilly shelter of a hedge in the light just before dawn. Hantz was still sleeping. Pomme had her face in her nosebag a few feet away and was chewing contentedly.

I sat up. Something had disturbed me, but I was not certain what. Not the cold, as I was used to that. This was not the first winter night I had spent in the shelter of a hedge beside a dying fire. The clouds had that low, leaden look, purple-gray and cool, as though snow was not far away. Max's storm was rolling in.

Certainly it was cold enough. The temperature had already dropped in the night. In the half-light I rolled out of my blanket and cloak, and chafed my hands together, gathering up the cloak. I trundled off into the woods to relieve myself where Hantz would not see if he suddenly awakened, finding a huge pine tree some little way away. It was absolutely still in the woods, the browns of dead leaves and the green of the evergreens the only color in a grey world. No birds moved, not an animal scampered.

And then I heard the thunder in the slate-colored sky. I looked up, counting, one thousand one, one thousand two, one thousand three, one thousand four until I reached seventeen. It was not thunder in the sky. It was the thunder of our guns.

It was not much further before we began to catch up to men on the road, wagons of our baggage train hurrying forward with all dispatch, artillery pieces and caissons urged forward by sweating carters. In my blue coat and buff breeches I looked like some lieutenant of chasseurs if one did not look too closely.

"Sergeant!" I called to a heavy quartermaster sergeant with the wagon train, riding up beside him. "Which unit is this?"

He took in my blue coat and boy's face. "14th of the line's baggage."

"Who are you attached to?"

"Marshal Soult. Taking these supplies forward to the Corps hospital."

"I'll join you then," I said. "I need to get back to VI Corps headquarters from their baggage train." It made it sound as though I were one of Michel's couriers, but I had not precisely said I was.

"Are they behind us on the road?" the sergeant asked

"About eighteen kilometers behind me," I said truthfully. "Doesn't look like you're going to wait on them though."

"Not likely," the sergeant said. "But if you're looking for VI Corps headquarters, I don't know where you'll find it. Staff and all were over at Alt-Reichau, and then they went to attack the Russians."

"Where are they now?" I asked.

"Don't know. Somewhere up ahead."

"Thank you, sergeant," I said, touching my heels to Pomme and trotting along the side of the column, passing the slow caissons laboring over the frozen ground. Hantz followed me.

Perhaps three kilometers further along we come upon the hospital, such as it was, not VI Corps', but Soult's. It was a mongrel collection of tents and wagons filling up the square of a small village I did not know the name of. And here were our wounded, the first of them, five wagons filled with moaning men brought back from wherever the action was, a pair of Larrey's Flying Ambulances holding the worst. I dismounted, picking my way through the square, leading Pomme by the rein among the injured and the dead. Yes, there were those too, a wagon or two, their faces covered with handkerchiefs or a bloodied red pelisse trimmed with fur.

They reached for me as I walked past them, reaching with feeble, dirty hands, smelling of urine and vomit. "Brother, won't you give us water?" one man said, his fingers closing about my forearm.

"I will be back with some," I said, gently taking his bloody hand from my sleeve. His other arm was soaked in blood, held to his body with a ruined hussar's jacket.

I stepped over them. The surgeon was under the flap of the tent, one eye bandaged with linen, as though a shell had impacted further back than expected. "Jesus, get this one out of here," he said to the orderly, dropping the man's arm limply across his shattered belly. "He's gone. Get somebody on this table I can help."

"Doctor?" I said.

He glanced at me sideways. "What do you want? We can't move. I have too many here to pull out. If Soult wants us to pull back, to hell with him."

"Sir," I said, "I only wanted to ask your permission to leave some money for you. I know provisions and medicines are expensive, and I have plenty." I reached in my pocket and drew out my purse. "Please take it."

The surgeon took it with a bloody hand. "Son, are you trying to get on the good side of the Almighty today?"

"I'm going forward to join my unit, sir." Now more than ever I needed to catch up to VI Corps. I turned, leaving the purse in his hand, and walk back to Pomme.

The wounded man grabbed at my arm again. "Water, boy, for the love of God." His fingers were still very strong.

"I have a flask of brandy instead," I said, handing him my pocket flask and unstopping it for him. "Will that do?"

He actually smiled as he lifted it in his good hand. "Better than anything."

The man next to him was watching with undisguised envy, so I gave him my other flask which was full of Madeira. "Thank you, son," he said gravely in a quiet voice more at home in the drawing room than the field. He was very pale from blood loss and shock. I wondered if he would live, though he could not be so gravely wounded as some.

I nodded to him and walked away. Pomme and I still had far to go.

Just as I reached her, other troops begin to crowd the road in both directions, pouring through the town as best they could. Ahead on the road I could see one of Soult's heavy guns stuck in the mud with all the gunnery company around it trying to drag it out.

Hantz started to say something, but I didn't wait for him. "Let's go on while we can," I said, swinging into the saddle.

There were dragoons posted along the route acting as signposts for the reinforcements and for VI Corps' baggage behind me. Despite the scene at the hospital, the troops on the road did not seem particularly discouraged. No one attempted to stop me or question me, looking as I did like a courier, and they had no idea where I belonged or where I might have a legitimate errand. I passed through the lines coming forward and up a hillside with as much tranquility as if I were out for a pleasant jaunt in the Bois de Boulogne.

Suddenly the shelling was much closer. Ignoring Hantz' cry of protest, I wheeled Pomme sharply toward the higher ground. Beneath me, the order of battle unfolded as suddenly as a painting in the Académie, bright uniforms and bright blood against the winter ground, punctuated with the deafening roar of thirty massed pieces of artillery. An infantry division got into motion. I could see the white smoke of their guns as the first row fired. Without even losing step, they opened to the middle, left and right, and fell back to the rear as the second row advanced between them, taking up firing stances in turn. They stepped over those who had fallen.

As though the guns shook loose the clouds, the snow began to fall, thick damp white flakes twirling on the wind. I need to get off this hill, I thought. It was too barren and I presented too good a target.

I turned and went down from the hilltop, and Hantz and I turned to our left, down a back road which it seemed might take us parallel to our lines, for it was clear to me now that VI Corps was on the left wing, while we were instead behind Soult's IV Corps. After twenty minutes of travel along this road, the sound of the guns became fainter. I drew rein.

"Hantz," I said, "I think this veers too far to the north. We need to get back to the main road." The snow was now falling in thick, heavy flakes, and if we did not find our way soon it would become much harder. Across the track there was a partially burned house and cattle byre, deserted and empty.

I swung down. "I will wait here," I said, "while you see if this road veers back to the left around that bend."

He clenched his teeth with Saxon stubbornness. "Madame," he said, emphasizing the feminine title, "I can't simply go off and leave you alone here. Anyone might happen upon you."

"If they do they will see a courier, as everyone today has," I said.

"Maybe they will, and maybe they won't," he said.

"Certainly they will. Hantz, I have done this a dozen times."

"What if they don't?" he asked. "You, a lone woman, out here by yourself? It isn't right."

"I am perfectly capable of looking after myself," I said, leading Pomme in a slow circle to cool her off. "Do as I have told you." Pomme was sweated and I could see that she was tired though still game. The cold bothered her, as it did Arabs.

Still he hesitated stubbornly. "Even if you aren't the least bit afraid of what might happen to you, I am. Dead or alive, I'm not leaving, Madame."

"Hantz," I began, but a sudden clamor and shouting startled me, and I remounted quickly. A cavalry unit came along at a trot, cuirassiers, of a regiment I did not recognize, but clearly they knew where they were going and were hell-bent on getting there as quickly as possible. "Come along," I told Hantz, following them.

Only a half-mile down the road, we were back on the field in a section of the line that was beginning a general advance. The cuirassiers we had been trailing fell in behind a squadron of Montbrun's division.

We advanced at a walk over the muddy ground to the movement and roll of the drums. Ahead, the shells were falling far short. The Russian gunners did not seem to be very good, or perhaps they could not see us very well yet, what with the snow and the powder smoke. It was flowing away from us, and our vision was perfectly clear, but it enveloped the guns completely.

Hantz dragged at my elbow, but I brushed him off. "Madame, what are you doing?"

I felt that familiar prickling and fear inside me, but I would not turn aside for anything now, not now as each moment, each second, became clear as wind to me. I was frightened, oh yes, but more than that, alive, each sense tuned to the highest point. It took all the time in the world for each step of Pomme's foot as we went forward.

"Madame St. Elme!" someone shouted close behind me.

I pulled Pomme about to see Colonel Calend, the baggage master of III Corps, gesturing at me wildly, his horse prancing in the press. Making sure Hantz was still behind me, I pulled out of the line and trotted over to him. He was a fine man and a distant member of the Lodge though not one I had seen often, as he had never been with Michel's Corps. "Good afternoon, Colonel Calend!" I called to him. "I trust you are well?"

He came up beside me, his salt and pepper moustache quivering. "You're a damned fine wench! What the hell are you doing in the midst of this?"

"Warsaw was rather dull so I thought I'd come down here and keep you company," I said. "I'd hoped I would arrive before the ball was over and I could have a dance or two."

"We've kept them warm for you," he said, looking at my surly servant. "Lad, you ought to know I've run into your lady here on one field after another. Stay by her! She's got a good luck charm that never fails. I suppose the first was Hohenlinden?"

"You were with Moreau then," I said. "I remember."

"And a fine ball that was," he said. "Weather pretty much like this, as I recall."

"Where is Marshal Ney?" I asked him. "I know where VI Corps' infantry is, but he is not with them."

"He's running after Woronsof's grenadiers. Way out on the wing. If you want to take supper with him you will have to go rather far to find him." Calend winked at me. "If you've come all this way, I'm sure it won't be too far for you."

"It won't be," I replied.

"Indeed, Madame," grinned Calend, sweeping off his hat as though I were in the foyer of the Opera. "Do not let me detain you."

"Good day, Colonel," I said.

"Good day, Madame," he said, and with a gesture for the astonished Hantz, I cantered off toward Montbrun's Imperial Guard cavalry.

They were forming for their charge, their plumes bright against the winter sky, mettled horses dancing, held in with a touch. Before I could more than catch up with their rear, the colonel's saber shook in the frozen air, the bugle call answering his gesture, and with the thunder of a thousand hooves the cavalry leapt forward with one breath, the beginning of a perfect flying wedge following a single point. I kicked Pomme and she sprang forward with a trumpet of challenge, as mettled and game as I.

"Stop!" I heard Hantz yelling behind me, but I paid him no heed. My saber was free of the scabbard, flashing clean in the air, every fiber of my body singing that this is what I was born for, this ancient and deadly dance with death. The music of our hooves was like drums, like the beating of my heart, and the shells that passed overhead were slow compared to our passage. Meanwhile, the thinking part of me realized they could not depress their guns as quickly as we could cover ground, and already we were beneath their angle of elevation. Ahead, between the pounding horses, I could see their infantry, too scattered to form squares.

Then we were among them, smashing against the first grenadiers like a wave. I could not see what I was striking at, but I felt the jolt as my saber caught, and I jerked it clear. In a moment there was another before me, green uniform, dark face. His bayonet had the reach of me, and he was to my left, usually a problem for a cavalryman who is not left-handed, but Pomme lunged forward too quickly for him, and my saber struck his right arm above the elbow. And then we were past him, Pomme dancing to avoid the bodies beneath. Someone grabbed at her rein from the right, and I switched the saber across, striking at his hands. They came apart under the blow.

We were wedged too tightly, the horses shoulder-to-shoulder. A guardsman's horse stumbled into Pomme, and she shied to the right. For a moment she stumbled, and I thought she would fall, shoved by bigger horses. If she did I should be trampled under the horses' feet. Hauling on her reins I disengaged to the right, but not quickly enough.

A grenadier's bayonet struck me over the left eye, most of the force of the blow taken by Pomme's leap away. My head shook on my neck, my ears ringing from the force of the blow. The guardsman to my left lunged forward, spitting him in the chest with his saber. I could not see for the blood in my eyes, a sudden veil across my vision. It didn't hurt, although the sudden cold clarity in my veins told me that the blood was mine. I dashed it away with my sleeve as Pomme backed frantically as a warhorse should, feeling the slackness of her reins.

I could see a little from my right eye. In that moment of calm in the midst of the storm I hoped that it was not my vision gone. I could feel no pain, none at all. The Guard was still forcing ahead, the melee past me now.

Suddenly Hantz grabbed my bridle. "They've half killed you!"

"No, they haven't," I said. "Give me her reins back. I can ride, damn it." The Guard was well ahead now, forcing forward toward the Russian batteries. There was no one else here but the wounded and the dead, ours and theirs alike, in the ruins of their half-formed squares. "Give me your kerchief," I said.

Pomme stood quiet, out of the press, head up and calm. She saved my life. If she had not leapt away of her own initiative, that blow would have opened my skull. I had a moment's macabre vision of my grey brains oozing out from under my blond curls. I wiped the blood out of my eyes.

I could see from the left eye as well. Not in the eye, then, but above it. "Hantz, where is the cut?" I asked.

He took my head roughly in his hands. "Across the forehead above your left eye and running up into your hair over the left temple. It's long, but I don't think it broke the bone. Deep enough that I can see white at the scalp. Bleeding a lot. Should need sewing, I would think. It's a wonder you still have your head."

"Best bind it up then," I said, making a wad of the kerchief and holding it to the wound. I pressed down as hard as I could to stop the bleeding, as tightly as I could bear it. White at the scalp, the glint of my skull beneath the thin layer of hair and skin and muscle. I felt light but wonderfully clear-headed. "Let us go over there."

In the wind shadow of another tiny hill with three stunted trees, a wounded French Guardsman was kneeling on the ground, holding his wadded jacket to his shoulder.

"Are you all right?" Hantz asked.

"Better than this fellow here," the soldier replied, gesturing to the Russian grenadier on the ground. It was easy to see that the Russian was dying, his body too shattered for use.

Pomme jerked her head, disliking the stench. Still holding the kerchief to my forehead, I tied it there with my own scarf, drawing the knots as tight as I could. Scalp wounds are never as bad as they look, I told myself.

The Russian was murmuring, begging and pleading in a language none of us could understand, spittle running out of his mouth.

"What do you suppose he wants?" the Guardsman asked.

"Water. It's what they all want. That and their mothers." Gingerly, I slid off Pomme's back.

"Help me lift him up then," the Guardsman said. "He can drink from my bottle."

That is as well, I thought, because I had already given away both my flasks. Hantz and I lifted his shoulders a little, trying not to give him any more pain than he must already have. Or perhaps he felt nothing. I still felt no pain in my head. The Guardsman unstopped his flask and put it to the Russian's lips.

The Russian looked up into my face, smooth as silk, discoloring purple from the blow, stained with my own blood. "Mother," he whispered, a word that is the same in almost any language. His wet lips moved in half a smile, and slackened as his eyes went empty.

"Here, fellow," said the Guardsman. "Have a little more."

"He is dead," I said quietly, and closed his eyes with my fingers.

The Guardsman looked at me, and wiped the top of the flask. "You're a woman, aren't you?"

"No, my friend," I said levelly. "Not me."

"Then you must be a pretty boy. Well, you are a good fellow all the same." He restopped the flask. "Let us go to the ambulance together then."

We had a hard time of it trying to get back to the hospital. Night was falling while we were still on the road, only Pomme stepping along bravely as though she had done nothing more strenuous today than walk about the avenues of Paris.

The snow was falling heavily and it was full dark before we reached the village without a name. By now my face was beginning to throb with swelling. It was still bleeding a little, and the kerchief and scarf were entirely soaked. My hands and feet were colder even than the snow warranted, a sure sign of having lost too much blood. The Guardsman looked worse off than I was.

The hospital was no longer there. I looked about the square with a sense of defeated disbelief. Soult, I thought. The surgeon was expecting orders to move, and he must have gotten them.

There were other French there, however, men who came to where they thought the hospital was. The Poles had taken them in. There were fires lit in the houses, warm and dry, a door half ajar. When I knocked a young woman opened it, blood down the front of her dress. "Come in," she said in Polish, beckoning because I would not understand. "It is well. Come in."

There were four of our men there, two sitting by the hearth, one with another man's head in his lap as he lay prone, the fourth man sitting on a stool as a man with a beard laid a pad of bandages to his upper arm.

I sat down heavily on the floor by the fire with the others. "See to my friend first," I said in Polish, hoping that Hantz was tending to Pomme outside, "I am lightly wounded." The Guardsman had a musket ball in his shoulder just above the collarbone, far worse than a scalp wound. It would require a proper doctor to get it out without dangerous bleeding. Outside the wind was picking up.

The young woman bandaged him up with a poultice on his shoulder and made him comfortable for the night, one of the two men she put to bed in her own bed. Afterwards, beside the fire, she washed my head clean of the dried blood, her hands deft and quick. "It should be sewn. I can do it for you."

"Do it then," I said. The world was beginning to take on a curious unreality, as though I watched all from a distance.

"I will have to draw your scalp together, and your forehead. You are lucky it did not get your eye." Her hands were gentle. She must have been little more than a girl, with wide blue eyes and a light blue dress stained with gore.

"Do you have any vodka?" I asked. "It will help for the pain."

She handed me the bottle. "I pour it in the wound as well. It hurts, but it's better in the long run."

"I know," I said. The pain which had evaded me for hours was coming on at last.

She looked at me more closely. "You are a woman, aren't you?"

I glanced over at the Guardsman sleeping in her bed, his eyes closed and his face still drawn in sleep. But we were speaking

Polish. "Yes, I am."

"I thought so," she said. "Your voice gives you away. What is your name?"

"Elzelina," I said, yelping with pain as she poured the vodka into my raw scalp, trying not to cry.

"Not a French name," she said. Like a good healer, she kept talking the entire time she was working, keeping my mind off what she was doing. She threaded a sewing needle and passed it through a candle flame. "We do that out of tradition," she said. "It's said to help."

"What is your name?" I asked. Distraction.

"Judith," she said, digging the needle into my flesh.

"Jews?" I asked.

She nodded, "My husband and I. There is a French boy too. An officer. He is asleep now. It's hard to believe that the French have officers who are Jews. Gentiles really serve under them?"

"Yes," I said. "Under our law any may lead and any may serve." I was trying to ignore the piercing pain of the needle that was lancing into my head.

"You should not have gotten this so dirty," Judith said.

"I couldn't help it. There was a battle."

She smiled, her hands still working on my head. "You'll live, Elzelina. But this scar is not going to enhance your beauty any. I do good work, but it's right over your eye."

"I'm thirty. It won't make a difference."

Judith laughed. "Let me tie it off and bandage it. Then go to bed. There's room here by the hearth. It's going to swell, and when it does, I'll put a poultice on it. For now, the best thing is to let the vodka work."

I was asleep almost before I hit the floor.

Aftermath

The next day I sent a message to Michel. Or rather, I sent Hantz.
"I don't like leaving you here, Madame," he said, glaring around the little kitchen suspiciously.

I took a deep breath, which in itself was enough to make me dizzy. "I can't ride," I said. "It's safest not to move someone right after a blow to the head if it can be helped. And this time it can be helped." I was certain I would be quite safe where I was. Judith and her husband had five soldiers staying in their small house, as did most of the villagers, and her care was as good as any I would find in a hospital. "I will be fine here. And the Marshal will be worried." That, at least, made an impression on Hantz. Michel's wrath was something to be avoided.

The storm had blown itself out and the skies were clearing. It was still cold, but the snow was not very deep, ten or twelve centimeters, though how long that would last was anybody's guess.

"If you are going to go, then now is the time," I said. "The roads and the weather are not going to get any better, and they may get worse." Which was certainly true. At the moment the cold had at least firmed up the surfaces of the roads. "You will have to find the Marshal, and that is not going to be either easy or quick." I had no idea where Michel might be, or rather where VI Corps headquarters was. We had seen a few men through the village from this unit or that, but other than reporting that the battle had been won and that the Russians had pulled back, they could tell us nothing.

The next three days were long indeed. Hantz left and did not return. My head was throbbing, and I feared that for all Judith's care it was festering under the bandage. Needless to say I could not see it, over my eye as it was, and Judith would not say. She just kept pouring on the last of the vodka and frowning. I felt continually lightheaded, whether from the loss of blood or because the blow had indeed addled my brain.

The fourth day after I sent Hantz away a carriage arrived. By then I was more than a little unsteady and began to fear that I was shivering with more than the cold. A fever was sure proof of infection.

The driver was an older trooper with a pronounced limp, the sort of thing that leads an otherwise able-bodied man to a job that requires little standing and walking. "Charles Van Alyde?" the driver called out in French, looking around the room full of wounded men. "I've been sent down from headquarters to fetch you."

"That's me," I said, staggering to my feet. "Let me get my things." There was only Pomme and my saddlebags to bring.

I had many thanks for Judith. She had been more kind to me than necessary, and her skill had probably saved not only my life, but the other Frenchmen here as well. I gave her the rest of my money, though she protested and did not want to take it. "For the price of all that vodka," I said, and pressed it into her hands over her final token protestations.

The driver was chewing tobacco and leering at me, having obviously concluded that I was someone's pretty boy. Which of course I was, but not in the way he thought.

We tied Pomme on behind, as I was not about to leave her under any circumstances, and the driver could hardly do it himself. When he tried to take her rein she tried to bite him, then pranced back with her ears laid back and regarded him with a gaze one could only call malevolent.

"There, my darling," I said, reaching for her bridle and tying her on. "There, dearest. It's all right." She came along for me as docilely as a lamb.

"That's a mean 'un," the driver said.

"You're lucky," I said as I pulled myself inside the carriage. "A man tried to steal her once and lost a finger."

It was a long drive, all day, over the worst roads I had ever seen, even in Poland, pitted by the ceaseless traffic of carts, caissons, and artillery pieces. My head bounced with every bump, and even stretched across the threadbare seats, there was no rest. We only stopped once, in early afternoon, and I could do no more than take a little water. My stomach heaved at the thought of food, for all that I was horribly thirsty. I knew this was not a good sign.

Just after dark I dozed off, then woke to feel the stickiness of fresh blood oozing down the side of my face. We were still bouncing over Polish roads. Of course it had torn some stitches loose. Outside the windows there was no light, only the shadows of bare tree branches against the snow, pale in the starlight. The movement of the horses was monotonous, clattering over frozen ruts no faster than a man could walk. Of course I couldn't walk. I was shivering with cold or with fever, and I began to think that perhaps this time I had gotten myself into serious trouble. "Shit," I said to myself, and leaned back again, pressing on the bandage to stop the bleeding, nodding off to sleep and then jolting awake as my hand slipped until at last sleep took me.

When I woke it was in heaven. The carriage had stopped, and I could hear men's voices outside in the wide courtyard shouting to one another in French. The door to the carriage opened. It was Michel, his face lit by the torch someone was holding beside him.

What he thought looking at me I did not know, my hair matted with dried blood, my face swollen and purple and swathed in bandages, as filthy as a pig and twice as smelly. The expression on his face would have killed any Russian in a hundred miles. What he said was, "Jesus Christ. Dery, help me get her out of here."

The torch bobbed, and he reached across me, sliding his nice clean uniform sleeve around my waist. "Elza, can you put your arm around my neck?"

For some reason my voice wasn't working, but I could slide my arm around his neck, feel it weakly against his hair. Dery was moving my feet free of the door, an expression of concern on his face. I ought to tell them that I can walk, I thought, but I felt much weaker than I had that morning. A day on Polish roads had done me no good.

Michel lifted me up and out of the carriage, effortlessly it seemed. I must have lost weight for him to lift me so easily, as I was not a small woman by any means. I felt as though I was flying. Surely if I were borne away to heaven it would be like this, in a wide, cool courtyard with my cheek pressed against the gold braid on his shoulder.

I closed my eyes against a wave of nausea while he carried me into the building and up two flights of stairs, Dery coming after, and into a low-ceilinged parlor, where he laid me down on a horsehair couch. He put me down as softly as a child.

"How is she?" Dery asks.

"She's burning up with fever," Michel said, his voice cracking for some reason that seemed mysterious to me. "Get me a basin of water. And get Duplessis out of bed. She's pulled her stitches loose. At least I hope that's what it is."

Dery disappeared from my view as Michel knelt down beside the couch. I had gotten a brown stain on his clean uniform where I leaned against it. I tried to apologize for it, but only a harsh croak came out.

"Don't try to talk, Elza," he said quietly, smoothing my matted hair back from my eyes. "Don't try to talk. You're going to be perfectly fine." There was a tic working furiously in his jaw. I wanted to reach up and smooth it away, but I did not have the strength.

Dery burst back into the room carrying a pitcher, towel and basin. "Got it, sir. Dr. Duplessis is coming. He stopped to get his kit."

Michel took it out of his hands and put it on the floor beside him. He poured some water out in the basin and dipped the towel in it. "I'm not going to move the bandage. I'll just wash around it. I'll leave the bandage for Duplessis."

I could smell the water. I croaked again, trying to reach for it.

He knew what I wanted. "Yes, you can have some water. Dery, go fetch a cup!"

Dery was already out the door.

His hands were soft and cool on my face, the smell of water in my nose. "We'll have you fixed up in no time. Just lie still, Elza." He was washing the blood off my face. I could see the towel staining more each time it passed my eyes.

Dery thundered back in again holding a filigreed glass

champagne flute. "Will this do, sir?"

"Fine," Michel said, taking it from him and pouring water into it from the pitcher. My hands wouldn't seem to hold it steady in the wavering room, though I tried to use both of them, so he held it for me, lifting it to my lips like the Host. "Dery, where is Duplessis?" he demanded.

"I woke him up, sir," Dery said. "He's dressing and then he'll be right here."

The water was cool and clear as springtime. It was all the water I had ever drunk in my life, all the water there was in the world. I could have washed away on it. I swallowed, pushing the goblet away for the moment. "Pomme," I croaked. My poor dear, faithful Pomme. I hoped she was still tied on behind, not lost or stolen, not left standing sweated in the cold courtyard, forgotten by everyone.

"What?" said Dery.

"Dery, see to the lady's horse," Michel snapped. He never spoke to aides less than politely, and I was surprised both that he did, and that Dery seemed unbothered by it.

"Right away, sir." Dery tore out of the room.

"Here, Elza," he said, and lifted the glass to my lips again.

"There you are," Max said, coming in, still putting his glasses on his nose. He hadn't shaved, and a heavy shadow of beard lay across his chin and cheeks.

"She's torn stitches loose, I think," Michel said, moving to the side and letting Max kneel down where he had been. "And she's got a fever."

"I can see that," Max said quietly, his fingers seeking the pulse at my wrist, his familiar professional competence reassuring in itself. "Elza, can you speak?"

"Yes," I whispered.

"She asked for her horse a moment ago." Michel was hovering just out of sight.

Max nodded, his eyes still on mine. He lifted a candle and moved it close, and I winced at the sudden light. "Both pupils responding. Good. Can you tell me who I am?"

"Dr. Maximilien Duplessis," I said. He wanted to know if I had my wits about me.

He nodded again, putting the candle down on the side table.

"And where are you?"

"I haven't the faintest idea," I said.

The rest of that night was a blur to me. Max's hands, soaking the bandage of crusted blood off my head, the snip of his scissors trimming back my hair from the wound. "Whoever sewed this did a nice job," he said.

Somehow without moving he was gone and there was only Michel there, lifting me up and easing me out of my stained coat and shirt, tugging at my boots. Somehow I was in a different room and there were shadows that moved along the walls, a cold that would not stop.

We are in Rome, my parents and my brother and I, all sick with the summer fever. Charles is dying, and somewhere across a river there is a funeral pyre staining the sky with smoke.

And then I am running along a path, torches flaring in the gloom behind. Behind me, Reille and Subervie are standing shoulder-to-shoulder with drawn swords, watching the doors before them heave with every blow, waiting for the bar across them to break. They look at one another, and Reille grins as a man will when he sees his fate beside a friend. And I am running down the path through the trees, fire flaring across the river. Countess Walewska sits in the stern of a boat, a child in her arms, looking up toward the torches and I barely gain the side before the bargemen push off...

...and then we are rowing on the sea in a ship's boat, the little boy's head beneath my chin as he sits on my lap, the ribbons of the Countess's bonnet flowing in the sea air, sailors in their striped shirts manning the oars as beneath the bright sun the island draws nearer ...

For some reason, Michel was there talking to me softly, easing one of his own old shirts over my head. I tried to explain to him that he could not be there, that he did not belong in that story, but he did not listen. "You can't be there," I insisted. "If you had it would all have been different."

I was naked beneath the shirt, and he was bathing my body with the cool water, trying to break the fever. The water was cool on my skin. "I promise I will never fail you," he said, his voice low and quiet. "Never again. I will never make those mistakes again. I promise you that upon my immortal soul."

The last thing I remembered was being lifted up, up, up, like flying. I could almost hear the sound of mighty wings.

When I woke it was to the sounds of close-order drill in the courtyard. The slanting light through the window had the look of late afternoon, and I was lying on sheets in a fine cherry bed, wearing a man's worn shirt and wrapped in a soft blanket. I lay quietly for a moment, watching the play of light on the ceiling, listening to the familiar commands in the courtyard. The coffered ceiling and large window with damask drapes, the fine furniture, all spoke of a great house that was being used for headquarters. And yet I had no idea what town or city this might be. Cautiously, I turned my head.

It was still swathed in bandages, and the movement made my vision waver for a moment before it steadied. I was also starving, and surely the absence of nausea was a good sign.

Winter sunshine poured in the window, making a patch of light on the fine Aubusson carpet. There was a beautiful Sheridan chair beside the bed and a wad of damp towels on the marble-topped nightstand. Across the room there was a cherry wardrobe with the doors open, some of the uniforms looking suspiciously familiar. Michel had put me in his own room. I wondered where he had slept since I was taking up the entire bed. I wondered *if* he had slept.

I heard the door creak open. "Michel?" I quavered.

"Ah, sleeping beauty awakes!" Jean-Baptiste Corbineau said, lounging in and sitting down in the chair beside the bed. He crossed his legs. "I wondered if you were going to sleep the day away. Your mare is in the stables, frisky and feeling fine. I must say she looks better than you do."

"Jean-Baptiste? Do I look terrible?" I asked.

"I've seen you looking better, but I can't remember where." He grinned. "What did you get into, Elza?"

"An Imperial Guard cavalry charge," I replied. "Against some unfortunate Russian grenadiers. They're dead. I just look like a mummy someone dug up." I tried to push up in bed, conscious of needs that I would have rather not needed Jean-Baptiste's assistance with.

"Be careful," he said. "You were pretty sick last night."

"So I gather." I settled the blankets around me more modestly. And more warmly. "What happened?"

"Last night?" he said.

"No, at the battle. And since then. I heard the Russians retreated. And where are we anyway? We must be somewhere near Konigsburg now, aren't we? I think so, as I think we were going north yesterday."

Jean-Baptiste stared at me. "You and him. Just alike. Half-dead one minute, and the next minute wanting troop dispositions. Every time he's shot it's the same thing, and now you're doing it too. He said I wasn't to tire you, and I won't. I just came to look in on you and see if you were awake and needed anything."

"So where are we?"

"Brunsberga," he said with satisfaction. "Which is only a few kilometers from the Baltic, in case you didn't know. And yes, near Konigsburg, though how you'd guess that in the state you're in I can't imagine."

"And the battle?" I asked.

Jean-Baptiste's face changed. "It was a mess," he said. "The Russians withdrew, so we'll call that a win." He stood up and paced over to the windows, shading his eyes as he looked down at the courtyard below. "We lost about fifteen thousand men. So did the Russians, but who's counting?"

"Fifteen thousand?" The number seemed incredible to me. "Half an army corps?"

"More or less." He didn't look around. "It's the worst setback we've had since…. I don't know when. Since the Directory. They say you win some and you lose some." There was something wrong in his voice. "Luck of the draw, I suppose," Jean-Baptiste said. "I suppose it would be better if we had more to show for it. But one can't win them all, can one? Not even Napoleon can win them all."

"Jean-Baptiste, what is wrong?" I asked.

He shrugged, his shoulder still turned to me. "Nothing that isn't always wrong. Men died. It is just unfortunate…." He stopped and then went on, his voice perfectly even. "Only one of them was that great lout Claude. He told his friends at breakfast that morning that it was his deathday and he was right. He was taking an order from the Emperor when a cannon ball…" His voice broke, and he leaned his head on his arm against the window.

"Oh my dear," I said, trying to get up so that I might at least put my arm around him.

"For God's sake don't get up," he said, turning about. "The Marshal will kill me if you fall out of bed and hurt yourself."

"Then come and sit here where I can touch you," I said. "Jean-Baptiste, I am so dreadfully, dreadfully sorry. Your brother…"

He sat down on the edge of the bed beside my legs, not even bothering to dash the tears from his face. "He was all of twenty, you know, when the revolution came, when he promised the parents he'd look after me if I came to war with him. I was sixteen, and the moment we were out of sight he said, 'Here you are, child. It's your neck, not mine. I'm not your chaperone.' Mother would have killed him if she'd known he let me go for a message rider, underage and not having ever fired a gun!"

I folded my fingers around his and let him talk.

"It's just so Goddamned stupid. One of those things. You're talking to people one moment and the next a cannon ball comes along and renders all immaterial. I suppose at least it was fast. There is that to be thankful for. At least it was fast."

"Oh, my dear," I said.

He shook his head, wiping his eyes with the back of his hand. "He won't nag me about getting married anymore. He really was a bit of an ass sometimes, but he was my brother. My big brother…" He closed his eyes, and I shifted forward, getting one arm about him and letting him fold onto my shoulder.

"Jean-Baptiste. I am so sorry. So horribly sorry." We sat there for a long while, his face against my shoulder, my arm about him. There never is anything that one can say at a time like that, nothing that will mean anything ultimately. The only thing that matters is that one is there.

After a while he straightened up, squeezing my hand and then letting it go. "I shouldn't tire you," he said. "I came up to see if there was anything you needed."

"I could use a chamber pot," I said truthfully.

Corbineau blushed. "Of course. I should have thought of that. There's one behind the screen. We haven't a maidservant, or anything like that…." His voice trailed off.

"I can manage for myself, thank you," I said, sincerely hoping so. "Why are they doing close-order drill in the courtyard?"

"You know the Marshal. Can't have anybody sitting around bored," Jean-Baptiste answered. "Actually, it's a disciplinary thing. An artillery unit lifted some plate from a church near here. Nobody will say what happened to it. So the whole unit is drilling all afternoon, and all tomorrow afternoon, and so on until we go into action again or the plate turns up."

I smiled. "I see."

Jean-Baptiste got to his feet. "If you need any help with anything…"

"I will be quite well," I said, and thought that it was probably true.

It was eight days before I was able to be moved. I did not see much of Michel in that time, as needless to say he was quite busy. As Corbineau had told me, our losses had been terrible. Thankfully, half of the men were wounded, not dead, but the logistical needs of that many wounded men were daunting. I only saw him a few minutes at the beginning and end of the day, though for the first few I hardly noticed as I slept nearly around the clock. Sometimes I would wake in the night and he would be there. And sometimes he would be gone.

He came in quietly the night of the 21st and put his gloves and the candle on the nightstand. "Are you awake, Elza?"

"Yes." I lifted my head gingerly and looked at him. The light was not complimentary. He looked drawn and exhausted. "Are you?"

He smiled and sat down carefully next to me. "Max says that you can travel now. Listen to me, Elza." He took my hand in his. "We are going to be on the march soon. In only a few days, maybe. We will have to move fast and unencumbered. I'm going to send you back to France. I would do the same if you were a man."

I nodded. I knew what I could do, and what I could not.

"I don't have the time or the means to take you with me. And it would not be safe for you. I have a carriage that I am going to send you in and a reliable driver. You seem to have made quite an impression on that Saxon of yours. He's determined to have the job of driving you."

"Hantz?" I asked. "Oh, not again. Michel...."

Michel was smiling, stroking my fingers absently. "He says he can keep you entirely out of trouble."

"He didn't before. I don't know why he thinks he can do it now," I said tartly.

"He had better do it." His voice was serious. "Elza, I mean it. I want you to go straight home where it is safe. All hell is breaking loose around here, and I want you out of it. I am sending you home, and you are going."

"Of course I am, Michel. I never said I wasn't," I replied. "I'm not a fool. I know I'm not up to another campaign right now."

There was a knock on the door, Dery's voice through the wood. "Sir? A courier has just arrived with urgent dispatches."

Michel stood up, letting go of my hand. "I'll be right down." He looked down at me. "This is the only hour I have. You have to go, my friend. As soon as you can travel."

"I know, dear," I said, watching him as he went to the door, oddly touched that he called me his friend. Of all the endearments I have heard, that one was the sweetest.

I left VI Corps headquarters on the morning of the 24th in an old carriage drawn by a pair of nags Michel had bought from someone. Hantz drove the carriage armed with a huge pair of pistols, and my dear Pomme minced along behind on a lead, prancing and impatient with the pace we kept. It was cold and raining again.

By the time we were four days out, I began to wish I was back with VI Corps. Surely all this jolting over ruined roads couldn't much improve my health! It was freezing, damp, and even with the money Michel had given me, one could not buy food where there is little to be had. Hantz was surly, as if he had not volunteered to drive me from Poland to France in the first place.

By the time we reached French soil and pressed on to Nancy I was ill again, a rising fever that left me shivering and shaking even in a good coat. We stopped for a few days at a clean inn there before going on. It was beginning to seem that there would never be an end to muddy roads, throbbing head, drizzling rain, and cold.

I didn't even know what day it was when we took to the road

again. The towns and villages passed in a blur of winter grayness, inns and marketplaces marking our stops, Bar, Chalons, and Thierry. At Thierry I was shivering again, fever still coming and going. Stopping again seemed horrible beyond belief, confirmation that this journey was indeed endless. Leaning out of the window into the cold rain, I told Hantz to find a change of horses in Thierry and to press on through the night. I did not even hear him agree before I fell again into a feverish sleep.

I woke at dawn, and through the window I could see the fine, clear sky glowing rose and hear the first birdsong I remembered in months. I opened the carriage window and drank in the warming air. Ahead, a familiar church tower was silhouetted against the morning sky. We had reached Saint Denis, and springtime.

Shadows Past

The rest of March I took to my bed, hardly caring what happened outside, sleeping and eating egg possets prepared by my house-keeper, Rachelle, who was also temporarily my maid as well as Claudine was still in Warsaw with all my clothes. Since I couldn't seem to get rid of Hantz any other way, I sent him back with instructions and a purse for her so that both she and my wardrobe could come home. And mostly I slept.

It was April before I bestirred myself. In the parks the tulips were blooming, a sea of yellow and pink and white. I stood one day at the open window, simply breathing in the spring air, and thought to myself that I should like something I had not had since my last days with Moreau, a little house with a garden, rather than a city apartment. Perhaps I could now afford to rent something if it were out of town rather than in a fashionable neighborhood.

To that end I rented a little house in St. Cloud, small but with a beautiful garden crowded with the sprouts of summer flowers and a peach tree. It was not convenient to the Right Bank at all, but then proximity to the theaters was no longer a priority.

Indeed, I thought as I looked in the mirror, it would probably never be a priority. The angry red scar began just above my left eyebrow, puckering slightly at the bottom where the bayonet had turned on the brow bone, and running fully the length of my middle finger up into my hairline. On a gentleman, it would have been thought evidence of a noble wound. On an actress, it was disfiguring.

Well, I considered, pushing my hair back from my brow and turning my head this way and that, at thirty my days on the stage were numbered anyway, and it was not the only damage I had taken. My skin was coarsened by exposure and my cheeks no longer held the firm, smooth roundness of youth. At the moment I looked positively emaciated. But even when I had not been ill I would not have the looks to compete with eighteen, not anymore.

I took a long breath, meeting my own eyes in the mirror. And would Michel care? He was a rich man now, a Marshal of France, famous and distinguished, and hardly old and unpleasant to look at. He could have his choice of beautiful young mistresses. For that matter, his wife was beautiful and some years my junior. He would be kind, as he always had been, but it would not be unexpected if his attention strayed. I had never asked him to be faithful. That had not been our arrangement, not now or ever. And yet I thought he had been, except for Aglae. Or if not, it had been of such minor importance that it did not trouble the seas at all.

I squared my shoulders. I did not need the stage to provide me with a living. I was the Emperor's agent, wounded in his service, and he had never cast off any such. My value lay in my utility and, scarred or not, I could serve.

I unclenched my left hand, suddenly realizing I had been clenching it so tightly that it hurt. My hand was whole, and yet for a moment that seemed strange to me. I could almost see it swathed in bandages, splinted and wrapped from some other wound, while I wondered if I should be useful still. I pursued the thought, but it eluded me. Some other wound, some other time. I did not know how to reach for it, how to bring the memory into sharp focus.

But perhaps there was something I could do about that. M. Noirtier had promised me a letter of introduction to his master, Dr. Mesmer, should I ever have time and leisure in Paris. At the moment I had little else. The Emperor was still in Poland, and I could hardly convince myself that I was fit to travel. I must regain my strength, and while I was doing that there were other skills I could improve besides, questions I might answer that would satisfy more than my idle curiosity.

Thus it was with some trepidation, armed with a letter from Noirtier, that I presented myself at the residence of Dr. Mesmer on a beautiful morning in May. He lived in a lodging house near Les Halles, hardly the place one would expect for a distinguished doctor of medicine. And he lived on the third floor. As I climbed I considered that perhaps, despite his past notoriety, fame had provided little in the way of lasting financial reward.

He opened the door himself, a little old man with a watery smile wearing the wig of the last century, his brown frock coat brushed and tidy but cut in a style at least ten years old.

"Dr. Mesmer?" I asked as his rheumy blue eyes searched my face.

He broke into a wide smile ornamented by ivory false teeth. "Mademoiselle Versfelt! What an unexpected surprise!"

At that I nearly fell over. I had not used my maiden name since I was twelve, and there was no one in Paris who had ever heard it, except perhaps for the Minister of Police in his blackmail files.

He reached out and drew me into his small parlor. "I hardly expected…. But of course I should not be surprised…. You are a grown woman now. Time does pass." He stood back a few steps and looked me up and down from my straw bonnet to my striped linen dress, carelessly dressed hair that covered my forehead. "Of course you grew up. It must be twenty-five years!"

I stared at him in utter astonishment. "Dr. Mesmer, I have no recollection of ever meeting you! How do you know my name?"

"You're Leo Versfelt's little girl. I never forget a face." He smiled triumphantly, displaying the ivory again. "Elzbieta, was it? For his mother, as I recall. Such an interesting young man. I hope he is well?"

"My father has been dead for many years," I managed.

"A terrible shame," he said. "But it happens, I suppose." He puttered around a little table with a pretty English teapot on it. "Do you take tea? Such a civilized custom, I think." His apartment was cluttered with books and papers, a few old but nice pieces of furniture well-dusted, if a bit crowded in the small space.

"I should be happy for some tea," I said. "And please tell me how you knew my father. And me, for that matter."

He gestured to one of the chairs and I sat down while he fussed with the tea service. "You were in Milan, as I recall. It was shortly after I had left Vienna for my health and I traveled a bit. Your father asked me to come for a consultation with your mother. You were a beautiful child! Golden curls and so precocious! Three or four, perhaps? Utterly fanciful and it was clear your father doted upon you."

"A consultation about my mother."

He handed me a cup of tea. "I understood that she had some sort of nervous condition, some sort of neuralgia that made her prone to melancholia and strange fancies. I had made enormous headway in Vienna in treating disorders of the nervous humors through the application of magnets, the most new and revolutionary of treatments! Your father hoped that I might be able to effect a cure of your mother's condition."

"Oh." I did not pick up the tea to drink. The fussy little apartment seemed strangely warm and uncomfortable suddenly. "I take it that you did not."

Dr. Mesmer put down his own cup on the tray and looked at me keenly, nothing dithering in his bright blue eyes. "My dear girl, I did not. There was nothing I could do." He took a long breath, as though he were looking into the past itself, seeing some scene far beyond me. "I do not know how much you know of your mother's history, but it was a very sad case."

"Tell me," I said. My mouth was dry.

He was still for a moment, then nodded. "If it would ease your mind." He picked up his cup again. "You know your mother was orphaned as an infant. Her father drowned in a shipwreck and his wife committed suicide soon after. She leapt from the highest window of a town-house in Amsterdam and split her skull open on the cobblestones below. The baby, your mother, was given to her uncle to raise, as indeed he was the nearest kin."

I stilled my hand so that the cup would not rattle against the saucer. I thought I knew what was coming.

Dr. Mesmer's voice was very careful, the voice of a physician of many years' practice. "Some men entertain perverted desires for very young girls, and this uncle was one such. He preyed upon his young niece in the most depraved fashion until, at the age of sixteen, she escaped him by running away from home with nothing but the clothes on her back and no means to make her way in the world except the obvious one that is always open to a pretty girl of sixteen. Perhaps it was better the devil she didn't know rather than the one she knew all too well, or perhaps she underestimated the dangers of the streets—I cannot say. But she ran. And sometime thereafter she took up with Leo Versfelt, a common mercenary armsman of twenty-five, a sometime fencing teacher and card sharp. They made their way to Italy together and he was her faithful protector. I am sorry to say that many of his schemes were little more than confidence games. Yet they seemed to do well enough together, and it is there that you were born. You and your ... was it a brother?"

"My brother Charles," I said, and was proud that my voice was even. "He would have been a baby when you knew us."

"In any event, your mother was plagued by fits of melancholy that were extremely profound. Sometimes your father feared for her life, and he hoped that I might be able to improve her condition."

"But you could not," I said.

Dr. Mesmer shook his head. "I could not," he said with his eyes on mine. "There are some damages done to the mind that cannot be remedied, some wounds that cannot be healed. Your mother ..." He looked away again, that same distant expression as though he relieved some part of the past. "She believed there was a curse upon her house. She believed that she saw ghosts and the dead spoke to her. She relied upon her phantoms for companionship and solace, just as she had growing up in her uncle's house. Then she had believed that the ghost of a dead girl who had been buried beneath the foundation was her best friend, and that a woman who took the shape of a cat urged her to run away. Her fancies were so integrated with her sense of self, with her beliefs about the world around her, that there was no way that rationality could penetrate them. She did not want to be free." Dr. Mesmer shook his head again. "Regretfully, there was nothing I could do."

I felt chilled to the bone, utterly frozen as though Polish winds scoured me. "My mother was mad," I heard myself say. "And I fear that I will go mad too."

Dr. Mesmer looked at me straightforwardly. "Perhaps you will," he said. "But it won't be the same way."

"What?"

"The natural state of humanity is bliss," he said. "Just as the natural state of your arm is straight." He reached for my left hand and lifted the fingertips from my lap until my arm was held out before me. "It is possible that some accident or injury could cause your arm to be broken. It is possible that it might not heal fully and completely, or that you would be left with a bulge or knob where the bone knitted. But that would be the result of the injury, not because it is your natural state. Injuries to the mind may likewise cause invisible scars, but they are the direct result of the injury, not of some natural predilection. You cannot possibly go mad in the same way as your mother because you have not sustained the same injuries in childhood. You are a grown woman in your prime, and you will never again be a child or vulnerable as a child is."

I blinked. I had not thought of it that way.

"The natural state of humanity is bliss," he said again. "Nature creates us whole. It is the events of our life that disfigure us. The electrical fields of the body may be as impaired by injury as the flesh, even if they are not visible."

I frowned. "I do not think I understand what you mean."

"Our bodies create and contain vast reservoirs of electrical and magnetic energy," he said. "This energy moves within our bodies, and those who are sensitive enough can detect its flow." He pinched the tip of my finger slightly and I twitched. "There," he said.

"There what?"

"When I pinched your finger an electrical impulse ran from your finger up your arm and into your mind. Another then returned, and your finger twitched in mine."

I blinked. "How do you know that?"

"I can feel it," he said. "I am very sensitive to the movement of minute amounts of electricity. It is the movement of these currents in the body that allow electrical applications to be effective."

I thought I saw where this was going. "You mean like the direction of energy in esoteric work."

Mesmer snorted. "Bah! That's Noirtier's lodge games, not science! He's as bad as that fraud, Cagliostro! I am speaking of science, of the science of medicine, not silly games with angels and oracles. I will tell you as a matter of prophecy derived from pure knowledge that in time it will be possible to bring a man back from the dead by the application of electricity!" He waved a finger at me. "You scoff, but you will see! The application of a sufficient amount of electrical current delivered to the heart muscle will cause the heart to begin to pump again even after death has just occurred. I can see precisely how to do it, and indeed I could do it myself if I could generate a current of sufficient strength! I have tried it, but

I am not strong enough. Yet I rest assured that in time this will be entirely possible, and human life will be greatly extended as a result." I must have looked skeptical, for he cleared his throat. "But that isn't why you came to see me."

"I came to see you because I wish to learn your techniques of mesmerism," I said. I wished Noirtier had told me that Mesmer did not believe in the work of the lodge at all, but perhaps it was an embarrassment to him.

"I do not teach those techniques," Mesmer said, but there was a tone in his voice I knew well from my father, the huckster beginning to bargain. This apartment was not very nice.

"That's terribly disappointing," I said. "As I was prepared to pay well for lessons."

"They are very demanding and require utter concentration and a very serious mind," he said. "After all, they represent a medical breakthrough that allows men and women to live free of pain and compulsion both!"

"I assure you I will well recompense you for the waste of your time," I said. "And perhaps you will not find me so frivolous."

"I want to be very clear that this is not one of Noirtier's scams," Mesmer said. "I am a doctor, not a charlatan."

"I have every confidence in that," I said.

"I cannot teach you to see the future or move things with your mind, and I cannot teach you to manipulate electrical current unless you have a natural aptitude for the same. This is medicine, not witchcraft."

"I am very clear on that, sir," I said. "Now will you teach me or not? I am quite prepared to pay your customary consulting fee. Three times weekly for lessons, if that suits you."

I could see him turning the money over in his mind. Three times weekly was not a small sum of money, but I would consider it well spent if I could learn to control this oracular talent. What did it matter if, like my father, he did not believe such things existed? I would take knowledge wherever I could get it and consider all stories of worth.

"We will try it," he said grudgingly, as though he did me a great favor. "And see if you are capable of learning what I have to teach."

Thus I took up my apprenticeship with Dr. Mesmer, though it was certainly not the only thing I did that summer. As studiously as I had applied myself to pistol shooting in the past, now I applied myself to the study of the esoteric, which was rather more difficult. To begin with, one could not simply seek out a well-thought-of instructor. Those who publicized themselves, like Lebrun, were charlatans, and those who did not were not easy to find. There were any number of books for sale, and I bought a few with high hopes.

However, one June afternoon, sitting beside the open window in my little parlor looking out at the garden, I put the book of the day by with disgust. "The Book of Fate," I said aloud. "What a load of shit! 'Signs for foretelling the weather: if there be large masses of heavy cloud upon the horizon and the weather is cold, snow is portended.' Surely any idiot can guess that!" I could only imagine the young lieutenant consulting the Book of Fate from his saddlebags, concluding that the snow clouds rolling in would lead to snow.

I put the book down and got out my cards instead, which had finally arrived from Warsaw care of Claudine. I shuffled them and turned the first up, bright paper against my white tablecloth. The emperor sat enthroned, the orb of the world in his hands.

"Clear enough," I said, and turned the next card across it.

The female pope stared up at me, the veil stretched between two pillars behind her, the horned moon on her brow. Across the base of her throne there were carven letters half-covered by the hem of her flowing robes, Isis Invicta.

"I don't understand," I said. "Truly I don't. Show me what this has to do with me. Show me what oaths bind me."

A turn of the card. The Sun, boy and girl twins playing in a garden beneath a cloudless sky.

"I am bound by happiness?"

No, I thought. Not by the metaphorical meaning of the card, but by the literal meaning. By the twins, brother and sister. There was something dark there, some tale of murder and danger, some oath left unfulfilled. A child I had promised to guard? And yet I had failed. I was certain of that. I had failed and that promise bound me still.

I laid the cards aside. Perhaps I was going about it wrong. I should learn the thing that no one else in the lodge knew, not the thing that they all knew. I should learn history. What use to know the words to open the doors to the past, as Noirtier had in that ritual in Boulogne nearly two years ago, if no one had the wit to understand what it meant? Of all of us, only Max and Honoré had enough formal education to be able to trace the path of this Great Story at all. At least a career on the stage had given me a passing familiarity with Classical history, as the plots of so many plays were drawn from the myths and history of antiquity. Perhaps what I should read was not The Book of Fate, but Pliny and Suetonius, Diodorus and Arrian. Perhaps I should read Caesar. Perhaps I should read that new work by Vivant Denon, the director of the new Museé Napoleon housed in the old palace of the Louvre, A Journey Through Upper and Lower Egypt. I should undertake the study of the Story.

Ludicrous, of course. I was no scholar, but a woman and an actress and a courtesan. I knew no Latin or Greek, had not attended school so much as a day. And yet stories ought to belong to those who claimed them. If I should not be turned from war because of my sex, why should I be turned from scholarship? There were Latin tutors aplenty in Paris, and I should not need Latin to read Denon. I could probably track down an introduction to the man himself, but first I would need to become conversant enough with his work to know what to ask.

Yes, I thought, with a strange stirring of excitement, Egypt was where I would begin.

I went into town that very afternoon to seek out an expensive bookshop that would carry Denon's work, two volumes with numerous illustrations and a price to match. Dear, but I could not resist. I opened the first reverently, letting the pages fall where they would, an engraving of strange carved animals and beast-headed men, a boat floating on a sea of night. Below the caption read, "A likeness of the astrological ceiling of the Temple of Hathor at Dendera, rendered in the era of the great Cleopatra."

The bookstore owner had been regarding me suspiciously, and now he came over. "Do you wish to purchase this book as a gift, Madame?"

"Oh yes," I said airily. "Hold it for me a moment. I'd like to look a little longer."

While he carried it away I closed my eyes. *Isis Invicta*, I said in my mind, *if that is your name, show me what you want me to learn.* I turned about, eyes closed, and took a few steps until my hand touched a leather clad spine. I opened my eyes. Beneath my fingers the title was picked out in gold, The Aeneid of Virgil.

DISTANT THUNDER

It was soon after this that news came of the great victory at Friedland, fought against the Russians on June 14. The *Moniteur* reported breathlessly on the action, quoting someone or other as saying that Michel "appeared as the God of War incarnate." I thought this was probably a bit of an exaggeration, but I did indeed know what they meant. He had that fatal concentration, that serenity in slaughter, that many found unnerving, all the violence at the depths of his soul unleashed in pursuit of victory.

And yet you would not know to expect that, meeting him elsewhere than the field, a calm and rational man who loved his children and his friends.

He was not wounded at Friedland, though many were of course, even with a great victory. But this was not Eylau all over again. The Russians had taken 25,000 casualties to our 7,000, and a few days later sued for peace.

I heard all this in Paris. Summer had come and my strength was returning. In addition to my studies and my appointments with Dr. Mesmer, I added my customary fencing and shooting, reminding my body that nothing was wrong with muscle and bone save for several months of disuse. The scar across my forehead remained angry and red, though I supposed it would fade to white in time. I decided upon a new hairdo, one with softly curling bangs that covered the forehead. At least that way it wasn't the first thing one saw when I appeared.

I also needed new clothes, as my male wardrobe had suffered greatly in the last campaign, and of course the styles changed somewhat with every season. This year the vogue was for striped cottons, and I ordered a summer dress with pale green stripes from my dressmaker, a transplanted Bavarian who did a very credible knockoff of couturiers for a price better suited to my purse, as after all I was not a Marshal's wife who could afford Leroy.

I went to my dressmaker's for the final fitting on a steaming hot afternoon in mid-July. It was so hot that even in my thinnest cotton gown I was soaked with sweat before I got there, and the ribbons on my bonnet had wilted like yesterday's flowers. Eager to get out of the blinding heat of the street, I barged straight into her shop, setting the bells she had tied to the door jangling. "Good afternoon, Katrin," I said, untying my bonnet strings. "I'm ready for my fitting."

"Late again, Madame St. Elme," she said, getting off her tall stool and coming around her counter of pretty ribbons and trims. "I have better things to do than make appointments that ladies are always late for."

"I'm not so very late, am I?" I asked. The shop was nice and cool. There were four stories above it to take the brunt of the afternoon sun.

"You are." She opened the curtain that divides the front room of the shop from her fitting room and I followed her back. "Not that I should be surprised today."

"Oh?" I started stripping off my dress and dropped it onto the chair with my bonnet and reticule. "Katrin, you know I give you more business than anyone else."

She looked at me sideways, not really angry but just a little annoyed. She pulled the half-finished dresses off a hanger, holding the pins in her mouth.

"Besides," I said, standing there in my shift, "I give you more interesting business than anyone else. How many hussar's uniforms do you have to make for women? How often do you run up everything from men's clothes to ballgowns to nun's habits?"

"If I'd wanted to run up everything but the Pope's robe I would still be working in the theater," she said, dropping the green-and-white-striped summer cotton over my head. "There is a little problem with the sleeves."

"Oh?" I looked at it in her mirror. "I can't see anything wrong."

"That's because it's not finished," she said, tugging at the binding of my right sleeve. "You see how this fits? It's not supposed to be that loose. Your measurements have changed."

I shrug at myself in the mirror. The bangs did not entirely cover the scar. "I suppose I lost muscle in my arms this spring. I don't know that it looks wrong, though?"

Katrin patted me on the back patronizingly as she lifted my arm to pin something beneath. "You tend to the army and let me tend to fashion. I'm sure you have too much on your mind today to even be bothered."

"Do I?" I asked.

She stopped pinning for a moment, looking at me in the mirror. "You haven't heard? A certain distinguished military man of your acquaintance arrived this morning through the Porte de Clignancourt."

"Really?" My voice was perfectly disinterested, but my heart gave a treacherous leap. It did not do to provide food for gossip. "I hadn't heard."

"One of my morning customers said there was quite a little to-do up there earlier. She lives that way, you know." Katrin was pinning away, not watching me. "They do put on quite a show, don't they? A fine entrance with a military band and everything."

"I suppose so." I stood perfectly still so that I did not mess up her pinning, but inside I was leaping and cavorting.

"Do you need to hurry off?" Katrin asked, looking up as she twitched my sleeve into place.

"Whatever for?" I asked innocently. That would keep her guessing. In reality, there was no point to hurrying. Michel was regular as clockwork about some things. Today he would report at the Tuileries and pay his respects to the Empress, and tonight he would be with his family in the Rue de Babylone. Tomorrow night he would be mine.

The next day was even hotter, though the afternoon did hold some promise of rain with the thunderclouds building in the north towards Montmartre. Not a leaf was stirring in St. Cloud, and my cook, Rachelle, was complaining enormously about having to cook in the heat.

"Never mind, Rachelle," I said. "Just make a little light cold supper. I shouldn't imagine we would want more than that. It is too hot to eat all those rich dishes anyhow."

"Madame," she ventured, "There hasn't been so much as a note from the Marshal. Do you really want me to..."

"Lay a nice table for two? Yes, I do. And use my good china and plate. If I'm serving informal food, at least I can do it beautifully." I fussed with my hair in the hall mirror. The humidity made my curls flat and limp, my bangs hanging in a soggy mass rather than fashionably covering the scar on my forehead. Even a hot iron couldn't make them curl right.

"You put so much work into that man," Rachelle grumbled.

I gave my hair another twitch. "Of course I do. Men like it when you put work into them. But make it look effortless." I turned and smiled at her, and kissed her lightly on the cheek. "Dearest Rachelle, I think he comes as much for your cooking as for me. Don't think I don't appreciate how much work you have put into everything too."

"It's my job, Madame," she said, "That's what you pay me for. But I'll be damned if you can't be the most charming creature when you want to be."

I gave her a hurt look. "Rachelle, you know I'm not."

"I know you are. But you just save that charm for him, and don't waste it on me. You'll be in a pretty pickle if about eight o'clock he hasn't shown up." She went off to the hot kitchen a little mollified.

I was not, though I said nothing. There had not been a note. What if he didn't come?

He did, of course. About six-thirty, under bright summer sun still slanting under the building thunderclouds I heard the sound of hooves and ran to the window. Michel was dismounting from a pretty dun mare I had never seen before, and Hantz came out to take his reins. They stood talking for a moment by the gate. Michel had lost weight again, I thought, and his pristine white pants were loose on him. He often did in the field. He must have just come from some official function, blue uniform and gold braid and a dress sword. He and Hantz were talking, grinning at each other. Michel said something and gestured towards the house. Hantz laughed and led the mare off.

I gave my curled bangs one last arrangement over my forehead and ran to open the door. "Why Michel!" I said breathlessly, "What a surprise! I had no idea you were even in Paris! Please come in.

I'm afraid you've caught me all unawares."

He grinned and shut the door behind him. "Liar. Hantz just told me that you have been driving poor Rachelle since nine this morning. And you've been dressed for three hours."

"It isn't fair for him to give away my logistics," I said, stepping closer and putting my hands against his chest. Real. Solid. He smelled of sweat and horse and Hungary Water.

"I believe you have an intelligence leak," he replied, his arms settling comfortably about my waist.

"Don't you want to get out of that wool coat?" I asked. "I would think you would be about to die."

"Very near to it," he said, stepping back and unfastening the coat and laying it carefully over the hall chair. "It's hot as hell, even for Paris in July. You look beautiful, Elza." He took off his gloves and put them down beside the coat.

"I'm glad to know that I didn't waste all that preparation," I said.

He reached up and brushed the curls away from my forehead.

I grabbed his hand. "Don't."

"Why? I've certainly seen it much worse," he replied, tracing the scar on my forehead with his thumb up into my hairline, his eyes following the track of his fingers.

"But not here in the drawing room. Everything is different out there." I pulled away and straightened his coat on the chair to save the blocking of the shoulders. "I'm afraid dinner is not ready yet. I didn't expect you quite so early."

"It's going to rain," he said. "I didn't want to ride out from Paris in a downpour."

"That was a good idea," I said. I wasn't certain why it bothered me so. Vanity, perhaps.

He put his arms around my waist from behind, pulling me back against him. "One thing isn't different."

"No," I agreed, and turned in his arms to meet him, bodies and souls touching in one long, languid, sensual kiss, tasting of each other and melting together, white-on-white and flesh-on-flesh in the dark shade of my hall. I closed my eyes. This was right. This was what it was supposed to be.

"Let's go upstairs," he said, his hand on my neck, turning my face up to his.

"Dinner," I whispered.

"Isn't ready."

But he was. I could feel him against me, wanting and impatient. It had been five long months since he rode back to Warsaw for a reprimand, five months since we shared a bed with me more than semi-conscious. Rachelle and Hantz would have a good laugh at our expense, but I found that I didn't mind.

"Take off the sword belt, then," I said, my fingers moving to the buckles. "It's really a bit much."

"Is it?"

"I prefer something a bit smaller," I said rather breathlessly, still trying to unfasten the buckles while he kissed his way down my neck.

"How much smaller?"

"Less than a meter would be nice."

At that he burst into laughter and undid the buckles himself, propping the sword against the chair with his coat and hat and gloves.

"Come upstairs," I said, "And you can muss my hair to your heart's content."

Sweet and hot and hurried, stripping off clothes in the heat of the room, rolling together on my featherbed with the sun through the open window making a molten path across us, red fire behind my closed eyelids as I lay back breathless, heart pounding and hips lifting.

"Is this a..." he began, sounding breathless himself.

"Not a safe time," I said. "On the night table."

I tilted my head and opened my eyes to see if he found the box of letters without delay, watched him tear the paper open, old white scars across his chest and upper arm. That one was before my time. The long bayonet scar down his leg wasn't, nor the one to his left forearm, a defensive wound in a tight melee, when there was nothing else to guard his vitals with.

He looked round at me, unrolling the letter and putting it on, paler than the organ it sheathed. "What are you thinking?"

"That you are beautiful," I said, and drew him down to me.

Afterwards, we lay in the stillness of my room. The heat was just as oppressive, but the light had changed, the purplish light of the approaching storm, and a breeze twisted the leaves of the peach tree outside. He turned onto his back, carefully rolling the letter off without snagging it to wash it out and use again, while I stretched sensually against the sheets, reveling in our mingled scents as I watched him. "Michel, what if we didn't?"

"Didn't what?" He dropped it over the edge of the bed and turned back to me, propped on his elbow.

I hadn't thought I would say it, but I did. "Stopped using the letters."

To his credit, only Michel's brows twitched. "I thought you didn't want any more children."

I let out a long breath and drew him down, arranging his arm beneath my head, one hand idly resting on the horseshoe-shaped scar in the middle of his chest. I wanted to touch him if we were going to talk about this. "My oldest son was born when I was thirteen," I said quietly, "and the second not much later. I was a child myself. I had no desire to be a mother, and I was content to leave them to their nurse and only play at motherhood once in a while, like a child playing with dolls. But that was a long time ago." He had been the one who wanted children before, the one to whom it mattered consumingly.

His breathing was slowing, and one hand traced a lazy pattern on my back.

"But I'll be thirty-one in the fall. We've been together, on and off, for seven years now. It doesn't feel the same."

His voice was quiet, as though he were choosing his words carefully. "You know that I would treasure any child of ours, and that I would support it and give it the best start in life that I could. I can afford it and I wouldn't be cheap."

"I know that, Michel," I said. He had once given me half of everything he had. I had never doubted his generosity.

"But you don't have to do this for me," he said. "I'm staying, child or not. And what would happen about you going in the field?"

"We're at peace," I said. "The Russians have asked for terms, and the Austrians and the Prussians are beaten. We're at a stalemate with England. They can't field an army on the continent, and we can't beat their navy, so we glare at them and they glare at us like zoo animals kept in separate cages. I can't imagine there would be a better time." I settled against him, running my fingers lightly over the twisted red hair on his chest. "Admittedly going on a campaign pregnant wouldn't be a good idea, but plenty of women who have had children follow the army. I could get back in form soon enough. I've had two, remember?" And the one I didn't have, but I had never told him about that. I had never told anyone.

"I do remember," he said, his arm tightening about me. "This is the one you could keep, the one whose father would never take it away."

For some reason that made my eyes sting. He wouldn't. He would never. Not Michel.

"If you want we can leave them off and see what happens," he said. "Let nature take its course."

"Yes," I said. It only made me a little frightened. It was not nearly as bad as a grand battery.

Outside the thunder rumbled and he tensed, every muscle in his body going taut, his face turning toward the window.

"It's only thunder, Michel," I said, running my hand down his arm and feeling the muscles jump beneath my touch.

He took a deep breath. "I know. It's been a long time since I was home."

"You're home," I said. "The war is over."

Another roll of thunder split the air, closer and more substantial. The curtains moved in the freshening wind.

He did not react by act of will. "And duly rewarded," he said. "The Poles gave me 18,000 francs on the treasury of the Grand Duchy of Warsaw in reward. If we are parasites, at least we are gilded ones."

"And what does that comment mean?" I asked.

"Nothing," he said, and turned his head away from the window. "A long war."

"Friedland?"

"Eylau." His arm tightened as the thunder spoke again. "I've never seen such a useless slaughter. But you know. You were there."

"I was," I said. And I had been, but I was not responsible. It was one thing to do it oneself, to risk nothing but one's own life, and quite another to have every soul upon one's conscience. "And yet."

"And yet I love it." His eyes met mine. "What manner of man can say that?"

"One who is suited to the task before him," I said. "You harness your nature for the good of your people, and what more can one do than that? You cannot change your nature."

His hand covered mine, tightening on it, his gaze on my face. "And surely if the devil were to tempt me it would be with a succubus like you, with honeyed words to lure me back into the bloodbath."

"I should rather I was your Venus," I said, unaccountably hurt.

"You are." He bent his head. "Forgive me, Elza. I'm not saying anything right today."

Outside the sky opened up and the rain began, pounding against the leaves of the peach tree. The lightning flashed across our faces, brisk air blowing in through the window and cooling our heated flesh.

"Yes, you are," I said, and folded against him, holding him in the imperfect illusion of peace that was the best I could create.

It was dark before we got up and had dinner. The rain was still falling, cool and sweet, blessed relief from the heat. We didn't bother to dress completely. After all, if one can't dine scandalously with one's lover, when can one? I put on a long sapphire blue robe à la chinoise, and he wore only his ruffled shirt and white breeches like some oversized angel. Rachelle served us in silence.

He smiled at me and poured the wine, his touch light on my hand as he gave mine to me.

I looked up and met his eyes, raised my glass in the light. "Absent friends," I said, my voice shaking a little.

He raised his glass gravely and touched it to mine. "Absent friends."

It was full dark, and the rain made a quiet noise against the trees outside, against the eaves overhead. "So what have you been doing?" he asked. "Other than not dying, but I don't imagine you've simply been resting."

I took a bite, smiling back at him. "Studying with Dr. Mesmer. Noirtier gave me an introduction. It's quite fascinating really. And studying history, especially ancient history. I thought it was distinctly unfortunate in Boulogne that only Reille seemed to be able to tell the difference between Tudor England and Alexander the Great!"

Michel glanced quickly at Rachelle, who was bringing the next course in, but of course she had no idea what we were talking about. "It was fortunate he did," Michel said.

"And rather embarrassing if he hadn't," I said. "Who knows what you might have said next?"

"Things I'd rather not consider too closely," Michel said, looking down at his plate, and I thought it best not to mention anything I'd read recently involving Alexander spending too much time 'between Hephaistion's thighs.' "I'd rather put myself in your hands than Noirtier's, if it comes to doing it again."

"I don't entirely trust Noirtier," I said. "Not the way I trust you and Lannes and the rest. It seems to me it would be useful to have more than one person who can conduct such an operation. You're going to have to learn the method from me."

"I am?" Michel looked up, startled.

"I'm the Dove," I said. "I can't very well take myself down. Someone's going to have to learn how to guide me."

"Noirtier's not going to like that," Michel observed.

"What, because it wasn't done that way in the Pleiade?" I shrugged. "Lots of different things have been done by lots of different people, and no one understands half of what the ancients did. Even famous rites, like the Eleusinian Mysteries, are lost to us. I don't doubt that later scholars have created plausible reconstructions of various things, but there's no particular reason their interpretations are sacred. Our interpretations may be equally valid. Or for that matter better. There has never been a thorough and scientific survey of Egyptian sites before Denon, only a few treasure hunters here and there rather than systematic sketching and recording. Our current information on Egypt is better than anything available in Europe in a millennium. Perhaps one day soon the writing of the Egyptians will be deciphered as well."

Michel had stopped eating and was staring at me.

"What?"

"Good Lord you sound like Reille!" He shook his head. "I had no idea you were such a bluestocking!"

"It's context, Michel. It's story." I lifted my glass. "That's all history is—the stories of the people who came before us, our own stories half- forgotten. If we want to steer the course of history, we have to know how we came to this place."

"I'm not disagreeing," he said and lifted his own. "Only envious."

"Envious?" Of all things he could have said, that was unexpected.

Michel shifted in his seat. "My father was a cooper for the vineyard in Saar Louis. He wanted better for me. He hoped I might be a clerk. He sent me to school until I was twelve so that I could learn to read and write and figure, and then found me a job as a copy boy for the coal mine. Ten hours a day at a desk, copying orders and receipts—you can imagine how well that suited me at twelve! I played truant and lost the job, so he found me another, copying in the office of the foundry. The day after I turned sixteen I took off and joined the cavalry. He didn't speak to me for two years." He took a long drink of his wine, his eyes meeting mine over the top of the glass. "I should have liked to have learned Latin and history and to have had more of mathematics than a smattering here and there. I should have liked Greek and geometry and the rest. But my father couldn't afford a school beyond the Jesuit grammar." He shrugged. "That's why the most important thing we've done is free education for all children. That's our future. That's the fruit of the revolution that's worth dying for."

"And independence for women," I said. "That I might have my own money in my own name, that any woman might have custody of her own children, that she might sue in court and even divorce her husband. That's what I will die for."

He touched his glass to mine again. "For the future."

"Yes," I said. "For all the things that we might build." I searched for the words, wondering if he knew them too. "Alexander dreamed of his Successors, of an army of the children of his soldiers and their mothers from all over the world, and instead what he got was Alexandria. Instead of an army we built a city. We built the greatest city the world has ever known, the freest and the wisest, and it endured for centuries. Let us build a new Alexandria! That's my dream."

Michel ducked his head, a bemused expression on his face. "Not a city, but a world," he said, and I realized he was quoting someone else. "A continent united by law, where every government respects the universal rights of man and religion and birth are no barrier to any man, with one currency and one system of justice, so that borders shall fade."

"Who said that?" I asked.

"Who do you think?" Michel said. "The Emperor. When I asked him what Eylau was for."

I shook my head at the enormity of it. "It seems absurd," I said. "A century and a half ago we all nearly killed one another in wars of religion, and the persecutions have not stopped in many places. The Inquisition still holds sway in Spain! It is unthinkable for anyone but us and the Poles that Jews should serve in the army! Even England's precious navy wouldn't take Max because he's Lutheran, not Anglican! The idea of a world where these things did not matter surpassingly…."

"Is no more impossible than your Alexandria seemed on the eve of Gaugamela," Michel said with a smile. "Do you think then we knew what we were about?"

"I didn't," I said, and the memory fit together like pieces of a puzzle. "All I wanted was to impress you."

He reached for my hand and held it across the table, fingers entwined beside the shining plate. "I think you did."

"I think I did too," I said.

Rachelle coughed in the doorway, a large silver bowl in her hands. "Peaches and Cointreau, Madame. You'd better eat them before they spot."

Michel laughed, still holding onto my hand. "Bring them in, Rachelle! It wouldn't do for them to spot! Don't mind us playing lover's games at the table!"

"You are incorrigible," I said as Rachelle began to serve. I lifted his hand and kissed it quickly.

"You're going to start that, are you?" he asked, lifting my hand in return and with his eyes on mine kissing my fingers exactly at the break, warm and leisurely, his tongue just darting between the middle finger and the ring finger so that I caught my breath. "Two can play that game."

"Can they?" I said, very aware of Rachelle beating a hasty retreat.

"I merely submit to my master's hand."

"Do you now?"

"Come upstairs again and I'll show you just how submissive I can be," I said feeling the craving begin anew with such sharpness that it nearly took my breath away.

His smile faded. "I'm sorry, Elza. I can't."

"You can't?"

"I have to go home."

To Aglae. To his wife who expected him. "You could stay."

"You know I can't."

"I do know." I had him to myself on the campaign. In town I shared him. I understood that. It was the bargain I had asked for. "You will come again soon, won't you?"

Michel nodded. "I will. As soon as I can. Later in the week?"

"Send me a note and tell me when," I said. "I have a lot of things to do."

"I know," he said. He stopped, then began again. "You know I wish…."

"Don't," I said. "Eat your peaches before they spot."

ILLUSIONS

I ran through empty streets, free as a bird in flight, my feet pounding on the uneven paving stones. Somewhere far away there was music, violins and cellos and all the rest, but I ran away. It was night, but the moon made the empty streets bright as day, strange houses with no roofs, wide streets with no people, and nowhere a single light.

Dimly, the part of me that was sitting in Dr. Mesmer's apartment was aware of his hands on mine, sitting knee to knee, almost touching. "…a happy memory of childhood," he said. "A time when you did something you enjoyed very much." He was teaching me how to go into the past, my own past, seeking a happy memory to demonstrate how clear the past could be made.

"I ran away from a party," I said. "Into a beautiful place." My voice seemed very far away, far less real than the moonlit street.

I turned a corner, dancing between the curious stones across the street like stepping stones with a slot between them, my long hair escaping from its ribbons. Free to explore, and no one knew where I was! Houses with no doors, only boards propped against stonework, occasionally shored up with mason's scaffolding, a village of empty houses bright under the moon. There was a sign on one that said "Attenzione!" and more words I didn't know, but I ducked under it and went inside, through a little room with columns into a courtyard open to the moon.

It was all white marble, glittering and pale, an empty pool in the floor ahead. The walls were painted with fish and boats, a marble plinth stood empty where a statue should have watched me. I wandered through room after room, from one house to another, empty rooms calling to me, beautiful and frozen, like some story I had heard.

"Once," I said to the empty rooms, "there was a princess who was doomed to sleep for a hundred years, and so the whole kingdom went to sleep too." But that wasn't the story. I ran my hand along stone seats set into the wall of a dining room, scarlet paintings chased out on the wall bordered in gold, people feasting in long white robes, women with ribbons in their hair. One of them carried a shield with a head on it, and I traced the cool plaster with my finger tip.

"Once," I said, turning and going through another doorway, "there was a dead city that slept beneath the moon because the gods had deserted it. Sand crept in and covered the pictures on the floor, whispered through every brazen tower, buried every scroll and every statue, until all that was left was the story."

The part of me that still sat with Dr. Mesmer whispered on, things my child-self did not know to think but somehow knew. In memory I stretched my hands to the moon, reaching high in a roofless chamber, as though I could grab it from the sky.

And then there was a light. I saw her across another courtyard, a woman with long dark hair in a white dress, a lamp in her hand. She smiled at me and passed through a doorway.

"Wait!" I said, and ran after. I thought I knew her, at least for a moment.

I ran through the door and down a hall, pausing to wonder which way she had gone. There was a faint glow one way, as from her lamp, and I pelted after.

When I got to the corner she was already across the street, but she stopped and beckoned to me, then turned the next corner.

"Wait!" I called.

"Come," she said, and I hurried. She had a white scarf over her hair and the lamp wavered in her hand, her face beautiful and warm. "Come."

I got to the corner and she was gone, halfway down the street disappearing between two buildings. Somewhere up ahead there was music, like men singing. I ran again.

And plowed straight into a man, bouncing off his midsection and looking up. He was a middle aged man in an expensive dark frock coat, and his wig had two rolls over his ears. He had a very fine nose which he was looking down at me. "Who are you?" he asked.

"Elisabeth Tolstoy," I said. My father had been very clear on what I was to say if anybody asked my name.

"The Hungarian Count's daughter," he said.

I nodded. My father was being a Hungarian count this month. I was absolutely not supposed to say he wasn't. "I was lost so I was following the lady with the light," I said. I thought it sounded better to say I was lost than I was running off.

"The lady with the light."

"Yes. She had long dark hair and a white dress and a veil over her hair." I nodded again. Nodding a lot makes you look truthful.

A peculiar expression crossed his face. "Perhaps you saw this," he said, and led me into the first room behind. There on the walls was a painting of steps and pillars and plants in radiant sunshine, a dark-haired woman with a white veil raising her hand in blessing to all of the people who waited. Her smile was warm and secret, but she was only paint.

"It's paint," I said, lifting my hand to touch it.

He grabbed my hand. "Don't! It's not for children to touch. That painting is nearly two thousand years old!"

"She was real," I said. The woman I had seen was no painting. And I had not imagined the singing. I heard it still coming from deeper within the house, ten or so men chanting together like a men's choir.

His face stilled. "Are you a blank slate then?"

The words poured from me though I did not understand them. "I have never been an empty vessel, even when I was chosen as Her host. And I am not some urchin you can keep. I am Count Tolstoy's daughter, and he is looking for me."

And then his face was ordinary again, a middle-aged rather affable man, a scholar or a diplomat. "You are," he said. "And no doubt your parents are worrying about you. I will show you how to get out of this maze. The city can be rather confusing. It is no wonder you were lost."

"Thank you," I said, and let him lead me away from the singing, away from the painting, back the way I had come.

"It's not very far," he said. "You must have wandered from the party."

"Yes," I said, but did not touch him. There was some power

there that I did not fear, but was properly respectful of.

"...up the stairs from the past. Madame? You must ascend." Dr. Mesmer was talking to me, pulling at me as though I were a dog on a leash, pulling me away from the past. I opened my eyes.

"You stopped speaking," he said. "I grew concerned that you might have fallen into an unpleasant memory."

"No," I said, shaking my hands out where they were numb from lying along the chair arms. "No, simply very deep."

That had happened. I remembered it vaguely waking. There had been some confidence game in Italy, some game of claiming a nobleman's title and spending the carnival season in a round of card games and investments in horse breeding. There had been a party and I had run away, and wandered about until a gentleman brought me back. My mother had been worried and asked me a thousand times if he had done anything to me, if he had taken my clothes off or touched me. Which he hadn't. Nothing had been wrong. I had walked around looking at things and then someone brought me back. I did not tell her about the lady with the lamp or about the singing. And after all, those were not the things she asked.

"A pleasant memory?" Dr. Mesmer said.

"Yes," I replied.

His brow was furrowed as though he didn't quite believe me, but there was nothing I could think to ask him.

"About my childhood in Italy," I said. "I don't know quite where we were." I ran over the pictures in my mind. Not a city, but a ruin. Rome? Perhaps the Colosseum? But surely Rome was not so uninhabited? "It was very pleasant," I said firmly.

"Good," Dr. Mesmer said, and stood up stiffly from the chair he had been sitting in at my knees. "Next time we will discuss learning the induction technique that I used."

I arrived home just shy of three o'clock. Rachelle came out to greet me before I got to the front door. "Madame, the Marshal is here."

"What?" Michel never showed up without sending a note first, not since we stopped sharing an apartment together five years before, and he had specifically said the night before that he would see me later in the week. Which did not mean ten hours later and unannounced.

There was a frown between her brows. "He's been here for more than an hour. He just turned up and said he'd wait. I've offered him coffee but he said he didn't want anything."

A cold dread settled over me. "Thank you, Rachelle," I said, and went in, untying my bonnet strings as I went.

Michel turned from where he was looking at the clock on my mantelpiece as I came in. He had not come from an official function this time, and he looked horrible, unshaved and bleary-eyed, wearing an old brown civilian coat.

"Michel!" I said, closing the parlor door behind me. "What in the world has happened?"

He'd taken his gloves off and had dropped one of them on the rug without noticing it. "Aglae was waiting for me when I got home at four."

The cold became ice. Utter, painful clarity. I could take it. I could take what was to come. "And she has given you an ultimatum," I said evenly. My voice did not shake at all. "You have come to give me up."

Michel blinked. "No."

"No?"

"Why would you think that?" He looked perplexed.

"You're not here to give me up?" I could almost feel sensation returning to my hands.

He looked away, toward the fireplace, and I thought that he blinked furiously. "I'm here because I don't know…. Because I don't know where else to go."

I could breathe. Yes. I took off my bonnet and put it on the chair. "She's thrown you out and she's asking for a divorce?"

"I wish it were that simple," he said miserably. "That would at least make sense."

I took my own gloves off and tossed them on the chair with the bonnet, came forward and took his hand. "Come and sit down and tell me what happened." I drew him down next to me on the sofa. "Tell me what happened from the beginning."

"I got home about four," he said. He took a deep breath. "Aglae was awake and waiting for me. She asked me to come in the library and shut the door. She said that it was embarrassing for me to come home at that time of night, that servants had to stay up and that they gossiped. That it was disgraceful for a marshal of France to sneak into his own house before dawn, and that if I were visiting my mistress I should at least consider appearances." He glanced at me. "She said I shouldn't bother to deny it, that you had the most piercing perfume, rose and ambergris. And that it was uncouth for me to come home smelling of you."

I winced. "Did you deny it?" I asked.

"Of course not!" Michel's mouth twisted in a wry smile. "There's no point denying something when you're caught red-handed. Besides, I've never lied to her. I've just not told her all the truth."

"And she told you to give me up?" That seemed the next logical step in this dance.

"No." He shook his head. "She said that I had to hear her out, that I owed her that, and I allowed that I did. She said that I didn't chase the nurserymaids or sleep with her friends, didn't go to brothels and bring her diseases, but what was she supposed to think, this one woman for all these years? That she knew we were together two years before she married me, that you were older and not as pretty...." Michel looked at me apologetically.

"I know she's young and pretty," I said. "I've seen her." I had certainly made the comparison myself, and I could hardly blame Aglae for coming to the same conclusion.

"She said she would rather I had a stable mistress rather than affairs with her friends, and much rather than the dangers of brothels, and that you seemed well-bred enough not to create scandals for me. Therefore I should not create them for myself by behaving embarrassingly, like Berthier and Junot and other new men did. Instead of sneaking in at four in the morning I should simply spend the night and come home in the morning shaved and dressed and irreproachable at a time that caused no comment. And that I should take a bath."

I winced again. It was true that one got used to going without in the field, and I did not find the lingering scent of sex objectionable. But I supposed I might, were it my husband coming home from his mistress.

He took a deep breath. "She said that we got along well, and that we might go along in perfect comfort and respect for one another. That I should not embarrass her, and she would not embarrass me.

That when she took a lover she would be likewise discreet and give no cause for gossip or humiliation." He looked down at his hands.

"Does she have a lover?" I asked. I had not heard anything, but that signified little it seemed.

"She says not." Michel looked up at me. "But she says she will, when she has met someone that she loves, and that I owe it to her to allow her to pursue her inclinations as freely as she allows me to pursue mine—discreetly and with dignity, preserving our affection and our friendship. And that this is best for our children." He stood up abruptly, pacing to the front window with his back to me. "Elza, this is not what I wanted!"

"I know, my dear," I said.

"I haven't seen my boys in a year. They're four and two and the baby's not quite one. The older boys don't remember me and Eugene's never seen me before! I'm a glittering stranger. I can't get five minutes with them. They're their mother's children, and that's all right. She loves them and she's a wonderful mother and they're warm, happy little boys, as much as I can tell. But they're not mine!"

"And she's not yours," I said.

"She doesn't love me."

"I know." I stood up and went to him, put my hands against his back. "It's an aristocratic marriage, Michel. That's how it works."

"I thought she'd be furious about you."

I pressed my palms against his coat. I had responded the same way once, when I realized that my husband did not love me and never had. I had expected him to be jealous, rather than tell me he didn't care if I had a lover. Perhaps Michel and I were more alike than I thought.

And yet I thought I understood Aglae far too well. "Michel, she's a child of the revolution. Remember, Josephine rescued her and her little sisters from prison when she was eight. She went to live with Josephine when Josephine was Barras' mistress. She spent years living in a house with a foster mother who was the mistress of a man she hated, a man who had blackmailed her to keep her children safe! I was there, Michel! I met Josephine in those days! Aglae was not too young to understand. She must have been fourteen or so when…" I broke off. When Josephine wrote that letter to Therese, the one Fouché had paid dearly to get. But Michel knew nothing of that. "She's not that much younger than I am. When I was twenty, she was fifteen—not five! Aglae knows what's what."

He didn't move. "I thought she was so innocent."

"She may have gotten to your bed a virgin, but none of us are innocent, Michel. We could never afford to be."

His shoulders squared. "I think she was technically a virgin, yes." He hesitated and then went on. "Things happened. When she was in prison. When she was a child. Before Josephine was thrown into the same prison, her mother's friend who looked after her. She was there alone for a week before Josephine." He took a deep breath. "Aglae is...very brave. And very determined to have a life that she wants, free of shadows."

He should not have told me those things, not talked to me about his wife, about things so intensely private. And yet who else could he talk to? As horribly inappropriate as it was to talk to me, Reille or Lannes or Max would be worse. I would not speak of it, and he knew that.

"You have given her a precious gift," I said. "A good man who was gentle with her to begin on, someone kind and honest who did not mistreat her or beat her. And you have given her the children." Aglae's sons, like my two sons I had lost.... I blinked, but nothing crept into my voice. "And now she wants the freedom to seek a love of her own. She's twenty-five, Michel, and her heart has healed enough for her to think about happiness. You have given her this gift, and believe me when I say as a woman who was much less fortunate in her marriage that it was no little thing!"

"A marriage of convenience...."

"A marriage based on respect and agreement, rather than passion," I said, and went around him to see his face. "Respect, and your children."

His eyes didn't meet mine. "She said we could continue to sleep together sometimes. That she didn't mind and that she would like a daughter."

"Oh Michel."

"All I wanted was to marry someone I loved and have a family together. How did this get so complicated?" He took both my hands in his.

"We made a mess," I said. "I should have trusted you and you should have waited for me."

"And you have two sons you can't ever see, and I have three sons who don't know me, and we have none together and you have a dead husband and I have a wife who wants a lover and..." He started laughing at the absurdity of it all.

"And here we are," I said. "And we must make the best of what we have." I could see too clearly where this had gone wrong. In my anger and my bitterness I had said that I never wanted to marry him, that I didn't trust him and couldn't. I had likened being with him to slavery. And so of course he had turned away. I had chosen my own life, good and bad, and I could blame the bad on no one except myself. "Forgive me," I said. "Forgive me for not trusting you. For assuming the worst of you because other men had treated me badly, other men who were not you and who you bore no responsibility for."

His face sobered abruptly. "Forgive me for not waiting. I should have been patient. I should have understood that it was too soon, and that *no* did not mean *never.*"

"I meant for it to mean never at the time," I said.

"But it doesn't mean never now."

"No," I said, and I reached into my heart. I did forgive him, a thousand times over. "And I forgive you for not waiting."

He bent his forehead against mine and closed his eyes. "So what do we do now?"

"We go on as we've begun," I said. "All three of us. Aglae doesn't want a divorce, and I don't see you about to divorce her."

His eyes flew open. "How could I do that? She's the innocent party!"

I shrugged. "As you say. So there we are. You are married to Aglae and I am your lover. And one day she'll have a lover as well, and you'll be a good sport about it."

"And I'll be true to the two of you?" he asked with an ironic smile.

"If you like," I said. "But I never promised to be true to you. Nor will I. That is a thing you must understand about me. No one who loves me will ask me to be faithful, no one who knows me as I am."

He put his hand to my face, and I closed my eyes, my lips against his palm. "Have there been others?" he asked quietly. "Since Boulogne?"

"No," I said. "But there will be."

"Well." He stepped closer, his other arm about me. "Then I suppose I shouldn't be jealous about Aglae either. And I'll stand stud to both of you like a prize stallion."

I opened my eyes at the vaguely smug sound in his voice. Yes, he was smirking. "Oh you rat," I laughed. "You like that. You like the idea of women lining up to get a bit of you!"

"I can't help it if everybody wants the best," he said, his grin broadening.

"Conceited man."

"You like it that way."

"I do," I said. "I like your pride and your mettle. And your form and your stamina."

"Now you really do make me sound like a horse."

I put my forehead against his chin, laughing. "A big blood bay. Sixteen hands and well hung!"

He tightened his arms around me, picking me up and spinning me around. "How do you always make me laugh?"

"By loving you," I said simply. "And there is one good thing in all this. You don't have to sneak around anymore and you can actually stay the night."

"There is that," he said. His eyes caught mine mischievously and we both said it at the same time. "And take a bath."

THE WIDOW'S SON

Summer turned into autumn, golden and warm and sweet. September blew in with clear skies and cool nights, days that were warm enough for riding or anything else one wanted. The Russians had signed the Treaty of Tilsit, and we were almost at peace. The army was home.

Michel stayed with me two or three times a week, spending the rest of his time with his children. He was being a bit more aggressive, I thought, about insisting on time with them, refusing to leave for the evening's events until after bedtime in the nursery. He was, after all, the master of the house, and no one could actually throw him out if he wanted to spend time in the nursery. It made him happy. There was quite simply a glow about him when he talked about Joseph and small Michel, an animation as he described their small struggles and triumphs, their emerging personalities. Joseph was dark haired, like his mother, and at four-and-a-bit was curious and thoughtful. He considered before he did. Michel was his father in miniature, red-haired and daring, two years old and prone to screaming temper tantrums and beating on people with his fists. He also nearly killed himself falling six feet from the stair banister and cracking his head on the floor below, an accident involving two days in bed in a darkened room, though apparently his head was as hard as his father's and in a week he was preparing to face the banister again.

Michel related each story with delight, presuming I would like to hear them. Which I did, and I didn't. I had deliberately missed those days with my sons. I had been very young and their care had seemed a bother to me, one easily passed on to older and more competent caretakers. It pained me a little to think that it might have brought me such happiness and I had cast it aside. But perhaps it wouldn't have, not at that age. And perhaps it still would. We laid aside the letters, resolved to let nature take its course. I had not been entirely regular in many years, though less so in the field than in town, and a week's delay in my courses at the beginning of September filled me with both dread and elation. And then they came on hard, a false alarm. But what, after all, was one month? One could not expect these things to happen instantly.

With the army and court both in town, there were glittering entertainments almost every night. Needless to say I was not invited to the same dinners and card parties as Michel and Aglae, not moving in those exalted social circles, though larger events like the balls at the Tuileries I could almost always manage to attend. I had a good many friends among the young officers who were still bachelors and did not expect my favors but simply a pleasant escort—Corbineau was such a perpetual favorite that it greatly increased his stock among his fellows to be thought screwing a Marshal's mistress behind his back!

There was one set of events I did attend with Michel, however. As the army was back in town, so was the Lodge. Just before eight o'clock on September 21st, we alit from Michel's carriage before Lannes' townhouse in the Rue de Varenne, a grand showplace that often held the most fashionable parties planned by Lannes' second wife, who was a notable hostess. I was nervous. Indeed I had been with the Lodge in Boulogne, and three or four impromptu things in the field since then, but I had never attended a proper meeting in Paris that involved the full lodge. Also, this was one of the quarters of the year, the fall equinox, which I was gathering was a high holiday, and additionally it was to be an initiation ritual well above my grade, as Honoré Charles Reille was taking Journeyman's oaths. And of course I was the only woman. I wasn't entirely certain who had agreed that I should be there besides Michel, and almost assuredly Lannes, since it was his house. At least I hoped so. Surely Michel had asked Lannes?

"Does Lannes know I'm coming?" I hissed as Michel handed me down from the carriage in front of the magnificent entrance of the Hotel de Rohan-Chabot.

"He invited you," Michel said, squeezing my hand and reaching back for the leather bag containing his change of clothes. The footman dashed around the carriage and seized it just before Michel did. He would never learn that a marshal didn't carry his own luggage!

"Good," I said. "That's one thing."

"Elza, nobody is complaining about you. There are lodges in the past that have admitted women. Yes, not many and most of them have been dodgy, but..."

We reached the top of the steps, the nimble footman ahead again to open the outer doors. For a moment I thought he was going to announce us as though it were a ball. It ought to have been. It was a palace. And for some reason this was far more intimidating than going to the Tuileries, and the heights much more surreal. "Oh God," I whispered to Michel. "This was the house that belonged to the Prince de Soubise before the Terror! It belonged to a Marshal of France!"

"It still does," Michel whispered back, and gave me his arm.

The entrance hall was filled with mirrors and gold leaf, a magnificent life-size statue of Venus in white marble in the very center. I had only a moment to consider whether it was a Hellenistic original or a Renaissance copy when Lannes himself came around the corner. He was of medium height and whippy rather than heavily built, with light brown hair and a classically handsome face. Lannes looked as a knight ought to look, I thought, with a face that ought to be carved on the magnificent Charlemagne Sarcophagus in Aix la Chapelle. He held out his arms and Michel came and embraced him, kissing him on the cheek. "Good to see you on this happy occasion!"

"Let us hope so," Michel said, more soberly. "And I've brought Madame, as you see."

"Madame St. Elme." He bent over my hand quite properly, his eyes twinkling. "You will be happy to know that I have procured a proper robe for you and shan't make you wear a sheet!"

"I'm grateful for that, sir," I said, more reticently than is my wont.

He glanced over to include Michel in his words. "I've sent Louise off to the theater and the beasts are in bed, so other than two dozen servants or so we have the house to ourselves."

"The beasts?" I asked. "You have children?"

"Five of the little creatures," Lannes said cheerfully. "Age six on down, but they won't bother us. Duval, kindly show Madame St. Elme to a room where she can change."

I left Michel talking with Lannes in the foyer and followed the footman upstairs and down a long corridor, trying to act as though I visited dear friends who happened to own palaces every day.

"This way, Madame," he said, opening a door to the right. "I trust that you will ring if you require anything."

"Thank you," I said, and went in and closed the door. For this house it was no doubt an ordinary guest room, and not the best one, thoroughly splendid in the style of the last century, with an enormous bed draped in azure satin and mirrors of Venetian glass in gilt rococo frames everywhere. A painted screen showed shepherdesses dancing in a bucolic landscape, little lambs frolicking beside them, while tiny fat cupids stooped overhead with pan pipes and strategically placed clouds. If this was Lannes' taste I was utterly flabbergasted.

Lying across the bed there was a white robe and I picked it up. It was thick Lyon silk satin, heavy as a church vestment, the collar facings done in white velvet, long sleeves cut full rather than fashionably tight. I undressed and put it on, acutely conscious of wearing nothing beneath it, the whisper of heavy cloth against my body sensational, though it could not have been more modest. I turned and looked in the mirror. It did indeed cover me from neck to ankles, the pointed neckline coming down only just below my collar bones. It was loosely cut, as of course Lannes had not had my measurements, flaring like a medieval gown from the waist into a fuller skirt, the material thicker by far than any fashionable dress. And yet I was intensely aware of my nakedness beneath it. I ought to have been wearing acres of petticoats beneath something like this. It reminded me of my first days with Moreau, and how humiliating and arousing I had found it to wear ordinary clothing with nothing beneath.

And that was a train of thought that was inappropriate in the extreme. This was supposed to be filled with deep spiritual purpose, not one of Lebrun's fake séances designed as much to titillate as enlighten. With that in mind, I composed myself and went downstairs.

Barefooted. The contrast between wooden parquetry and cool

marble, between marble and thick carpet, was fascinating. At the bottom of the stairs I heard voices and followed them through one salon into another. The scene that met my eyes was strange in the extreme.

The salon was more or less round, half of the room defined by tall windows draped in gold satin curtains now closed against the night, matched on the interior walls with tall mirrors framed in gold. The ceiling was painted azure and trimmed lavishly with gilt, roundel paintings of the Olympian gods around the room between the tops of the windows and the ceiling, nearly a century old and still drawn as bright as when they were painted. There was an enormous chandelier, but it was not lit. Instead the diffuse light came from twelve massive gilt candle stands, each holding three pillars that looked as though they belonged in Notre Dame, set about the room in a circle that mimicked the shape of the chamber. Gilt side tables stood at each of the cardinal points, and on a bronze tripod a gilt-and-glass censer smoldered. There was no simplicity, no making-do here. This was high ceremonial at its highest.

Nearly twenty men stood about gorgeously robed, most in pure white as I was, but a few with sashes in bright colors like the ones worn with a sword belt, marks of their rank within the circle. Michel's was scarlet, a Journeyman in the service of the Archangel Michael.

Jean-Baptiste Corbineau turned about from a little knot of men gathered near the door and his face lit. "My dear sister!" he said, winking at the old joke. "Come and meet one of our partners in crime that I don't believe you know. This is Charles Lefebvre-Desnouettes, a rascal and a rakehell after your own heart."

He bent over my hand as though we were in the drawing room rather than a rather stranger situation, dark hair, blue eyes and a very prominent nose. "So you are the amazon Jean-Baptiste speaks of so often! He did not tell me that you were beautiful." He gave Jean-Baptiste a look of mock reproach. "I confess that I am enchanted."

"The pleasure is mine," I said. The game always was intensely fun to play. "And what do you do, besides behave as a rascal and a rakehell?"

"I'm one of Marshal Lannes' brigadiers," he said. "And he's had me to some hot dances."

"I imagine so," I said. Lannes did like to promote flair.

One of the other men in the group was better known to me, and Gervais Subervie came forward to kiss my cheek rather than my hand. "It's so good to see you," I said, giving his arm a squeeze. "How is your family? How is Nestor?"

"Nestor is quite well," Gervais said. "Jean has decided that he is the best horse that ever lived, his own Bucephalos. They trot quite credibly around the ring, which is to say that Nestor does his business and Jean stays on him, but what can you expect at his age?"

"I'm glad to hear he's happy," I said.

Lefebvre-Desnouettes looked from one of us to the other. "Do you know Madame well?" he asked curiously.

"A bit," Gervais said. "She kept me from falling over a cliff once."

"She did not," Jean-Baptiste said indignantly. "I kept you from falling over a cliff! She only helped haul you back up."

"You both kept me from falling over a cliff," Gervais temporized. "And I appreciate your efforts, both of you."

"Dare I even ask how this happened?" Lefebvre-Desnouettes asked.

"Probably not," I said. I had been on the Emperor's service at the time, something that was not widely known even in the Lodge.

A very young and very pretty young man in a plain white robe came up deferentially, standing about in the style of an aide who has quite a lot of practice at politely interrupting generals. "Sir?" he said to Gervais. "I'm sorry to disturb you, but Marshal Lannes wonders if you might assist with the preparations in the inner chamber?"

"Of course," Gervais said. "Got to finish setting up. I'm coming. Give me a hand, will you Jean-Baptiste? You'll be wanted too."

They trailed off after the aide, and I looked after them. I didn't know the boy either. "Who is he?" I asked.

"Another Charles," Lefebvre-Desnouettes said. "De la Bedoyere, a lieutenant by rank. He's Marshal Lannes' new maid-of-all-work. A good boy."

"Ah," I said. I thought I'd seen the gleam of interest in Corbineau's eyes, but had no idea whether or not there was any hope in it. Probably not, as Jean-Baptiste ranked him by far too many grades, and that would be distinctly injurious to discipline. Lefebvre-Desnouettes, on the other hand …

"And how did such a beautiful lady find herself in such bad company?" he asked. "A dangerous thing, for a mermaid to venture among so many sharks."

"Say rather an amazon," I said, "and one quite adept with pointy arrows. It is an unwise huntsman who mistakes me for prey."

His smile broadened. "Never that, dear lady. If half the stories Jean-Baptiste tells about you are true, I should be in mortal terror!"

Michel cleared his throat behind him and came around to take my arm. "Are you ready, Elza? Lannes is trying to begin."

I nearly laughed aloud. Lefebvre-Desnouette's eyebrows rose almost to his hairline. "I'm quite ready, dearest," I said.

We were twenty strong in the circle, de la Bedoyere running about like a proper aide telling people where to stand. I was one place to Michel's left as he stood at the southward quarter while people milled about talking and finding their spots. "What in the world does Lannes' wife think we're doing?" I whispered.

Michel leaned over and replied, "Drinking vast quantities of Armagnac, refighting Marengo, and eventually pissing in the cuspidors."

I looked at him sideways. "Really?"

His mouth twitched. "I generally spare the cuspidors."

"Can we get started?" Lannes shouted, his voice pitched to carry over a melee. "It's nearly nine."

At that people began to quiet down and Subervie went to shut the doors so that the servants could not look in, nor the curious "beasts" if they weren't as snug in their beds as their father thought. There were many familiar faces around the circle. Max Duplessis gave me a cheerful nod and pantomimed coming over to speak with me after, and I happily pantomimed talking back. Charles Dery was also present, conferring with de la Bedoyere before they both took their places. Honoré-Charles Reille stood two places to Michel's right looking nervous and adjusting his collar again and again. The one I did not see was Noirtier, which surprised me as I thought he was the master here. But he was not, nor was there any space left for him as at Lannes' nod Subervie extinguished all but the guide candle set upon the side altar and stepped silently into his place.

For six long heartbeats there was nothing but silence, the sound of each of us breathing into the dark. Michel reached for my hand and I thought it odd until I felt the tentative fumble on the other side, de la Bedoyere stepping into the place beside me and reaching for my left hand. I took them both, realizing belatedly that we had all joined hands around.

It was like a jolt of electricity, like standing in the middle of a storm, energy running through me from right to left, as though the circle were a mighty river and I were caught in its current. And yet it flowed. It was powerful but benign. It was like the moment before a charge, all energy held in check, all tamed by discipline. And, like that, it was an incredible rush.

"Raphael, Angel of Morning, Angel of the bright light of the mind, illuminator and friend to humanity, grant us your benison!" It was Max Duplessis at East, beginning the first calling, the guide candle in his hand as he lit the pillars in the massive candle stand, his face transformed and filled with brightness, his glasses reflecting the flames. "As we prepare to witness the oaths of our friend, Honoré-Charles Reille, please grant us the very great honor of your presence this night."

He reached for the censer, taking it up with a practiced hand so that the smoke of the incense rolled over the sides in a vast wave, a tide of frankincense and myrrh through the room, and a shiver ran through me. I had never heard angelic presence called before, except for that once with Lebrun. This was like a silent wind, the hairs on my arms standing on end as Max slowly and carefully trod the circle, passing behind each of us as we faced the center. When he returned to his place I felt it close like a clap of thunder.

And then it was Michel, turning in place as precisely as if he were in drill, going to one knee to light the pillar like a knight before his lord. "Michael, Angel of Bright Noontide, Captain of the Hosts of the Most High, defender and friend to humanity, grant us your benison!" From the floor beneath the candle stand he lifted up his own sword, not the fine dress sword he wore for court occasions, but the saber he'd had for all the years I'd known him, its hilt wrapped with cord long since stained with sweat and blood. He drew it still on one knee and held it up so that the bar of the hilt just touched his lips, as though kissing a cross of steel. "As we prepare to witness the oaths of our friend, Honoré-Charles Reille, please grant us the very great honor of your presence this night."

With that he stood, graceful as a fencer, and began to trace a line about the room, walking the same path that Max had trod, the light flaring off the blade. It was Michel and not Michel, a presence not fully enfolded but about him, a numinous shimmer just below the threshold of sight. I caught my breath in wordless wonder. That was what it looked like, a glimpse of the divine in each of us, a glimpse through the veil at our souls unmasked.

A tear ran down my face as he stepped back into his place, laying the bared sword on the altar.

Lannes' voice was grave, his head bent as he poured clear water into a silver goblet. "Gabriel, Angel of Evening, Annunciator and Font of Compassion, comforter and friend to humanity, grant us your benison! As we prepare to witness the oaths of our friend, Honoré-Charles Reille, please grant us the very great honor of your presence this night." He lifted the water as though it were the Host, his eyes never leaving it as he paced the outside of the circle, and the scent of the sea followed him.

Thus we came to North, and Subervie took a deep breath, his face stilling as he reached for a gilded dish filled with salt, its elaborate lines proclaiming a treasured antique. "Uriel, Angel of Night, Angel of Death, final guardian and friend to humanity, grant us your benison! As we prepare to witness the oaths of our friend, Honoré-Charles Reille, please grant us the very great honor of your presence this night." I saw it settle about him like a cloak, impenetrable and infinite, as though he wore the night sky in his face. It transformed him, this ordinary man I had known in Boulogne, and it was all I could do not to sink to my knees and bow my head. *On your knees to Death.* To serve that would be to be consumed.

Or not, something whispered beside me, as though Michel had spoken, though he had not, a voice like his and yet unlike. It was like a warmth at my back, a touch of fire that did not burn. *Welcome home, Elzelina.*

At that my eyes overflowed, tears streaming down my face. Welcome home. This was where I stood, in the circle of my friends, beside my lover in the heart of the world. I had weathered every storm to come to this moment where I rested, complete and whole, at the bosom of my master.

You are my master, I said in my silence. *You are who I serve in this life, here and now, with a full and grateful heart. Michael. I will put myself in your hands and fight as you show me, that I may be your instrument on earth.*

You have been for a very long time, he said, and I thought that he smiled.

"The Lodge is open in the First Degree," Lannes said solemnly.

I did not remember much of what passed next, lost in something of a haze of wonder. There were many passages and responses and a short dramatic story about the building of Solomon's Temple as a metaphor for perfecting the world acted out by Lefebvre-Desnouettes and Corbineau with much feeling but little acting ability. Lefebvre-Desnouettes did have a nice, clear speaking voice though. "Once, in that time, there was a young man who was the son of a widow, and when he was an infant, his mother had taken him away to dwell alone in the marshes for she feared that his father's enemies might also harm him. And in that time when he was grown, he stood before his mother and he said, 'Let me go now unto the kingdom of my father, for its people suffer beneath the lash, and the blood of the slain cries out for justice!'"

I felt that I had heard this story somewhere before, but I could not place it.

You knew this story well in times long ago, He said behind me. *Often you have told the story of the Son of the Widow and how his mother bore him in secret and raised him to save his people. Often you have walked the paths of this story with one or another. And perhaps you will again.*

I don't understand, I said.

I know. His voice was contemplative. *But perhaps within this current lifetime you will read the story again and it will be told in its original form, not as these pieces of lore transformed and transfigured through many peoples. The keys are in your peoples' hands, and for that matter in your own. Perhaps someday soon someone will read those words again. They have been waiting for you for a very long time.*

Lost stories, I said keenly. *Lost stories that have been waiting for me...*

But for now listen to the retelling, He said. *Learn the story so that you can tell it.*

To whom? I asked.

There was a flicker to his voice, as though there were something he did not want to tell me. *To a child yet unborn,* He said. *For whom, if all goes well, you will open the gates of the Underworld.*

"Honoré Charles Michel Joseph Reille," Lannes said clearly. "Are you resolved to walk the path of the Widow's Son?"

"I am," Honoré replied.

"Know that you will be tested, and if you are found wanting you will not go on as you have been," Lannes said.

"I consent to the testing." Honoré's head was high, his dark eyes bright, and for a moment I thought I saw someone else standing there, some shadow of another—or another and another and another.

"Then kneel." Honore sank to his knees, his white robe about him. Subervie stepped forward with a black kerchief in his hands and bound it about Honoré's eyes. He did not flinch, not even when Michel stepped out of his place in mirror and seized Honoré's wrists, binding them roughly and tightly behind him.

"You are the sacrifice," Michel said. "Your life is forfeit."

"My life belongs to my country, to my friends, and to the service of the Most High," Honoré said. "And for those things it is gladly forfeit."

Subervie reached down to drag Honoré to his feet none too gently. "You will be taken from this place to a place of trial, and there you will suffer." Holding Honoré by the arm he led him from the circle, Michel and Lannes and Max and two others following, all the ones who wore colored sashes over their robes. Max slipped ahead to open the doors that led from the room into some adjoining one, and they hustled him through and closed it behind them.

I looked at Corbineau with something like astonishment. "What now?"

"We can't go," Jean-Baptiste said. "We haven't achieved the degree ourselves. Obviously if we saw it now it wouldn't be any suspense to us when we get there."

"Ah," I said. It wasn't that I thought they would really hurt him. At least not in any physical sense. And yet what they did was real.

This was a true testing. "So what do we do?"

"We wait," Lefebvre-Desnouettes said. He leaned back on his hands. "We wait."

I did not know how long it was before they returned. There was no clock in the room, and the pillars burned slow and steady.

When they did, the doors were thrown open in triumph and Honoré led the way out, a scarlet sash about his waist weighted with heavy gold fringe like the sashes of the Army of the Republic. He seemed lighter, as though buoyed up by a delight he could not contain.

"The candidate has been tested and found acceptable," Lannes said solemnly. "Welcome to our fellowship, Journeyman."

"Thank you," Honoré said, and he stepped back into his place with a smile.

Michel reached over and clasped his arm, and he bent his head to Michel's shoulder for a moment in embrace. "Well done," Michel said. "So well done."

"Are there any here who wish to make a Profession of Apprenticeship?" Lannes asked loudly in what was no doubt intended to be a ritual question. "Are there any who wish to set their feet upon the path that Reille has already walked?"

De la Bedoyere swallowed and stepped forward, no doubt prepped for this part. "I do," he said. "I wish to pledge myself to stand amid this fraternity in our service together."

Lannes looked about the room. "Is there any person who objects to the inclusion of Charles Angelique François Huchet de la Bedoyere in our fellowship?"

Of course there was none. They must have all known that he was going to say this.

"Then welcome to our fellowship," Lannes said warmly. He looked about. "Is there any other?"

"I do," I said.

Everyone stared at me, not the least Michel.

"I do," I said more strongly. I could feel the flame at my back, feel the rightness of it. "I wish to pledge myself to stand amid this fraternity in our service together."

Subervie's jaw dropped and Lannes looked nonplussed.

"What?" Max said.

"She's done as much as any of us," Honoré said. "And more than some. We needed her in Boulogne and she came through. I don't see why not."

"She's a woman," Lannes said. "We've never..."

"Then it's time we began," Jean-Baptiste said. "And hang the traditions of the Pleiade! My vote is for Madame."

"Noirtier will have apoplexy," Max said.

"Is Noirtier the master here?" Michel asked, his eyes meeting Lannes' across the circle, as though exchanging some thought of their own. "Or are we?"

"We're not his damned Jacobin club, if that's what you mean," Gervais said. "It's time we decided which drum we're dancing to."

Lannes didn't look away from Michel. "And you're for this?"

Michel shrugged unapologetically. "Yes. I've seen what she can do." He looked around the room. "We're going to need a Dove again, and where do you think we'll find a better one? If we turn her off, then what?"

"Point," Max said.

"We ought not be having this conversation in front of the candidate," Honoré pointed out.

"Better in front of my face than behind my back," I snapped. "I'd like to see who doubts my honor."

"I'm in then," Lefebvre-Desnouettes said. "I don't know Madame St. Elme as some of you do, but I like the sound of that."

De la Bedoyere looked spooked, and I doubted he would vote at all. But then Lannes was the one who had to be convinced, as apparently this would occasion a break with his own Master, a breach of discipline and possibly a breach of orders.

"Does anyone seriously doubt she can do the work?" Jean-Baptiste asked. "This isn't about that. It's about whether we follow the rules or make the rules. I think it's time we grew up and made the rules."

Lannes' eyes flicked to Corbineau and then back to Michel. "Is there then any person who objects to the inclusion of..." He stopped, suddenly realizing that he did not know my full name.

"Elzelina Johanna Versfelt," I supplied. I would never claim my husband's last name again.

"...in our fellowship?" Lannes concluded.

Of course not a person answered. Which was not to say that they all agreed, but none objected enough to stand forward.

"Then welcome to our fellowship," Lannes said, but it was Honoré who took my hand and embraced me like a brother.

LOST STORIES

We took Michel's carriage back to St. Cloud, as it was very late. Since his conversation with Aglae, he was less reluctant to stay with me. The coachman and the footman might tittle-tattle where he'd been, but since the only one he cared about knowing that was Aglae, there wasn't any point in sneaking.

He waited until we were well underway, the carriage wheels rattling across one of the river bridges, the reflections of light on the water playing across his face. "I wish you'd told me what you planned to do," he said evenly. "You could have trusted that I would be on your side. You didn't have to put me on the spot to have my support."

"I didn't plan it. Truly." I looked over at him, in profile by the window, and it came to me that perhaps he was hurt. In some ways he was very easy to hurt accidentally. "I didn't intend to do that."

He glanced at me. "Truly?"

"Yes."

He nodded. "I thought we'd come to that eventually, but that it would go over better if everyone in the Lodge knew you first and were used to the idea. That before we got to Noirtier we could show solid consensus." His eyebrows twitched. "It will be Lannes who has hell to pay with his own master, and probably a break with the Tradition as well. I'd hoped we could ease into that, but as usual you blew everything to hell."

"I am so sorry," I said. "Michel, I didn't realize. And I had no thought of doing it until…"

"Until?"

I searched for words, but there were none except the true ones. "Until you invoked Michael's presence."

He did look at me then, sharply and then his face fell into familiar lines again. "You heard the drum and you had to follow."

"Just so," I said. "I had no idea I was messing up any plan of yours. You might have told me you had one."

"And say that I thought that many of my friends would not consider you worthy?"

"Michel, I know that most men don't consider me worthy because I'm a woman." I shook my head. "That thought has occurred to me before. It's the exception that is surprising. I would not have expected your friends to automatically exempt me from the rules."

"Not exempt you," Michel said. "Not Charles, the only exception. But to change the rules entirely."

I put my head to the side, not certain he could mean what I thought. The tenor of the carriage wheels changed as we rolled off the bridge and onto the streets of the left bank. "You want women in the lodge? As a general practice?"

"I think we'd be better for it," he said. "Honoré and I've talked about it. A better balance of energies and abilities. We've always had major problems balancing certain quarters, and while it's not true that there are no men who call upon Venus or the Archangel Raphael, we're fire heavy and that's unavoidable when half the circle are cavalry. We'd do better with a mix of skills and affinities. We're not the Pleiade, with a sole Dove who is supposed to be a blank slate for the magician to write on. And there are any number of women who would be candidates besides you. You're the simplest to get in because you've worked with us before and they know you, but you're not the only possibility."

"Like who?" I asked.

Michel shrugged. "How about your friend Isabella Thibault? Auguste would bring her in a heartbeat if he could, and she's a different sort altogether, all water and earth. She's Auguste's wife and he's shown her things privately."

"You have actually thought this through," I said.

"Give me a little credit, Elza."

I took his hand and squeezed it. "I should not underestimate you so."

"No," he said. "You shouldn't."

"I'm sorry," I said. "Please don't be angry."

"I'm not. Very." He squeezed my hand back to show he wasn't, then held out his arm and I cuddled up next to him, my head on his shoulder. He dropped his face against my hair for a moment.

"Next you'll tell me you'd commission women in the army," I said.

"I'd commission you if I could get away with it," he said.

I looked up at him and boggled. "What?"

"You're perfectly capable. There's not so much talent in the world that we can afford to throw it away. And what's the difference between throwing it away because it's a cooper's son or a busboy, and because it's a girl?" He shrugged. "But I'd never get away with it. Not unless you lived as Charles full time."

I thought my mouth was hanging open. "Where in the world did this come from?"

He frowned. "If I tell you truly, will you believe me?"

"Yes," I said.

"There was a girl," he said, and took a long breath as though steeling himself for something. The lights of the town moved across his face with the carriage's motion. "Or rather, I was a girl. That's the thing that's hard to say, isn't it? A hundred years ago or more. A young widow with lands to hold and two sons to protect and the Imperial army bearing down on me..."

I caught my breath, for I could see her in my mind's eye, red-haired and slender, blue eyes that snapped anger and provocation, but never fear. A dusty black dress and an autumn morning, a cloud of powder smoke rolling away to the west ...

"I was still me. Do you understand?" There was a note of passion in his voice that was hers, a rising note I thought I knew. "I was still me. Three thousand years of experience, three thousand years of knowing in my gut how to command armies, how to win—but none of that mattered! The only thing that mattered was having a woman's body. Because I had breasts I was no longer fit. I could do nothing but hide behind someone else, find a man to be my voice and to do the things I could not. Because I was nothing."

I swallowed. "And you found a man," I said. "To be your consort. To be your voice. A mercenary captain who had never had a home."

"A landless and lawless man who could do whatever he wanted with me and mine."

"And did he?" My voice caught in my throat.

"Not so much." His arm tightened around me. "Not so very much. We came to terms, I think."

"And perhaps he loved you," I said. "As much as he was capable of loving anyone."

Michel bent his face again to my hair. "I had an object lesson, I think," he said. "I'd like to think I'd learned something from it and wouldn't be cruel to someone else so unfortunate."

"Michel, being a woman is not a misfortune," I said.

He craned his neck to see my face. "Isn't it? Wouldn't you rather be Charles if you could be? If you could simply change your body and be male, wouldn't you?"

"No," I said slowly. "I don't believe I would." And that was a new thought to me. Ten years ago, five years ago, I would have given anything to be Charles, to forever bury Elza and be done with her, my weaker and less worthy part. But now... "I am Charles and Elza both," I said. "Both parts are my soul, and neither is better than the other. Neither is stronger. I'm not 'really male' or 'really female'. I'm both. Both sides of the coin, both pillars of the Temple, sun and moon alike." I spoke what I knew in my heart, and trusted he would understand. "We are all made in the image of God, male and female alike, and we give that power different faces to suit our needs, to make it easier to think about with our mortal minds and to understand with our mortal senses. But to exalt one over the other is ultimately blasphemy."

"Or to say that I should not love my children now as I did then because now I'm a man?" Michel said. "Or that you should no longer follow the drum because you're a woman?"

"To say 'this is male and this is female and they are in opposition' is to create war within ourselves," I said. "Because we are all both. And in time we will all live lives in either body. We all have."

He put his face against my hair again. "We have all been wife and husband. We've all been master and slave. We've all been killer and victim."

"And we will be again." I pressed my cheek against his shoulder. "The story of humanity is the story of our souls, even if we do not remember the story in full. There are so many stories that are lost." I thought of what the angel had said then, of the secret warmth in his voice as though he remembered me fondly, like a father who reflects on moments in babyhood that one has forgotten. "Languages no one can read, stones buried in the sand waiting for someone to decipher the stories."

His lips brushed my brow, and then he straightened up, reaching for his bag beneath the opposite seat. "I was going to give this to you for your birthday next week, but I think I'll go ahead."

I sat up too as he rummaged in the depths. "Michel, you don't have to…"

"No, it's the time," he said upside down. "Like I said, this was for your birthday, but it won't hurt to be a few days early." He sat up with a dark blue leather case in his hands. "Here. Happy birthday, Elza. And besides, it's customary to give your Entered Apprentice a gift."

I took it but didn't open it, a jeweler's case and quite heavy. "Am I your Entered Apprentice?"

"My eromenos," he said with a boyish smile that lit his face. "Open it!"

I did, and for a moment I ceased to breathe.

It lay on white satin, beads sensuously curled in coils like a snake, a double strand of them with gold spacers, while in the center…I could barely touch it. It was a gold beetle fully the length of my thumb wrought of pure reddish gold and pierced for the chain, stylized and smooth, its wings folded just so. I lifted it up with trembling hands, felt the deeply incised carvings on the back and turned it over, squinting in the half-light of the carriage. A long oval enclosed a crouching lioness, a bird, a feather…

"What do the words say?" I asked.

"No one knows," Michel said, and reached for the necklace to lift it up before me. "Egyptian hieroglyphics have never been deciphered. But I saw it and I knew it was for you." He put it gently around my neck, fastening the clasp.

"Where did it come from?" Its weight settled around my neck, the scarab resting unerringly on my sternum, just at my heart.

"A soldier brought it back from the Egyptian expedition. He bought it in the souk from a man who sold antiquities to Europeans. When he ran short of money last year he sold it to a jeweler in Paris. I had it strung for you with lapis lazuli just the color of your eyes."

He looked at it lying on my breast, looked up at my face. "I hope you like it."

"It's utterly magnificent," I managed. "Oh my dear Michel."

He touched the scarab with one finger. "No one knows what it says. But I know it's for you."

"A lost story," I said, blinking hard.

"Perhaps you'll find it," he said.

"Perhaps I will," I said, and reached for him with a full heart.

Autumn came in earnest, blown in on winds and rain after the equinox, tinting the poplar trees with gold in parks and on street corners. Winter came after, scouring the trees of leaves but with no more than a trace of ice. And I was happy. My strength had returned and I could ride and shoot and dance as I had before Eylau. The scar faded to pink. I had my studies and my consultations with Dr. Mesmer, my lover and my friends.

In November my courses skipped completely, and once again I hoped and feared. I had almost decided to tell Michel when they came on with a vengeance on the first of December. Another false alarm? Or a pregnancy that began and didn't take, gone after seven weeks? One could never know. All I could know was that I was not pregnant now.

Michel was to spend Christmas with his family, and I reconciled myself to a very lonely holiday indeed. I might have been blessed with good news, cosseting early pregnancy and being fussed over. I might have had someone to see the year turn with. But of course, I did not.

It came to me that surely there were others of my acquaintance who were not married and who would not begin Christmas morn with the excited cries of children, and perhaps rather than feel sorry for myself I should throw open my doors to the rowdy crowd of bachelors. Jean-Baptiste would be glad of Christmas Eve dinner, and so might Honoré, who had no family except his sister and her son. At the last moment we acquired Max and his sister, a studious spinster nearly my age named Annette, and then Jean-Baptiste turned up with Charles Dery in tow, proclaiming that poor Dery had been planning to spend the day alone and he could not leave him to his fate. In the end we made a merry party of six, Annette shyly flirting with Honoré and Jean-Baptiste turning all his charm on the apparently oblivious Dery, and I found that I hardly missed Michel at all.

I began the new year with a summons from the Emperor. On the second day of 1808, a young aide arrived with a note for me from Marshal Duroc, directing me to present myself at the Tuileries the following day at ten in the morning. This time I was well prepared. Appropriately dressed and with my heart beating fast, I reported fifteen minutes before the appointed time, wondering what was in store. It had been a year since my last formal assignment, though I had spent a good deal of that recovering from the wound sustained at Eylau. Where would he want me to go? What would he want me to do? Not England, surely, as my English was rudimentary at best. More likely east than west....

I was shown into his study at precisely ten, something I did indeed appreciate. But then Napoleon never had needed the trick of making one wait endlessly in order to establish his authority. He didn't need games and didn't indulge in them for fun. "Sire," I said, sinking into a deep courtesy.

He looked up from the papers on his blotter and wiped his hand on a handkerchief where he had got ink on it. I noticed that his white breeches were liberally spotted with ink. "Madame St. Elme," he said, with a smile. "Come and tell me how you are enjoying Paris this winter."

"Very much so, sire," I said, taking the offered chair before his desk.

"What do you do with yourself? Plays? Opera? What sort of thing?"

"I enjoy the Opera very much," I said, wondering what this line of small talk was for. "I like horse racing too, and the faster the better, even on a hard-frozen track."

"Do you wager much?" he asked.

"No," I said, "For I find that I always lose, and there are more pleasurable ways to spend my money than losing."

He laughed at that. "And you have your friend," he said.

"If you mean that I entertain Marshal Ney, yes." Again, I thought he knew this quite well.

"Dances, card parties?"

"I am rarely invited to the events of the season," I said. "Except when I enjoy your benevolence through the generosity of a friend. But I amuse myself well enough with my own set."

"Bachelor officers," he said. "Well, there is no harm in that."

"I hope not, sire. Many of them are devoted to you."

He waved a hand as though to dismiss any concern. "I do not question their loyalty. Just their judgment."

"Sire..."

"I know. You will defend your friends!" He smiled again. "And are you willing to take on an assignment for me?"

"It would give me great pleasure, sire," I said.

"Good." He shifted some papers around on his desk. "Four weeks from now the Countess Walewska will arrive in Paris. She is, as you may be aware, the wife of Count Anastase Walewski, a Polish gentleman of some note."

"I am aware of that, sire," I said, blinking.

"She will be traveling with only her brother, Benedict, and will live very retired in an appropriate house in a suitable neighborhood. By her request, she will not be presented at court and will not attend any official function on behalf of anyone."

"I see," I said, and I did. The countess had left her husband, or at least done so in all but name, and now she would live as I had when I came to Paris for Moreau. Of course she would not be presented at court! That would be a horrible affront to Josephine, who I had thought he loved. Perhaps he did, and that was the root of it. Why should I expect the Emperor's life to be any less complicated than mine?

He did not look at me as he shuffled papers about on his desk. "While the Countess will not be visiting in any official capacity, I do not want her to think that our capital is devoid of pleasures or lacking in anything that might make it amenable to her. The Countess does speak French, and her command of the language is improving, however I think it would be a comfort to her to have a companion who is fluent in her native tongue." He did look up at me at that. "You speak Polish, I understand?"

"I do, sire," I said. And I understood now what he was about. Unlike Moreau, he did not mean to throw Countess Walewska to the dogs. I had been left to make my own way among the likes of Therese with no friend, with no one who could guide me in this treacherous world, no one who shared my status as more than a casual affair of the heart and less than a wife. I should make a better friend for his Maria than anyone had been to me.

And still he spelled it out. If I had not known him better I should have thought that he was uncomfortable, and yet eager to speak of her, eager for her arrival. "She will wish to visit the best modistes," he said. "I understand that is best done with a lady who may give solid advice. I should like for her to have a companion for the theater. She is very eager to enjoy some of our best productions, and it is entirely respectable for her to attend with a female friend."

"Of course," I said. No young officer could be detailed to that without looking as though he were paying court to Count Walewski's wife, since they were maintaining that fiction, but a female friend should be perfectly permissible.

"I trust that you also will advise her as to the character of those she meets," he said, shifting from one foot to another. "As not all of our ladies are worthy of her regard."

"I am well aware of that, sire," I said. Therese had hated him much more than she hated me. In her heyday I had been for the most part below her spite, while he had not. He had not been such a fool as she thought, this penniless young officer without a dress sword, unworldly and awkward, who her friend had lowered herself to. If he wanted me to warn Maria off the likes of Therese, I should do so and consider it a boon to society.

"I don't know how long she'll stay," he said, and for a moment looked less like the Emperor than that young man again, ridiculous young Bonaparte that Therese and Moreau had laughed at together. "It might not be for long."

There was nothing I could say to that. She would leave when she liked. Certainly he could make her stay, but he wouldn't, no more than he had made me stay with him that evening in Milan. "I will do my best to ensure that she enjoys her visit," I said, and with that our conversation concluded.

Michel was, predictably, not surprised. "I don't know who else he'd get," he said. "About four ladies speak Polish. He can't ask someone's wife if he means for her to be his mistress, he can't ask any close friend of Josephine's, he can't ask anyone with a bad reputation or who looks like they're for sale or who is still on the stage like La Grassini...."

"La Grassini used to sleep with him herself," I said. "That wouldn't do."

Michel grinned. "I suppose you're it! Ambassador to Poland without portfolio."

"That's not amusing," I said. "There are currents and currents in this. She's not a singer or a courtesan. She's a foreign noblewoman of good family that he very well could marry."

"She's already married," Michel said.

"Her husband is nearly eighty," I said. "Reasonably, how long can one expect before she's respectably widowed?"

"He's married."

"In a civil service with no witnesses," I said. "It could be annulled in a heartbeat. Josephine planned it so."

Michel frowned. "Why?"

"So that she could divorce him," I said. I could say that much. It was old news. "That cuts two ways." I could almost put my fingers on a pattern, almost see the shape of the mountain.

...a mountain, and a door that led into the depths...a passage winding into the heart of the earth, cut from living stone, and a prince who would go that way behind a woman who walked in darkness, two companions at his back...

"The Widow's Son," I said.

Michel blinked. "What?"

I hardly heard him, lost in the vision. *A lean Roman reclining on a couch, his blond bodyguard at his back, the lines of his face animated and clear. "I can give you what no one has," she had said, and my sister's voice was serene. "I can give you a son."*

"A son," I said, the last piece falling into place. "An Emperor needs a son."

Michel's expression was serious. "He can't have a son," he said. "He's never fathered a child, not with any woman. We talked about it once, years ago. There's something wrong."

"He's perfectly capable," I said. I nearly added, *and I ought to know, having slept with him myself years ago,* but that would just muddy the waters.

"Of making love, yes," Michel said. "But nothing ever comes of it. Nothing ever has. Not with Josephine, not with a single lover. He's consulted doctors and none of them can find anything wrong, but all their tonics and preparations do nothing. Not one of his women has conceived."

"What about that child born to Caroline's little reader?" I asked. "Eleanor or whatever her name was? Gossip said her baby was the Emperor's."

Michel shrugged. "Murat was in that too. Anybody could have a black-haired baby boy. It did the Emperor good to have it talked of, and Murat certainly wasn't going to put a sou out for the child, so he gave him an annuity for his support. But he didn't seriously think the boy was his." Michel put his arm about me carelessly. "He's reconciled himself that it's not to be. I can't imagine anything could convince him otherwise."

"I can," I said grimly, but I said no more. I knew one woman who had conceived by him—Josephine. And I knew what had happened. I took a breath. And quite possibly I was the only person in France besides Josephine herself who knew what might happen. Countess Walewska was no lightskirt also in bed with Murat, and she was no actress or courtesan whose child could never be an heir.

I tilted my head back. I would have banged it on the ceiling if I could have. "Not Roxane," I said. "Cleopatra. She gave in so that he would fight the Russians for Silesia. So that the Emperor would restore Poland."

"And he has," Michel said. "In all but name. The Grand Duchy of Warsaw is a lot better than nothing. But let me tell you that territory cost lives."

"And what is that," I asked, "Compared to her country? Compared to an ancient kingdom fallen into servitude that might be saved by its daughter? Oh my God, Michel! How could I, of all people, have missed that? She goes to him and promises what only she can give in return for her people's freedom! She is the sacrifice, laying her heart at the feet of the Queen of Heaven!"

Michel took both my hands. "Elza, what in the hell are you talking about?"

"Caesar came to Alexandria hunting Pompey and found the

kingdom in chaos. He restored Cleopatra to her throne and placed the Kingdom of the Ptolemies under Rome's protection, under his personal protection, and she sealed the bargain with Caesarion, blood of the Caesars and blood of the Ptolemies in one!" I put my hand to my breast, feeling the scarab heat against my skin. "Michel, haven't you ever seen the play? Antony and Cleopatra?"

"No," he said with rather too much heat. "I hate that entire period! I've never seen the play and I don't mean to!"

"It's gorgeous," I said. "Well, except for the end. 'Was this well-done by your lady?'"

He swallowed hard as if I'd slapped him, his face white. "Very well," he said. "As befits the last of so many noble kings."

I stared at him, my veins ice. "How do you know it then?" I whispered.

"I don't know," he said slowly. "I don't want to. And neither do you."

I took a long breath, my hands tightening on his.

"It doesn't matter," he said. "It doesn't matter what Cleopatra did or what Caesar did or that Antonius was an utter idiot as a naval commander or that Polio tried to explain to Agrippa what Octavian would be...." He closed his eyes. "It doesn't matter. This is here and this is now, and we do not have to take part in this drama if we don't want to. We can choose who we are and who we will be."

"Yes, Michel," I said, my hands holding his and the scarab warm against my breast. "We can choose. We all have second chances. And we can make it right." I felt tears start in my eyes. "And if there is a child I will never, ever, let anything happen to it. By sun and moon and the sons of gods, I will make it right!"

"We will make it right," he said, and his eyes on mine were a pledge.

CANDLEMAS EVE

Countess Walewska arrived in Paris on the second day of February, a date both portentous and inconvenient. It was the old Feast of the Churching of the Virgin, meaning that it was one of the eight major lodge meetings of the year, and only the third since I had been formally admitted. I should probably have to miss it. I doubted I could possibly leave the Countess in time to be at Lannes' house by nine.

I had been alerted to her impending arrival by messenger from the Emperor, who had been kept abreast of her journey by semaphore since she crossed the border, and therefore I presented myself at the house he had rented for her at Number 2 Rue de la Houssaye, a pretty little townhouse built in the last century in a very respectable part of town. At the moment that I arrived, two footmen were unloading the trunks from the traveling coach, and I noted that while they were certainly nice ones, there were only three—an absolute paucity of luggage for a grand lady traveling, especially since one of them must belong to the brother who accompanied her. There were also four or five Polish lancers in splendid uniform loitering about in front along the street, presumably additional security on the Emperor's orders. They were as unobtrusive as a bunch of swans amid a flock of pigeons, and already some passersby stopped to see what was going on. I presented myself to the lieutenant in charge of the detail, who passed me through. Everyone had been quite thoroughly briefed.

The butler was also Parisian, and I wondered for a moment if the Countess had brought any of her own staff. Presumably her maid, at least. He led me into the foyer and announced me in a grand stentorian voice. "Madame St. Elme to see the Countess."

Maria Walewska turned. She was ten years my junior,

twenty-one instead of thirty-one, but not wearing the deliberately virginal white gown in which I had first seen her, she no longer looked like a girl just out of the schoolroom. She wore a traveling dress of dark blue broadcloth and low boots topped with gray fur. Her honey-colored hair was coiled at the back of her neck. She had broad cheekbones and fresh, clear skin flushed from the cold or perhaps from the excitement of arrival, and her eyes were the same wildflower blue as mine. It struck me forcefully that we looked very alike. My face was sharper than hers, my cheekbones higher and my nose longer, but our coloring was just the same. She stood a few centimeters shorter, perhaps the width of two fingers, but our builds were identical. If I had been introduced as her elder sister no one would have doubted it in the least.

"Countess," I said in Polish, and dipped a shallow courtesy as befitted her rank. "It is a very great pleasure to welcome you to Paris and to place myself at your disposal."

"Madame St. Elme," she replied in the same language, and I saw confusion cross the butler's face. Of course none of the household staff the Emperor had hired spoke Polish! It was not so common a language in France, and certainly not among skilled domestics. She drew herself up and her eyes were not warm. "So you are the one who is to teach me to be a dishonorable woman."

I straightened up from the curtsy like a duelist from a bow. To flinch from her would be a mistake. "I may lack virtue, Countess, but I do not think I lack honor."

At that she colored, her cheeks brightening, not so certain of herself as she had sounded.

"My loyalty to those I love is unimpeachable," I said.

"Marshal Ney," she said, and I saw the butler's eyes flicker. The name at least was close enough to the French for him to take the meaning.

"I have been his friend for nearly eight years," I said. "And it is not a regard I take lightly. I am not a whore, Countess."

She flinched. I had used the rudest word I knew in Polish. "I did not say that you were," she said.

"The Emperor does not mean any insult by sending me to you," I said. "I am the friend of one he esteems greatly, and he hoped that I might provide companionship for you in Paris. But if my presence is displeasing to you, I will take my leave." I once again made a curtsy of just the right depth and turned toward the door.

"You do not need to go," she said, and I stopped. "Perhaps I have misunderstood. We do not do things this way in Poland."

I nodded, letting the steel drop from my voice like dipping the point of a blade. "How is it done, then?"

"Every woman of worth has a husband," she said. The color was still high in her face. "Someone appropriate is found. The last king of Poland had a friend, Madame Grabowska, and she was married to his general even though her children were brought up in the castle. Everyone knew, but she was the general's wife and had a place even if it was a convenient fiction. You have no husband?"

"No," I said. "Nor want one. I can tend to my affairs myself, and some poor third party does not have to be dragged into a marriage of convenience." Well, other than Aglae, I thought, but it was best not to open that discussion.

The footmen were standing about with hatboxes and trunks, and she turned to direct them, telling the butler to take them upstairs and show them where things went, that her maid had already gone up to see to her toilette. Her French was quite good, if accented in a way the Emperor no doubt found charming.

She turned back to me. "I saw you with Ney," she said. "At the Foreign Minister's ball. Countess Potocka pointed you out and said that you were happy. Why should I not be so happy, she asked. Surely dishonor did not bring a life of misery and sorrow when you lit like a flame at his approach?"

I almost felt myself blushing, except that I was much too old. "We had been weeks apart," I said. "And I did not expect him to be there. The Emperor called him in unexpectedly."

And suddenly that made sense. Michel came in from Silesia to make a report in person that he could perfectly well have sent by courier at the Emperor's request. And why did the Emperor suddenly want him at Talleyrand's ball? For this, of course. He did not need me to join the chorus persuading Maria into his bed, but to provide an object lesson in the pleasures of concubinage. He had only to make certain that our reunion was in front of Maria, and Michel and I would carry on embarrassingly enough to make the point that such passions could give great pleasure if indulged! Oh he had used us again! And he had done so in a way that gave us nothing but delight while securing his own agenda!

All of this passed through my mind in a moment while Maria walked over to the foot of the staircase, listening to the bangs and noises upstairs as the footmen tried to get things through narrow doorways. "You looked at him as if he were God," she said.

"Not quite God," I said. "Perhaps an angel."

She looked over her shoulder at me swiftly, as if not certain how to take that. "I do not think I can do that," she said.

She was honest, and honesty was best with her, honesty and a swift decision. And what was the use of knowing things if one did not use them? "Have you come to Paris for yourself, or for Poland?"

"For Poland," she said, raising her chin, but her eyes did not meet mine.

"That is a noble purpose," I said. "For we must fight as we can in our women's bodies and use the weapons that nature gave us."

Maria smiled then, shaking her head. "You sound like Countess Potocka. 'Why do you think God made you beautiful?'"

"To entrance a conqueror," I said. "To preserve your nation by making it dear to his heart. Why else would Frenchmen bleed to keep the Russians from Silesia?"

Her eyes were sharp. "And why would our Hussars come to Paris and place themselves under his command wherever he may need them? It is through our mingled blood that peoples are made one."

"Blood may be shed side-by-side on the battlefield," I said. "But the only place it mingles is the womb."

The color faded from her face. "And from that?" she said.

"A world reborn." I took a step closer. "There is a reason alchemists revered the final product of their interactions as a newborn baby, and a reason why the infant born in the darkness of winter speaks to all hearts. Where is the hope of the world except in the shining face of an infant, who unites all blood and brings peace?"

"Even if it be by his death?" Her eyes did not waver from mine. "The Prince of Peace was born at Christmas to die upon the cross, and his mother wept and rent her hair as he suffered. The hope of the world he might be, but it is still her son that died."

I dropped my eyes as there was no answer to that.

"To give a child to a great man is to give a hostage to fortune," Maria said. "It is to lay one's heart upon an altar and know that it will be destroyed."

"It is true that the Emperor has many enemies," I said. "But he has many friends too, and they are not inconsiderable." I thought it worth it to throw the dice and see. "And he loves you."

She turned, pacing away with her hand on the bottom of the stair rail. "Perhaps for the moment."

"This is the moment you have," I said gently. "Time is always racing away."

"You are very effective at persuading me to his bed," she said.

"If you did not mean to go to his bed you would not have come to Paris," I said.

She turned, and she was smiling, pure pleasure and enjoyment as though this game were something she enjoyed very much.

I shrugged. "Surely there were a thousand reasons to stay in Poland."

"There were."

"And so you are here, but now you must steel yourself for what comes. You wonder if he will be the same as he was last year, if you will be the same. If you will love, or if it will be a sad shadow of what there was and you will both wish that you had never seen each other again."

"Last spring…" Maria drew herself up. "Last spring I joined him at Finkelstein Castle outside Konigsburg. I stayed for two months, though no one knew I was there except his valet and Duroc. It was as though I had entered an enchanted underworld of secret rooms designed for my pleasure, and there was nothing but him."

"But now you must compete with the court," I said. "With thousands of beautiful ladies and with all the demands on his time. This is no enchanted idyll, but real life, messy and complicated and prone to sully the most wonderful memories. And you wonder if there will be anything left once you have left that underworld and walk again beneath the sun."

"Can there be?" she asked.

"I think so," I said honestly. "But then I think that enchantments are wrought. Beautiful moments come because we strive for them and learn to make them, because we cultivate them as a musician cultivates his skill or a writer his words or a Hussar his lethal art. It is the marriage of craft and inspiration that gives us timeless beauty. Whether he will love you forever, or you shall love him, I do not know. But I know that an idyll such as you describe was created. He created it for you. He is very adept at seeing how to give someone pleasure or how to manipulate their feelings into gratitude and delight. In many ways that is his gift, and he has never had any other."

Maria frowned. "How well you know him!"

"I have known many who were devoted to him for a long time," I said, which was no more and no less than the truth. "And I have willingly placed myself at his service." I might as well say that. She would guess it soon enough, and I thought Maria valued honesty.

She nodded slowly. "And you say that he loves me?"

"I think he is just as nervous about seeing you as you are about seeing him," I said. "I think he is afraid that all will be changed and you will not love him now, that he will think he was mistaken about you and that everything between you will have vanished like last year's snow. I do not think this requires fates or God or Poland in it. I think that is what lovers think when they have been apart and fear that their beloved has changed." I smiled at her. "I think you are very ordinary."

"He sent a note when I arrived, but he did not ask me to come to him."

"If you came to the Tuileries it would be nothing but gossip," I said. "It is not like Finkelstein Castle, believe me! Everyone in Paris would know you were there and how long you stayed and what you wore and what you said to one another and what the sheets looked like after."

Maria colored.

"He will come here tomorrow night, when you have had a chance to settle into your house and put your things away and have a good night's sleep that is not in an inn. That is how it is done. To stand on the steps like a schoolboy would embarrass you and also be unkind." I looked about the foyer. "And so the enchantment is yours. This is your stage but only you can make the scene."

"I see," she said seriously, and I thought she did.

It was after ten before I got home, living in St. Cloud as I did. It had been too late to make the lodge meeting, and it was far more improper to arrive late after the doors had been closed than not to arrive at all. And Michel knew where I was and would make my excuses to Lannes.

Rachelle had gone home. I made some tea and got some bread and cheese and sat down for a little cold supper in the kitchen, musing upon the day. I would not be wanted tomorrow. Maria would spend the day preparing for the Emperor's visit. She said that she would appreciate my company for shopping perhaps the day after, as there were things she had not brought because she had thought she would get them in Paris, and I of course had said that I would be delighted to spend the day in a round of shops at her convenience.

There was a knock at the door and for a moment my blood pounded. I did keep a pistol in the dining room cabinet, primed and loaded. Then I saw the carriage and went to the door.

"It's nearly midnight," I said.

Michel waved his coachman on and came in. "Sorry. The lodge took a while this evening. We missed you."

"I didn't expect you," I said. And he had not known I would be home. He had driven all the way out to St. Cloud in hopes that I might be here. It was more than a little touching.

His mouth quirked and he put his hat in its customary place on the hall chair. "Oddly enough there's no staff meeting at the Tuileries tomorrow afternoon. I suppose the Emperor has other plans. And Aglae has taken the boys out to see her sister in Versailles, so there wasn't much point in going home."

"Make yourself comfortable then," I said. "I'm eating bread and cheese in the kitchen. I take it you left before Lannes' buffet to be here now."

He shrugged sheepishly. "I just thought…"

"That I would be very happy to see you, which I am," I said. "I have some nice Camenbert."

We put our feet up on the fender of the kitchen fire and ate bread and cheese and a pot of chestnut cream that I found in the larder and went up to bed, curling sleepily together in the cold stillness of the night. It was cold enough to snow, but the skies were piercingly clear and I opened the drapes so we could see them, Orion parading proudly across the night sky with his belt of light.

"What shall we do tomorrow?" I asked, my head on his shoulder, hand open against his chest. "An entire day when neither of us have to be doing something else. A whole day to spend together."

"Anything," he said. "There's nothing I particularly planned."

"Not shopping," I said. "I'm supposed to take Maria around day after tomorrow."

"I could take you somewhere nice," he said. "Café de Chartres?"

"Mmm," I agreed, contemplating their likely menu in February. "And the salle earlier? We could have a bachelor day?"

"If you like," he said. "That could be ideal."

It more or less was. We got up early and went into town with me in my best dove gray breeches and a rather elaborate waistcoat with a pattern in cherry toile and a very tall beaver hat that I could see Michel thought was far too dandified, but then his taste in civilian clothes tended to be dowdy in the extreme, like some rusticated country gentleman who had no idea what people were wearing this year. I found that amusing, since his taste in uniforms was certainly elaborate enough.

An hour or two at the salle of M. Vincenzio passed pleasantly enough. He had at last decided I was female, but as long as most of the patrons of his establishment remained ignorant, he did not see fit to enlighten them. Besides, he made a lot of money promising to teach young gentlemen to fence like Ney! Throwing me out would not have endeared him to his stellar client.

I was quite thoroughly sore and replete by the time we had finished and changed, emerging into the noonday streets with the air of those whose time has been well spent. Our reflections paced us in shop windows, a young dandy with blond hair too long for the current fashion and a swagger to his step, and his friend up from the country, tall and rather looming. Despite my desire not to do extensive shopping, we did step into Á la Civette in the Rue St. Honoré on our way to lunch. Cigar shops were not something I could regularly patronize dressed as a woman. It was always enjoyable to watch shop assistants who would have given me nothing but glares hurry to help me when I appeared as Charles. It amused Michel too, who not being recognized played the country friend to the hilt, asking my opinion on everything as though he had never been in a proper shop before in his life.

The Café de Chartres was more of a challenge, as I had been there many times in female dress, and once or twice with Michel. They did recognize him, and we had a very nice table and very prompt service. Nothing was too good for M. le Marechal! It was quite gratifying to him, and so I could not resist sitting a little too close and leaning in a little too intimately, my knees brushing his beneath the table. The waiter was far too well-trained to notice, though the wine steward stared at me a bit when he thought I couldn't see. "If I'm not careful," I said in a low voice, leaning in, "they'll get the impression that you are not faithful to Madame St. Elme."

"Heaven forbid," he said, looking amused rather than annoyed. "I think I hardly register as a scandal given the activities of my brother officers. I take it you heard about Junot falling off the trellis departing Caroline's house? He broke his arm, which Murat could not fail to notice."

"I did hear," I said. "And that the Emperor has packed Junot off to Spain until the talk dies down. After all, it's his own sister."

"There's a post I don't envy," Michel said. "Our fortunate allies."

Some years ago we had entered into a treaty of alliance with Spain, as the one thing that was a constant in Spanish foreign policy was their hatred of England. It was not an easy or comfortable alliance. Spain was an absolute monarchy ruled by the House of Bourbon, with laws that were far worse even than those that Frenchmen had overthrown in the Revolution. The Inquisition still held sway, and as little as a decade ago they had still burned unfortunate women at the stake as witches. Not only did Jews lack civil equality, but they were also subject to conversion or the flame. There were no civil courts or laws, only ecclesiastical ones. Women were quite simply property and had no rights at all, no more than a cow or a horse. Consensual sodomy carried a mandatory death sentence, though sometimes this was waived if one of the parties were under fourteen and made a plea that he had been corrupted. In short, it was as though the middle ages had never ended, and the profound differences in values made our alliance uncomfortable at best. The king, Charles IV, and his minister Godoy, paid lip service to the idea of reform but made it clear that they actually intended to do little.

In the last year we had sent troops into Spain ostensibly to pressure Portugal, a traditional ally of England who had refused to join the continental trade embargo against them. They served a double purpose. Ferdinand, the king's son, was more conservative than his father and Godoy, and there were intrigues and rivalries. Our troops were to bolster Charles' position against his son as well as pressure Portugal. It was into this situation that the luckless Junot had been exiled.

"I'm glad you're not there either," I said. "I heard the Emperor is also so mad at Murat for making a scene about it that he's packing Murat off to Madrid too."

"God help the Spaniards," Michel said, raising his wine glass.

"I thought you liked Murat," I said.

"I like him well enough," Michel said. "He's a lion in the field. Unfortunately, he's got the common sense of a housecat. He's a Congreve rocket. You point him at the target and watch him explode, but don't expect him to figure out how and why."

I allowed that might be so. But truly it could not matter so much. I was much more interested in telling Michel about Maria and talking over the business of the lodge.

It was nearly three when we finished lunch, and clouds had rolled in smelling of snow. There was a biting edge to the wind and I wished I'd brought my overcoat even if it did spoil the line of my trousers.

We took Michel's carriage back to St. Cloud, arriving just as the first flakes began to fall. "Come in and get warm," I said.

"Your coat is thinner than mine," he said, but he cheerfully stood before the parlor fire while Rachelle bustled about complaining that Claudine had not lit the fire upstairs in my bedroom yet and that she had no idea what she'd make for dinner as she hadn't known I'd be in. "We shan't want much," I said. "We had an extraordinary lunch."

We left her to her quandary and went up, watching the snowfall through the still-open curtains. He leaned against the glass, looking out, and I thought with a pang how lovely he always seemed to me, my dearest friend and my best companion. Even now, Maria would be preparing her stage, evoking perfection for a lover she had not seen in eight months. I had told her that the time was flowing, but that was as true of me as of her. Today these moments might seem endless, but they were finite.

And so we must seize them with both hands and make a memory to hold in colder days.

I went to the window and drew the curtains, standing behind him and reaching around him to do so, and he looked down quizzically at me. "Why are you closing them?"

"So that no one will see," I said, letting my body brush against his from behind. "I expect you'd prefer it that way."

Enough light came in around the edges of the drapes for us to see one another clearly, but no one could look in.

"I would?" He still looked quizzical.

"You would," I said, and lifted my chin in Charles' best affected expression, lips slightly parted in a smile that was not at all pretty. Charles was still a very charming young man, even though he wore his hair back from his forehead to display a duelist's scar that didn't look harmless at all. On him it was ornament.

I felt Michel's breathing quicken and his eyes closed for a second, masking whatever was there. Lust, I thought. Perhaps leavened with a bit of shame. It was one thing to go about town together like boys who were lovers, and quite another to admit it. Not for anything would I hurt his pride.

And yet there was something I could give him that no one else could, something that if I were entirely honest I knew that I wanted too, half glimpsed in those moments a few months ago when we had talked about the girl he had once been. I could imagine her all too clearly, long red hair and creamy skin, the shape of her breasts against my arm, her white thighs and the curve at the base of her back like a cello. No, I could remember her all too clearly. And what it felt like to have her.

"I will have you," I said, my voice low. "Any way I like, any time I like."

A slow flush rose in his face, the pulse jumping at his throat, and he didn't move.

"Wretched creature," I said, my hands working at his waistcoat buttons, opening it and pulling his shirt untucked. "With your pretty blushes and useless protestations. It's time for you to stop playing games and stand and deliver. There's a word for one like you." I had to stretch on my toes to say it into his ear, a breathy whisper. "Cock tease."

I felt the shudder run through him, felt him lean back into me.

"You've pushed me too far, pretty one," I said, unfastening his trouser buttons at either side of his waist. "Now you're going to get it."

His head bent back, the long line of his throat working.

"On your face on the bed," I said. "I want to see your ass in the air."

He knew what I meant. He had said it to me, a feature of certain games that I now turned the tables on. And yet I saw the tremor as he complied, felt him shake when I knelt behind him, pushing his knees apart with my soft gray trousers. He wore nothing but his shirt, and I shoved it up like a girl's chemise, feeling for his nipple as though I meant to work a breast roughly. "You like that, don't you, pussy?" He could take that either way, as though I meant that he was a girl and a whore, or a boy who put out. "Answer me."

"No," he said breathlessly.

"You do." I pressed against him from behind, pubis bone against his ass, and then slapped him hard across the buttocks.

He nearly cried out, which would have been a bit indiscreet with Rachelle and Claudine in the house.

"Enough teasing. I'm going to teach you a lesson." I wished he'd give me some indication of which direction his mind had gone. I'd play it either way, but it was not clear which. I put one hand at the small of his back, against the smooth flesh there, as redhead fair as the girl I remembered, and slapped him again.

He bucked, head going back.

"Keep your knees apart." I shoved them apart again, seeing that he was erect and ready, straining as he tried to get some friction against the sheet. That decided me. "What a whore you are," I said in Charles' most indolent tone, reaching between his legs negligently and playing with him. "It gets you hard to be mastered as you deserve. But this time you've bitten off more than you can chew, my darling."

He groaned, a noise that would surely carry. But hopefully

Rachelle was in the kitchen. Or not. I didn't care just then.

"I'm going to have you," I said, still working him with one hand as I unfastened my own trouser buttons and dropped the front flap. Oh yes. Skin against him, pressing against his right thigh. I shifted, straddling his right leg so that I could press more closely, still working him left-handed as I leaned to the right. Yes, there on the night table on the shelf beneath the concealing white embroidered doily. Ready to hand, as I liked it. "I'm going to have you."

He looked sideways, amply aware of the things kept there, and his mouth opened and closed, some inarticulate sound emerging.

"Oh yes," I said, turning the smallest of my toys in my hand, lace cuffs falling back as I brandished the dildo. "You're going to take it and like it." I straddled him still as I opened the little bottle of olive oil and let it dribble down the shaft.

"I can't..."

I put one hand to his cheek. "Yes, you can, sweet boy. You'll like it once you start."

He closed his eyes, surrender written in every muscle.

So tight, so resistant. What was small and easy for me must seem enormous to him. He stiffened as I thrust gently, and I touched him again, spreading the olive oil on my hands up and down his length, slick friction as I worked the dildo in.

"Wicked boy," I said, holding it there. The tension was building in me, warm but still bearable, still something I could think through. I rocked my slit against his thigh, parting the lips and pressing against his skin. Yes, this was something like it. This was something like what it would be to take as a man did, still dressed except for my trouser flap, like a rake who means to have and run.

He cried out, his entire body stiffening, and I felt him come in my hand, collapsing against the sheets as though his knees would no longer hold him. He groaned again as I drew it out, the muscles in his buttocks working.

"There, sweet," I said, running my hand down his back as though to gentle an anxious animal for all that I was close to the edge myself, flirting with temptation on the very brink. "There now. You did very well."

He turned over, eyes closed and chest heaving. "Oh God."

"There now," I said again. I crouched over him still, biting down on my upper lip to keep from working myself against his thigh, rubbing against him the way I would against a girl, wicked tribadism, slicked with my own wetness.

He opened his eyes, blue so luminous I thought I could see to the bottom of his soul, and I bore down against his leg while he lay there, arms slack at his side and organ flaccid with use, shirt pulled up in obscene exposure, ravished and ruined. With that I ground down, a wave of utterly incomparable lust carrying me with it, crying out my own release as I rubbed against him, each internal spasm feeling as though it would never end.

At last I slumped forward. I rolled into the space beside him, feeling as though I should shake in every muscle. Cool sheets beneath me, and the kiss of cool air against my pubis, lying on our backs side-by-side. The light crept in around the curtains and the fire hadn't been lit.

My hand found his or his found mine, our fingers entwining though we touched at no other point. Anything else would be raw. I wondered if this time I had finally pushed him too far.

"Are you all right?" I whispered. "Was that too much?"

"There is no too much," he said.

HANDMAIDEN

Spring came early that year, trees bursting into bud before February was done, a lace of blossoms that tossed in the warm air. I accompanied Maria to the theater and to the best modiste in town, Leroy, who designed clothes for the greatest ladies of the court. The Emperor had opened an account in her name with unlimited credit. Even my eyebrows rose at the thought of unlimited credit. The Empress did not have unlimited credit with Leroy. The Emperor had imposed a very generous limit.

However, after I had gone with Maria to her first appointment, I understood better. She might have anything, and she should—the mistress of the most powerful man in the world. Instead Maria ordered five dresses. They were all lovely, and certainly none of them were cheap, but compared to the bills that Josephine routinely rang up they were practically nothing.

The most expensive was an evening gown of pale blue Lyon silk, a thicker underlayer in a gray blue with a thin overdress in a slightly lighter shade so that when she walked the colors shifted like the movement of water. The sleeves were short and gathered above the elbow, the décolletage providing the merest hint of cleavage. It was elegant, simple, and utterly tasteful.

Leroy himself came to the fitting, turning her about and poking at this and that while she stood before three mirrors. "Primavera," he said with satisfaction. "You should always wear blue, Countess." From him this was high compliment.

I waited while she tried on other things, glancing at the sketches pinned to the wall, other gowns conceptualized or on order. I could not tell who most of the gowns would belong to. A few I could, where the artist had rendered the lady plain in just a few strokes. Caroline Murat, the Emperor's sister, should have a rose pink gown for summer, cut low in the front and back alike, displaying her beautiful shoulders, a setting for her expensive jewelry. Lannes' wife Louise would have a day dress in white India cotton, a note written on it that said, "Must wash!!!!" With five children I expected that was a feature the lady insisted on. And there was one for Josephine, the few lines of the sketch rendering her plain, a ballgown in deep crimson red like her beloved roses, the skirt solid and the bodice a brocade in the same shade. It was entirely different from Maria's dress, and outstandingly beautiful. They were March and August, the first breath of spring and summer full blown in its complexity. Leroy translated into fabric the things I did not have words for.

How would this city look, I wondered, when Maria came into her own, a solar system with two suns? Or would she replace Josephine? That would be a cruel irony, the cruelest I could imagine, that Josephine would at last be divorced for barrenness as she had wanted all those years ago.

Maria seemed happy and yet serene. That was not a combination that I had imagined. She was patient and watchful, and once again her eyes spoke when the Emperor came up in conversation, but she never said anything intimate, never made a single confidence. I reminded myself that I was not her dear friend, not a childhood confidant dear as a sister for her to speak of private matters to. And perhaps she would not have spoken of them if I had been. She was not the kind of woman who discussed her man with her friends, and perhaps she never had been.

And yet it was only six weeks before she sat with me in the spring sunshine outside Patisserie Dalloyau, a cup of strong black coffee before her, tilted her face up to the sun and said, "I'm returning to Warsaw in a few days."

I was astonished. Here, in a public place, I could not ask anything personal. "But why?" I asked. I had thought that she was happy. It did not seem to me that the Emperor's interest had waned, nor hers.

She met my eyes squarely. "The situation in Spain has worsened," she said. "He thinks the men he has sent are making mistakes and they are provoking a war that is ill-timed and ill-considered. He means to go himself with his best men and see to it." She turned her coffee cup around in her hands. "It will take many months, he expects. All summer. I do not want to stay in Paris alone, and there is no need for me to."

"No, there is no need," I said. "And those who have the means often leave town in the summer anyway." And it preserved her position to return to Poland. Let him go to Spain, and then wait for her return in the fall, rather than sitting waiting for him! Let Caesar come to Cleopatra if he wanted her.

"So I will go in a few days," she said. "Ida, I do appreciate that you have done your best to make my stay enjoyable."

"It has been a delight," I said warmly. "Truly."

Her eyes searched my face. "And you are not jealous at all. Not of the gowns or the gifts or…"

I shook my head. "No. I am a vain woman, but such things have never meant as much to me as love. I should follow my Michel were he a sergeant." I did not know how to put it so she would understand. She was the age I had been when I was with Moreau. "When you have been very poor, when you have thrown away all advantages of your own free will, such things bind you very little after that. I like to eat in nice places and wear nice clothes, but I don't want to so much that I would be the friend of a man I dislike or compromise my honor."

Maria nodded slowly. "Every ruler needs a servant like you," she said. "Someone who cannot be bought."

"Or rather say that I cannot be bought with anything that most people can offer," I said, and to my horror my voice choked. My courses had come on heavily that morning.

"And what could you be bought with?" she asked gently.

"A child of my own body. To be with child today and have it go well." I looked away, focusing my eyes on carriages passing in the street, the hat on the head of a gendarme directing traffic at the corner of the Rue de Faubourg St. Honoré. "But that will be or not be, and there is nothing anyone can do about it."

Her face changed. "I am so sorry," she said quietly. "I had no idea."

I shrugged. Traffic passed in the bright spring sunshine. "I have hoped for half a year and there is nothing."

"Sometimes these things take time," Maria said.

"I am not so old! He is not so old! I'm thirty-one and he's thirty-eight. He's gotten healthy children on his wife! I don't know what's wrong with me! I seem to be in perfect health, but nothing, month after month after month!"

"Sometimes there is no explanation," Maria said gently. "It's in God's hands and there is no reason we can understand." Her face changed, that inward-looking expression she got when she was not speaking of the Emperor. "Others have this problem too, though nothing seems wrong and they enjoy good health. I should like a child too."

I could not say it. I could not betray Josephine, though perhaps I should have in that moment. Perhaps this was the moment when the truth should have been told. He believed he was infertile. He believed he could not give her a child. And I knew it all rested upon a lie.

"But that's neither here nor there," Maria said briskly, raising a hand for the waiter like a true Parisian, and the moment was gone. "What will be, will be. But if he is going to Spain I will go home, and who knows when I will see you again? I hope it will be soon."

"So do I," I said, and realized I meant it.

Maria left for Warsaw on the seventeenth of March. Four days later the Emperor sent for me. Once again I reported at the Tuileries at a reasonable hour of the day, part of the routine business of the state. I assumed he wanted to talk about Maria.

"Sire," I said, sinking into a deep curtsy in his office. I waited a moment while he finished signing his name to the document an aide held for him, until he looked up.

"That will do," he said to the aide, who hurried out with the paper. He dusted his hands off on his breeches and looked at me. "I trust your duties this spring have not been onerous."

"No, Sire," I said. "I enjoyed my days with Countess Walewska very much."

"Good." He got up from his chair and paced about the room, stopping to look out the windows that faced the river. They were open and the curtains moved in the fresh spring air. "I'm afraid my next job for you will not be so pleasant." He glanced around at me sharply. "Unless you have some reason you may not undertake an assignment at this time?"

Maria had told him, I thought. Well, of course she had. "No," I said quietly. "There is no reason at this time."

He nodded, and I thought I saw sympathy there, a kinship that of course he would not speak of, the fellowship of the infertile. "This is a very dangerous assignment," he said. "Nothing like looking after Maria. It could easily cost your life. I tell you this to begin with, and if you refuse it I will take that as no stain upon you."

"I am willing, Sire," I said. Truly, what could be more dangerous than what I had faced in the field? I would do that again in a heartbeat, even the charge at Eylau.

"Are you acquainted with Claude-François de Malet?" he asked.

I frowned, trying to place the name. I could not. "His name is familiar," I said. "But I do not believe I know him. Or if so I met him on some occasion but had no reason to take note."

"And Jacques Oudet?"

I let out a long breath. That was a name I did know. "I knew him once, sire. But I cannot call him a friend."

"Tell me," he said.

I had nothing to hide. "When I was with Moreau all those years ago, a decade and more now, he was a lieutenant with the Army of the Rhine and was one of Moreau's aides. I remember him from headquarters. He was a very brave soldier, they said, and certainly he did his work with great energy."

"But you did not like him?" The Emperor's back was to me, looking out over the river.

"I did not," I said. I searched for the words, not knowing if the Emperor thought well of him or not. Either way I should be honest. "He was … too intense. He was too passionate in ways that seemed … inappropriate." The Emperor turned and I went on. "There was once when everyone was drinking Moreau's health, as one will, and he stood up and made an impassioned speech about how he would die for Moreau. Loyalty is all very well, but it was too much. He was too enthusiastic. It was uncomfortable. And he made me uncomfortable as well."

"How?"

It sounded silly when I spoke of it, fancies of the girl of nineteen I had been then. "He wrote me several letters," I said. "Declaring his love for me."

The Emperor's brows raised.

"I had barely spoken with him," I said. "And I was with his general. I gave him no encouragement. Indeed, I did not reply to the letters at all! I said nothing to him and avoided him. There was something...I do not know how to say, sire. He knew what I liked to eat and when I got up in the morning. He spoke as though I were his lover, someone who he had entered into relations with, when I was almost a stranger. It was too much. It was strange."

"And what did you do?"

"It was soon after that when Moreau sent me to Paris," I said. "I received one more letter from him, which I threw away. I have not seen him since then nor communicated with him in any way." I met the Emperor's eyes. "There was something wrong about him. It unnerved me. What has he done?"

"Well you should ask," he said with a smile. "This Malet, who you did not remember, was also with Army of the Rhine. He was a captain at the time, but with a forward unit, under General Moreau but not attached to headquarters. It is possible that you briefly saw him at some moment or heard him spoken of but did not meet him."

"That is likely," I said.

"You had no reason to think they were especially close to Moreau?"

So that's what it was about—Moreau's treason four years ago, though from all I had heard Victor lived quietly in New Jersey. "Not particularly," I said, and I made a guess. "They are in a Royalist conspiracy?"

The Emperor's smile broadened. "A theory, but to the wrong side. A conspiracy to the left rather than the right."

"Which has always made more sense to me," I said. "Moreau would plot to return to the Republic, plot with his old Jacobin friends, but I could not see him plotting to restore the House of Capet. I believe he knew there was a conspiracy to assassinate you and chose to do nothing, rather than that he instigated it. After all, if you were dead, perhaps he would step into your place."

"That is what I concluded too," he said. "Hence his exile to America rather than the firing squad he would face for plotting to assassinate the head of state. I think Moreau's role in that conspiracy was peripheral, as it is in this one."

"But there is a conspiracy," I said.

"Yes, Madame. There are always conspiracies, but this one is particularly pernicious." He put his hands behind his back and paced over to the window again. "Malet and Oudet belong to an irregular Masonic lodge called the Philadelphes. They claim that they are the heirs to ancient Egyptian mysteries and that they may manipulate occult symbols to bring down the government. But the real danger is that they use this lodge to recruit within the army for a Jacobin conspiracy that intends a military coup d'etat. I cannot stress enough that this is a serious matter."

"I know it is, Sire," I said. "I know Moreau would gladly have taken part in such, and indeed he may expect to return as a savior if and when it succeeds. It costs him nothing to encourage former subordinates to treason from where he sits in America!" I did not know what to make of his dismissal of the occult aspects of the Philadelphes. Certainly I believed the work of a lodge could be real. Whether this one was or not, I did not know. There were indeed fake lodges and charlatans. And there were real ones.

I saw the Emperor's purpose then. He needed an agent who could tell the difference. He needed an agent who could fight magic with magic.

"I need a very particular agent for this," he said.

"I see," I said.

"Several agents have attempted to infiltrate the Philadelphes before," he said. "Three of them have been unable to gain enough trust to know anything, though they labor on. The other two are dead." He looked at me squarely. "One of them drowned accidentally, poor man. Another was shot. A terrible mistake by a sentry. He was taken for the enemy and killed. Such tragedies happen."

"You believe they were murdered," I said evenly.

"Yes." He rested one hand against the window frame. "But I believe you can get in where they could not. You are a woman, and moreover you were Moreau's mistress. And Oudet would want very much to believe that you remember him. What could be more natural? Abandoned by your lover, filled with bitterness at his betrayal, cast off to make your way in the world, your thoughts turn to the noble form of Oudet, a young man you knew years ago whose honorable devotion you were unworthy of because of your liaison with Moreau? You humble yourself. You write to him. You tell him of your mistreatment and your disillusionment. You speak of how you miss the old days, of how you regret that Bonaparte rather than Moreau became Consul! Oh if that had not been! Oh if nobler sentiments had prevailed! You are alone in the world, filled with sadness for all that might have been! Would he be so noble as to forgive the foibles of a weak and shallow woman who regrets her youthful follies?"

"You are writing a novel, sire," I said dryly.

"I attempted one once," he said cheerfully. "In my younger days. It was full of tragedy and unrequited love. This requires an actress of some note to carry it off, and also one who has been in the right place at the right time, as well as one who possesses certain skills now."

"In bed," I said grimly.

"I meant with a pistol," he said. "I will authorize you to do whatever is necessary, a license to kill."

"I will have to sleep with him," I said. "I confess my skin crawls at the prospect."

He waited and said nothing.

"It is possible," I said slowly, "That the Philadelphes are not all hot air. It is possible that they have some actual knowledge that is important." I did not know how much he knew of our lodge, or how much he believed, but I found it impossible to believe he knew nothing, as close friends as he and Lannes had been for years. "I will need to find that out. There are two pieces, sire. There is the political conspiracy which may cause much trouble, and there is the possibility that they are indeed using some actual efficacious method."

"And you can do both," he said. "That is why I need you, Madame St. Elme."

"I am yours, sire," I said. I took a deep breath. "Marshal Ney…"

"Is about to receive his orders for Spain," he replied. "It's a mess, and Alexander must have his Hephaistion!"

I opened my mouth and shut it again. There was no reply possible to that.

"Ney will take a corps command in Spain this summer, and while I know you would like to follow the army, you may have your own work."

I nodded. If we were two men we would not always be posted

to the same command, and one could not whine about it. "So he has broken my heart. I will need to tell him that."

"You will need to enlist his assistance, I should think," the Emperor said. "If it is to be plausible. And I will send you to my sister, Elisa. She's in Florence and is well known to have a soft heart. You have impressed her with your sad story and she will give you a post as a reader in her household out of pity for the cruelty of men!"

I thought he was getting a bit carried away in the melodrama of it all. "She knows?"

"She'll know you're my agent and that she is to render any assistance possible, personal as well as financial. But she won't know the details of your assignment. No one will. And she knows Malet."

"Does she?"

"After Malet left the Army of the Rhine, he retired to civilian life. He joined the diplomatic service and for a while was our consul in Rome. Unfortunately he was arrested for running a black market profiteering scheme involving stealing supplies from the army depot and selling them. He's currently serving a nine-month prison term for profiteering. He's due to be released on the 30th of May."

"And you want to see what he does then," I said.

"Exactly. By the 30th of May you will be in Florence, reading Young Werther to Elisa and weeping on her shoulder."

"And where is Jacques Oudet?" I asked.

"He's currently a colonel assigned to Lannes' corps."

"Where Lannes can keep an eye on him," I said grimly. The murder of the agents must have taken place practically under Lannes' nose, which made it all the more clear why my involvement would be welcome.

"But Lannes cannot run around Italy chasing Philadelphes," he said. "Nor will they ever trust him. You can get inside."

"I will do my best, Sire," I said.

Michel was not pleased, though he was philosophical. "I knew I'd be for Spain sooner or later," he said. "Junot's making a mess. I'd hoped you'd come with me."

"And I would like to," I said, taking his hand and raising it to my lips. "But."

"You have your work and I mine," he said. He shook his head as though amused at his own foibles. "If you were Charles…"

"If I were Charles we'd suck it up, and so we will," I said. "And besides, it's only a few months. One campaign season. Come Christmas we'll be together."

"True enough," Michel said. "We have time enough for everything."

I hope so, I thought. But I did not say it.

I would leave for Florence at the beginning of May on the Emperor's service with a license to kill, spy and magician.

ON THE EMPEROR'S SERVICE

As I crossed Grand St. Bernard Pass, bound for Italy again, snow still lingering in the crevasses along the route, my heart soared. True, I would miss Michel, but we had had a year together spent mostly at leisure, something that could not last, and despite all public protestations that I was heartbroken at being cruelly cast off, our private parting had been as tender as I might wish. Certainly I was not looking forward to Oudet, who had always disturbed me, but I could manage him, I thought. And there was a part of me that relished the danger. I was a Companion on a critical mission, and how could I want anything else?

It had been many years since I had been in Florence. My parents had lived there briefly when I was a young child and Charles had been born there, but I barely remembered it. We had left Florence for Naples when I was three. It was almost entirely new to me, though occasionally I would catch a glimpse of some street or building and it would come back to me that I had seen it before. I took a room at a respectable penzione that catered to traveling gentlewomen and sent my credentials to the ducal palace, thinking that it would not be long until I moved and therefore there was no need to make a long-term plan. I should wait upon Elisa.

Elisa Bonaparte Levoy, the Grand Duchess of Tuscany, was my age exactly, eight years younger than her brother the Emperor. Consequently, they had not been companions as children, for he had been sent off to school before she was six, but he had said laughing that she had been his little shadow, the one who wanted her big brother's attention and considered his games of far greater interest than the games of five-years-younger-still Caroline. There had been affection between them if not closeness. Now she was thirty-one, and was the only one of his sisters to wield real political power. Grand Duchess of Tuscany was not an empty title, and the changes and reforms she instituted in her realm were likewise real. Most particularly she had a passion for education. She had founded the only free boys' secondary school in the province and by law had made the education of girls aged five to eight compulsory so that at least they should learn to read even if they went no further. She had started a school to teach the silk farming trade and created a body of female teaching inspectors whose job was to certify the many convent schools and ensure that they taught an academic curriculum.

It was rumored that her own marriage was unhappy. She had married Felix Levoy at twenty, back in the days of the Directory, when he was a captain in one of her brother's brigades. Now they lived apart, and their only child was a little girl three years old, also named Elisa. An older boy had died, and I had been cautioned not to speak of him, a warning I appreciated.

Michel had said that of all the brothers and sisters she was the one most like Napoleon, and ushered into her private salon in the palace I could see it in a moment. She was dark haired and very thin, the top of her head barely reaching my chin, small breasted and almost as light as a child. Next to her I appeared to be an enormous brawny valkyrie. Her eyes were dark brown and keen as a hawk's, looking at me over the papers in her lap with an expression like her brother's as she signaled for the footman to leave us.

I sunk into an appropriate curtsy. "Your Highness," I said.

"My brother," she said. "Says you are a secret agent." She put the papers aside on a little scrolled side table. "I've met his agents before, but you seem rather different."

"Different how, Your Highness?" I asked.

"You're not a Corsican thug. I generally expect brass knuckles and blackjacks."

"I try not to employ them except at need, Your Highness," I said.

She glanced at the papers again. "He says in the most melodramatic language that you are engaged in a mission vital to the survival of the Empire and that I must render you all possible assistance, but he fails to tell me what your mission is! I do not appreciate being left in the dark as though I were ten years old."

It was best to speak, I thought. She would be a very bad enemy to have and it would be easy to alienate her. "I am to infiltrate a conspiracy within the army," I said. "Several of the gentlemen were formerly close to General Moreau, and the Emperor believes that they may trust me because of my former association with that gentleman."

"You were his mistress for some years, my brother says." Her eyes did not leave my face.

"I was," I said, and did not blush.

"And now you sleep with Ney." Her brother seemed to have briefed her quite thoroughly in those papers.

"I would, were he not in Spain and I in Florence."

"My brother 'requires' that I shall take you on as a reader and grant you every intimacy."

And that was what had her back up. She was a sovereign duchess, and still her brother demanded as though he were fourteen and she six. "Your Highness, I do the Emperor's bidding, and I do not know what he wrote. I shall try to be very little trouble to you."

At that she put her head to the side, considering. "He's written you a blank check. Any money you may require, any assistance, any person. For what kind of agent does the Emperor do that?"

I was surprised myself, and also touched by the confidence. It was like Maria's account at Leroy, I thought. He had concluded that I would not ask for too much, so there was no harm in giving me whatever I wanted. "Not for what agent, Your Highness," I said. "But as a measure of the gravity of the situation."

Elisa nodded slowly. "Then he considers it very severe indeed."

"I believe so," I said truthfully.

"And I am to provide your cover story. You are my reader, a member of my household staff, because I have been moved to such sympathy by your plight. He describes your desertion by Ney in such touching terms!"

"I am sure he was very imaginative, Your Highness," I said diplomatically.

Elisa shook her head. "At one point in his youth he desired to emulate Goethe," she said. "It's probably a blessing that he did not. When he finally did meet Goethe, the poet was much taken aback by my brother's adulation." She picked up the papers again, folding them along the creases. "Very well. You are my new reader, and I shall do as my brother asks."

I had never before held a respectable job. It was certainly a change A reader, like a governess, occupies a peculiar middle ground in a household, neither servant or friend. Like a governess, she is generally gently born and her tasks do not include manual labor. Yet, like a governess, she is paid. She is not a member of the family or even a poor hanger on, but a servant like the governess and the tutor and the nurse. True, her clothes are nicer, and she is addressed as Madame St. Elme rather than by her first name alone as though she were the chambermaid, but she is nonetheless a servant.

I had been an actress and a soldier and a courtesan and a spy and even in some desperate days in my youth little better than a streetwalker, but I had never been a servant. My room was tiny and had one dingy window, but it was no worse than a junior cavalry officer would have expected as a billet. I was told when I could take my meals and with whom, when I should attend on the Grand Duchess and when I would not be wanted, given one day a week off (it was Tuesday), and told that my clothing must be inspected for its suitability by the Grand Duchess' chief lady in waiting and that anything she disapproved of could not be worn. I must not speak with men while on duty, and I absolutely must not have men in my room at any time. Such was grounds for dismissal. The chief lady in waiting sniffed. "We are not a brothel," she said with a tone that suggested that such a setting would better suit me.

In short, I hated it.

Still, for me it was a cover story for a mission of importance, not a way of life. How I pitied the women who had to live this way every day, and who could imagine nothing better than sinking slowly into lonely spinsterhood, a dreary round of being a reader or a governess or a paid companion! How this should be preferable to the life of the baggage train I could not imagine.

In the afternoons I sat with the Grand Duchess and her ladies in the salon, reading aloud from some improving tome while they generally talked and ignored me. I could not, of course, converse, as I had to keep reading. Thankfully, the third week we finished the improving work in question and moved on to Goethe's Faust—not quite Young Werther as the Emperor had joked, but very nearly. I also read aloud various newspapers and occasional bulletins, and that at least caused the ladies to look around and listen, their light refreshments just out of reach and entirely forbidden to me.

It was thus that I read of the troubles in Madrid. There had been a riot and a number of French troops had been killed. Murat, in his usual style, had reciprocated by shooting a like number of civilians in retribution. Rather than cowing the citizens, instead he had sparked a general uprising. The heir to the throne, Ferdinand, was raising an army against his Francophile father, who either fled to Murat or was taken into protective custody, depending on whose account one believed. Thanks to his mishandling we now had a full-blown war on our hands rather than an uneasy alliance.

Personally, I hoped the Emperor had him whipped. Michel would have to go into considerable danger as a result, not to mention those others of my friends now sent to Spain in the wake of this disaster, Honoré, Gervais, Max, and Jean-Baptiste. If any of them were killed, I should lay the blame squarely on Murat where it belonged.

I read and I read and I read. By the middle of June I was ready to slit my wrists. Fortunately, at that point I received a letter from Oudet. I had written to him as soon as I arrived, a very short letter asking if he remembered me and saying that I was now a reader for the Grand Duchess and that I hoped he was well as I cherished his memory. It was perhaps a bit overdone for a bare acquaintance from ten years ago, but I did not think the tone was wrong. From his response I knew I had been correct.

Dearest Madame St. Elme,

Of course I remember you! How could I forget the things we shared, a passion cut short by capricious fate? I am quite well and touched to be ever in your faithful prayers, though I do not put much stock in them as Popish folly. I have prospered in these years and am now a Colonel. But I am more yet, as you will not be surprised to know. One day I will stand at the pinnacle of fame and fortune! You will wish that you had sacrificed all for me rather than for one unworthy.

Yours as always,
Jacques

I folded his note and put it by. "Oh dear," I said. This was not going to be pleasant at all.

One expects that being a secret agent involves a great many dangers and excitements. Unfortunately, that is hardly ever true. For the most part it requires weeks or months of boredom as one works through the particulars of a case, learning who and what and where, pursuing false leads and maintaining one's cover. In that regard, the Emperor's secret service was much like any other branch of his service—four minutes or four hours of heart-stopping terror in the carnage of a cavalry charge out of ten months of drill and garrison duty.

In this case, I began with the four months of boredom. All through June, July, August, and September I read for the Grand Duchess. I endured the sniffs of her ladies in waiting, who considered themselves far above me, and the complete tedium of a well-run noble household, while accomplishing very little except establishing myself as a poor and deserted woman with a series of white lawn dresses and a certain pride in an interesting past which, alas, had now deserted me along with my youthful looks. I could not fence or ride or shoot, and with no sensual pleasure available to me at all except for the table I could feel my dresses getting tighter. If I truly could not spend my days and nights in hard exercise I should be plump in no time at all!

There were, of course, occasional letters from Oudet, perhaps one every two weeks. He would write to me and then I should wait for its delivery, then I would reply immediately and wait for him to receive it and return. I could not rush the mails, nor make this process of cultivation too swift or it would seem suspicious. And he was my entry into the Philadelphes.

There were also letters from Michel, more irregular than Oudet, as he had the habit of writing several in a row and then sending them by the same courier. I might get three or four at once and then nothing for three weeks. They were very long letters, tender, chatty, filled with service gossip and stories of the camp, with private jokes between us and digressions onto some bit of history of interest. If my letters to Oudet smacked of a woman seeking a lover, my letters from Michel sounded more like a best friend, albeit a best friend who shared one's bed, a bedfellow as the rankers said.

I kept them in my room in my trunk, neatly folded and tied with ribbon in the order they had been written, as I often read them over and over in my loneliness. One afternoon I returned when Elisa had dismissed me as she went to dress for dinner to find that they were moved from their accustomed place and their order in the stack had been changed. Someone had been reading through them.

I checked quickly to make certain that nothing was missing and hurried down to find Elisa.

She was in her boudoir, and when I knocked her maid admitted me reluctantly. "I should like to speak with the Grand Duchess, if I may," I said, already pushing past her. After all, a reader ranked a maid, even the Duchess' own.

Elisa turned, wrapped in a pale green silk dressing gown, having discarded her day dress but not yet dressed for dinner. It made her look very young and really very pretty. I wondered entirely irrelevantly if she had a lover since she and her husband separated. She looked at my face and then past me to her maid. "You may go, Annette. I will ring for you."

I waited until the door closed. "Someone has been going through my things," I said.

Her eyebrows rose. "Was anything stolen?"

"No," I said. "But my letters have been read. That is not a servant. A servant might go through my trunk and pocket some valuable, but an Italian domestic would not read letters in French."

"I presume you had nothing incriminating in them?"

I shook my head. "Of course not. They were personal letters from Ney."

Elisa nodded gravely, an expression that was exactly like her brother's when he considered some serious matter. "One of the ladies, then. Jealous or curious. A boarding school trick."

"Perhaps," I said.

"Surely you do not suspect my ladies?" Her voice hardened.

"No," I said quickly. "But that does not mean I trust every man who might be associated with them. The Emperor believes this conspiracy cuts deep, and many a wife or daughter or sister has been pulled into schemes not her own." Which was more tactful than saying no, I did not trust her ladies and thought some of them snakes. They were Elisa's friends. It was time to take the bull by the horns. "Your Highness," I said, "this is not working. I have established my cover and entered into a correspondence with one of the conspirators who does indeed seem convinced as the Emperor hoped. It may be that in time he will introduce me to his fellows, but for that I would need to be in some place where his fellows are! And I cannot find out anything while spending every afternoon in the salon reading."

It was not as though she actually wanted me for a reader. "I suppose I can find reason to send you on unspecified errands. That will give you greater latitude."

"That will do very well," I said. "And there is the other thing, though I am not eager to do it. Oudet needs to come here. There is only so much I can do without seeing him in person. I think the safest course would be for him to be sent to Florence on some pretext so that we may meet." Elisa's brows rose and I went on grimly. "I hope I may rely on your chaperonage as an excuse not to have to spend time together too intimately."

Elisa put her head to the side like a curious bird. "You really are afraid of him, aren't you?"

"Yes," I said. "But it must be done."

She nodded. "What kind of man is he?"

I looked past her out the window, assembling my thoughts. "A petty bully," I said. "The kind of young man who thinks he deserves everything and is filled with resentment that his successes are not as stellar as he wishes. True, he is a colonel and has a reasonable measure of worldly success, but he thinks he has rare genius that should be appreciated. Why is it that other men his age are brigadiers or Imperial aide-de-camps? Why do they advance faster than he, never mind that he is already ahead of most. He should be first because he deserves it."

"And that is what leads to revolution?"

"I think," I said. "Your Highness, as a people we believe in justice and liberty. We were born of the genuine grievances against Crown and Church, against the abuse of the poor and the exploitation of our sex, and so it is hard for us to say that not all grievances are legitimate. But they aren't. Simply because someone claims that they deserve more than they have using the language of liberty does not make it true! In his letters he raises the Liberty Tree as nothing more than a hatpole for his own resentments. He deserves a better posting! He deserves to be decorated! He deserves what some other man has earned! When the truth is that he does not. He is not sent to the galleys or condemned to the chain gang, or even wallowing in agricultural servitude. He simply isn't making as much money as he thinks he should. Other men are richer. And he is better, so he should be richer yet."

"You truly do dislike him," Elisa observed coolly.

"I do. And I shall probably have to sleep with him," I said. "Regretfully, I will have to send to Paris and ask if the Emperor can arrange for Lannes to fortuitously send him on some errand to Florence."

"The Emperor is in Spain."

"Then I will have to send to Spain, which will take longer." Weeks, I thought. Weeks to get this matter to the Emperor's attention and then for him to write Lannes and then for Lannes to come up with a pretext and send him off. I should be lucky to have him in town before Carnival. Which might be just as well. "And in the meantime I will work on the Philadelphes. Unfortunately, it's very difficult to research a secret society in a town in which they have never operated."

"Clearly," Elisa said.

"Perhaps Madame St. Elme needs to go to Lucca," I said. "To visit her aging former governess in a convent there. The poor woman is ill and you have allowed her this mission of humanity!"

"You have been taking lessons in melodrama from my brother," Elisa said dryly. "But of course I will let you visit your old nurse."

And so it was that on the fourth day of October, 1808, a young man named Carlo Tolstoy took the road for Rome. He was the son of Leo Tolstoy, a Hungarian gentleman and a distant cousin of a cardinal now deceased who had been for some time resident in Rome. He rode a fine horse and his clothes were the latest style from Paris, his fair hair combed back from his face to display a dramatic scar over one eyebrow, trophy of either the field or an affair of honor. He wore a pistol at his saddle bow and a worn epeé at his side, and carried a Florentine passport from the Grand Duchy of Tuscany which opened all gates without fuss.

Carlo Tolstoy established himself in a good hotel and he was free with his purse, mentioning once or twice in passing that he had come into a good deal of money of late, courtesy of his mother, who was an heiress. In Rome one was discreet about many vices rampant in Paris, or so they said. Among other things, one could not find an open and aboveboard Masonic Lodge, Freemasonry having been legalized only five months earlier when the French Emperor abolished the Papal States, thus giving Rome its first civil government since the Visigoths. It might now be legal to be a mason and no longer carry a jail term, but most masons were still not certain that this state of affairs would last and preferred to be discreet.

Which was not to say there weren't masons and more besides. A young man with money to spend who professed a desire to find out what his future held could garner all matter of tips from concierges and waiters as to those who might assist. Thus young Carlo Tolstoy spent the better part of a week hunting about Rome, visiting one genuine, certified completely authentic article after another. Most were complete charlatans, women of little means who read cards or looked into crystals and predicted wealth, advancement, and a happy marriage.

I had, of course, done this game myself, but I had no idea how tedious it was from the other side, sitting in some tiny rented room rendered atmospheric by drawn curtains listening to an old woman predict that I would sire five healthy sons, an implausibility that certainly made me skeptical of the rest of her prophecy. I paid her what we had agreed upon and I made my way down the back stairs to the alley, wondering if this plan were futile. Certainly this seemed to be getting me no closer to the Philadelphes. Rome was where Malet had been stationed until last year. Surely there had been other Philadelphes here, some sort of organized lodge! And if so, surely somebody knew something about it.

Lost in my thoughts, I didn't hear the steps behind me until almost too late. I didn't hear them until the other man stepped out of the shadows before me. "Give us your purse, boy."

He had a knife. I heard the first man's steps behind me and

glanced around, a young boy perhaps fifteen, also with a knife.

"Take this instead," I said, drawing my epeé and rushing the boy behind me.

It is a hard thing to stand when a man attacks you with a sword for the first time, doubly so when you have only a knife. He was not an accomplished thief, just a boy, and he made the mistake of standing his ground. One swift beat and his blade was to the side, the second opening up the back of his hand where a guard would have been if he had a sword. He screamed and dropped the knife. Before the other man could reach us I had him, my right arm about his throat and the point of the epeé against his testicles.

"Drop it," I said to the other man.

He did, his face white beneath his beard. "Signore, don't do this!"

"Why shouldn't I?" I snarled. "You were planning to rob me and slit my throat."

The boy wet himself in his fear, the smell of it pungent in the alley.

The first man stood still, his hands raised, his eyes on the boy every moment. "Signore, he is my younger brother. I ask you in God's name to spare him. I give you my word we did not intend murder!"

"Just robbery," I said. "And what will your mother say when you bring your younger brother home gelded?"

The boy whimpered, and I pricked his thigh just a bit with the point. "I have been in the French Army for five years," I said. "And I've done a lot bigger than you, little pisser."

"What do you want?" The older brother's voice was desperate. "Do you want our money? You can have our money, Signore. It's not much."

"I want information," I said. "About some men called the Philadelphes. Their leader was that Malet who went to jail."

"Revolutionaries." The older brother's eyes were sharp. "What about them? Who do you call lord?"

"That's not your concern," I said. "But your brother's welfare is. I want information and if it's good enough I'll let him keep his balls."

"You wanted a fortune teller," he said. "That's why you went to

Mama Stella. But she's not the real thing. There's a woman the man you speak of used, that man Malet. La Colombina. She's the real thing. That's all I know about them, Signore! I give you my word!"

"Where can I find this woman?" I demanded. He might make something up, but I didn't think he had presence of mind to. And certainly someone who knew nothing of the business would name her The Little Dove.

"She works for a milliner in Traviatore. For La Voga. That's the shop. Her name is Ana. I don't know any other name for her. Please, Signore! My brother is only fifteen. I got him into this. It is my fault, not his!"

"You should take better care of him," I said, and I shoved the boy toward him, catching him in the back of the knees so that he went on all fours in the filth, and backed swiftly away. I did not stop until I had gone several blocks and looking back saw no pursuit. Of course not. The boy's plight was distraction enough, though I thought the cut across the back of his hand was not that bad. All soldiers had those scars eventually, defensive wounds.

I plucked disdainfully at my cuffs and trousers where I had held the boy against me. I would have to go back to my hotel and change before I visited the milliner's shop. I could certainly not walk in like this, reeking.

La Voga was a very respectable looking shop, though quite small. The window was filled with expensive looking hats, tasteful, and entirely fashionable. There was a bell that jangled when I opened the door. The walls were painted cream and pink, the woodwork picked out in cream, and the counters held ten or twenty bonnets, including a magnificent mourning bonnet with attached yards of veiling and black-dipped peacock feathers. One would expect it of a Marshal's widow, a thought I mentally suppressed the moment it flew through my head. Bad luck to even think of such things.

I looked about negligently, Carlo to the hilt. Perhaps he intended a present for a pretty mistress.

In a moment a girl looked out of the back room. She scarcely looked older than the boy in the alley, but she was very pretty, tall, and curving with long dark brown hair pinned up on her head and a lower lip wider than her upper lip, a curiously sensual detail that

I couldn't help but mark. "May I help you, Signore?"

"I hope so," I said with my best Charles smile, leaning on the counter with my elbows. "I'm looking for Ana."

Her smile faded. "I'm Ana."

Of course she was. The Little Dove. Malet had been using a dove barely into her teens, as it had been done of old. And chances were that it had not been pleasant.

"I am so glad to have found you," I said. "I hoped that I might."

Her face was closed. "Why, Signore?" She carefully kept the counter between us.

I lifted my purse and placed it on the counter, opened it and carefully piled up the gold coins, enough to buy every hat in the store. "This is a dowry for a young girl," I said. "Enough that she could marry respectably or whatever she liked. Enough that she could have her own shop."

Her eyes did not leave the stack, though her hands didn't move. "And what would I have to do to earn that?"

"Not sleep with me," I said, thinking it best to get that out of the way first.

"I didn't think so," she said, lifting her eyes to mine, dark as night and for a moment unfocused, as though she were blind. "You are no man."

"No," I said, and stood up from the pose, Charles falling away from me in a heartbeat. "I'm not."

"You are the same thing I am," she said. Her eyes did not move, her pupils unchanging, and I felt a chill run down my back. She was, at last, the real thing. I wondered if Noirtier had felt the same when he had seen me.

"Yes," I said. "I am a dove from a line of doves."

She shuddered at the word. "I am the Sibyl," she said.

THE SIBYL

She would not tell me where she lived. I gathered she shared a room with some other girls and she did not want them to think she was seeing a rich young man and a foreigner. There was, after all, only one thing she could be doing to earn a large sum of money from such as Carlo Tolstoy! Instead, when the shop closed, we walked out and sat by the fountain at the Spanish steps, a popular place for meetings and a very public place. It was perhaps a bit risqué to meet me there, but not a complete loss of reputation. We sat in the last sunshine, the sound of the fountain covering our voices, her feet tucked under her like a child.

"I came here from Naples nine years ago," she said. "My grandmother brought me. I was seven." She reached out to touch the surface of the water, the ripples spreading, reflecting the setting sun, fire and the memory of fire. "She was afraid what would happen to us when the Parthenopean Republic fell. You know that hundreds of people were executed in the counter revolution and many more jailed. I don't know why she thought she was in danger, but she did. So she brought me with her to Rome. We did all right." The light danced across the water. "She died three years ago. I've been on my own since then."

"And you're a sibyl."

"The Sibyl," she said, looking up at me. "My grandmother said so. She said I would be the Sibyl after her. But then she got sick and died. And I don't know how to do it." She took a long breath and I waited for her. "I met this man, the French consul in Rome. He said he knew what I was."

"Claude-Francois Malet," I said.

She didn't seem at all surprised that I knew his name. "Yes," she said. "He wanted me to see for him. He paid me good money and he didn't take any liberties." She glanced at me swiftly to see if I believed her. "He said I had to stay a virgin."

"Obviously not," I said dryly, "As your grandmother was a grandmother."

She shrugged. "I only tell you what he said. And I was thirteen, so I was glad of his protection."

"And what did he want you to see?" I asked gently.

She looked at me swiftly. "He wanted me to see the downfall of the French Emperor. The one you serve."

"And how do you know that?" I asked, unnerved.

Ana smiled, sudden and gamine. "Don't you believe in what you, yourself, can do? It's written all over you. You serve for love, not money, and you are bound by your word."

"I do," I said. Was I this frightening? Truly? "And did you see it?"

She shook her head. "These things are written on the wind. There are too many pieces in motion, too many decisions yet to be made. I can't see a clear path, only possibilities, shadows of things that might be. He may fall or not. That depends on many things."

"And how did Malet take that?"

"He didn't like it. He wanted me to forecast sure success for him. Which I could not truthfully do." Ana splashed her hand in the water and raised it, droplets falling tinged with sunset's flame. She was using it as a focus, I realized. She was using the reflections of light in the water the way I used a candle. "I told him that if he wanted a true Sibyl then he would have to hear the truth."

"You are very brave," I said.

Ana shrugged. "I couldn't make up things for him because I didn't know what he wanted. So I told him the truth." She looked at me. "You know how it is. You see bits and shadows of things, things that may be the future or the distant past, and only God can open the true doors. That's not something that you can make happen."

"I know," I said. And I did know. I had never before met someone like me. "What did you see?"

"I saw a city of brass," she said. "I saw a place that was not a place, or it was many places at once, the gates of the underworld opened by deep magic within the earth, tying this place to others that have been. I saw a city on the horizon, long walls sleeping under slanting sun, domes gilded in the fading light."

"A real place?" Cold touched me for all that we sat in warm sunshine on warmed stones. Had I dreamed this? Or had I only dreamed it in some other life?

Her eyes were unfocused, a voice like a dreaming child. "A palace in summer heat, winged bulls thrown large on the walls, blue and green and gold mosaics cool under my feet. Mother says we must hide. She says that the king is dying and we do not know what will happen. We must hide, my brother and I, until our father comes. No one must see my eyes. No one must see my eyes...."

My veins were ice. I could see her, dark head bent, a little girl of seven or so, another child spirited away in the night with revolution and fire behind her, the long road stretching out before us under Ishtar's horned moon....

Ana looked at me. "You were there when Alexander died," she said.

I swallowed hard. "I was."

"And you will be again," she said. "When the dream comes full circle. You will walk into the wasteland and it will kill you or change you." I said nothing and she put her hand on my arm, her fingers real and callused against my sleeve. "Do I frighten you?"

"True prophecy is not gentle," I said. "I know that. And if my destiny has been coming, then it will come. All I can do is face it with honor."

Ana nodded. "Yes. And there is no point asking me what will happen after."

"I know," I said. "That's written in the wind. But I must take action for the future I want. And I would like your help."

She raised her face to mine. "It is of no importance to me who sits on the throne of France."

"No," I agreed. "But I can give you many things you might want. I have money to spend and the freedom to go where I like. What is it that you want from life, what thing that is impossible? Now is your moment to ask for it."

"I want to go home," she said simply. "I want to go home to Naples. Surely whatever danger is past now and King Ferdinand is in exile. I would have gone before now but I have no money and a poor young woman can't travel alone. That's what I want. I want to go home."

"I can take you to Naples," I said. "Though it may have to be some time from now. I am on the Emperor's business and I must soon return to Florence. I am a reader in the Grand Duchess' household and cannot absent myself forever. But as soon as I may I will take you to Naples." That was a road I could easily see stretching before me. Naples. I had been there long ago with my parents, and now I could see the path turning southward again, as though a line had been drawn straight through the ancient walls of Rome, straight as the Via Appia cutting south through the countryside. "I will take you to Naples and give you this dowry if you will help me."

"Help you to do what?"

"To catch Malet, or at least to make a start upon it."

Her gaze was even. "He will kill me if he thinks I betray him."

"You'll come to Florence with me," I said. "I can get you a position in the Grand Duchess' household. You're a milliner. She has hats. A ladies' maid is a perfectly respectable position. And then when I can I'll take you to Naples."

Ana's eyes searched my face, and I don't know what she saw there. Why should she trust this stranger who offered to take her away from all she knew? And yet she did. "Agreed," Ana said.

Ana at last agreed to return with me to my hotel that we might continue our conversation in more comfort and with a meal. "After all," she said disingenuously, "It is not as though you can actually do me harm since you're really a woman."

Untrue, but I would not disabuse her of it. Besides, I was not in the habit of seducing sixteen-year-old girls.

Though there was an appeal to it, in a way that made both desire and guilt crawl up my spine together. She was very pretty and entirely innocent, and I would leave her technically a virgin at the end of it…. Oh, Michel, I thought. Is this what it is to be a man and constantly have one's judgment at war with one's impulses? He would not do this, and therefore neither would I.

I ordered dinner brought up for us and Ana settled into a chair with no outward discomfort at the fine surroundings. But then, she must have seen many fine houses when she worked with Malet. It was a good meal but not an extravagant one, not the kind of thing that would seem a bribe, but more like what I would have requested were I alone. Of course the footman thought I was going to have her, an apparently respectable girl, and his disapproval was writ large on his face though he said nothing. "That will be all," I said, and sent him off. We could tend to the rest ourselves. He sniffed and gave her one last doubtful look before the door closed, as though he didn't quite dare to rescue her.

Ana was watching me. "How confident you are!" she said. "I would never guess from your manner that you aren't a man."

"Confidence is the greatest part of it," I said. "We assume that people are what they seem. My father taught me that."

"Most of being noble," he had said, "is manner. We believe someone is an aristocrat because they act like one, not because of the cut of their coat or the price of their stockings. Many a noble doesn't have two lira to rub together, but their blood's as blue as the sky back to the Holy Crusades. If you want to be taken for quality, Elzelina, the only thing that matters is manner." We had been in Naples then, I thought. There had been some scheme or another, a grand title to which he pretended. "You are the daughter of a very noble man of a very noble family, and you are used to having your way, Elisabeth Tolstoy, the daughter of a count."

It was a con, of course. But he'd never pulled off anything as high stakes as the games I now played.

I helped myself to a second glass of wine, the lace on my cuffs falling back from my hands with a gesture that was now entirely natural. "Can you tell me about the Philadelphes' lodge?"

Much of what Ana related was entirely standard. They had been working within much the same framework I was used to, both with Lannes' lodge and the fake one Lebrun had originally trained me in, the framework of the Masonry of the last century. There were, however, fascinating points of departure.

I put my elbows on the table, leaning forward. "A trap door?"

Ana nodded. Her face looked a little flushed from wine and good food. "A trap door in the floor beneath the altar. I never saw it opened. They called it the megara."

"And you never saw it opened? You have no idea where it led?"

Ana shook her head. "Perhaps to a basement or cellar? We were on the ground floor of the house. But I have never seen a fine house have a trap door to the cellar in the library room."

"Nor I," I said. "I confess I'm puzzled." Surely if one wanted to actually keep a prisoner one would use an ordinary cellar door? And yet there was something that seemed familiar about it, about the word megara that I ought to know. Some story prickled at the back of my neck just out of reach. "You're certain they used it?"

"They spoke as if they did," Ana said. "But they did not open it while the lodge was open in this degree, whatever that means?"

I nodded. "It means only certain members were allowed to see, those who were most senior. That's a fairly standard practice." And one above my head, I thought. It did not bear mentioning that I was only an Entered Apprentice in my own lodge. Perhaps someone further along would make more sense of this than I.

"They said their rites were Egyptian." Ana shrugged eloquently, as if to say who knew what that might mean. "That they had been passed down from the builders of the pyramids."

"Everyone says that," I said. "It's one of those things no one can verify." I took another bite of my dinner. "No one can actually read a word the ancient Egyptians wrote, so anyone can claim that they have secret Egyptian knowledge."

"They had a manuscript," Ana said slowly. "Only Malet and one other were allowed to touch it, but I saw it. It was a book with painted illustrations. They said it had been made by a man now dead who had been their master."

"A book?"

Ana nodded again. "They said it was by someone named Count Cagliostro. And that he wrote it after he returned from the dead."

My eyebrows rose of their own accord. "I doubt it was after his literal death. Perhaps his death and rebirth as a Mason." His was a name I knew, one that Noirtier had bandied about and so had Mesmer. They, at least, thought he was the real thing. But surely he had not been involved with Malet recently. As best I remembered, he had been dead some fifteen years.

"I don't know." Ana looked troubled, and her eyes rose to mine. "These things they were doing—they were real things. They truly worked." She shook her head. "I don't know if you can believe me or not. But they were real."

"I believe you," I said simply. "How could I not?"

At that she looked more confident. "Malet wanted me to see things for him. I gathered there were other meetings when I wasn't present. And some of the things he wanted me to see happened a long time ago."

I frowned. "How long?"

"Twenty years perhaps?"

"That kind of long ago." Before she was born. Before one was born is always long ago. I had feared she meant a thousand years ago or more. Certainly we had done that kind of work. "What kind of things?"

"Whether some operation undertaken by Cagliostro and his students worked. I didn't understand it all. But I understood more than they thought," Ana said.

"How is that?" I asked.

"I'm the Sibyl," she said. "My grandmother was the Sibyl before me under the mountain."

"In Naples?" I said, and she nodded. "Your grandmother was the actual Sibyl at Mount Vesuvius?" It was almost unbelievable. And yet I believed it.

"Yes," she said. "I told you, we fled to Rome when the Parthenopean Republic fell. But I didn't tell Malet that. I told him my grandmother had the gift of prophecy and that was enough for him."

"Of course it was," I said grimly. It was far too easy to underestimate a pretty girl. And hadn't Michel warned me that I always did?

"The cave is a real place," she said. "I promise you that it's true. It is really a gate to the underworld."

"I know," I said, and I knew it in my bones. There was a real cave and this girl was its rightful keeper. "And a real manuscript." It was too much to hope that Malet had left the manuscript in Rome. Of course not. Something that valuable had to be entrusted to an advanced student, someone who would guard it correctly. And with no idea who that might be, I had reached a dead end.

"I think ..." Ana began and then stopped.

"Yes?"

"I am only guessing," she said.

"I would like to hear what you think," I said. I knew well that the hunches of someone with this gift should not be ignored.

"I think they thought that they could attach something to the thing Cagliostro and his group had done, something to turn it to their own ends. Something to bring down the French Emperor. But I have no idea how they thought that would happen or how one would do such a thing! Can that even be done?"

"I don't know," I said thoughtfully. "I wish that one of my colleagues were here. Honoré is much better at this sort of thing than I. To piggyback something onto an older and more powerful working to turn it to one's own ends.... It might be done? But I would need to know both what they did and what the original working was."

"Would the manuscript help?" Ana asked.

"Of course," I said. "Don't tell me you know where it is!"

"No." Ana shrugged.

"Well, then."

"But I might know where another copy is."

I put my head to the side. "Really? How do you know that?"

"This man, Cagliostro, lived in Naples for a time. It was before I was born, but my grandmother spoke of him. He paid her some, you see. He wanted her to see for him, but she only did it a few times because she did not agree with what his friends wanted to do. And so she told him no more. They said they did not want her anyway, some old Italian woman who did not cooperate, not when they had their English Dove."

I put my wine glass down. This was all starting to sound maddeningly familiar. "Do you have any idea who was in this group?"

"Don't you?" she asked. "One of them was Count Tolstoy."

"My father." I blinked. "But that was a scam!"

"Perhaps for him," Ana said with another shrug. "But some of the gentlemen took it very seriously. They gave Cagliostro and his associates a lot of money. Very rich men, rich Englishmen with much to spend on games and treasures."

"On treasures," I said slowly. "We were in Naples. My father was no count, Ana. He was a con man. But he might have known Cagliostro. He might have entered into a game with him. I don't remember." She waited while I cast my mind back. I had been a child and it was not very important to me at the time. I was six. We had been in Naples, staying in another beautiful house that belonged to a stranger...I could not quite remember the name of it.

"I think there is another copy of the manuscript," Ana said. "The Englishman had a copy, Cagliostro's patron. It may be there yet. Who knows?"

"Who knows indeed," I said. I could almost remember. If Dr. Mesmer were here, he could help me remember. For that matter, if Michel were here he had learned enough of the technique from me to guide me down. But I could not guide myself. Yet there were more ordinary ways of remembering. "I will take you to Naples now," I said. "Tomorrow."

"I thought you did not have the time," Ana said.

"I need to find out what the Philadelphes were doing," I said. "And it seems my best chance of doing so is to go to Naples. Perhaps I will recognize the place I remember."

The English were out of Naples now, of course. The Kingdom of Naples was no longer a Bourbon kingdom. It had been recently given to the Emperor's sister, Caroline Murat. But that didn't mean the manuscript wasn't still there, buried in the library of a great house that had been passed on to one owner after another who had no idea what was in it. The chance that Caroline or anyone in her entourage read enough Latin to understand it was unlikely. "To Naples," I said. "I will take you home, and that will at least right one wrong."

We had gone to Naples when I was six. It was the season of Carnival, in 1783, and my father had a scam. Some old gentleman he knew intended to con rich Englishmen, and he wanted a continental noble to provide his bona fides, to play the wealthy student who was likewise investing in his schemes. The Englishmen were not to know that the wealthy student was no real noble and was also in on the scam.

I was entirely unclear on what the English thought they were spending their money on, but I understood my role. I was Elisabeth Tolstoy, the pampered and spoiled daughter of a Hungarian count. My brother, Charles, was likewise a prop, albeit one without a speaking part, as he could not be counted on to remember what he was supposed to say and what he wasn't. I was to describe my beautiful home in Hungary and the gardens and white pony that I had there, and to decry the filth and heat of Naples at every opportunity. Perhaps I overdid it with the descriptions of my ten dogs and my horse that looked like a moonbeam, but people took me for a fanciful child.

"I don't speak Hungarian," I said to my father.

He grinned, his brown hair falling out of his queue at the sides, a handsome man still only in his early thirties. "All well-bred girls speak French," he said. "And if you have to, just say something in Polish. The English won't be able to tell the difference."

How could this bright young man, this enthusiastic family man, be a con artist? Of course Count Tolstoy was a wealthy student whose single-minded pursuit of knowledge led him to come to Naples with his Master, bringing his lovely family with him!

His master was a fake. My father said so. He said there was nothing occult, nothing frightening. It was a game, he said. A scam. A play put on for the gullible English who would give them lots of money. And in the meantime we were the guests of one of them. Sir William had a beautiful villa almost on the slopes of Mt. Vesuvius, a charming place full of airy rooms and lovely views with a long loggia where children could run up and down even on days when it rained. Charles and I ran races there.

Once, we felt the earth tremble. We might have been afraid, but we weren't. "It's just warning us," I said. "It's just reminding us that it's only sleeping." I put my arm around Charles. "There is a monster down there in the dark and sometimes it rolls over in its sleep." His eyes were very wide. "It won't wake up today," I said. "Not today."

Sir William was a widower. His wife had died the year before. Her rooms were quiet and cool, just as she'd left them, but with the furniture shrouded with dust cloths and her clothes packed neatly away. I liked to walk through them and pretend they were mine, the big canopied bed and the dressing table with Dresden shepherdesses, the mirrors framed in white. I never stole anything. Elisabeth Tolstoy didn't steal. She was a very rich little girl and her parents could buy her anything she wanted.

It was Carnival and there were parties. Charles and I didn't go. We were much too young. I loved to watch my mother get ready, to stand behind her at the dressing table and watch while her maid powdered her fair hair, sweeping it up into grand styles held with dozens of pins, while she affixed a little patch in the shape of a heart at the side of her mouth and dusted her bosom with rose scented starch.

At night Charles and I shared a little room on the second floor that faced the back of the house, its one small window framed in ruffled curtains that matched the ones on the bed. We curled together like puppies in the warm night, watching the stars rise bright and thick over distant trees. Perhaps it was the sound of music that woke me. Perhaps I was merely curious and wanted to see the party. Downstairs a hundred guests were finishing a midnight dinner, masked and glittering with jewels paste and real.

I wanted to hear the music, and I heard my mother's voice, so I went to the top of the stairs. Below, the diners were coming from the dining room, laughing and stumbling, talking of cards and dancing. The music was thrilling, bright arpeggios that rose and fell, mingling with laughter.

I followed her voice. The library door was open a little, and I heard her laughing, heard her speaking Italian breathlessly, a soft moan.

Two men were holding a woman on the library sofa, her spangled bodice opened and her breasts spilling out, a golden half-mask across her eyes that did not hide the heart-shaped patch at the corner of her mouth. One of them held her wrists lightly, his head bent to suckle at her nipples, black domino flaring across her. The other knelt between her legs, his mouth on her privates, her skirts clutched in his hands. She moaned and leaned back, one leg akimbo clad in white stockings.

I knew the brown hair that spilled behind the Diablo mask of the man who held her wrists, whose mouth caressed her breasts, knew his shoulders even in the domino, but the other man I did not know. I just saw how he pressed against her, his fingers leaving red marks on the white flesh of her thighs.

I heard her moan his name and I knew it, our host, the man who owned the villa. She moaned again, her mouth hanging slack, her back arching, mound of Venus riding up against his mouth.

I watched. I wanted to see.

When she collapsed limp in my father's arms moaning, "Leo, Oh Leo," I stepped back, deeper into the shadows of the hall. I did not want them to see me. But I still saw when the masked man sat down beside my mother, her boneless form almost in his lap, when my father unbuttoned his breeches and took him in his mouth. I saw, and then I slipped away.

There were other revels, of course. There was a party on the slopes of the mountain and one that I was allowed to attend as being suitable for children, an illumination of the buried city of Pompeii. The empty streets were lit with torches and came in a procession through the long-buried avenues to a house lit up with a hundred lamps, the colors of the paintings on the wall vibrant and real and living. Men and women in evening dress walked through fine peristyle courtyards sipping wine and looking at the frescoes while a string quartet played in a Roman dining room with crimson walls.

I behaved myself. I pretended I was a great lady myself and walked through the rooms looking at the pictures, monsters swimming in a green river with little boats upon it, palaces crowding the shores.

One of the other Englishmen was talking with Sir William, their voices low but carrying. "I don't understand what you hope to accomplish," he said.

"My dear fellow, how can you look on all this and not see it?" Sir William asked. "This is nothing compared to the contemporary splendors of Rome or even a provincial capital! This is Rome's Brighton, not London! And yet you see what is here. Pompeii has shown us artistic triumphs that we can not yet equal. Can you claim that there is any modern sculptor who approaches the perfection of the art we have found here? Any Reynolds or Romney who can equal what these gentlemen had on their dining room walls? We can aspire, my friend. And aspiring, we can make it manifest—a new Augustan Age!"

They paid me no mind. I was a child. I do not even think they saw me properly.

"These workings will simply nudge the course of history into the correct path, an act of restoration rather than change, actually."

"Pax Romana?" the other man asked, a note of cynicism in his voice.

"Say rather Pax Britannica," Sir William said. "An orderly, sunlit Age of Silver in which all arts and industry shall flourish, each thing in its proper place."

I did not like things that were orderly. That was the simplest explanation as to why it made my skin crawl. After all, I had never heard of Augustus.

"And the Sibyl?"

Sir William shrugged. "She's not very cooperative. Perhaps Count Tolstoy's wife will be so kind as to step in."

"Much more charming," the other agreed. "If reluctant. Ignorant Italians may be picturesque, but there is only so much picturesque one wants!"

They moved away, and I did not follow. They wanted my mother to do something she didn't want to do, and I could not quite imagine what, only that it must be like the thing at the masked party, thrilling and disturbing at once. It gave me a strange feeling in the pit of my stomach to think about.

If I were grownup, I thought, and for a moment it was as though a grownup woke up inside me, someone bright and kind who knew what they were talking about, someone who had walked through rooms like these and who was unintimidated by the splendors they described. If I were grown up, I thought…. *I would kill your world before it began. I am your enemy, and I do not sleep. I am still here, still following you, and I will best you yet!*

I ran my hand along the wall, feeling paint two thousand years old under my fingers, the plaster cool against my hand, painted river and painted crocodiles and painted boats. *You will have your Roman peace over my dead body.*

Buried Things

I told Ana of the things I remembered the next day as we journeyed toward Naples. The Emperor had said I might draw any funds I needed, and that certainly stretched to renting a carriage and horses and hiring a coachman, as Ana couldn't ride. A private carriage was entirely in character for Carlo Tolstoy, and it made it much easier to talk than a public coach would have.

Ana listened quietly while the press of travelers about the gates of Rome thinned out, the road stretching before us under a golden autumn sun, following the course of the old Via Appia southward through the countryside. How much had it changed since Pompeii was buried, how much since...what? Since some other me had passed that way? I could not remember, could not reach for it yet.

"I think the Master you mean was Count Cagliostro," she said. "What you say matches what my grandmother said of him. I think the English gentleman you call Sir William must have been Sir William Hamilton, who was the British ambassador to the court. I was only six when I left Naples, but he was still there then, though he had remarried. Everyone said his wife was the most beautiful woman in the world."

"Emma Hamilton," I said, a piece fitting into place. "The woman who became Admiral Nelson's mistress, his Circe, the cartoons in the papers said. But surely she was too young then? She could not be so much older than I!"

"Perhaps ten years older," Ana said, looking at me critically. "But she was much more beautiful. Red hair."

I nodded. It did not hurt my vanity to be compared to a great beauty and be found wanting. "Sir Joshua Reynolds painted her as Thais the Athenian," I said. "I've seen the engraving. She is very beautiful. And he..." I dredged up the tails of dinner conversations a year or more old. "He wrote a book on volcanoes? He has studied them to help predict eruptions. And also excavated the places that were buried."

Ana kicked her feet up on the opposite seat cushion. "Everybody knew that. He got King Ferdinand to stop letting people dig for treasure. The old city had to be dug out carefully by workmen in his pay. There were men who drew everything before it was moved and when they found a cavity they were to pour it full of plaster before they dug any further. He had so many statues and tablets and things that when he tried to flee Naples with the British fleet, they could not fit in them all. Admiral Nelson said that he did not have room for seven hundred statues!"

"Seven hundred," I said. The number was incredible.

"They said there were thousands of tablets and tens of thousands of pieces of clay, bowls and dishes and pitchers and everything."

"What happened to them?" I asked.

Ana shrugged. "The British took the best ones. The others are still there. And they could not take the houses, of course, nor the temples. But I don't think they dug up everything there is. I think there is still lots more. The Parthenopean Republic didn't remove anything."

I knew very little of the Parthenopean Republic in Naples which had played such a large role in Ana's life, the fall of which had sent her grandmother fleeing to Rome and had doubtless scattered Cagliostro's former associates, as its rise and fall coincided with a tumultuous period in my life, those months immediately after my association with Moreau ended. I had been busy with my own concerns, and events in Italy had skimmed across like a stone on the surface of a pond. Lately, of course, I had made it my business to learn something of recent events in Italy, but I had put the brunt of my attention to the politics of northern Italy and in particular to Tuscany where I had been sent. I counted myself no expert on the affairs of what had once been the Kingdom of the Two Sicilies.

Twenty five years ago, when I had come to Naples with my parents, it had been one petty kingdom among many, ruled by King Ferdinand who was of a cadet branch of the House of Bourbon, and his queen, Maria Carolina, who was a sister of Marie Antoinette. Like her more famous sister, she was Austrian by birth and her tastes were much at odds with the tenor of the country she actually ruled. Unlike her sister, who had been blamed for economic problems she had little to do with, Maria Carolina actually ruled Naples. Ferdinand was an ineffectual man concerned with little besides the pleasures of the hunt and the table, and everyone knew that it was the queen who made policy. It was, at least, a policy that was easy to articulate. Hereditary nobles, more than seven hundred noble families in a realm the size of a French province or two, lived in great luxury. The poor of Naples were, as the poor most everywhere, illiterate, disease ridden, and without expectation of change—more than 40,000 were considered homeless, living in the streets of the city on charity and day labor, a number that would have shocked even the most jaded pre-revolutionary Parisian. There were also some small groups of people who were neither noble nor poor, tradesmen and craftsmen, owners of fishing boats and taverns, or who catered to the hordes of tourists who flocked to Naples from abroad to buy cameos and cloth at bargain prices and to enjoy the beautiful weather. In very recent years, some came for another reason as well.

Ten years before I was born, a day laborer had gone to the residence of the British Ambassador in Naples, Sir William Hamilton, with a vase that he had discovered while digging in a field. He had heard that the crazy Englishman would pay good money for old things, and he had hopes that it might be worth a little bit.

It was a first century Roman amphora in pristine condition, still bearing the seals that had labeled it.

Sir William knew what he was looking at, and not only bought the vase on sight but wanted to know where it had come from. Hearing that "oh yes, Signore, there are many, many more where it came from, they come out of the ground like bones," he hurried out to see for himself.

What he saw was almost unbelievable. There, beneath the ground, was a complete Roman city, Pompeii, still preserved beneath the layer of ash that had covered it when Mount Vesuvius erupted in 79 AD. It was a city lost in time, everything frozen in that moment of destruction, dishes still on the tables, dogs still tied to the doorposts, bread still in the ovens. Nothing had changed since those fateful hours when the ash began to fall, a story known from the letters of a Roman gentleman named Pliny whose uncle had commanded a squadron of ships that had tried to evacuate the residents by sea. Some had succeeded, breaking oars against the piers and taking aboard those they could, but most had failed. Most perished with the townsfolk, including his uncle the admiral.

And now it was found, a city where time had stopped and Rome had never fallen, preserved forever by the mountain like something out of Virgil's underworld. Sir William got the king to give him the right to excavate and to refuse to allow treasure hunters to dig at all. The city was his. He was the one who could walk its streets dreaming, the one who could kindle lights where none had been in nearly two thousand years. His were the bronzes and the mosaics, the marble beauties drawn pristine from the ash, still perfect and unbroken. Rome might live again. How could it not, when it only remained to draw it forth from its encompassing shroud of ash, its restoration the work of many lifetimes?

This was the city I saw as a child. This was the memory I recalled in Dr. Mesmer's stuffy parlor, a new Augustan Age—Pompeii uninterrupted, a life continued. Why should the temples not echo again to flute and tambour? It is such a little thing to bring the dead to life!

But statues do not embrace, no matter how beautiful they are. Ten years, fifteen, and they still do not. Frescoes never move. The gods go on dreaming and they do not speak. It must have grown unbearable, I thought, to walk each day among the memories but be unable to give them substance, to touch each artifact as the first hand that has done so since their original owner and know that they will not shine again in use. The music fades and the city is still a ruin. Unbearable, to have it so close and yet to worship at a tomb.

She came to Naples, the English Dove, Emma the red-haired beauty who shared his bed. She brought the statues to life. She was a sensation as an actress, performing attitudes from antiquity, transforming with the twist of a scarf or the movement of a shawl into Medea or Circe, Penelope or Ariadne, fury or sacrifice. When she was Iphigenia they wept, and when she was a bacchante they caught their breath in delight and passion. Who knows what private attitudes she struck, his own personal Galatea coming to life beneath Pygmalion's hands?

I could guess. But then I was also both Dove and courtesan.

We shared a secret, she and I. The dead are not here, buried two thousand years with their wine cups and their statues. We are the dead. We return, but we are not pristine. Centuries of use have changed us. The admiral may come home at last to save the city he failed long ago, but we have not been waiting for him. Our souls are battered and worn, transformed by the alchemy of time into new elements that only partially resemble those we once were. We are not blank slates for the magician to write on, Galatea with no memory of her own. But then, we never were.

Michel said I underestimated women, but I did not underestimate her, this woman I had never met, Emma who became Lady Hamilton, Sir William's wife and Nelson's mistress, the woman who was perhaps most responsible for the failure of the revolution in Naples. I did not underestimate her, England's Circe, painted as Venus of the Waves who blesses the ships with her love. Even the cartoonists who hated her drew her thus, the Lady of the Sea weeping for Nelson's death. If this manuscript I sought had belonged to Sir William's set, I had no doubt that she had something to do with it. After all, I had been in Boulogne in the summer of 1805, just before the Battle of Trafalgar, when we strove against the witches of England. I did not underestimate that power at all.

And so it was with due care that I came to Naples with Ana on a warm day at the end of October 1808. In the last ten years since Emma had reigned supreme as the British Ambassador's wife and confidant of Maria Carolina, there had been five governments. In 1799, as French forces engaged the Austrians in northern Italy, some of the nobles and the small middle class of Naples had embarked on revolution, emulating the stormers of the Bastille. Frightened of sharing her sister's fate, Maria Carolina and her family had fled to the arms of the British navy and Admiral Nelson had evacuated them all to Palermo. After the flight of the king, the Parthenopean Republic had been proclaimed and the city gates were thrown open to our troops.

However, the loss of Naples was a strategic blow to the British, a key Mediterranean port that could not be ignored. Financed by the exiled king and facilitated by the British navy, a loyalist cardinal had been landed in Naples to foment a counter uprising. To me, this made little sense. Why in the world would the poor of Naples, including forty thousand so poor that they had no homes, rise up in defense of a Bourbon monarch who had absolute wealth and absolute power? Why would they provide themselves as cannon fodder for a king who gave them nothing against a government who offered them equality under the law and who planned to provide public education and opportunity? It seemed incredible to me that it had happened, that this Cardinal Ruffo had succeeded in inspiring a counter revolution.

And yet it did happen. The Parthenopean Republic lasted six months before it fell in bloody street fighting that killed thousands, and the British navy swept in and restored King Ferdinand. Seven hundred were executed for their support of revolution, including some hanged by the British, something so beyond the pale that the Whig leader, Charles Fox, denounced it in Parliament in London.

This restoration did not last, of course. Two and a half years ago, after our defeat of the Austrians at the Battle of Austerlitz, the king and his family had again fled to Sicily. We had taken Naples with barely a shot fired. The Emperor had at first given governance of Naples to his brother Joseph, but a few months back had instead made it the province of Marshal Murat, who was the husband of his sister, Caroline. Murat had made such a mess in Spain that it no doubt seemed politic to send him off somewhere he couldn't do much damage, and Naples was far from any center of war. Naples had a new king and queen now, and I wondered how well that could possibly go. Caroline was no Elisa, and Murat's talent for government went without saying. Still, I supposed with proper advisors they could hardly do worse than the way things had been, such a disaster the government of Naples had been for the last half century!

Ana, for her part, was delighted to be home. Well-dressed in a new gown of flowered muslin, alighting from a nice carriage in front of one of Naples' fine hotels, handed down by Carlo Tolstoy, she looked like she'd done well by herself and acquired a wealthy protector. It would hurt her reputation irrevocably, and I told her so.

Ana shrugged. "And should I gain more by arriving in a wagon of produce with bare feet? None of it will change who I am. I have no intention of pretending to be other than my grandmother's granddaughter, and that already means I have enemies."

I frowned. "Why?"

Ana looked at me as if I were stupid. "Because she was the Sibyl. And because she supported the Republic. My grandmother was Annunciata Setti, who spoke before Caraciccolo and the Assembly. She was a very beautiful and educated woman in her day." Ana looked about at the city, façades of the houses painted pastel colors against the brightness of sea and sky, ready and waiting for a tourist watercolor. "I'm proud to be her granddaughter."

Once we were settled into a tidy (and expensive) set of rooms, Ana took her leave of me. "I will come to no harm," she said. "And it's better if I seek friends and family without you. You are not exactly unobtrusive."

Which was certainly true. I ordered an elegant meal brought to my suite and sat beside the window looking out over the blue curve of the bay of Naples while I sipped claret, a loaded pistol near at hand. My lace fell back from my cuff just so. Overhead the stars came out. The sky was cloudless except for one faint puff of mist shrouding Vesuvius' peak. The cool sea breeze lifted my hair.

And I missed Michel. All the beauty in the world was sterile when one saw it alone. I yearned to hear his step, to lean back against him as he stood behind my chair, feeling his solidity, smelling the warmth of his body.

Oh my dear, I thought ruefully. When did I fall so thoroughly in love?

I had hoped this would be a short assignment, but May had turned to October with no end in sight. I took another sip of claret. On the road like this, as Carlo, I did not even get his letters. They would be waiting when I returned to Florence, and he would wonder why there was a pause in mine. Hopefully he wouldn't worry. I certainly couldn't put where I was going and how in the outgoing mail!

My ruminations were interrupted by Ana's return. She came in gracefully, her face flushed with happiness, and sat down in the opposite chair at the table by the window.

"I take it that all went well?" I asked.

"Very well," she said. "I found my cousins living just where they used to, and I found my grandmother's friend alive and well! Oh it is so good to be home!" Ana was alive with delight, and I listened to her tell me of all her cousins and their doings while she ate just a little something more, having been pressed to eat with almost everyone she had spoken to.

At last, when full night had fallen and Ana tucked her foot up under herself in the chair, I ventured to get to the heart of the problem. "And did you find out anything about the manuscript belonging to Cagliostro?"

Ana nodded rapidly, her mouth full of sweets. "I should have told you that first! I'm sorry! Yes. You were right that the book belonged to Sir William Hamilton. My grandmother's friend, Ignacia, knew that. She remembered it very well. She remembered how they used to do pageants out of it, she said. Pageants were what she called them, anyway."

I nodded. "That's good to know. Did she happen to know where the book was kept?"

Ana helped herself to the claret, looking decidedly too young in her pretty muslin to be doing anything of the kind, a fresh Italian schoolgirl waiting for a painter to render her in bright oils. "She said that the last she knew it was in the library at the Hamilton hunting lodge at Caserta. Sir William never sold the villa because he thought he might come back to it. Nobody has lived in it for the last seven years except the staff. But a few months ago a bunch of books and antiquities and things were removed and taken to the palace."

I drew a breath. "We don't know if this book was among them?"

Ana shook her head. "We don't. But the property of the former British ambassador was deemed spoils of war. At least the queen decided so."

"Caroline," I said. She wouldn't have let valuable things sit unattended in a hunting lodge, not if they could adorn her palace. Statues and vases made sense, but books? The prickle down my spine told me there was more to this than I liked. "I would take any odds that our book was among them," I said.

"There's more." Ana popped another sweet in her mouth and talked around it. "Ignacia said that someone else was asking about the books just a few days ago. That seemed very ... coincidental."

I frowned. "It is indeed," I said. "They're left alone for seven years, and then two people ask about them within a few days? Who was the other person?"

"A young Englishwoman," Ana said. "A governess. She said her name was Miss Carew."

"An English governess?" I blinked.

"Some of the noble families hire them," Ana said. "It makes you very important, very refined."

"Was asking about this book?"

Ana nodded again. "She said she particularly wanted to know about the book Cagliostro gave Sir William. She called it *St. Germain's Dream*. And she also wanted to know about a book by someone named Henricus Agrippa. And a book called *On Cause, Principle and Unity*. And one called *The Ash Wednesday Supper*."

I shook my head. "I have no idea."

"She thought that Sir William had all four of these books. That's what she asked about." Ana tipped the claret back. "I suppose they're valuable? She said that some of them were old."

"I suppose," I said. "Though Cagliostro's wasn't. It couldn't be more than thirty years old at most. How old was she?"

"A little younger than you, I suppose. Ignacia said twenty-five. She was very English looking."

"What does that mean?"

"Modest dress, plain bonnet, brown hair, pink face." Ana smiled at me over the rim of the claret glass. "See? I'm good at being a spy."

"You are," I said. "Did Ignacia tell her the same thing she did you? That some valuable books had been taken to the palace?"

"Yes." Ana shrugged again. "She had no reason not to. And Miss Carew paid her."

"I see," I said. Not idle interest then. Something was most definitely not right. And on the morrow I would have to investigate in earnest.

Opposite Number

On sober reflection over coffee the next morning, I considered that it was most likely that the woman in question was in the pay of the Philadelphes. After all, an agent who could appear British would seem entirely unlikely to be connected with a radical Jacobin plot. Did we not know that all Britons were Tories? Certainly the Duke of Portland's government would like everyone to think so, and for the most part it worked very well. It was easy to lose sight of the fact that an opposition party existed at all, much less that it had been vociferous in its condemnation of certain adventures, like support of the Cadoudal plot. There were, in fact, a significant number of Britons who did not feel that their government ought to be conspiring at the assassination of foreign heads of state, much less that this was best accomplished by setting off a bomb in a crowded shopping street on Christmas Eve! More than fifty people had been killed or injured, including five children killed. In our outrage, we tended to overlook that some Members of Parliament had strenuously demanded an accounting of just what sort of involvement and support Cadoudal had received from Britain's secret service, not that anything ultimately came of their demands. Still, the involvement of a woman who appeared British would lead any observer haring off in the wrong direction, hunting British agents high and low, rather than Jacobins. Miss Carew, or whatever her name really was, was much more likely working with the Philadelphes rather than the British.

It was, of course, possible to ask about her. A man like Carlo was the sort to go leering after every pretty girl he saw, and so it aroused no suspicion for him to mention that he had met her and ask after her with the desk clerk, the breakfast waiter, and the guide he hired to drive him and his little Italian mistress out to see the sights of

Pompeii, armed with a picnic basket and champagne.

Miss Carew, it seemed, had only been in her position a few weeks. She had been hired by the Bianchi family to tutor their daughters, Sophia, aged 10, and Teresa, aged 8, in English, drawing and deportment. Her given name was Emily, and she was said to be a spinster of some twenty-six years who had never been in Italy before, but whose references were spotless. Since her arrival, she had ventured forth with her young charges to draw the vista over the bay, to make sketches in several churches, and to visit several very respectable shops that catered mainly to tourists. She was, they informed Carlo, very pretty but quite unapproachable.

Therefore what I should do was approach her as soon as possible. This was not as difficult as it might seem. There were, after all, only a limited number of prime tourist spots in town to which it was possible to take two little girls without a carriage, and if she had a penchant for sketching in a place where children could run about, it was unlikely she would choose the churches. It required only two days of lounging about town before I found her—two little girls with sketchbooks open, solemnly drawing the vista of the bay, the curve of ocean and Vesuvius in the far right corner. Or at least that's what the elder was drawing. The younger appeared to be drawing a girl wearing a dress with giant panniers and a tiara and fanciful butterfly wings.

The governess' drawing was rather more competent. There was the bay and there Vesuvius, there the ships in the harbor and the line of the forts, precise and technical as a military drawing, and just as free of distracting people or nature. If it were not for the fact that the fortifications of Naples were hardly secret, I would have thought her sketch very informative indeed.

"You have a very keen hand," I said in Italian, putting my best foot forward negligently and holding the pose, a dandy hoping to impress.

She did not look up.

"A very keen hand indeed," I said. "If lacking the flowery flourishes that young women seem to find necessary. You should do well at engineering drawing."

Miss Carew did not lift her head. "I do not speak with strange gentlemen," she said.

"Ah, but you have just spoken with me!" I came around so that she could see me, perching scenically on the carved stone balustrade of the terrace. "And I shall not be strange to you if I give you my name. Carlo Tolstoy, at your service."

At that she did look up, as she must to tell me off. Whoever had said she was plain was wrong. She was a beautiful woman trying to look plain, which is not at all the same thing. Her hair was brown and lustrous, even pinned back severely beneath a plain bonnet, and her face was a perfect oval with even soft features that any beauty in the world would have been proud of, but it was her eyes that startled. They were utterly extraordinary, one blue and one brown, not rendered such by an injury that left the pupil permanently dilated, but actually different colors, one sky blue and one molten chocolate. "If you think I will give you my name, then you are mistaken, sir," she said tartly.

"I know your name," I said, taking out a cloisonné snuff box and tapping it open. "You are Miss Emily Carew."

"I am not interested in your attentions," she said, drawing herself to her feet as if to prepare to remove herself and her charges.

Charm would not work. So perhaps directness. "I think perhaps you are," I said, dropping my voice. "Or at least you are very interested in some books now in the possession of Queen Caroline of Naples."

The startled expression that fled across her face was real. Perhaps she was not so long at this game.

My voice was low. "Some four books once belonging to Sir William Hamilton, and perhaps other things as well." I shook the snuff onto the back of my hand and took it delicately. "It so happens that I am something of a specialist in assisting people in the recovery of their lost valuable items. It is a positive mania with me, this need to be of service. Most utterly discreetly, I assure you."

She glanced left and right, making certain her charges had their heads buried in their work. "You are a thief."

"Such a terrible word," I said, touching my nose with the lace edged handkerchief. "I prefer to say that I am merely someone who provides a very specialized service for those in need who cannot sully their reputations. After all, can Miss Carew, a respectable governess, sneak into the palace and pilfer the library? I do not see how it can be done, by God! Not without able assistance, at any rate. Surely you have reached the same conclusion?"

Again there was a flicker across her face. Yes, she had. Miss Carew had absolutely no legitimate reason to get into the palace, and perhaps scaling walls and climbing in windows was beyond her. On the other hand, what legitimate reason did Carlo Tolstoy have? "And you think it is such a little thing to do this?" she asked, her voice dripping with doubt. "Why should I believe you?"

"Why shouldn't you?" I asked pleasantly. "How shall an unaccompanied woman, an English governess, present herself at the palace guardposts and be admitted to wander about unescorted? How indeed? On the other hand, a French lieutenant of chasseurs, bearing dispatches from Marshal Lannes to our holy sovereign Marshal Murat, might be expected to pass through the guard posts with complete impunity. Or if he were escorting a young lady whose presence the Marshal had requested the pleasure of for an intimate supper?"

Her cheeks did not flame. Miss Carew was beyond embarrassment. "You think you can be taken for a French lieutenant of chasseurs?"

"I know that I can be," I said. It was more than a matter of accent. It was knowing how things were done, the details of the guard protocol, of the shade of salute rendered, of how one walked and stood and shrugged. In truth it was far easier to be Charles than Carlo.

The elder of the little girls was watching her curiously.

Miss Carew ducked her head. "The church of Gesu Nuovo, tomorrow at noon." She raised her head again. "Sir," she said clearly, "If you do not remove yourself immediately I shall be forced to take steps. Sophia, Teresa, we are leaving." She gathered them up like an offended duck with ducklings and swept away, her back straight and without glancing behind. Carlo had just been cut dead.

Well, I thought, chasing after her will only attract attention. Either she will turn up at the rendezvous she suggested, or she won't. And if she won't, then I can still get into the palace. Only it will be much more difficult to find something when I have no idea what it looks like. A book. Well. Best to keep the rendezvous and see what happens.

The church of Gesu Nuovo was on the piazza of the same name, and it was not one of the grand churches. In fact, the exterior was unprepossessing. It was stone and rather plain, a neighborhood church rather than a grand cathedral. Arriving well before noon, I slipped in the back as the eleven o'clock mass was ending. The interior was baroque rather than medieval, with a fairly nice pipe organ and some pretty paintings, but not at all the sort of thing tourists liked to see, except perhaps for the most dogged.

I was clad less foppishly today, and did not attract stares as I sat down on a bench far to the side where I could see both door and altar and bent my head as if in prayer. The only remarkable thing about Carlo at the moment was being the only man in the church, bar the priest. The rest were elderly Neapolitan women in black dresses, and there were not so many of them. A weekday mass at a quiet neighborhood church did not attract great crowds.

Miss Carew arrived exactly at noon. She looked like precisely what she was—an English tourist with sketchbook and reticule and practical tatted gloves to go with her day dress. She walked about gazing up at the mediocre paintings, not making a genuflection toward the altar at all. Well, she was English!

The priest walked out with two of the old ladies, talking animatedly. He looked sixty himself. Perhaps they had offered him lunch. They seemed very good friends. The church was momentarily empty and silent.

I got up. "Miss Carew?" I said, as though I had just seen her, bowing very properly. "Fancy meeting you here."

She spoke French rather than Italian on this meeting. "M. Tolstoy. If that is your name?"

"It was the name of my humble father," I said with another bow. "Shall I take it that you are considering my proposal?"

The priest came back in, glancing at us on the last phrase. But of course I might have meant a proposal of marriage. And so I raised my voice again. "Emily, you are all my happiness! What can I do to persuade you of my good intentions?"

For a moment she looked startled, and then she saw the priest as well. "I am quite sure of your intentions, Carlo," she said. "But there are so many barriers." She sank down on the bench, drawing me down by the hand to sit next to her.

The priest glanced at us again as he went up the aisle, apparently concluding that young foreign lovers had chosen his church as a meeting place rather than somewhere more salacious. He should leave us to our ardent discussion of marriage and chaperone from clear across the nave, where he was joined by another old man in tattered clothes with a long sweeper's brush.

She looked over, then back, her eyes keen. They truly were the most extraordinary eyes.

"Begin at the beginning, Miss Carew," I said quietly. "If that is your name." I gave her a conspirator's smile.

She did not return it. "It is not my father's name," she said. "Nor did he ever use it, and there is the beginning of the story. I am not a thief, M. Tolstoy. I do not seek anything that is not rightfully mine."

I raised an eyebrow. "You do not appear to be Sir William Hamilton."

"Sir William Hamilton died five years ago," she replied. "His personal property quite rightly belongs to his widow."

"Ah," I said, a piece falling into place. "And so you are in the employ of Lady Hamilton."

"I am not," she snapped. "I am her daughter."

When she turned those blazing eyes on me I kicked myself for not seeing it before. Her coloring was different, brown hair instead of red, skin of purest ivory instead of fair peaches and cream, but the shape of her face was the same. No doubt if she had stood next to one of the famous paintings of her mother it would have been obvious.

"Sir William left various personal items behind when he left Naples, fully intending to return at some later date. Those items have now been confiscated by that parvenu who calls herself Queen of Naples. They do not belong to her! They belong to my mother, and I have come to get them."

"Like a good daughter," I said.

Miss Carew laughed, a bitter and brittle sound. "A good daughter to be sure. I've had little enough from her over the years, but now when the creditors bang down her door she begs, 'Emily, go and get these books and I will be ever so grateful!' as though I could be charmed."

"Then why do you?" I asked.

"For the money," she said, raising her eyes firmly. "My mother says that we will split the proceeds of their sale equally. It will be enough to buy me a life. Have you any idea what it is like to be a woman with no money?"

"I don't see how I could understand that," I said quietly.

She was angry now, the anger of weeks of silence that poured forth. "She was seventeen when I was born, seventeen and the mistress of a libertine who shared her favors with his friends, happy hunting weekends in the country with the Hellfire Club. But she played him false and had a lover of her own, Charles Greville, the man she swore was my father. Certainly he thought so—enough to pay for her lying in and to pop me off to a wet nurse and then to my great grandmother as soon as I breathed! And that was all I had from him. Ever. While my mother went about her fashionable ways on his arm. Painted by all the best painters, she was." A hint of an accent slipped into her speech, something not appropriate for a governess. "Sometimes she sent a little money. Once in a while she saw me for a day or two. But he gave nothing. Not a penny."

"Men are often that way," I said. I certainly could not imagine that any child of mine and Victor's would have received much tender attention, if it had suited him to let me carry to term.

"Oh, he's one of the best!" she said, looking up, her eyes bright and her voice hard. "So good, Mr. Greville, so virtuous! You know what he did when he tired of her?"

"No," I said. "How should I?"

"Sold her. Sold her like a slave." Her hands clenched about her reticule. "He had debts, you see. And his uncle was a rich old man. So he told my mum that he was going to meet her in Naples for a fabulous Italian holiday and sent her off like a parcel, his debts paid by his uncle and my mum the exchange. She gets here friendless, not knowing a soul on the Continent, not a penny to her name, and finds out she's to make the old man happy. Bought and sold."

I confess that I was shocked. I had been badly treated by Victor, but even he would have balked at that, if for no other reason than the censure of his peers. A man who treated his mistress of many years that way would be considered no gentleman. I could not imagine that even the most jaded company, even the likes of Talleyrand and

Moreau, would consider that acceptable. A business arrangement at least requires the woman's consent. Even at the worst I had never been Victor's property to sell as he liked without even knowing that I went to a new master.

"And people didn't talk?" I asked incredulously.

"Why should they?" Emily Carew's eyes snapped challengingly. "Do you think gentlemen care what happens to a working class woman? Do you think they care what happens to their own get if it's under the blanket?"

"Gentlemen I know do," I said. Talleyrand's natural son was right here, in the very palace I intended to burgle, aide-de-camp to Marshal Murat. He might not have his father's name, but he had an education and a commission and a good start in life. And Michel...

"I doubt that," Emily said. "You are who you're born, and that's it. No matter where you go or what you do, that's all you are. Even Nelson—do you think all that lot so eager to shake his hand three years ago when they were quaking in their shoes about Boney would honor his bequest to my little half-sister? Her hard luck, isn't it? But then what's a bastard girl worth? Especially since Nelson wasn't anybody. Not really. Just a parson's son who got above himself what with sinking the French fleet and all." She unclenched her hands from her reticule. "Greville's got Sir William's estate, and the government's not honoring Nelson's bequest, and my mum's hard up. It's not for her I'm doing this. But Sir William was kind enough to give some money for my schooling, and there's her, isn't there? Horatia. She's seven. She ought not have it like I did, feast or famine, wondering where the next meal's coming from or who'd be taking care of her next month." She gave me a reproving look, one that showed she believed in the authenticity of Carlo's title about as much as it deserved. "You've no idea what the Quality are like."

"I think I do," I said quietly. "It doesn't have to be that way."

"They run the world," Emily said. "And the rest of us live in it, God help us."

"There are other ways to live," I said. "Other ways to order society. It doesn't have to be that way."

Emily was unimpressed. "And who'll make it different? You?" She gave me scathing look.

"Yes," I said. "Me and my friends."

She snorted. "Some half-baked Italian revolutionaries on their way to being shot."

"Not hardly," I said. I could have said more, but it was better not. Tempting, but not.

"You're a thief for pay."

I shrugged. "We all must make our way, pretty lady."

"True enough." She lifted her head. "There were some books and other valuable small antiques that my mother said Sir William had left behind. I'll pay you to help me get them out of the palace, but I'm coming with you. No telling you what they are and hoping you'll actually bring them to me. I'm not stupid."

"Well enough," I said. "I have given this some thought. Marshal Murat has a taste for the ladies. He often arranges assignations, but of course he does so discreetly when it's right under his wife's nose. A young officer sent to escort the lady to his rooms and back again later, a quiet word to the guard here and there.... It's all very civilized."

"Quite," Emily said bitterly. "So I'm to play the whore and you the officer?"

I nodded. "We'll pass into the palace that way and then it will be quite some time before we're expected to depart. We can search the library and get the books and whatever else you wanted, then pass out again the same way. The guards won't make a fuss because it's supposed to be discreet, and I will carry off the questions." Heaven knew that I knew how it was done! I'd certainly seen how to get a mistress in and out of headquarters! "You've only to smile and look pretty."

"Until we get inside," she said grimly.

"It's so," I said. "Do we have a deal, Miss Carew?"

She hesitated and then shook my hand firmly. "We do, Mr. Tolstoy."

I had never been in the royal palace in Naples. Built in the era of Louis XIV, like so many foreign palaces it mimicked Versailles only on a much smaller scale. Fortunately, it was not surrounded by parks, but opened directly onto a piazza in the center of town. There were, of course, fences and guard posts, but this was hardly a remote castle protected by a curtain wall and moat. Anyone who wished could walk past, and approaching the guard post was a very minor matter. I trimmed my hair from Carlo's rather loose style into the more clipped Brutus cut ubiquitous in the army and put on the uniform of the Chasseurs à Cheval I had brought. Corbineau had said he'd have me for a troop leader, and I'd taken him at his word. At least I could convincingly portray one. The scarlet pelisse laced with gold braid was very fetching, and hardly what one would wear if one wished to be inconspicuous.

Certainly Miss Carew blinked at it. It was quite an ensemble, and after all Carlo had ample luggage space in which to carry it— buff breeches and a dark green tunic lavishly embroidered with soutache braid with scarlet facings, and a scarlet pelisse not only laden with braid but also ornamented with white fur, tasseled boots and white gloves and a glorious hat that added a full head to my height. I made my best bow to her, every bit of elegance the uniform required. "Mademoiselle, I am charmed."

"God help us all," Emily said. "Where'd you get that?"

"From a fine military tailor in Paris," I said.

She laughed. "You expect me to believe that?"

"Should I say my old mother ran it up for me?" I offered her my arm with a gallant flourish and led her across the piazza. "I shall if it pleases you, Mademoiselle."

"Saber and pistol?" I was, of course, wearing my own epeé.

"It is the uniform," I said.

Her dress was pretty if not revealing, a white satin that would do for a modest woman's evening wear, but with a cloak over it all that showed was the hem. She looked like a very young courtesan, the kind of fresh girl Murat liked.

She saw where my eyes went. "Do I need a bit more rouge?"

"No," I said, stopping in the shadow away from the gate, not quite close enough to be seen from the guard post. "Just to blush a bit." I leaned in and kissed her, feeling her sudden startled breath against my lips, soft and smooth and feminine. I didn't wait for her to push me away, but straightened up with a smile. "There. That will do."

"You're a scoundrel," she said, but there was color in her face, challenge but not fear.

"I expect so," I said. There was something deliciously satisfying about kissing a girl who did not know I was a woman.

"And a liar."

"Absolutely," I agreed, offering her my arm again. "You might also add cad. But is there any reason this shouldn't be a little fun? After all, how many times in your life do you intend to burgle a palace?"

She looked at me sideways. "You're mad," Emily said. "What do you intend to do if we get caught?"

"Cry for my mother, I suppose," I said.

It would be very awkward. No doubt this would involve a great many letters and unpleasant scenes before the Emperor sprang me from his sister with my female accomplice, and he would not be pleased that I had contrived to get caught, but I didn't think any real harm would come to us. Unless, of course, a guard shot us escaping with stolen goods.

Emily shook her head. "Mad."

We were at the guard post then, the senior officer only a lieutenant like me. I saluted him smartly, giving him benefit of seniority. "Lieutenant Mercier upon the orders of Marshal Murat," I said.

"You mean His Highness King Joachim?" the other lieutenant said, trying to catch a glimpse of Emily's face beneath her hood.

"The other title's better," I said staunchly. "As I was there at Austerlitz, and a hot dance it was too."

"You can say that, brother," he said, not asking for my papers. "Your business?"

"I am escorting Mademoiselle Charmante," I said. "To a private meeting."

"Ah." She looked up, her beauty speaking for itself, then looked shyly away. "Of course."

I gave a little half shrug as if to say, we all understand these things, and it's the senior officers who get the pretty ones.

"Go on then," he said, and waved us through, across the remaining stones of the drive and up the shallow steps. I hoped to the high heavens that security was better at the Tuileries! He had not even asked for my papers.

We made our way down the main corridor past footmen at attention before the doors of a dining room. Inside I could hear the sounds of cleaning up, the clink of glassware and trays. Dinner was over and the staff was removing the remains of the last course. "Which way?" I whispered. "Do you know where the library is?"

Emily gave me a sideways look. "To the right. Of course I do. My mother almost lived in this palace when she was the intimate friend of Queen Maria Carolina."

"Who didn't leave her a pension either, I should think," I whispered.

We turned the corner, Emily a step ahead. The candles in the gilt sconces were all lit, but there was no one in sight. Faint strains of music floated in from somewhere behind us. Presumably everyone was at the party, whatever it might be?

"Of course not," Emily said. "She thought she was an intimate friend and in the end she was just a servant. Do you think the sister of Marie Antoinette is friends with the daughter of a blacksmith?"

"You'd be surprised where the sons and daughters of blacksmiths may end up," I said. But of course they didn't, not in her world. In her world there had never been the revolution.

"Here," Emily said, stopping outside the fourth door on the side hallway. "I think this is right."

I eased it open. It was the library as promised, not so very large but dark and cool. There were no candles lit, and the heavy damask curtains covered the windows completely. We stepped inside and closed the door carefully, a little light creeping under it from the sconces in the corridor.

We waited, letting our eyes adjust to the dim light. I could hear her breath loud in the darkness, feel her hip not quite touching mine. It would be easy to just reach out and caress it ...

Emily stepped away, her skirts whispering against the thick carpet. "Give me a few moments to find them."

"Of course," I whispered. Some of the shelves were glass-fronted cabinets. I hoped they weren't locked.

Emily's movements were swift and sure. "Ah," she said, her fingers running over the books, looking for the method by which they were shelved. She pulled one out and handed it to me, a heavy old leather book written in Latin rather than English. I flipped to the title page, squinting in the dim light. "Three Works of Occult Philosophy?"

Emily didn't glance away from the shelves. "My mother has a buyer, Sir Harry Fetherstonhaugh. He's very interested in the occult. Apparently there are people who will pay a lot of money for that nonsense." She handed me the second book and I felt a cold prickle up my spine.

It was almost square, bound in plain dark leather. I opened it to the title page, in French rather than Latin this time—The Most Holy Trinosophia. Arranged about the title were small colored-block pictures, a sphinx, a palm tree, a falcon, checkerboard patterns and Hebrew letters. I flipped a few pages in.

At last I arrived and found an iron altar where I placed the mysterious bough. I pronounced the strongest words...instantly the earth trembled under my feet, thunder pealed...Vesuvius roared in answer to the repeated strokes; its fires joined the fires of lightning. The choirs of the genii rose into the air and made the echoes repeat the praises of the Creator. The hallowed bough which I had placed on the triangular altar was suddenly ablaze. A thick smoke enveloped me. I ceased to see. Wrapped in darkness. I seemed to descend into an abyss. I know not how long I remained in that situation. When I opened my eyes I vainly looked for the objects which had surrounded me a little time ago. The altar, Vesuvius, the country round Naples had vanished from my sight. I was in a cast cavern, alone, far away from the whole world...

I shut the book. This was the one, unmistakably. My hands shook and I clasped it firmly with the other.

"Here." Emily handed me two more, her back to me as she opened a drawer. "And this." She took out a leather case and opened it, scooping out the objects within. "These are from Pompeii."

I blinked at them. "They're dildos."

"Sir William wrote a book on priapic cults," Emily said stiffly.

"They're Roman dildos." They looked very modern indeed, carved of ivory and properly detailed, in three graduated sizes.

"Put them in your pocket," she said, handing them to me. Of course her gown had no pockets.

"That's one place to put them," I said.

Now her cheeks really were flaming. "Business, M. Tolstoy."

"Absolutely," I said. "I shall be delighted to conceal three dildos for you. And six books. But that is really enough if we are not to attract attention."

"That will do," she said.

Getting out proved very simple. We left through the side door near the ballroom, simply walking out arm in arm. No one prevents guests from leaving a ball, and in my uniform and her evening gown it was easy to wander out through the portico, past other couples strolling or calling for their carriages. No one even spoke to us. It is all confidence and attitude, as I have said.

We stopped several blocks away, near enough to the house where she was employed for her to get safely home, but not so near that she would be seen with Carlo, as that would cost her place. "And what do you do now, Miss Carew?" I asked.

Emily reached for the largest book that I proffered, an expression of satisfaction on her face. "I believe Miss Carew will receive an urgent letter from home. Her dear old mother is ill and she must regretfully return to England immediately." She balanced the book in one hand, looking up at me. "And there is the matter of your payment, M. Tolstoy."

"A trifle," I said, handing her two of the dildos and most of the smaller books, retaining the book I wanted as if by chance.

Her brows rose. "I would not think so."

"I would," I said, drawing my pistol with my left hand. "You see, this is the book I was hired to get, for which I thank you, Miss Carew. I could not have done it without your help."

Her mouth did drop for a moment before it tightened into a thin line, looking straight down at the barrel of the pistol pointed at her breast. "I see."

"You have five of the six books you came to get," I said. "And the antiques. Consider this one my fee and walk away."

"And if I don't?"

I shook my head. "You can't take it from me by force. And I should prefer not to shoot you, though I will if I must."

"Traitor."

"Unjust, Miss Carew," I said. "Of all the things I am, that is not one of them."

Her brows knit. "Who are you really?"

"Only in bad novels does the villain take the time to explain to the heroine all of his secret plans and machinations. Alas, this is not that sort of story, so you must be satisfied with my simple farewell. It has been a pleasure, Miss Carew. Pray give my regards to your mother, one blank slate to another. I hope that we may meet again under more auspicious circumstances." I made my bow as best one can while holding a pistol on a lady.

She said nothing, just stood there with her arms full of books and antique dildos, her eyes spitting fire, her white dress making a puddle around her on the paving stones, while I backed away out of range and then turned and walked away, Cagliostro's book safe against my breast.

Descent

My head was fairly swimming. "There are too many pieces," I said, "and I do not see how to put them together." Sir William Hamilton and the Philadelphes, Cagliostro and the Sibyl of Cumae, revolutionaries and scientists and mystics of all stripes.... How could I sort out who did what and when, and what the results of it might be? Months in Naples would not suffice, and in any event not all of the clues were here. There was only one way to ask that would be short, and I feared it and relished it at the same time. "I will have to go to the mountain," I said, and a chill touched my back.

Ana blinked. "Why?"

"That's where Virgil says the cave of the Sibyl is," I said, and I thought it was true. It felt true.

"He may have said that," Ana said. "But it's not." She shrugged. "Maybe it was once. I don't know. But that's not where it is now."

It was my turn to blink. "Then you know where it is?"

"Of course I do," Ana said. "Didn't I tell you my grandmother was the Sibyl?"

"I thought the cave was lost," I stammered.

Ana smiled. "There are an awful lot of things that aren't lost at all, just not available for every tourist to wander through sketching. Do you really think that these loud foreigners with their guides and books actually have any idea what lies beneath their feet or what the rites really are?"

"But Sir William Hamilton lived here twenty years and more," I said. "Surely..."

"He knew some of it, but not all." Ana gave me a sideways glance. "He didn't ask. And in the end they preferred their English Dove to my grandmother, who might have told them if they had asked the right questions."

I had to know. "Why are you telling me?"

"You're asking the right questions." Ana's expression was mischievous. "And you bother to listen to the answers." She sobered. "Also, I think it is for the Lady to deny you or oblige you, not for me to decide. You belong to Her. It's up to Her what she will tell you or not."

I took a deep breath. "Ana, will you show me the Gates of the Underworld?"

"Yes," she said.

We took a carriage by moonlight. I'm sure it was very romantic for Carlo and his lady, or at least so the driver thought. A picturesque drive by ruins was entirely in character. I expected that Ana would direct the driver toward Pompeii, on the other side of Mount Vesuvius, but instead we went westward along the bay toward Cape Miseno.

"What in the world?" I asked Ana as the driver carefully picked our course along a rutted road that seemed little used. "I didn't know there was anything along here except a few fishing villages."

"That's where we're going," she replied. "The fishing village of Baia."

I did not recall hearing anything of the place. "What is there?" I asked.

"A few pretty ruins," Ana said. "A dome they call the Temple of Venus. Views of the bay that English painters like to draw. Nothing much." She glanced at me sideways, her face unreadable in the darkness of the carriage. "And the Sibyl's cave."

We paid the carriage to wait beside the one tavern in Baia, a small place in a line of squat buildings along the beach, the curve of the sand marked by several piers, fishing boats tied up in rows. Behind the village steep terraced slopes were covered in grape vines, tier upon tier of them, neat as regiments on parade.

"We're going to take a walk in the moonlight," I said, and tipped the driver to wait. I put my arm about Ana's waist, and he winked.

"I'll be right here," he said, knowing what we were about. After all, why might a man like Carlo go for a walk with a pretty girl in a moonlit vineyard with a gorgeous view of sea and sky?

Ana picked up our little picnic basket, and we set off.

It was very quiet. Baia was a tiny town and, other than the tavern, there were no lights showing. The ruin Ana had mentioned was practically on the beach, and compared to Roman ruins I had seen elsewhere it wasn't so much. It was simply an octagonal building of modest size, weathered by time and salt air. I said as much to Ana.

"Long ago," she said, her voice quiet as we climbed the terraces, "Baia was a resort for the Romans. Very rich men built pleasure palaces here. Long, long ago. It survived the volcano and then dwindled away to nothing. No great disaster befell it. It simply stopped mattering."

"I suppose there stopped being rich Romans," I said. The terraces were quite steep.

"Things changed," Ana said. "As they always do." She was ahead of me so I could not see her face, but there was something odd in her voice, something much older than her sixteen years.

We had climbed nearly to the top. I stopped and looked back. The Bay of Naples spread out beneath the moon, Vesuvius looming on the far horizon, the lights of Naples bright against the sea. Below, the dome of the Temple of Venus shone faintly in reflected moonlight. About us the vines whispered, growing in lavish profusion, leaves dark as blood in the night. A sacred place, I thought, but not to any god I knew. It watched me, but it did not speak.

"Here," Ana said quietly. There was a little space between where the row of vines was tied up and the hillside, an atrium open to the sky, and at the back of it a shadow. She stooped and ducked in, and I followed.

I could see nothing. About me was the scent of earth, and I could not stand up straight. I felt her hand reaching back for me and grasped it, following her a few paces, bent over in darkness. My heart pounded. The earth above seemed to press down. I followed her.

In a few minutes the air seemed less close, and when I reached up I could raise my head, the ceiling a foot above. "We are far enough," Ana said. "We can light the lamp and it will not be seen." She drew a lantern from the picnic basket and I waited while she lit it. And then I gasped aloud.

Behind me was a dank tunnel. Ahead a white marble façade shone in the light of the lamp, arches and columns with elaborate carvings, acanthus leaves and hanging fruit.

"This entire hillside is riddled with palaces," Ana said. "It's very dangerous. There are drops and landslides and no one knows where everything goes. And the roof may come in at any time. It does after a heavy rain."

I glanced up at the ceiling involuntarily, though I knew it hadn't rained in several days. "Then all these vineyards…"

"Grow on the soil above," Ana said. "The volcano makes good soil for grapes." In the light of the lamp her face seemed very young. "I think these are houses, not temples. But you must come through here."

She led me through an archway between columns, a room half filled with rubble and sod. In places there was the trickle of new dirt, and once we had to almost crawl over tumbled stones. I was very careful. I should not have been surprised if our movements caused a cave in, as above seemed nothing but hard packed soil. At last we reached a lintel, a doorway that seemed to have a ceiling above.

"This is the old passage," Ana said. "I think when these houses sat at street level this was where the hillside was then."

I looked about. I could see what she meant, so perfectly preserved were walls and stones beneath our feet. "What was this?"

Ana turned and looked at me, the lamp in her hand. Her eyes were very dark. "A sanctuary of Dionysus," she said. "Built when his worship was illegal in Rome. There was another entrance, but it was filled in with rubble in the time of Augustus." She smiled, and it was not Ana's smile at all. "A man named Marcus Vipsanius Agrippa closed it."

I swallowed hard. "And what is he to me?"

"Is that what you want to know?"

I swallowed again. This was not Ana. She wore Ana's body like a gown, but she was no more Ana than those mighty presences called in ritual were simply my friends. "No," I said carefully. "I want to know what is needful. I want to know what I need to know to fulfill my charge."

Her smile widened. "And how do you address me, daughter?"

I thought I knew this, knew the invocation and spoke it aloud. "Isis Invicta," I said. "Unconquerable and Unconquered." Inexplicably, there were tears in my eyes. "I ask for your help. Please show me what it is that I most need to know."

She turned away, one hand tracing the line of the lintel. "Those others came here demanding answers."

"It is always a bad idea to demand answers of an oracle," I said. "And more so to think that one knows what the questions should be. That's always how people get into trouble."

"And so you ask what I think you should know," she said, and turned. "Humble and clever both. Dionysus would like you, trickster girl in your boy's clothes, deceiving and deceived. You must answer my question before I answer yours. What do you want?"

I blinked. "What? You mean right now?"

"I am asking what your heart's desire is. Everyone wants something of the Story. Everyone wants something of your Emperor, the living and the dead, even the gods themselves. If you could chain the lightning and claim your prize, what would it be?" She looked around at the walls. "Sir William came here knowing what he wanted—for Rome to live again. To save the city he once lost, to reclaim it from the ashes, to raise each statue and each dish, and fill every ruin with light and laughter. To remake the world in the image of the one lost—Pax Romana, with its art and its legions and its baths of clean water and its endless procession of ships from far away bearing back to the capital all that is best and most wondrous in the world! Orderly and serene as Apollo's gaze, wild and frantic as the bacchante's dance, London as the new Rome with its men of science and its benevolent order. Pax Britannia." Her eyes met mine. "What is it that you want, trickster girl?"

I took a deep breath, so many thoughts and so little had I put them into words. "I want a world in which I'm not an oddity."

She waited.

"I want a world in which I can be Companion and woman both. I want to be a paladin and a scholar and a lover and a mother all at once. I want a world where I can have lovers without having to marry them and children without losing them and where I can study anything I want and fight as a soldier without claiming to be a man. I want a world where people believe in gods and try to be good without burning each other at the stake. I want learning available for everyone without turning pedantry into a false god. I want the whole world open, every border and every nation, without any authority requiring that all men do one thing or another." It ran out in a torrent, and I stopped, shrugging my shoulders, as I knew how it must sound. "I know it's not possible. It's impossible that women should be ministers of state!"

"They were once," She said. "You were once, and your sister too. That which was may certainly be again."

"I want all religions practiced freely, every face of the divine," I said. "I want us all to learn from one another, no one compelled, no one enslaved, and no one isolated. I want to be what I am, soldier and courtesan and agent, with no contradiction. To be my true self without fear." There was a catch in my voice. "To be a treasure, not an abomination."

Her voice was as solemn as a judge's. "And you think your Emperor can make that world real?"

"More than anyone else," I said. "Without him what is there? Restoration of the Bourbon kings who wish it were 1780? A Republican government like the Directory only headed by Victor Moreau? Or Sir William's Pax Britannia, his new Augustan Age? Napoleon is my only hope, My Lady. A constitutional monarchy that at least guarantees freedom of religion and public education, that appreciates excellence and champions plurality rather than orthodoxy.... Of course it's not perfect. Nothing created by my friends is likely to be perfect! But better this vision of theirs than Moreau's or Sir William's!"

"You are as passionate about your vision as Sir William was about his," She observed. She stood aside, beside the door leading down. A strange scent rose, the brimstone scent of sulphur. "You have answered my question fairly. Now I will answer yours."

I looked at her. "What should I do?"

"Take the lantern," She said, "and descend."

For a moment I froze. There are few things I am afraid of. The heat of battle fills me with elation. Heights and storms hold no terrors for me, only healthy respect. But I do not like enclosed spaces, and the passage before me seemed barely wide enough for me to walk through, not to mention that it led into a treacherous maze at the heart of the hill, beneath tons of soil held in place only by crumbling stones that might dislodge at a breath. My throat closed and I stood in place. My pulse pounded in my ears.

And yet some part of me inside said, of course you are afraid. If you weren't, it wouldn't be a true initiation. It has to be something you really fear, and not for a moment would you fear the swords of your friends in Lannes' candlelit dining room!

Then why would Honoré have feared, another part of me wondered, but I knew as soon as I thought it. What Honoré feared most was failure. What he feared most was to disappoint those who believed in him, and so the examination held its own horrors for him. I, on the other hand, had never had much expected of me under the presumption I would come up short, so that trial could hold nothing that truly scared me.

This, then. Following the thought to its logical conclusion had steadied me. I could refuse, but I knew I wouldn't. I would never simply walk out of the cave leaving the Mystery behind. And so I should get on with it.

"I am ready," I said, and saw the smile in her knowing eyes.

She handed me the lantern. "Go on," She said. "I will come behind."

The passage descended at a gentle incline, the walls smoothed and squared, though every few feet there was a niche for an oil lamp. The air was close and hot. I should expect that it would be cool underground, but it was not. I walked very, very slowly.

"Once, long ago in the beginning of the world," Ana said behind me, or at least She who spoke through Ana said, "there was a king who lived in paradise. He had all that a man might desire—riches and plenty, a beautiful wife who loved him, and the hearts of his subjects. But there was some canker, some sore in his heart, and he desired more. He wanted to stand above the gods and to stand above the Law, above Justice herself, and he declared that she was no more. All the ancient rhythms, all the customs that had governed king and priest and commoner for a thousand years, should be no more and only the will of the king remained. Do you see the Mystery he profaned?"

I stopped, my hand on the wall. I knew this, child of the

revolution as I was. "The king is the servant of the people," I said. "He is the will of the people made manifest. Rulers exist to serve the people, not to be served, and when they forget that compact it is permissible to overturn them."

"The king is the sacrifice," she said. "King or queen alike. He laid that aside and said that story was not real. He said that compact didn't exist, and he built a new city in the desert where he would see nothing that was not to his own glory, where he would not have to walk the streets of his own people and hear their cries, and in those gardens he found bliss."

"Versailles," I said.

"The City of the Dead," She said. "The City of Brass. Long ago and far away."

I began to walk on, her hand at my back. There were stairs down, another passage, and then it widened into a chamber. I could scarcely see the walls, but the heat from a door on the other side rose up to meet me.

"And so a red man came out of the desert, a man beloved of Set, and he killed him there and cut his body into parts that he might never be venerated." Her voice was sad, yet steady. "Sometimes the fire must come. Sometimes the fields must be laid waste. There is a time for all things, even for pain. The world must be set right even at great cost."

"Even at the cost of torrents of blood," I said. I felt a little lightheaded, but perhaps it was only the heat. It was very hot. "You are saying that the guillotine was necessary. And I cannot accept that."

"Louis was not mad," She said. "And perhaps if he had compromised earlier, abdicated or agreed to a constitutional monarchy when it began...I do not know. But I am speaking of this other king."

"All the stories are the same," I said, and turned to see her.

"Because men are the same," She said. "Many men had free choices in your revolution. Some chose badly and some better. But the time to stop the fire is before someone knocks over the pot, not when it rages through your house. When the rulers forget that they are the sacrifice, that they live to serve rather than to reap the pleasures of others' work, the balance must be restored. And if it is not done by the hand of Justice, it will be done by Set. He too has his function, and it is necessary."

I nodded slowly. *A red man out of the desert, his chariot reins tied around his waist, a blue and white striped cloth upon his head...*

"The desert took the city," She said. "And there it still lies buried beneath the sands, though it haunts every dream." She took a deep breath. "But Set cannot rule. Do you see? The man who burns the fields may not make them green. The kingslayer cannot prosper. The executioner cannot rule. Justice must be restored. The Blameless Prince must come."

My breath caught in my throat. It was so hot in here. The air held the brimstone scent of sulphur. "The Widow's Son," I said.

Her smile widened, Her eyes dark as night. "Once, long ago, there was a boy from Avaris, a red-haired three-year-old whose grandfather was a common soldier of chariots and whose grandmother was an army wife named Tia. Once, there was a Blameless Prince, raised in the marshes of the Delta. Once there was a boy who pledged himself to this fire, to be the vessel of hopes and fears, to serve rather than be served, restorer of Justice. The gods rewarded him with long life and happiness to equal his burden, and so he chose it again and again. And when a thousand years had passed and once again he had scoured clean the temples of Egypt and restored balance, he was offered rest, to dwell eternally in peace rather than to toil and ache. What do you suppose he chose?"

The world seemed to narrow to a point, Her face shining in the darkness. I knew this, knew in the core of my heart the choice made in another underground room. "He chose to stay with those he loved," I said. "He could have become a god, but that would have parted him from those he loved. Better to take his chances, he said, for good or ill, than to leave the world he loved." My heart ached, but I scarcely knew why. "And so he returns, slave of the world, a wild magic that cannot be controlled."

Her eyes were dark as caves. "You pledged yourself to his service then and now. It is time to see what you chose." She took my hand and drew me down to sit facing her on the floor. The other door gaped wide just beyond the light of the lamp.

"What is there?" I asked. The heat was oppressive, hotter than the warmest summer day.

"The River Styx," She said. "I told you this was a temple of Dionysus. But he will not mind if I use it." Her smile was secret. "But this is not the day for you to cross that river. Look at the flame instead. See, and remember."

The lantern flame wavered, bright against the dark. I had seen it before, the same flame reflected in a blackened mirror. In a blackened mirror...

...it seemed to me I sat in Lebrun's parlor again, as I had eleven years ago, while Noirtier bent over me for the first time. "How shall fare Bonaparte's expedition in Egypt?"

I saw from above. Noirtier bent over me, a girl in a saffron shift, her pale hair pulled back from her face and her eyes dilated wide, though her voice was calm and dreaming. "He who would conquer Egypt must prepare to be conquered by it. There is a ship with an eagle spread upon its sail, great oars moving in unison. Caesar has come in relentless pursuit of his enemy, to conquer and be conquered. The Black Land does not give up her secrets easily, for we are older than time. We were old when last he came here, golden warrior, son of the gods."

Noirtier flinched as though he had been slapped. "Can you tell me more?"

"There will be fire on the deep," she said, "And Orient's loss will blind the eagle. It is not the sea that answers to his hand, but the deep-buried mysteries of the land. He has come to Alexandria now as he came to Siwa, seeking truths that only the Black Land can show him, and there he must find his destiny, in the place where he chose it once before, when he turned away from the rest that was offered." Her voice stopped, then went on, deeper and strange. "It is easy to descend to the underworld, but returning is the difficulty."

The scene changed. It was not the light of the candle, but the light of a torch. A black-haired young man carried it, holding it high to light their way. He wore the old uniform of the Army of the Republic, the tricolor sash around his waist with a curved scimitar instead of saber. He held the torch and looked back, waiting for two other men to join him in the shadow of the high wall beneath a starry sky. I did not know him, but as the others scrambled up the loose stones laughing, my breath caught in my throat.

"Hold a moment, Louis," the first said, whippy grace and brown hair, his bicorn hat in his hand, grinning as though they raced. Jean Lannes, I thought, but so much younger than when I had last seen him. Yes, this was

eleven years ago. His face had no lines. He was not yet thirty years old. He stopped, looking up at the stones above.

It was not a wall. It was a pyramid.

The Great Pyramid towered above them, tumbled stones about its base frosted with blown sand. The sky was cloudless and bright, the Milky Way like a path of light from distant horizon to distant horizon. The flame streamed in the desert wind. The third man clambered up. Bonaparte.

He was light as a shadow, two years younger than I had known him in Milan, his hair longer and his features rendered fine by the scarcity of a campaign. His white breeches were dirty from scrambling over stones.

"Slowpoke," the one called Louis said. His face was flushed with drink and activity. "Always hindermost."

Napoleon shrugged. "I'm not a gazelle but life isn't a footrace, Louis." He stood looking up, hands on his hips as he gazed at the pyramid. "Doesn't that take your breath away?"

Lannes nodded quietly. "It does."

The blocks of stone were enormous, each half the height of a man and large as a wagon. Over the entrance they were five times as big, set at an angle so they made two vast weight-bearing chevrons sheltering the dark door beneath, a space not quite tall enough to stand up.

Louis walked toward it, holding the torch outstretched. "We should have gone in today when we came with the scholars," he said. "It's a fine thing to see a pyramid."

"And how would I have looked to the army coming out covered in bat shit?" Napoleon said easily. "You can grub around as you like, but I have to try to look decent."

Lannes' face was serious. "And it would have been dangerous."

Both of the others turned to look at him. "You think it's dangerous?" Louis said incredulously. "You? The greatest idiot on horseback I've ever known?"

"This is an entirely different kind of peril, Desaix," Lannes said. "Who knows what's in there?"

"Bats," Louis said. "That's what the guides told us. Don't tell me you're scared of bats."

Napoleon had walked to the entrance and stood just outside, one hand on the lintel on a level with his brow. He bent, looking into the dark, his face entirely still.

"We don't know what the Egyptians built these for," Lannes said. "We

don't know what they do."

"They were tombs for kings," Napoleon said. He didn't look around. "The old king was buried at the very center with his son to accompany him into the darkness and then to return to daylight, pharaoh and god."

Louis Desaix's brow furrowed. "How do you get that?"

"One of the scholars said." He didn't look around. "That's what the passages do. They're the path to the underworld, to go and return. To leave the old king sleeping in the dark and come out anointed and consecrated."

Desaix snorted. "We're done with all that," he said. "Kings anointed in Rheims as if they were Solomon. The Revolution ended that. Kings die like other men."

He didn't turn around. "Consecrated to service," he said. "To restoring the land. Mopping up the seas of blood and restoring the worship of the gods. Taming the flood."

"The flood of the Nile is a dangerous thing," Lannes said, coming and standing beside him. "If the water overtops houses as well as fields." He looked into the darkness. "We come when the flood comes."

The torch shivered in the desert wind. Napoleon bent on the very threshold, looking back at Lannes with a half-smile on his face. "Do we, Jean?"

Lannes said nothing, just shrugged.

"Madmen and prophets, revolution and martyrs, saints and soldiers and old gods." Napoleon looked up at the pyramid above. "We may as well be madmen ourselves. Who knows what we'll find in this world gone mad?"

"A hole full of bat shit," Desaix said.

Napoleon laughed, reaching out and clapping him on the arm. "Not afraid of a little bat shit, are you, Louis? Or you can stay out here and wait."

"And let the two of you wander off?" Desaix grinned. "I suppose I'll have to keep an eye on the pair of you. I'm not sure how I'd explain to the army that I misplaced the two of you in a pyramid and let the bats eat you!"

"Bats don't eat people," Lannes said sensibly. "Bats eat fruit. And mosquitoes."

"You might fall in a pit."

"We'll try not to." Napoleon took the torch and held it in front of him, glancing back over his shoulder. "Coming, Jean?"

"Always," Lannes said. He laid his hat carefully on the stones outside

and stepped into the darkness, the torch glimmering ever smaller and fainter before them…

I gasped, seeking breath. I stood in the long passage beneath the hills of Baia, Ana clutching my arm. My linen shirt was soaked through with sweat, my hair hanging in lank pieces around my face. The heat was so great it was difficult to draw breath, though I thought it was less than it had been.

And we were in the passage, not the chamber below.

"How did I get here?" I gasped.

"I helped you," Ana said. It was her voice alone, her eyes empty of any presence save her own.

We came along a few more steps and then out into the larger chamber with the marble façade. A cool breeze came along, filtering down the hole from the vineyard. I took deep breaths, trying to clear my head.

"Sometimes the gas from the volcano is very bad," Ana said. "My grandmother said that in ancient times there must have been ventilation shafts, but those are all closed up and lost."

I nodded.

"From the chamber we were in there is another passage down to a hot spring," Ana said. "Sometimes the water there is almost boiling."

"The River Styx indeed," I said. I could think again. I could breathe.

"Come out and sit on the hillside," Ana said. "Sit in the vineyard and cool off."

We made our way laboriously outside and I sat down as soon as I could. Beyond the vines the sea stretched away, the stars scarcely moved from when we went down. The grape leaves whispered in the ocean breeze. I took the bottle from the picnic basket and tipped out a libation, red wine running about the roots of the vines. "Ave, Dionysus," I said. "Thank you for the use of your temple."

Ana sat down beside me, her white dress dirty from climbing about. I supposed sitting on the ground could do it no more harm. "Did you find out what you needed to know?" she asked.

"Yes," I said quietly. "Yes, I did."

THE WHITE HORSE AND THE BLACK

I left for Florence the next day. I took my leave of Ana, emptying my purse to her of everything except what I thought I would need for the trip back. "Are you certain you'll be all right staying in Naples alone?" I asked.

Ana smiled. "I'm home," she said. "Home with my family and friends where I belong. Don't worry about me."

"And the Shrine," I said.

Her face sobered. "And the Shrine," she said. For a moment her eyes were dark as night. "He is not immortal, your lover. And he is all too willing to be the sacrifice."

I caught my breath. "Michel?"

But her eyes were normal again, her hand on my arm warm. "Take care of yourself," she said.

"I will," I promised.

There were letters waiting for me in Florence—three from Michel, which I saved until last to read, knowing that I would savor them. There were also assorted others from friends, one from Corbineau, one from Reille, and one which purported to be from very small Jean Subervie but was actually from his mother, Marianne. *Jean loves to get letters from the army and he wanted to tell you all about Nestor, so I hope you will not mind replying.*

There was also one from Oudet.

...your letters demonstrate that you are a woman of taste and refinement despite the crudeness of your circumstances. You must know that there are others who labor for liberty and also have been betrayed by those who turned the revolution to their own ends. You say that you love freedom. There are others who do as well, and who realize that true

freedom cannot be achieved until all of the institutions of the dark ages are utterly and completely abolished. That the king went to the guillotine was a beginning, but it is beyond my understanding how we can have the Pope in our power, yea and all the College of Cardinals too, and not send them there as well. Surely the complete decapitation of the Church which has oppressed millions for centuries would be a blow struck for the freedom of humanity! It was a mistake to allow religion back into France at all. We should instead raze every church, every cathedral and abbey and synagogue—future generations would thank us for forever freeing them from the tyranny of religion.

I put the paper down, my hands shaking not with fear but rage. Burn the synagogues in the name of freedom. Execute priests in the name of humanity. How should this make us any better than those we fought?

Years ago I had fallen in love with Michel before I met him because of what Colonel Meynier said that he had said, "If we are the agents of liberty, then we must act like it."

Yes, Emily's society was rotten, a pretty confection over layers of mud that benefited no one except the privileged few at the top. But what did Oudet and his friends want instead? A sea of blood, a sea of unmaking, the destruction of every institution that provided comfort and order in the name of a world where it was every man for himself, or where a new orthodoxy reigned instead. I had not forgotten the hundreds who went to the guillotine for differing from revolutionary orthodoxy, or even simply disagreeing about the particulars of reform.

And what idealist should they install in the position of ultimate power? Moreau? Knowing him intimately as I did, I found it hard to believe he would rule more compassionately than a Borgia pope.

Or perhaps there should simply be an assembly, or a return to the Committee of Public Safety, a representative government that had murdered thousands who refused to give up Catholicism? How does one have the rule of the people when what the people want is revenge? In less than two short years, the Terror had resulted in the execution of close to 30,000 people. Thousands more had been jailed or brutalized like Josephine and Aglae. It was so satisfying, I am sure, for the downtrodden to avenge themselves on a pretty eight-year-old girl who, after all, deserved it for the crimes of her ancestors.

The government we had was not perfect. It was the fallible creation of fallible men. But all religions were equal before the law and so were all men. We had a legislative branch, and while our deputies and senators did not have as much power as their counterparts in America, they were indeed duly elected without bloodshed. We were a constitutional monarchy, albeit one where the emperor exercised great power. The transition from absolute monarchy to constitutional monarchy had only been achieved at a great price, and its maintenance in the face of the concerted efforts of the powers of Europe was still extremely costly. I knew, as I had bled for it, and I bore the scar on my forehead still. They wanted to return us to Emily's world, and that I would resist with every bone in my body.

Meanwhile, Oudet wished to plunge us into the Terror again. And I would resist that too.

It was the card in the tarot deck, I thought, the Chariot. The Emperor drives the chariot of state pulled by a white horse and a black who pull in opposite directions, left and right, and only his will may keep them yoked together, the chariot rolling forward despite all.

I put aside Oudet's letter and got out my deck, sitting on my bed in my little room in Florence. I closed my eyes and shuffled. The images from Cagliostro's book rose before my eyes, sphinx and golden bough, a tree standing straight and tall in the desert night. *Asherah*, some part of me whispered, supplying a word I had never heard. I shuffled, feeling the cards' smooth surfaces beneath my hands. The chariot drove over a path of light, not Roman triumphal arches before it, but pillars on each side, each shining with brightness, each a different color, red and blue and gold and purple....

"What is the middle path?" I whispered. "How do we make it manifest?"

And then, eyes closed, I laid out the cards and opened my eyes.

There, at the center was the Emperor enthroned, the orb of the world in his hands. To one side lay the Devil and to the other the Pope, not so clear as it might seem at first, an obvious choice between good and evil. But Devil and Pope alike were replete with meanings. The Devil represented chaos, being chained to the world, subject to our worst natures, to our short-sighted desires and petty spites. The Pope represented the desire for conformity, for acceptance and position at any cost, for success according to the judgment of the world.

"Well enough," I said aloud. "The Emperor stands between two temptations, to use his power for petty desires and pleasures, and the desire to be considered great. What can one aspire to when one is Emperor except to be remembered forever, another Caesar or Alexander or Charlemagne, Napoleon the Great?"

And the next position—how may it be manifest? Temperance. An angel poured water into a chalice, inexhaustible refreshment. Self control. Restraint. Moderation in all things.

Clear enough, but the reading gave me no course. Perhaps the question I had asked had been so grand in scope that even with the force of will behind them I could not make it plain. I scooped the cards together and shuffled again. "Show me," I whispered. "Show me what I need to know."

The first card was the Sword Queen, a woman standing in the tempest, her sword upraised before her, my own card. Across her lay the Moon, a dog baying to its shape half-veiled by clouds, conspiracy and hidden things, deadly secrets.

"Stop the Philadelphes," I said. I touched the card with my finger tip as if it would sear like ice. "Whatever the price."

Oudet did not arrive in Florence until Twelfth Night. It took two months for all the letters and orders to fly back and forth between Italy and Spain and Paris and Austria, which was really acting with remarkable dispatch on the Emperor's part. I had a letter from Lannes the day after Christmas, short and to the point: "Your request has been honored as of this moment." Thus I had a little warning before he arrived, as he gave me none.

The first I knew was in the evening. I had just been dismissed by the Grand Duchess, who had gone to her rooms to change for the festive dinner, and I was going back to mine to feel decidedly sorry for myself that I was spending yet another holiday among unfriendly strangers when I might have spent it with those dear to me. One of the little pages came running after me, telling me that there was a letter for me that had been dropped at the door by a soldier. Mindful of Lannes' warning, I tore it open immediately.

I have this moment arrived in Florence with orders of urgent importance. As I am sure you understand, while it is my responsibility to undertake matters of grave concern, I hope to have some few hours of leisure while I am in the city, and hope that I may give my regards to you. I have been told that my rank renders me among the honored guests at tonight's musical entertainment, and despite the services you render the Grand Duchess, I hope that you are allowed to attend. If that is the case, perhaps I might see you there and renew our acquaintance.

Your servant,
Jacques Oudet

I had not liked him years ago, and I did not like him now.

It was nothing about his appearance. Oudet was handsome enough, a bit taller than medium height with hair an unremarkable shade of brown and a fashionable moustache, brown eyes and even features. Perhaps one might have said that his chin was a bit weak, but that would have been unfair. He was certainly better looking than most of my friends, and I did not sit about considering that Gervais Subervie would no doubt be bald as an egg before he was fifty, or that Corbineau's nose was a bit beaky. The truth is that anyone I like is beautiful to me. Their faults fade into oblivion, and their fine points seem magnified into rare beauties. Subervie had extraordinary eyes in a beautiful light hazel, and his physique was a pleasure to watch in motion, never mind whether or not his hairline was retreating. Corbineau's profile was exquisite and he had cheekbones to die for in addition to a pleasant animation of face that filled one with delight.

Of course I had no doubt Michel was beautiful. Or at least he was so to me. I could attempt to look at him as a painter might look and yes, I was aware that ginger hair was not considered particularly handsome. His face was square and plain, a very ordinary face actually, with something of a tendency to be jowly. He sunburned at the slightest provocation, and so anywhere except in the depths of a Polish winter one could expect his nose to be as red as his hair. And yet I was quite certain that he was the most perfect specimen of manhood to walk the earth!

It is a gift of mine to see beauty where others see flaws, golden Aphrodite drawing a haze over all. I do not need to pretend to desire when the world is filled with beautiful mouths smiling at me, lovely faces and wonderful bodies, amazing and irresistible. With Oudet I should have to pretend. I did not like him, and the magic did not work.

I smiled and he smiled, and when he bent over my hand and his fingers were just a little too tight it wasn't provocative but merely annoying.

"I am glad you are well, Madame," he said, drawing me to the side of the room away from the piano and the space where the string quartet were arranging their chairs and music stands.

"I trust you had a pleasant journey?" I asked. The salon was large and there must have been fifty people present. No one was paying us the slightest attention. There were plenty of officers of one regiment or another in attendance, all in their best uniforms. It was something to spend Twelfth Night in a Florentine palace, even if one was a humble reader. And I must unbend a bit. I feared that I seemed grim and old rather than that gay heedless girl Moreau had brought to Paris. That was how he remembered me, and I must somehow find her again if I hoped to get anything from him. I blinked up at him with what I hoped were wide, guileless eyes. "It worries me so much to think of you in the field amid terrible dangers and privitations."

"It is not so much," he assured me, his eyes lingering on my face. I hoped that the curls I had carefully arranged on my forehead did indeed cover the scar over my eye. "I've had worse." He raised one hand and brushed them back.

"Don't," I said, jerking back. The window sill was right behind me, just at my knees, and I did not have to pretend to my discomfiture.

"How did that happen?" he asked, taking a step forward. His legs did not quite touch the flow of my dress, too close for propriety but hardly indecent.

"Need you ask?" I said, pouring bitterness into my words. "Did you think I would be as fresh as you remember me?"

His brows knit, thunderous. "You mean to say that…you have been ill-used?"

I supposed it did look as though someone had struck me in anger, and the violence to Michel's reputation was less than what I should have to do. I looked away as though in confusion and shame. "I would rather not speak of it."

Oudet took a deep breath. He was still crowding me against the window. "I'm appalled," he said flatly. "I had never imagined that one could have so utterly abandoned all principle…" He shook his head. "…that one who had begun life as a bourgeois could have so far adopted aristocratic disdain as to hit a woman."

"I said I did not wish to speak of it," I said, turning away. At least I could face the window. Somewhere in the background the string quartet were warming up. It was a crowded room. Oh Michel would not like this when it got back to him, as it inevitably would! But what else might I say? And surely ill-use of the sort that marred one's beauty forever would be a plausible reason for my disillusionment. "You already knew of the circumstances in which I find myself."

"Alone," he said. "And friendless."

"I am not friendless," I said. "After all, I have the steadfast generosity of the Grand Duchess." I did think it bore making the point that someone cared what happened to me. There was such a thing as being too much bait. "But it is true that I have no friend who cares for me as a woman desires to be cared for."

"Ah," he said. I thought perhaps that was the right touch, but dared not look around.

Double or nothing, I thought. I let my voice choke a little. "I had such beautiful dreams, Colonel! And now they are nothing."

"Perhaps not," he said. "You are still young and you have much to recommend you anyway."

And thank you so much for bearing with it, I thought acidly. Michel did not reckon a scar such a loss, or at least I thought not. If he did he would never say it. "You are too good," I said.

Behind us the musicians burst into full measure, the crashing opening of something by Beethoven, rendering all conversation useless. I slid around Oudet, turning to face the musicians politely and getting out from between him and the window. I opened my fan. It was already breathlessly warm in the salon between the candles and the press of bodies. The footmen had already opened one of the French doors that led to the courtyard, a formal little square between buildings with walks framing a bit of manicured lawn and a small fountain. The cool air was very welcome.

"Will you walk with me?" he asked.

"Of course," I said. There was a footman at the doors, and there were others seeking release from the confines of the salon. It was more private, but hardly deserted. We strolled out, my light shawl trailing fashionably, talking of one thing and another—how nice the music was and was indeed that Beethoven? He didn't know, and I professed not to know either, though I was almost certain it was. The light from the doors spilled out golden across stone paths, but other than that the garden was in silver beneath the light of the moon. It was very romantic. Or would have been, had I not been on pins and needles.

"Are you so dear to the Grand Duchess?" he asked.

I cast my eyes down modestly. "She has been all amiability to me," I said. "I can hardly profess my gratitude strongly enough."

"I see," he said. Once again his brow furrowed. "And does she have your loyalty, then?"

I saw the trap. Was loyalty to Bonaparte's sister loyalty to Bonaparte? "If it were not for her friendship, I do not know where I should be," I said carefully. "But let us speak instead of your travels and travails. They are certain to be more interesting than mine, confined as I am to the company of women and the tedium of domestic life!"

"I remember you always did like the road," he said, and I wondered how much he had watched me in those heedless first months with Moreau.

"Oh, rather," I said, as though it meant little to me. "But I must make the best of what I have." Plucky, I thought. But hopefully not too much a virago.

"And you have no particular friendship for the Grand Duchess?"

I looked up at him. "She was kind to me when I needed a place," I said. "She is a difficult taskmistress, and her court is far from lively. But I cannot complain since she has overlooked my faults."

"Then I would ask what you make of this," he said, stopping

walking and withdrawing a paper from his breast pocket. It was the second page of a letter and he unfolded it. There was no signature, but that didn't matter. I would have known that spidery, elegant hand anywhere.

I would most strongly advise you against taking Madame St. Elme into your confidence in any way. She is a tiger, and any profession of frailty is most likely false. Moreover, she is far more intelligent than she appears. She may play the innocent or the wronged woman, but that is no more than one of her many poses, a game that she is quite adept at. I cannot guess what game she is playing or whose employ she is in, but she is not to be trusted. She is duplicitous in the extreme and far more worldly men than you have been her dupe.

My heart raced. I paused, leaning over the paper as though it took me a great deal of time to read it.

He took a step closer, near enough for me to feel the heat of his body. "What do you say to this, Madame?"

That son of a bitch, I thought. But on the heels of that thought came the next—he had not thought Oudet would show it to me. Oudet had just confirmed to me Moreau's place in the conspiracy. Moreau was in league with the Philadelphes.

I looked up at Oudet in what I hoped was pretty confusion. "Who says such terrible things about me? Jacques, who? I can't imagine why anyone would hate me so much!"

"You are not a duplicitous woman?"

I handed the paper back to him with a certain amount of injured dignity. "Not in the manner this awful person describes! Yes, perhaps sometimes I have my petty fibs, an excuse for a glove lost or a breakfast overslept, but I hardly think that makes a conspirator of me!" He did wince a little at the word, amateur that he was, and so I went on in full flow. "Only once—once, Jacques! Once I have deceived a man who loved me with another. Once I was swept off my feet by a man's ardor and did not consider my duty. I paid for that lapse dearly. But to say that I am a liar and a tiger? Who would say that about me for such minor crimes? I beg you, tell me the identity of the person who tarnishes my name so!"

I saw him believe me. He wanted to. He wanted to be right.

Moreau had touched his pride, saying that there were better men who had been my dupe. He meant himself, of course. Moreau could never understand people well enough to command loyalty or he would have known that Oudet considered himself Moreau's equal.

"Say that you do not believe this awful letter!" I pleaded.

"I don't," he said. "He mistakes you."

"I wish you would tell me who," I said.

He folded the letter away again carefully. "It doesn't matter," Oudet said. "I see that there is malice in it."

"Surely you may trust your own judgment of me," I said, an appeal to his self-worth. "How may I show you that my esteem for you is real?" I thought I knew the answer to that.

The conservatory was empty. There was no need to dwell upon the details. I did what I needed to do. At least with my face employed somewhere below his waist he could not see clearly, certainly not in the shifting shadows of the carefully tended palms and orange trees in their ornamented terracotta pots. Afterward I pled that surely I would be missed, an excess of belated modesty that I thought becoming, and that also got me out of his presence before I could no longer keep up the pretense. He asked to see me again and I said that I could if the time I owed the Grand Duchess permitted. It is always best to leave while one is still wanted, and it was far too risky to start asking questions about secret revolutionary societies. Even a man so full of self-love as Oudet couldn't help but find that suspicious.

I went back to my room and washed my mouth out in the basin, spitting a dozen times to get the taste of him out of my mouth, and then I stretched out on the bed still fully dressed.

There had been those I desired and those I was indifferent to, those I adored and those I made the best of, but no one I had truly actively disliked. Jacques Oudet made every nerve in my body scream to get away from him. There was something that shrieked danger to me. I had not thought I would fear him. I never feared anyone.

And so I stared at the ceiling, my racing heart slowing. Sometimes one's duty is not pleasant, I told myself sternly. He would only be here a few days before he had to return to Lannes' corps. I had little enough time to use him, and if I had to use myself hard in the process then I would do so.

MASQUES

It is not so easy as all that to worm one's way into a man's confidence in three days. Oudet was not stupid, and if I pushed too
hard he would grow suspicious, particularly with Moreau's warning. And so I endeavored to make myself very pleasant and very
empty-headed, a frivolous woman who liked masques and talked of
little except theater and gossip. It was at least easier to do this since
the times of day I could see him were perforce controlled by the
schedule of my work for Elisa. Of course she knew what I was about
and didn't actually require anything of me while Oudet was here,
but it would have seemed suspicious if a reader had carte blanche
to do as she liked for several days in a row. As it was, I contrived to
meet him in public places and at the Grand Duchess' masque which
began the season of Carnival. For the next five weeks we should
live like there was no tomorrow until Lent came crashing in.

The following day he was off for Austria again to rejoin Lannes'
corps, so I thought I should have to put out. Also, perhaps a general
air of drunken debauchery would loosen his tongue. Fortunately,
or perhaps unfortunately depending on how one looked at it, there
were very few truly private places in the palace for one of my status,
and he shared a billet, crowded as it was with guests enjoying the
season. It was safer to manage half-clothed in alcoves where the act
could not be prolonged. I would like to think that for him it added
an air of spice, a whiff of the exotic, a masked lady's hand on his
privates behind a loose screen of statue and greenery, three hundred
people within earshot. For me it was merely nerve-wracking.

But I did go through with it. The mask hid my face very well,
an upswept affair in black satin ornamented with gold, some sort of
demoness in a black domino.

Afterwards, leaning back against the wall to catch his breath, his eyes focused on me again. "You want something from me," he said flatly.

"Of course I do," I said, leaning against the wall beside him as though also breathless. "You know what I want. A way out of this life. I want to return to Paris comfortably established. Do you think I like being a reader when I might be the mistress of a handsome and powerful man?"

Oudet digested that a moment, and I wondered if I had overplayed. "You're very calculating," he said.

"Of course I am," I said. "I must take care of myself. Do you think there are so many like you?"

At that he chuckled and put his arm about my waist as though to draw me near fondly. "You have no idea the heights I might rise to."

My heart beat a little faster. "Indeed I might," I said. "You're very talented. Moreau always said that you were the most talented young officer he had. I think perhaps he was a little jealous of so much potential in one so young." I tossed my head. "I don't see why you might not rise to the heights of command. A general, a marshal..."

Oudet snorted. "Little chance of that. That bastard Lannes has it in for me. Three years I've been a colonel, and I ought to have been made brigadier long before now! I ought to have been appointed an Imperial Aide de Camp a year ago. But the bastard hates me and so he passes over me with every opportunity."

"That's so unfair," I said.

"They're all the same, these new men who've embraced the trappings of aristocracy like they were born to it! They might have started out peasants, but now they're as spoiled and grand as any aristo. Now it's all caution and moderation. They're Bonaparte's cronies and that's all."

"You don't have to tell me that," I said, casting a silent apology to my friends that I wronged. "They're venal and small. I thought once that we would do better."

Oudet looked at me as though examining what of my face the mask exposed. He was only a year or two older than I, but in that moment he seemed very young, a faint sheen of sweat still clinging to his cheeks. "You're a failed idealist."

"Very failed," I said.

"You believed in the Republic."

"I still do," I said. "But that hope is vain. We have a new monarch now."

"That may not last forever," he said.

I started in alarm. "Jacques! Do not say such things. It's dangerous."

"Dangerous to speak of Caesar and to imagine the Ides of March?"

I did not need to pretend to shudder, as a long chill ran through me. "I don't dare imagine..."

"I do," he said grimly. "I dare to. And I am not alone."

"I can't believe that," I said. "It is too vague a hope."

"Take heart," he said. "Even now wheels are in motion. Caesar's tyranny may not long survive the efforts of true Republicans who yearn for freedom. There are more than you think who would embrace a worthy cause and follow a more worthy leader."

"Moreau?" I said.

Oudet smiled. "How about me? Moreau may think that I dance to his tune, but why shouldn't the student surpass the master?"

I blinked. In that moment, looking at him, I felt sorry for him.

Moreau was using him and when he was done Oudet would take the fall, this conceited young man who believed that he had the ability to rule a nation! He knew nothing of government, nothing of coalitions and politics, nothing of balancing the white horse and the black. He was not even a terribly talented soldier. He was simply a rather ordinary young man who thought too much of himself and who believed he should have prestige he had not earned. He was not willing to learn the work of governing, the complex business of treasuries and logistics, of trade and highways, of stocks and alliances. He simply wanted it given to him on a plate—to be a prince for no reason at all. Those men he envied had worked for their laurels.

And Moreau would use him up. When the time came, he would be a pawn in the game of princes.

"Ah, Jacques," I said, and for a moment there was real regret in my voice.

"You don't think I can do it?" His face hardened.

"I fear for you. That is all."

He nodded. "As a woman will. You have not lost womanly feeling."

He was, of course, still an ass. Just a doomed one being led to the slaughter, unknowing and unconsenting. I searched his face. "You promise me that there is hope?"

"There is," he said, and clasped my hand, which was unfortunately still sticky. "There is a fellowship of men devoted to restoring the Republic. I cannot tell you more, of course, as it would be far too dangerous for you, but you may rest assured that when our plans come to fruition that France will be once again remade. We will be purer, better! We will dig out for once and all the roots of superstition and tyranny that run so deep, beliefs that should have died with the Dark Ages."

"You are speaking of the Church," I said, while I wondered to myself how one could use a magical system while believing it superstition. Surely that wouldn't work? "And silly superstitions like magic."

"Oh that," Oudet said. "People don't understand what they're talking about. They imagine old witches wandering about curdling their neighbor's milk. Real magic is just a way to make things happen. Anyone can do it if you know how to command."

A shiver ran down my spine again. To command, to summon, and to believe one had dominion…. "You frighten me, Jacques," I said softly. "Have you never heard of Faust?"

"A fable of German poets," he dismissed. "We know what we're doing."

"And what is the price of Bonaparte's life?" I asked. It was hard to remain still when every muscle wanted to shake with chill. "Your soul?"

Oudet shook his head at my frailty. "You speak as though there are such things. Men have no souls to lose. That's just a pious platitude to make the weak feel better. There is no such thing."

"And so you may promise with impunity that which does not exist?"

He squeezed my hand. "Don't worry about me," he said. "We know what we're doing." He straightened up. "But we should return to the party before you're missed. I wouldn't want to get you into trouble with the Grand Duchess."

"Of course," I said.

Oudet left for Lannes' corps the next morning, and I sat quietly in my little room writing my report and putting it into cipher. The Emperor would be very interested in what I had to report, little as it was. I confirmed that Moreau was the leader of the conspiracy, or at least one of the leaders, and told him all I knew about the plot. I assured him that Oudet did not suspect me and that I would continue to work on him. It would be easier, I said, if he were nearer by. He could not be sent to Florence very often, and our correspondence took a long time.

When I had finished my report for the Emperor and burned my notes in the grate I began a second letter, this one not in cipher and hence composed very carefully.

My dear Marshal Lannes,

The visitor you recommended to me has arrived and departed, and I am even more greatly interested in the theatrical entertainment he suggests. It seems that it is to be a production of Shakespeare's Julius Caesar. He suggests that I may in fact be perfect for the role of Portia to his Brutus! Alas, I do not yet know who the other main players are to be, other than the title role. I am certain, however, that strong actors will be cast as Cassius, Casca, et cetera, and that the production will be entirely worthy of your interest. I do know that the old trouper I once performed with shall appear in the role of Octavian, who of course reaps the harvest in the end, but that is a minor role in this play.

I appreciate so much that you have taken the time to recommend this man to me out of the goodness of your heart and concern for my well-being.

Please know that I am ever in your debt, and your humble servant,

Madame St. Elme

I hoped that all made sense to Lannes, but it ought to. After all, he had once played this drama in earnest as Asinius Pollio and ought to respond with as much dread as I! In Boulogne, when the Lodge stood against the witches of England, we had invoked the story of Julius Caesar and his successful invasion of England. Now it should be little surprise if the Philadelphes invoked the same story. Indeed, perhaps their working could piggyback on ours, strengthened by the correspondences we had already laid down. That would be a terrible irony, but there was nothing we could do about that now. Julius Caesar was a story everyone knew, the assassination of a tyrant who would be king by a group of freedom-loving republicans.

Of course fewer people remembered the story of the fifteen years of civil war that followed, tens of thousands of Romans and subject peoples dying as purge after purge and battle after battle swept across the Roman world as the conspirators and the other powerful men of Rome fought one another. In the end, the conflagration consumed empires. Egypt, the richest and oldest of the kingdoms, had died last, her heir murdered and her queen a suicide. Marcus Antonius had gone down, and Pollio had finished his life in obscurity while Octavian and Agrippa danced on graves. Someone won, but it wasn't Brutus and Cassius. The Republic ended and the Empire began under an emperor far more cruel than Julius Caesar had ever been.

A fine model, I thought. I wished that Oudet had learned a bit more history before he invoked it. Brutus killed Caesar, and then he failed and died while Octavian swept the board.

And so would Moreau. He risked nothing, safely in New Jersey. Oudet and his friends would run all the risks and, on the off chance they succeeded, Moreau could sweep in as the promised leader. If they failed and were shot for treason, it was no harm to Moreau. It was, I thought, a typical Moreau plan—clever, and risking nothing that actually belonged to him.

I packed up both letters and went down to give them to the Grand Duchess, who would see that they went out by courier immediately.

Elisa was still in her boudoir wearing a wrapper of sprigged India cotton. Her little girl, a sprightly thing four years old, was jumping up and down on the featherbed, falling over and begging to be tickled, which Elisa was indulging with a great deal of laughter while the child's nurse looked on. For a wonder the nurse was young and cheerful and didn't look stern at all.

Elisa plucked herself out of the pile of covers, managing to show a great deal of leg in the process, and smoothed her hair down as the child jumped and yelled for more. "You look terrible," she said to me with something quite a lot like sympathy in her eyes.

I didn't think that I did. "I'm sorry," I said.

She scooped the child off the bed and handed her to her nurse despite pleas and giggles. "Mother has something she must do," she said firmly, and I was reminded once again that she actually did rule a province. "Go on now. I will see you in a little while."

The child pouted but allowed herself to be led out by her nurse. When the door closed behind them Elisa turned to me again, taking the proffered letters without glancing at them. "I hope it was worth it."

"I hope so too," I said candidly. I felt unaccountably choked up at what was merely a friendly word. I had spent far too many months here with no friend at all, with no lover to confide in and no one to trust or laugh with.

Elisa shook her head. "My brother should not ask this of you."

"I knew what the mission required when I agreed to it," I said. "He did not deceive me in any way. Nor did he tell me how to accomplish it."

"He bound you with praises rather than threats." Elisa laid the letters on the corner of the dressing table. "So what do you do now?"

"I wait," I said. "Oudet has returned to his regiment. I'll write to him and continue to fish for information. Hopefully he'll be sent back here soon, but I can't imagine it will be sooner than a month."

"Then you will take a few days for yourself," Elisa said decisively. "There is no need for you to attend on me when he isn't here to see the masquerade. If you wish, you could go take the waters or something."

I blinked. I had no idea where I would go. I knew no one in Italy besides Ana, who was now comfortably in Naples considerably further away than I could go in a few days. "That is very generous, Your Grace, but..."

"Go on then," Elisa said, waving a hand. "I'll see you on Tuesday. In the meantime I'll get these letters on their way today."

"You are all kindness, Your Grace," I said, and curtsied myself out.

And what would I do with myself? I went back to my cheerless little room and sat on the bed. This was Italy, not France. An unchaperoned woman did not have very many entertainments open to her. Besides, it was the dead of winter and raining hard, which made taking to the open road seem rather less attractive than otherwise. What I wanted was to be in Spain with Michel, preferably in garrison and tucked into a huge featherbed of our own, with nothing to do for a few days except please each other. Barring that, I would like to be at home in Paris with my friends and my own things, with restaurants to eat in and amusements of all kinds, or at least with my hearth and people to share good brandy with. Both of those were utterly impossible.

What I should like that was within reason was a change of scene from this miserable room, a luxurious inn with good food, and a long, warm bath. That at least was possible.

For Carlo, not Ida.

And that was an idea worth pursuing. Perhaps Charles Van Aylde should take in the sights of Florence, or at least enjoy a fine hotel for a few days. It would be simple enough to use the papers I already had for him and I had Carlo Tolstoy's wardrobe. The fading woman on the make who read for the Grand Duchess would disappear for a few days and there would be Charles instead.

Charles Van Aylde was a very dangerous-looking young man. His fair hair was a little longer than the current fashion, brushed back from his forehead and darkened just a little with pomade, a dark honey color between blond and brown. He had a dueling scar above his brow and he no longer moved like a dandy. His polished hussar boots had no spurs, but he walked like he was wearing them, the slight slide of the foot with each step taken first onto the ball of one's foot. He walked like cavalry, and no one would have been surprised to find out that he had been.

His evening clothes were conservative for Paris, which of course meant that in Florence he seemed the height of style, midnight blue coat and a waistcoat with gold and blue stripes and an excess of snowy white linen. If his cravat was tied in such a way that it filled out the neck of his waistcoat entirely, disguising the cut of it, perhaps that was how it was done in Paris these days. He had a room in the best hotel and immediately had the concierge secure a stall for the opera.

I had been in Florence for eight months without setting foot in a theater. Madame St. Elme, impecunious reader for the Grand Duchess, had neither the money nor the leisure to go to the theater. Besides, in Italy respectable women did not go alone, and other, closer companions of the Grand Duchess were always chosen to fill out her box.

The opera was Don Giovanni, which I had never seen and always wanted to. I have never had to pretend a love for theater in general and opera in particular, fashionable or not, from the most elaborate productions in Paris to the theater of the camps. Don Giovanni was reckoned one of Mozart's best, a brooding masterpiece that, though it was more than twenty years old, still proved extremely popular to produce, possibly because it had a leading role for the baritone, who usually was stuck with the villain's parts. The overture was glorious. I simply closed my eyes in my stall in the second tier and gave myself over to enjoyment, for a moment laying aside all thought of my mission or my work. Beauty transcends all momentary pain.

So engrossed in the opera was I that I did not even look around at the other boxes until the inter'act. To my surprise, there was one box occupied by a woman alone, a box in the first tier below and somewhat closer to the stage, so that I saw its sole occupant in profile. She was younger than I, perhaps twenty-five, with smooth black hair drawn back into a simple knot at the back of her neck and held with pearl pins. She wore a white gown also lush in its simplicity, for where on another it might have seemed plain, on her it served to exalt her perfect figure much as a white tablecloth sets off beautifully prepared food. Her breasts were half exposed by the square neckline, at least from above, smooth and ripe, ornamented by a rope of pearls holding a teardrop that sat just at her cleavage. Her fan was folded, clasped between her hands like a rosary, and she leaned forward in her chair, her gloved forearms resting on the edge of the box as she looked over the edge toward the stage, rapt attention apparent in every line of her movements. As the curtain swung shut she blinked like a dreamer awakening, stretching as she looked around like a cat.

I couldn't help but catch her eye. How could one look away from such perfection?

Instead of blushing she looked straight back, not with coquetry, but with interest, as though she were trying to decide who and what I was. I made a graceful bow to her from the box, all attention. She did look away then, turning her head and lifting her program as though to consult it.

I did as any man of fashion must—I rapped for the concierge and asked him who the lady was.

"Ah, Signore," he said with much amusement. "I should have thought that you would ask! Her name is Camilla Spinochi, but whether she should be addressed as Signora or not is a mystery to all."

"She is very beautiful," I said. "Is she then a stranger to Florence? Surely a woman so beautiful is married to some hideous old man!"

He laughed at my little joke. "One would think! It is always they who can afford the beauties! But she is not a respectable woman, as you can see. She is at the opera without so much as a cicisbe'o, what you call a cavalier servante. As to whether or not she is married, who can say? She is the mistress of one of your French officers, one Colonel Deshume. But he is not with her tonight."

"Not a respectable woman," I said. Which would explain why she had not been introduced to the Grand Duchess. Officers did not introduce their Italian mistresses at court. Madame St. Elme did not know her. But Charles Van Aylde might. "Do you think she would take offense if I visited her in the inter'act?"

The concierge spread his hands. "Signore, a good woman would. But a bad woman? I would be more worried that your Colonel Deshume might challenge you to an affair of honor."

"I see," I said. I did not want to be the sort of man who managed to give offense on first meeting, having seen rather too much of that sort myself lately.

"However," the concierge said brightly, "There is of course a way around it, if some respectable lady were to introduce you."

"Alas," I said. "I have only just arrived in Florence and I know no one who might do so."

"There is a lady, a former singer and entertainer." He looked at me with a waggle of eyebrow so as to make sure I understood the implications entirely. "Signora Martinaldo. She will be happy to introduce you to the lady if you are generous."

"I see," I said. "So if you will take some small token of my esteem to the Signora, then she will provide an introduction to Signora Spinochi?"

"You understand me perfectly, Signore," he said. "That is how things are done."

With a sigh I drew forth my purse and peeled off notes, handing him two for his own trouble. "I shall breathlessly await Signora Martinaldo."

"I will only be a moment," the concierge said, bowing out.

Of course he was several moments. The curtains were opening on the second act when he returned. The lady with him must have been sixty-five, dripping black lace and diamonds, including an extremely overwrought mantilla that made her look like the duenna in an opera. She looked like that rarest of women, an old bawd who lives comfortably and has not gotten hard.

I rose to greet her and she sat down in the second seat, arranging her rather ample self comfortably. "I understand you're another young Frenchman who wants to meet Camilla."

"I do."

"I don't arrange her affairs. She does that herself. And very credibly, too." The curtain was rising on the act, and she peered at the stage through a lorgnette. "Colonel Deshume keeps her very comfortably. And he's a good shot."

"So people keep telling me," I said, stretching out my legs. "But surely he won't shoot me for meeting her."

Signora Martinaldo shrugged. "Who can say what a Frenchman will do? I'll introduce you to Camilla, but I do warn you that she came here from Rome with Deshume and has been with him for several years. I don't think she's easily swayed."

"Better and better," I said. "I respect a woman who is constant in her affections."

"Then let's be on with it," she said, getting up. "I've told you there are no guarantees. It's an introduction."

"I understand, Signora," I said, and followed her out the door and down the stairs to the tier below, where she knocked upon the door of the box.

"Come in." Her voice was low and melodious. She turned around in her chair to see who it was, her face relaxing when she saw Signora Martinaldo, and then tensing again when she saw mine.

"Camilla, my dear, I'd like you to meet a friend of mine. He is a very distinguished *capo Franchese*, a famous duelist. This is Monsieur...."

"Charles Van Aylde," I said, taking her gloved hand in mine and bending over it. "I am enchanted."

"Are you?" she said, looking from me to the Signora and back. She wasn't fooled for a moment. "And what do you duel with?"

"My wits, most of the time," I said, releasing her hand. She was just as lovely in person, and the scent of tuberoses hung about her as though she had anointed her breasts with cologne. I was really quite taken with those breasts. "But they seem to have deserted me in your presence."

Her eyes flew to my forehead. "Someone's wits are sharp then."

"Sadly, that was a bayonet at the Battle of Eylau," I said.

"Are you in the army?"

"I was." I spread my hands. "But of course now we are at peace. So my humble services are not needed."

Camilla's eyes narrowed. They were almost black, rimmed in black kohl to make them seem darker still. "I am not sure I believe you."

"I assure you, Signora, that I am not in the army at present." I put my hand to my breast. "My word of honor."

"I see." She laughed. "And your desire to make my acquaintance is purely honorable?"

"My intention is to seduce you," I said. "But whether or not I am successful, it's a pleasant game, isn't it?"

At that she laughed again, glancing back at Signora Martinaldo with an expression that was pure mischief. "This one's saucy."

The Signora shrugged. "He's a rogue, and not a rich one for all his silver tongue."

"The rich ones have no need of it," I said.

They both laughed again, earning disapproving looks from the surrounding boxes.

"Very well," Camilla said. "You may watch the rest of the show with me. With the curtains open."

"I shall be very good," I promised, sitting down beside her. "In whatever capacity you prefer."

CAMILLA

We did not talk much through the remainder of the opera. Both of us wanted to watch. It was as beautiful and as chilling as I had heard, and my skin crawled when Don Giovanni was offered one last chance to repent of his wicked life and said instead that he was not afraid and that he should die as he had lived, libertine and unrepentant. He reminded me of Victor Moreau, a bit. Perhaps I had loved him just a little.

But I was not going to think about Moreau tonight, nor about the mission that had once again brought me into collision with him. Instead I made myself very witty and agreeable to Camilla, and hushed up in the good parts of the opera that we might enjoy them. I was quite aware of how tedious it was to watch with a man who believed that he, rather than the players, should be the center of attention!

When at last the curtains closed after the final bow, I turned to Camilla once again. "Would you do me the honor of joining me for a little late supper?"

"No," she said, and smiled anyway. "M. Van Aylde, you are a charming companion. But I know perfectly well what 'a little late supper' means!"

"Can you believe I would take advantage of you?" I asked.

"I believe you are a transparent rogue, and that half of what you have told me tonight are lies and the other half may as well be." Camilla folded her fan, her eyes dancing. "And so I am not about to accompany you anywhere. I am devoted to my Alfred, and I certainly would not want any rumor of misconduct to reach him."

"So it will be all right as long as he doesn't hear of it," I said.

Camilla laughed. "There will be nothing to hear of."

I put my hand to my heart. "Tragically. So tell me of this Alfred.

What sort of paragon is he?"

"He's a colonel in the French army, a cuirassier if you must know. We have been together for nearly four years, and I intend for this to be a permanent arrangement."

"Ah," I said. "Very serious then. Lucky man!"

"You may have gotten the wrong impression from Signora Martinaldo," she said.

"I did think that she…" There was no delicate way to put it.

"Once owned a house of ill repute?" Camilla spread her fan again. Around us the theater was empying. "She did. Nine years ago she was a madam of some note, but she has sold out now. I ran away from a convent, you see, and threw myself on the protection of a Frenchman. Better Signora Martinaldo's convent than the other!"

"And then you met Alfred Deshume," I said. "Who proved true."

"As I said, we have been together nearly four years. He brought me to Florence that I might be with him."

"I understand quite well," I said. "And do you like the life of the baggage train? It is a difficult life, but it has its rewards, not the least of which is sincere attachment if that is what one has. But more than that, it is so much more than the walls closing in around one!"

"Precisely," she said. "When I was in the convent I felt I couldn't breathe. I would never be free, not so much as a moment, not so much as choosing my own dress for the day or spending the afternoon in the open air!"

"Much less not knowing what will happen, what scene might be over the next rise, walking breathlessly into morning. The bad is all worth it for that. To escape from the circumscribed limits of a woman's life."

Camilla looked at me closely. "How is it that you know these things?"

"How do you think?" I asked levelly.

She studied my face carefully, her eyes moving. "It is nearly midnight, and there is no trace of beard on your chin."

"Perhaps I shaved before the opera."

"Perhaps you are one of the castrati yourself."

"Do you think?"

"No." Her eyes met mine. "I think you are a woman dressed as a man. You carry it off very well." She folded her fan again. "But why you would pay me elaborate compliments is beyond me."

"Perhaps I mean them," I said. There was no one in earshot, a few people still milling around down on the floor. Two stagehands had come out to quench the footlights.

"To what end?"

"Pleasure," I said with a shrug. "You know that you are very beautiful. It's certainly not a surprise to you that one might want to make love to you."

"Girl on girl?" Camilla laughed. "Like a Double Treat in a bawdy house?"

"Have you never done it?" I asked. "You might enjoy it."

"Might I?"

"Some women do," I said with Charles' elegant half bow. "All of the pleasure of being with a man with none of the danger. It's not as though I can get you pregnant. In fact, I don't understand why attentive mothers don't suggest it as a solution to their young daughters. Much more realistic to expect than chastity, and good practice, all in all. One learns what one likes and how to ask for it."

Camilla's mouth opened and shut.

"Besides," I said negligently, "If your Alfred does hear about it, it hardly counts, does it? My lover wouldn't think so for a moment."

"Your lover?" Camilla asked. "Your man wouldn't be angry?"

"If he could see me this very moment he would be both immensely amused and excited," I said truthfully. "If Michel could see me coming on to you dressed like this, it would make his month."

"How extraordinary," Camilla said, but I could see she was considering it.

"Think on it," I said. "And perhaps I will see you here again tomorrow night?"

"Perhaps," she said, and with that I had to be content.

She did turn up, of course. This time I insinuated myself into her box early in the first act. She would not allow me to drive her home, as the coachman would talk, but she let me in when I came around to her apartments later. "Just a taste," she said. "Because I'm curious."

"Of course," I said, and kissed her. She bent into me like a willow, lips soft and yielding opening beneath mine in an open-mouthed kiss, sweet as honeybread with the spice of cinnamon beneath. Passionate, yes, and far from innocent. A kiss is a kiss.

Her hair was like satin when I tangled my hands in it, pulled the pins and let it flow like a dark river to her waist. She caught her breath as I worked one nipple with my thumb through her dress, then pushed her back against the wall with my knee between her thighs and kissed my way down to it. A little tugging and it was free of the low cut bodice, red and pointed and obscenely displayed.

"Look at it," I said, and met her eyes, deliberately licking it with the tip of my tongue so that her back arched and she let out a little cry. "It's a filthy thing to do, isn't it?" I pulled at it, stretching the nipple and letting it go, teasing and releasing, all the while watching her face. "You want more, don't you?"

"Yes," Camilla said breathlessly.

"Then take off your dress," I said.

I had her over the divan in her little parlor, petticoat around her waist and chemise unbuttoned down to it, legs spread still in their pretty white stockings caught with garters above the knee. Her hair was very soft and fine, and when I spread her privates each fold was purpled with desire.

"Slowly," she said, her head flung back against the arm of the divan, her hair around her in disarray.

"As you wish," I said. I teased every nook and cranny again and again, now faster and now more softly, exploring each damp soft fold, brushing fingers against her pearl and then pressing ever so gently just behind her opening. The muscle there shook and her back arched, an incomprehensible sound coming from her lips.

"Just there," I said. A little more pressure. And then none. "Tell me you want it."

"God damn it," Camilla said, which I took for an answer.

One hand there, the thumb caressing soft flesh, and the other on her pearl, then a sudden rhythmic pressure.

She shrieked, bucking, her whole body tensing and releasing, hands clenching on her petticoats in tight fists.

"Like that," I said, and pushed her to it again.

It was glorious to watch her lose herself completely, to see private muscles tighten in a long, abandoned spasm. Glorious too to watch sense come back into her face, to see her relax boneless as a cat, a sleepy smile of satiation coming to her face. "And what do you want?" she said.

"A turn of the same," I said, hastily unbuttoning the drop front panel of my evening pants. "Please."

She lifted my shirt hem, man's clothes and woman's cunny, slick with my answering need. "Show me."

"Like this," I said, and seized her hand and put it where I needed it.

She'd been with men often enough, and she was a quick study. No doubt she'd done this to herself night after night in her narrow convent bed. And that thought was enough to tip me over the edge—Camilla in her little virgin cell, the moon coming in through a barred window while she sweated and twisted, working her fresh desires for all they were worth, white ass riding up as she spread her own juices.

It didn't take long, not aroused as I was. That was enough. I screamed out something, I don't know what, and came for her twisting fingers, my eyes closed against the darkness.

When I opened them she was leaning on one elbow looking at me curiously. "So who are you really?" she asked.

"Ida St. Elme," I said. "I'm a reader for the Grand Duchess." The world was still spinning a little.

"And you used to travel with the army?"

"I did," I said, getting my breath back. "With my lover. But he's in Spain now, and I have to have something to do until he gets back. Which I hope to heaven is soon!"

"You don't like it then?"

"The Grand Duchess is lovely," I said. "But the work is tedious. I won't be sorry to be rid of it."

"I see," she said. She didn't say the obvious—will he come back for you? That's one of those things you never say. It's the code.

"But I am here and must make the best of it," I said.

Camilla smirked. "And this would be what that is?"

"Why not?" I asked. "It is very nice, isn't it?"

"You do have a point," she agreed.

My liaison with Camilla definitely improved my sojourn in Florence, and not only for the obvious reasons. Madame St. Elme had no friend, a reader rather than a companion, not quite a servant but subject to their rules. When I had hours not spent attending on the Grand Duchess or waiting the weeks between letters from Oudet, I now had something to occupy myself. Signora Spinochi, as she was styled, was also less than a respectable woman but more than a servant. She too was outside good society, a mistress rather than a wife, an independent woman. There was no reason that I might not spend a free half-day in her company or that we might not attend the theater together. After all, her Colonel Deshume could not possibly be jealous of a female friend!

He was, I discovered soon enough, the commander of the French garrison in Florence, a small detachment of men sent to Elisa by her brother mainly to perform police duties. I met him before long, an energetic man of some thirty-five years, tall and dark-haired, with a decided limp. He was also missing the last two fingers of his left hand, a wound that didn't seem to slow him down much but perhaps accounted for why a competent soldier had been sent to garrison duty in some peaceful place rather than given a line regiment. I rather liked him.

As for bed sports, I thought I was more taken with Camilla than she with me. Her interest was purely in Charles, and without my male clothing she seemed decidedly lukewarm in her attraction. The thrill for her was Charles, the gallant beau that at the same time asked her to risk nothing of the security and affection she had found. A real male lover might be a disaster. A woman dressed as a man would probably only cause Deshumes to scratch his head in bemusement, if the thought ever occurred to him at all, which I doubt it did. Sometimes he came home when I was there, though mercifully not in bed, and he behaved with unfailing and absentminded politeness, as a man will when he would like a quiet evening alone with his established paramour and she has a friend chatting. Still, it was good to have a friend, even if it seemed that as Carnival ended and spring crept in that it was likely that the sensual part of our friendship would peter out soon.

That is where we were at the beginning of April when I received yet another letter from Oudet.

...you will be delighted to learn that I have at last been transferred! I

*am to take command of a regiment in the Army of Italy under Eugene de
Beauharnais, where perhaps I shall have cause to expect advancement.
Moreover, as we are to watch and wait for an Austrian advance from the
Tyrol, this will put me very near to you. I expect to see you much more
frequently in the future....*

"Oh good," I said sourly, folding the missive. I had told the
Emperor that it would be much easier to pump Oudet if I saw him
more often, so I could hardly complain that he'd taken me at my
word and transferred the blasted man to the Army of Italy! Now I
should indeed have to deal with him more frequently!

Meanwhile, Michel's letters were sporadic in the extreme. I did
not think this came from any lack of passion, or at least I hoped not.
There seemed to be no want of warmth in them when they came,
but now I might only see one every four weeks or less. I couldn't
berate him for not writing more often when every bit of news we
had from Spain was bad, and so I worried in silence.

Oudet arrived in person the next week. I would not go with him
to his billet, pleading decency, but we did steal off to the unused
morning room late at night for the expected events. I had steeled
myself for this and even brought the English letters rather than
relying on him to do so, passing them off with a smile and a word
about how I must have a care even though I had no doubt he was to
be a great man.

Afterward he was expansive, playing with my hair and
complimenting my beauty.

"I'm glad it pleases you," I said. "It's merely luck, not some sort
of magic. Though I'd like an enchantment to turn back time and be
twenty again!"

"Real magic doesn't do things like that," he said seriously. "It's
not for petty things like that. Real magic is about the fate of nations."

"Like war," I said.

"Magic is war," Oudet replied. "You would not believe me if I
told you the things that are true, the way occult armies meet and
clash."

"It sounds fantastic," I said. I leaned up on my shoulder on
the rug in the morning room in front of the empty fireplace. "Oh

Jacques! Do you really mean to give me hope that the Republic may be restored?"

"I can give you more than hope," he said, his hand sliding down my back. "I can give you assurance. There are no less than thirty good men engaged in this great work, and some of them at the highest levels of government. All of us have dedicated our lives to the overthrow of this tyrant! Moreover, once we are done, we will set about establishing an entirely different social order, one in which there is no superstition or idolatry and society is divided purely for the good of the people."

I looked at him with shining eyes. "I wish I could believe you! I wish it with all my heart! But I don't see how it can be done. Thirty men is so few compared to an empire!"

"Ah, but such men," Oudet said. "A cabinet minister, a marshal, how many do we need? It's having the right men at the right time. And of course this whole edifice is rotten. Bonaparte has no real heir, either in the flesh or to his power. If he dies, the entire thing collapses."

"That is probably true," I said thoughtfully. "But surely assassination is terribly risky!"

He shrugged. "The assassin must be pretty much expendable. But there always are men who are."

"I suppose."

"After all, an agent doesn't really expect any loyalty from their employer," Oudet said. "It's like caring about what your servant thinks of you. They're not anyone important."

"Who's to say who will be important in ten years?" I asked, and heard too late in my voice the echo of what Bonaparte had asked me in Milan. That was nearly ten years ago, and now I was a confidential agent in his service. I did not think I meant nothing to him, or that he would throw my life away more lightly than that of anyone else who served him.

Oudet looked at me sharply and I knew I had misstepped. "Not you," he said. "Despite being ambitious."

"I am ambitious," I agreed. "I have told you what I want—to be once again the mistress of an important man in Paris, the queen of fashion with a salon of my own. Is that so much to desire?"

"Not really," he said. But I could see in his eyes that he never meant to give me even that. I was just good enough for now.

I had little time to see him again or to push for any further information as he had to report back to his regiment almost immediately. The day before, the tenth of April, 1809, Austria had invaded Bavaria, which since the days after Hohenlinden had been our ally. We were at war again. It was to be expected that the Austrians would also attack south through the Tyrol, and Prince Eugene de Beauharnais, Josephine's son who commanded the Army of Italy, moved to intercept them. It did not go well, and he was forced to retreat nearly to Verona in order to regroup.

This sent an absolute frisson of terror through the Grand Duchess' ladies, though Elisa herself remained tranquil. "I have every confidence in the courage of our men," she said firmly. I was somewhat less confident privately. Our armies were equally matched in numbers, but the Austrian commander was Archduke John who we had so thoroughly routed at Hohenlinden. I expected he had learned a good bit in nine years. Though I heard nothing but good of Eugene, it was certainly true that he owed his command to his stepfather and had no real experience. He might be a bright young man, and indeed he probably was since he was Josephine's son, but that didn't make up for the kind of experience of war that was so critically necessary.

It was a tense two weeks before we heard that Eugene had this time fought an indecisive battle at Caldiero. Our losses were relatively light, but so were those of the Austrians. Mysteriously, however, Archduke John seemed to have had enough and began to withdraw toward the border with Eugene in pursuit. Many of the ladies concluded this was due to Eugene's skill, but I doubted it. Surely Archduke John had not invaded Italy only to turn around and run away because of the loss of less than fifteen hundred men!

"Something is happening," I said to Camilla. "Something we don't know about in Bavaria."

It was, of course. The Emperor had defeated another Austrian army at Eckmuhl, and Archduke John had been recalled. Meanwhile, Dalmatia was taking advantage of Austrian distraction to rise in rebellion against their Austrian overlords and, with the assistance of our General Marmont, were pushing the Austrians back first from Stoichevich and Gospić and then finally to Graz. The Austrians were considerably over-extended and the campaign in Italy was proving too ambitious.

Eugene tailed them closely and caught them at the Piave River, doing some considerable damage and capturing fifteen guns before their main body withdrew toward Carniola in Slovenia on the eighth of May. On the sixteenth, he caught them again at Tarvis at the foot of the mountains as Archduke John attempted to cross over to Graz and join forces with Austrian troops there. Again Eugene mauled him severely.

Couriers came and went. I had made my reports and sent them already, telling the Emperor what I knew—a cabinet minister, a marshal supposedly in the plot, but no names. Thirty men, but I did not yet know who. It was no doubt a very frustrating report to receive, but it was the best I could do. This was not the kind of mission that was easily accomplished, and the only way to do it was to go on and hope that he would impart greater confidences as time passed. I had only been with him twice for a few days each time. There was a limit to what he might reasonably have said.

I also sent a private letter to Lannes. I did not like the things that Oudet said about occult workings, and while I had no idea how much was bragging, I didn't like the sound of it. Lannes was the closest thing we had to a Magister and he ought to know. At least if he were advised perhaps the Lodge members who were with him in the field could put together a general working for the Emperor's protection.

I did not know if he never read it, or if he was simply too distracted to reply. Perhaps it arrived too late. Lannes was mortally wounded at Aspern-Essling on the twenty-second, a pitched battle on the banks of the Danube in the main theater of war. Both of his legs were amputated and he lingered in great suffering for eight days until he died.

It was the death Michel had feared, and hearing of it I had to go to my room and weep. It was not hard to believe Lannes was dead. I had lived with death for so long that there was no sense of unreality, no doubt. I simply wept because I had liked him and I would miss him, and doubly because of his suffering. That I could imagine too well. I wished it had at least been clean, like Jean-Baptiste's brother beheaded by a cannon ball in a moment.

I wished I might reach for someone's arms, but I could not expect that even from Camilla, friend that she was. I could not explain to her how I had known him. I could not speak of Boulogne or of the Lodge, of how he had trusted me in Boulogne or decided in my favor to join the circle at the expense of his own Magister's disapproval.

And so I said nothing as usual and went about my duties with a smile.

TREASON

I had written to Oudet too, of course, saying that I was terribly worried about him and hoped that he was well. I didn't dare fish too much in a letter. Therefore I was surprised when his answering letter to me gave me more than I had hoped.

...we will take Graz in a few days, of that I have no doubt. And then what? On to Vienna? Perhaps after the Austrians are suppressed for once and all, there will be the hoped-for changes we spoke of. I am assured by good friends that Marshal Bernadotte thinks most highly of me, and that I may hope for considerable promotion when his star rises...

I had to read it three times to make certain he had just said what I thought he said. My heart pounded in my breast. I had been here thirteen months cultivating this man, and at last I had something worthwhile.

I folded the letter again and tucked it in my breast and ran downstairs to catch the Grand Duchess dressing for dinner. I barged in regardless of her maid, who looked up startled.

Elisa regarded me calmly in the mirror, her long neck ornamented by a parure of emeralds.

"I need a courier to Austria immediately," I said. "To find the Emperor wherever he is."

The message was one word long: Bernadotte.

A few days later I was reading to the Grand Duchess. I believe it was a romance of some kind, a pastoral about young love growing untrammeled by civilization, when Elisa's major domo opened the morning room door rather apologetically. "Your Grace, Colonel Deshumes is here and says that the matter is urgent."

I looked up from my book, stopping in mid-sentence. The Colonel followed him in, four soldiers behind him. His expression was grim and he made his bow very stiffly. "I am sorry to interrupt you, Your Grace."

"What has happened?" Elisa asked, not starting from her chair, yet braced for fatal news of some military reverse. Her brother? Oh, surely, not that!

"I have a warrant for the arrest of one of your ladies," he said. "It is necessary to execute it immediately. Madame St. Elme, you will come with us."

I rose to my feet very slowly, utterly uncomprehending. "What?"

"What foolishness is this?" Elisa asked. "You can't arrest my ladies!"

Deshumes made his bow again. "I regret to say that I can, Your Grace. Madame St. Elme is wanted for very serious crimes."

Everyone in the room was staring at me. "I have no idea what you mean," I stammered.

"Let me see that," Elisa snapped, reaching for the paper he proffered. She read and then looked at me. Her face offered nothing.

"I have done nothing wrong," I protested, my arms at my sides like the heroine of a tragic play. "Surely there is some mistake!"

"Madame, you will go with the Colonel," Elisa said. "I am sure this will all be straightened out."

"But..."

"Come," Deshumes said and took my arm firmly but gently. "Don't make this any harder on yourself."

"Of course," I said. "But will you not at least tell me what I am charged with."

Deshumes' eyes met mine starkly. "Treason against the Empire," he said.

I was held in our garrison's jail rather than in the city, one cell which I had to myself. If there were others they were in another place, as I could not see them or hear them. The cell had a straw mattress on a frame, a basin and pitcher, and a rickety table and chair, quite nice as prisons go, I understand. There was a high barred window that was fully eight feet up. When I stood on the table I could just see out—the inside of the curtain wall and a patch of sky above.

Deshumes refused to tell me any more, saying that I would have ample time to discuss it later. I could not imagine what had happened. Unless somehow Bernadotte had learned that I accused him and turned the tables...But that was ridiculous! His best bet if accused was to simply deny everything. I had no evidence except Oudet's innuendo. Treating me as a threat would only make the accusation seem more credible. Besides, how would he know? Unless he intercepted couriers to the Emperor himself....

My thoughts chased themselves around and around. How could I have been framed? And by whom?

Evening came and then the next day. My meals were brought and the slops bucket emptied by a private who clearly knew nothing at all.

"May I please speak to Colonel Deshumes?" I asked him.

"I'll tell him," the man said, and left.

Night came again. I slept fitfully for all that it was warm enough. It was high summer and more likely too hot than too cold, though the stone walls did keep it somewhat cooler.

In the morning I was attempting to put my hair in order when I heard the jangle of keys in the corridor outside, no doubt the private bringing my breakfast. Instead, he let in Camilla.

She looked peaked and flustered, her shawl off one arm and trailing on the dirty floor. I had never been so glad to see her.

"Camilla!" I exclaimed and was happy to be claimed by her affectionate embrace, like one dear friend who visits another in great misfortune.

The private went back to the door. "Call when you want to come out," he said. Clearly he was a little in awe of the colonel's lady.

When the door was closed Camilla pushed back and looked at me. "Ida, how in the world did you get yourself into this mess?"

"What mess is it?" I asked. "I do not even know why I am accused! Surely I should have been told something by now."

Her dark eyes were very serious. "You've been accused of high treason," she said. "And there is evidence. And I have terrible news for you. The officer you were seeing with the Army of Italy was killed in action at the battle of Wagram a few days ago. Apparently he had letters from you urging him to treason and making it clear you were complicit in an attempt to assassinate the Emperor."

"What?" I could not even begin to list the reasons. My mind latched onto one thing. "Oudet is dead?"

She put her arm around me to offer her condolences. "I'm so sorry, Ida. He was a very brave man. They said he was shot from his horse in the front of a cavalry charge and he did not survive. It was in the bulletin too."

"He's dead?" All that work, all those months of insinuating myself, and now it was worth nothing.

"I'm so sorry," Camilla said.

"So am I," I said. "Letters?" Of course there were letters! How many times had I written to him egging him on, trying to get some further confidence from him?

"His commanding officer was packing up his effects and was appalled," Camilla said. "They seemed to indicate that you were in some sort of conspiracy with him and possibly with General Moreau. I suppose it's credible because you used to be Moreau's mistress...."

I looked at her levelly. "You believe it's true."

"I don't know what to believe," Camilla said, releasing me and pacing away. "Alfred says that he's ordered to hold you for transport to Paris. That this is a matter for the Ministry of Police. The Grand Duchess does not have jurisdiction."

"For the Minister of Police," I said. "Fouché." Fouché had no love for me since I'd betrayed him to Josephine over the Tallien affair some five years ago.

"He said the letters were very damning." Camilla turned and looked at me. "But I thought that you should hear of your lover's death from a friend. I thought that was best."

"You don't believe me."

"You haven't denied it."

I took a deep breath. "Camilla, I give you my word that those letters were not what they appeared. I give you my word that I am as loyal to the Emperor as anyone. I am not a traitor." I held her eyes. "I'm not."

She looked away.

Fouché. He had been a Jacobin once. Was he the cabinet minister that Oudet had meant? I could never get it out of Oudet now. But I was quite certain that if I were remanded to Fouché's custody I should never go to trial. Perhaps I would commit suicide in my cell and it would be very suspicious, just like the deaths of the agents before me. There was only one way to stop this, and for that I needed Camilla.

"I need your help," I said.

Camilla shook her head. "I'm not going to do anything that would compromise Alfred. You know that."

"I'm not asking you to," I said. "All I'm asking is that you send a letter for me in the next packet of dispatches." Elisa's hands were tied. Without her direct link to the Emperor, without the dispatches coming from her, I had no hope a letter to the Emperor would ever reach him. Michel was in Spain. A letter routed through him would reach the Emperor but it might take two months. By that time I might be dead. But there was one person I could count on, one person who stood steps away from the Emperor. "Will you send a letter for me?" I asked.

Camilla wavered.

"I will let you read it if you like. It will only say what has happened—that I have been arrested and what I have been accused of."

"If that is all," she said. Her mouth pursed, but I thought she would do it. "Who is it to?"

"An Imperial Aide de Camp, General Honoré-Charles Reille."

After Camilla left I lay down on the straw mattress. It was high summer, hot and still. Through the square of the high window the sky was almost white with heat. I did not expect to sleep, but I did. I slept, and I dreamed.

In my dreams I walked along the right bank of the Seine, the Tuileries on my left and the river on my right. A man walked beside me, brown haired and ordinary looking in a dark blue uniform coat, a saber at his side. I would have thought he was some young officer I knew, except for the shadow of folded wings. We walked in companionable silence.

Ahead, where the galleries of the Louvre should begin, was another building entirely. It was a vast block of stone, steps leading up to bronze doors guarded by a pair of sphinxes with a woman's head, serene and beautiful in their watch. I climbed the stairs. "What is this place?" I asked.

"A tomb," he said.

"Whose tomb?" I asked, though I thought I knew.

"Yours," he said.

I turned and looked at him. His gaze was kind, though power crackled behind it, an angel trying to appear mortal. "It's the test, isn't it? To go into the tomb. But why?"

He shrugged, looking up at the doors. "You want to know, don't you? But it's up to you. Nothing bad will happen if you don't go in."

"Except I won't know."

"Yes."

I took a deep breath. "And behind that door is…"

"Your memories." He put his head to the side. "You have the gift of memory, and though you will never remember as clearly in life as in dreams, you can remember more than most people can while wearing a body. What's in there…" he gestured with one arm, "…is your past. It's yours to claim if you want. Or you can leave it alone. That's up to you."

Once, I had run from this choice, run as hard as I could from what I perceived to be insanity. Now I was no longer afraid. "I want to know," I said. "I want all the stories." And I pushed upon the doors.

They swung open at my touch. I walked in, across the echoing stone floor, through the patterns of light made by the high windows. Paintings adorned the walls, carvings of animal-headed gods, while standing censers gave off the sweet smoke of incense. At the far end there was a sarcophagus. My heart beat faster. I could almost see this place full of people, hear women crying, almost feel a child's hand in mine.

"…your mother will go right there someday, like Alexander in his tomb or your grandfather in his," I said, my hand tight around the little boy's hand. "You see how it's carved with her royal cartouche. And over here on the floor are two cover stones, for me and Iras to lie behind her beneath the floor…."

There they were, the cover stones, and the royal cartouche on the sarcophagus, the crouching lioness and the feather and the other symbols, the same as the ones on the necklace Michel had given me, lost words that nobody could read. I knew them.

"Cleopatra Philopater," I said aloud, and in that moment the world spun. Like vast shards of broken glass, like cathedral windows destroyed by artillery fire, like all the mirrors of Versailles, every bright shard of memory leapt from slivers on the floor, reassembling themselves, whirling round in a vast storm.

She sat enthroned, my sister and my queen, a cape like golden wings around her as she sought my eyes above the dignitaries assembled. Iras bent over a papyrus, seven years old and deep in concentration, her braids falling forward as she read. Dion smiled and leaned upon my shoulder, showing me the drawings for the painted ceiling of the Temple of Hathor. Demetria nursed at my breast, her eyes closed in bliss. Caesarion ran across a peristyle courtyard chasing a ball, and beneath a bright sun boy and girl twins played in a garden heedless of anything that might come. Emrys bent his head to my shoulder, the first strands of gray in his long hair, and I gathered him to me. And others. There were so many others. Sigismund and Caesar, Philadelphos and Asinius Pollio and Asetnefer and Auletes worn and old. Marcus Vipsanius Agrippa, the last face I had seen.

I clung to the side of the sarcophagus, dimly aware that I had fallen to my knees. And gradually the world stilled.

The angel reached down and I took his hand, standing a little unsteadily. "Do you know who you are?" he asked.

"I am Elza," I said. My voice grew stronger. "And I am Charmian, Handmaiden to Cleopatra Philopater. With my sisters I was one of the Hands of Isis." I looked down at the floor, at the cover stones and their carvings. "This is my tomb. I lie with my sisters as I died with them."

He nodded gravely. "And?"

I grasped his hand, all the dark anguish of that day rushing through me again. "The children! Oh by all the gods, the children! They killed Caesarion. And they took the children. Helios and Selene and Philadelphos who was just a toddler and they killed them in Rome. They poisoned them. Only Selene survived." My voice rose into almost a scream, a wail from the soul. "I swore to protect the children! I failed. I swore to protect them. I promised!"

"You did everything you could," he said gently.

"But it wasn't enough. They cut Caesarion's throat in the temple and they poisoned the little boys. I have failed in my charge and I shall never know peace."

"No one is holding you to that account."

"I am holding myself. I am foresworn, and I did not protect them. I hold myself to that charge."

He held my hand, and it was steady as sun-warmed stone. "That is why you have a second chance."

"What?"

"A second chance to fulfill your charge. A second chance to save Caesarion."

I shook my head in confusion. "But that's the past, the distant past. It can't be changed."

"Not in the past. In the present."

The scene wavered, darkened. For a moment I could see nothing. Then I realized that was because it was night. I stood beside the window curtains in the bedroom of a grand house, a chamber all gilt and pale blue silk with a dressing table and mirror and a huge carved bed. My eyes adjusted to the dim light.

A couple were sleeping. They curled together, his body curved around her back and his arm around her waist, his face against her spill of golden hair. I knew them.

"Maria," I said. Maria, and yet more than Maria. She was my sister, my queen, my friend, and I had loved her before.

And the man—of course it was him. I had seen his face in repose this way myself, in Milan all those years ago, felt his arm about me though I did not envy her that. Napoleon slept beside Maria in the bedroom of some great house in Austria, far away from where I slept in a jail cell in Florence.

"What do you see?" the angel said. I had forgotten he was at my side. "What do you see with sight that is more than sight?"

They slept, the bright energy of their souls damped by drowsy slumber, like twin-banked fires. And a spark. There was a spark where there should not be, no more than a tiny pinprick of fire just beneath where his arm curled around her, a single miniscule point of brightness.

"Maria Walewska has conceived a son tonight," the angel said.

"Here, in the darkness after love, a seed has taken."

I brought my hands to my mouth.

"And when it is time for a soul to inhabit that body, it will be the boy you knew as Caesarion." The angel's voice caught. "He wants a second chance too, you see."

Something like a sob escaped me. "The Blameless Prince. The boy who is innocent of the Terror and its blood. The one who can heal."

"Maybe." He shrugged. "I can't see the future. I can only see what is. And what is possible."

"It is possible that he will live and rule?"

"It is possible. Anything is possible in this moment, all the good and all the bad."

I drew myself up. "What do I do?"

"I don't know. You'll have to work that out." He smiled at me, a quirky, sideways smile that reminded me of Michel. "I can give you a chance. You've got to figure out what to do with it."

That was fair. I had a second chance, and a chance was all I had ever needed. Not that it looked terribly easy to guard the life of a child unborn while sitting in a jail cell in Italy waiting for Fouché to have me murdered. "I'll take that," I said, and gave him a nod like a duelist. "And the memories? Will I remember when I wake up?"

"Not as well as you do at this moment, but you can always remember when you need to," he said. "You can reach for things and they will be there. You have claimed who you are, now and then."

"Fair enough," I said.

I woke in the quiet before dawn. Vivid dreams, and yet the substance of them did not fade with day. Maria had conceived. I knew that to be true as surely as I knew my own name. And the rest? Was it not conceit to imagine myself a role in one of the great moments of history? Was it not fantasy based upon the roles I had played in theater, when I had played the Handmaiden on stage?

I entertained those thoughts and then dismissed them. I had chosen to believe. With that choice came a strange peace. I had been promised a chance, and I would take what chance came. There would come a time to guard this child Maria did not yet know that she bore. In the meantime, I knew what my part must be, to stop the Philadelphes if I could.

Yet once the letter was gone there was nothing I could do except wait. As prisons go, I suppose it was not so bad. There was ample food and water, and Camilla was allowed to bring me a change of clothes and some books, so there were at least those small comforts. But even so, a prison is a prison. I paced its confines over and over, a million horrible scenarios playing themselves out in my head.

Fouché would probably not murder me here. I doubted he had an agent on the scene, and in any event Deshumes would ask questions. Better to wait until I was officially transferred to other custody. Then a million accidents might happen. Indeed, I might be shot trying to escape on the long road to Paris. Or I might kill myself in a tacit admission of guilt. There would of course be questions later, but nothing could be proven. Nothing could ever be proven with Fouché. And after all, I was legitimately charged by honest men for papers that were transparently treasonous.

How long did I have? Three days passed, then four. Camilla visited and told me that I was to be transferred to the Ministry of Police's men as soon as they arrived. What if the letter had gone astray? What if Honoré were detached and not at headquarters? What if he had been wounded at Wagram himself and was in no condition to read his mail? Who else could I write to? Corbineau was in Spain and also Subervie. So was Max Duplessis. So were most of the other Lodge members, even ones I did not know so well, like Charles Lefebvre-Desnouettes. Lannes was dead. Very junior men like de la Bedoyere did not know I was the Emperor's agent and in any event might not dare his displeasure.

I was in this welter of anxiety when the door opened. The transfer, I thought, and then I realized that it was Colonel Deshumes. He looked me up and down with a very peculiar expression, the thick white transfer order in his hand. "Never in my life," he said slowly, "have I seen such a thing." He unfolded it and spread it before me.

It was the original document, not a copy, creamy parchment with the seal pressed into the wax just so, with the signature in a flourish of black ink.

You are to release Madame St. Elme immediately and question her no further, nor examine her correspondence or personal property. You are to release all such property to her immediately and unconditionally. You are to discuss this matter no further with any person. You are not to ask her for any paroles or assurances nor interfere with her in any way.

Napoleon, Emperor of the French

I almost sagged over with relief. I reached out to touch the seal, yes, the full Imperial seal pressed into red wax, as though this were an order to move an army. My eyes unaccountably filled with tears.

I looked up and Deshumes was watching me closely. "Who are you," he asked, "to receive this?"

I took a deep breath. Who am I indeed?

"I cannot say," I said, gesturing at the paper. "Those orders of silence are for me as well as you. But I think you may surmise that I am in the Emperor's service."

"So I had gathered," he said. Deshumes shook his head. "I can't imagine what work could clear you of treason at the stroke of a pen."

"You probably don't want to," I said. I took the paper and refolded it, grateful that my hands were steady, holding it to my breast like a talisman.

"This came by special courier," he said. "Changing horses all the way from Vienna, the same man in the saddle for a day and a night. Jesus Christ!"

I said nothing. There was nothing I could say.

Deshumes spread his hands. "You are free to go, Madame. But where do you go?"

"Back to work," I said. "Where else?"

The Grand Duchess professed herself glad to see me. She looked at the order, her brows knitting together exactly as her brother's did. "Well," she said. "At least he's good for that." She regarded me solemnly. "You know that your position at my court is irredeemably compromised. Everyone has talked of nothing but your arrest for days, and your sudden release will only make them talk more."

I let out a long breath. Elisa's boudoir was a familiar and homey sight compared to prison. "I know," I said. "But Oudet is dead."

"Murdered," Elisa said.

I looked at her sharply. "What?"

"That's what they're saying. The rumor is that he was very slightly wounded at Wagram but that then he was stabbed to death in his hospital bed and that it was covered up by the Imperial General Staff."

"Why would the Emperor do that?" I asked. "He knew I was finally getting somewhere with Oudet. Of all the times to kill him!"

"I doubt that he did," Elisa said, sitting down at her dressing table, her eyes on mine in the mirror. "As you say, you had him on a leash and he was leading you to the others. Better to let Oudet run and see where he might lead you. I seriously doubt that he was murdered. This is the kind of wild story that somehow goes about. The Emperor has told one of his Aide de Camps to formally investigate it."

"Let me guess," I said. "Reille."

Elisa nodded. "The same."

"To investigate it, or to cover it up?" Either way, Honoré was the man for the job. "Or perhaps both," I said slowly. If someone else had killed Oudet, the Emperor would both want to know who and how, and also prevent anyone else from knowing. It would hardly do morale good to have it believed that officers could be murdered in their hospital beds. And I knew perfectly well who would want to kill him. Moreau would not hesitate if he thought that an underling was leaking like a sieve. Which Oudet was. But did Moreau have the means? At last confirmation he was in New Jersey, a very long way from Vienna. But surely all his confederates weren't.

"You can bet that I won't be told," Elisa said tartly. "After all, I'm only his little sister."

"I don't imagine I shall be told either," I said. "I will have to start over trying to cultivate some other member of the Philadelphes, if that is even possible." And that was a daunting task—to identify still another man I did not know and work my way into his confidence via his bed. Oudet had thought too well of himself and wasn't especially bright. Another man might heed Moreau's warnings. And certainly if the Philadelphes believed that Oudet had been murdered, they would be even more wary of me! If Moreau had not ordered him killed he would think that I had done so. I put my hand to my brow.

"You need to give it some time for the talk to die down," Elisa said sensibly. "Right now everyone is gossiping and there will be no chance of being subtle in anything you do. I think the best thing would be to go away from Florence for a month or more and give it time."

I nodded. "That is very reasoned," I said.

"Agreed," Elisa said. "Two months at least. Where will you go?"

There was only one option, only one thing that would do. "Spain," I said, and my heart leapt.

Afterword

The Marshal's Lover is based on the memoirs of Ida St. Elme, aka Elzelina Versfelt, a real-life courtesan, soldier and probable secret agent in Napoleon's service. Her story begins in the first book in this series, The General's Mistress, and continues in The Emperor's Agent and The Marshal's Lover. The next volume will continue her further adventures.

Most of the characters are real people, including her dear friends Corbineau, Subervie, Reille, Maria Walewska, Camilla Spinochi, and of course the love of her life, Michel Ney. While her memoirs illuminate many events, much was left out because she was writing in the 1820s as an act of defiance against the monarchy of the Restoration, and was duly careful about what she said about friends currently living under that government. I have therefore taken some liberties to fill in the gaps. For example, her letters to Oudet are documented, as is her mysterious full pardon by the Emperor himself, though no reason whatsoever is given for this extraordinary document.

As always, I am grateful for the help and support of many people as I continue Elza's journey. First and foremost is my wonderful partner Amy Griswold. I also owe much to my friends Melissa Scott and Kathryn McCulley. I am deeply grateful to first readers who reviewed sections of the manuscript in the works, including Wanda Lybarger, Nathan Jensen, Margaret Chrisawn, Tanja Kinkel, Lena Strid, and Anne-Elisabeth Moutet. I am especially grateful to Anna Kiwiel who found the story of the cavalry eating the roof for fodder and Ney's reaction to it in the town archives of Działdowo! Thank you for all your encouragement and help. All errors are of course my own.

About the Author

Jo Graham worked in politics for fifteen years before leaving to write full time. She is the author of the Locus Award nominated Black Ships and the Spectrum Award nominated Stealing Fire, as well as several other novels, including the Stargate Atlantis Legacy series and The General's Mistress. She lives in North Carolina with her partner and their daughter. She can be found online at:

http://www. jo_graham.livejournal.com.

Jo Graham Novels:

SGA-14 Death Game
SGA-16 Homecoming - Book I of the Legacy Series
SGA-17 The Lost - Book II of the Legacy Series
SGA-19 The Furies – Book IV of the Legacy Series
SGA-20 Secrets – Book V of the Legacy Series
SGA-21 Inheritors – Book VI of the Legacy Series
SGA-22 Unascended – Book VII of the Legacy Series
SGA -23 Third Path – Book VIII of the Legacy Series
The Order of the Air – with Melissa Scott
Lost Things
Steel Blues
Silver Bullet
Wind Raker
Oath Bound

Jo Graham Collections

The Ravens of Falkenau

Curious about other Crossroad Press books?
Stop by our site:
http://store.crossroadpress.com
We offer quality writing
in digital, audio, and print formats.

Enter the code FIRSTBOOK
to get 20% off your first order from our store!
Stop by today!